Praise for Scarlett Cole

"Scarlett Cole's characters pull you in from the very first page with real emotion and sizzling chemistry. Don't miss this action-packed thrill ride."

—Cherry Adair, *New York Times* bestselling author

"Nonstop action and heart-pounding romance—a must-read for romantic suspense fans!"

—Cynthia Eden, *New York Times* and *USA Today* bestselling author on *Under Fire*

"Fantastic characters, scorching sexual tension, and nonstop action make this one of my favorite reads this year! Highly recommend!"

—Laura Kaye, *New York Times* bestselling author

"Sizzling hot romance."   —*RT Book Reviews*

"Scarlett Cole truly knows how to get readers invested in her characters and in the story. H̶e̶r̶ ̶w̶r̶i̶t̶i̶n̶g̶ is excellent, and I'd lo̶v̶e̶ ... b̶o̶o̶k̶ ̶f̶r̶o̶m̶ ...

—*The ... der Fire*

"There is cate...   ...Scarlett Cole for ratche... ...y, ...and heart-palpitating thril... ...she can."

—*Romance Reviews Today*

ALSO BY SCARLETT COLE

THE LOVE OVER DUTY SERIES
Under Fire
Final Siege

THE SECOND CIRCLE TATTOO SERIES
The Strongest Steel
The Fractured Heart
The Purest Hook
The Darkest Link

THE PRELOAD SERIES
Jordan Reclaimed
Elliott Redeemed
Nikan Rebuilt
Lennon Reborn

DEEP COVER

Scarlett Cole

St. Martin's Paperbacks

This is a work of fiction All of the characters, organizations, and events portrayed in this novel are either products of the author's imagination or are used fictitiously.

DEEP COVER

Copyright © 2018 by Scarlett Cole.

All rights reserved.

For information address St. Martin's Press, 175 Fifth Avenue, New York, NY 10010.

ISBN: 978-1-250-12848-5

Our books may be purchased in bulk for promotional, educational, or business use. Please contact your local bookseller or the Macmillan Corporate and Premium Sales Department at 1-800-221-7945, ext. 5442, or by e-mail at MacmillanSpecialMarkets@macmillan.com.

Printed in the United States of America

St. Martin's Paperbacks edition / August 2018

St. Martin's Paperbacks are published by St. Martin's Press, 175 Fifth Avenue, New York, NY 10010.

10 9 8 7 6 5 4 3 2 1

CHAPTER ONE

Cabe Moss lay flat on his stomach, ignoring the stench of decaying seaweed and the flies attracted to it that buzzed around his head and landed on his hands, his M4, and the tip of his nose. In the darkness, he could hear more than see them.

One buzzed right into his ear. He twitched his head sharply to send them flying, but they didn't go far. Annoying little bastards. They were half of why this beach worked so perfectly for the people they were watching. Overrun with seaweed and difficult to reach down a jagged and narrow cliff-face path, it was rarely used.

With his night goggles on, the small boat looked almost white in the fluorescent green of the Pacific Ocean. The *putt-putt-putt* of the engine became clearer, more distinct. This was it, the drop they'd been waiting for. The one that could break the syndicate's back.

Cabe nodded to Six, his best friend since childhood, former SEAL teammate, and current business partner in Eagle Securities, the special ops firm they'd established with Mac, the third part of their triumvirate. From his spot behind a narrow strip of jagged rocks, Six adjusted his scope a fraction of a turn.

After thirteen months of trying to take down a Russian syndicate that had threatened their loved ones, they finally had a chance at hitting Konstantin Sokolov, the highest-ranking member and lynchpin of the organization, where it would hurt him most. They would relieve him of his latest cash shipment, denying the syndicate access to illegal funds they needed to operate. Sokolov was smart, too smart, but their intel was solid.

Cabe never took his eyes from the boat as it bobbed closer to shore. Tonight was *it*. The final nail in the syndicate's coffin, the last part of Eagle's three-point plan to eradicate it. The end of a thirteen-month effort to take down its members one by one and, with the help of the CIA and the FBI, disable systems that allowed the syndicate to operate, raiding warehouses, retrieving arms, and blocking trade shipments.

This was Eagle's riskiest outing yet, the organization's cash was bound to be well protected. Which meant a group of highly trained armed men with zero conscience. But if it got them a step closer to the organization that tried to kill Six's fiancée to get a chemical weapon and had gone after Mac's journalist girlfriend for exposing their arms shipment routes, then every moment of lying in the sand was worth it.

Lite and Harley, members of Team Three, the team Cabe led, were up by the road, scouting for the vehicle that would transport the money after it was brought off the boat. Capturing the driver *should* be a piece of cake. As always, Buddha had his fingers on the controls of a drone that was recording and giving them intel from above, its whir a faint sound lost among the buzzing of the flies and the crash of the waves. Jackson was with Mac on the other side of the cove, upwind from the rotting seaweed. Before assigning placements next time, Cabe would definitely pay better attention to wind direction.

The boat finally pulled into the shallows, its front hitting the small waves with a solid *thump* until Cabe heard the rough sound of the bow running aground. Somebody killed the engine, and aside from the soft *hush* of the gentle waves turning on the sand, the cove went silent.

Voices sounded faintly from inside. He could barely make out the words, his Russian passable on a good day. But tone was universal. And their tone sounded . . . jovial. That, he got. SEALs often relied on humor, even in crucial situations—the more inappropriate, the better.

"Vehicle approaching from the south," Buddha's voice whispered through Cabe's comms unit.

Cabe didn't need to respond. They all knew the plan. The team on the beach wasn't supposed to move on the boat's crew until after the vehicle was secured on the cliff.

The whispers from onboard amplified, as the boat began to rock from side to side from its occupants' movement. Their voices sounded forced, like actors on the stage attempting to project their words to the rear of a theater. An older man with a long beard appeared at the back and dropped the anchor. The splash echoed.

The sound of the approaching vehicle on the cliff grew louder, and a stream of light from its headlights hit the sand a yard in front of Cabe. He belly-crawled a few feet back into the darkness of the cove, with Six swiftly following. Both of them held their breaths, and Cabe prayed they hadn't been spotted. With minimum movement, he put his Steiner binoculars to his eyes and looked up at the cliff. There was nobody there, but that didn't mean they hadn't been seen.

The lights from the cliff flashed twice, then twice again. The man who had dropped the anchor raised his hand to shield his eyes and waved. Suddenly, he looked in their direction but thankfully the beach was cast back into darkness.

Cabe forced his shoulders to relax.

Two more men appeared from inside the boat and jumped off into the shallows. They were young, scrawny, and way too casually dressed in board shorts, their feet bare. The older man handed one of them a large backpack. It had to be the money. He handed a second bag to the other man, and they carried them to shore, holding them high out of the water.

Out of the corner of his eye, Cabe could see Mac and Jackson make their way along the shadowed wall of the cove until they were close to the water's edge. There was no real cover should they be spotted, the cliff to their backs. Their movements were painfully slow, and the beach was so dark that if he hadn't already known they were there, he wouldn't have seen them.

The reverb of something slamming into the car stopped the two men in their tracks. They looked up to the cliff and Cabe followed suit.

Damn.

Why hadn't anyone communicated that the driver was secure? What could have gone wrong? His mind flashed through scenarios: the targets had fought back, leaving Lite and Harley incapacitated or worse; they'd escaped; they'd . . . Buddha would let them know if there was a problem.

"Buddha?" he hissed.

"Nothing they can't handle," came the laid-back response. "Securing the targets now."

He said a quick thank-you to whatever geek had developed the drone.

He looked toward the two men. *Keep walking. Keep walking.* He didn't want them to stop. They needed to be farther away from the boat than Mac and Jackson were. The last thing they needed was for the two targets to have time to run back and sail away before Mac and Jackson could stop them, even if they had the drone following them.

Cabe held his breath for four seconds, then exhaled.

Something about the scene bothered him. The targets were too casual. They weren't scanning for danger, weren't looking around to check whether they were being watched or not. There was nothing furtive about their body language.

It couldn't fall apart. Not now.

"Car secure," Harley relayed.

That was their sign. "Go!" he shouted as he jumped to his feet and took to the sand at a run. "Down on the floor, down on the floor!"

No sooner had the words left his mouth, though, than he realized tonight would not be the night. And just like the unexplained feelings he'd had in a thousand different ops, feelings that had sent his men left instead of right or even saved his own life, he knew everything was off. The captain of the boat hadn't even moved from his position at the rear of the boat. There had been no reaching for a weapon or lifting of the anchor in an attempt to escape. He simply stood and waited as Mac and Jackson waded into the water and boarded the vessel. Meanwhile, the two men with the bags threw them into the sand as they dropped to their knees and put their hands to their heads.

There was no urgency. No look of panic. No fear etched into the lines of their faces.

"We're unarmed," the first man shouted, his Eastern European accent heavy as he rolled his R's.

"Unarmed," shouted the second. "Don't shoot."

It was all too easy. Too perfect.

He pushed the first man down on the sand and secured his hands with a cable tie. The target fell willingly and made no effort to fight back. Six did the same with the second man.

Without removing his night goggles, as they gave him anonymity, he reached for the backpack and unzipped it. It felt light . . . too light for a bag that was supposed to contain cool green American bills.

"Fuck," he cursed as he pulled out bubble wrap. A shit-ton of bubble wrap. The very thing people popped for stress relief had just sent his pulse to DEFCON 1.

He knew Six was doing the same with the backpack *he'd* retrieved, but Cabe knew better than to look. Nothing would be different.

"Nothing on the boat," Mac shouted.

"Same with the car and driver," Harley said through his earpiece.

The information the CIA had passed along was fake. No. It was worse. They'd been expected. The whole thing had been set up. Somebody knew they were being watched.

The target on the sand turned to him and smiled. Their intel had sent them to capture what he was certain now were the decoys. The real drop was somewhere up the coastline.

And they'd missed it.

There were days when it felt like Sokolov and his cronies were going to win. And there were days when his failure to find them felt like a blight on his otherwise successful career. He'd been sent overseas with the SEALs more times than he could count on the premise of protecting America from harm, always wishing for the chance to do the same on American soil, or in this case, sand. Yet having been given the opportunity, he'd been unable to fulfill his mission.

But worse than the failure, there was a very real risk that someone was going to get hurt as an outcome. The money was going to make it on to land, weapons were going to be bought, women like Six's and Mac's girlfriends were going to get hurt.

The need for vengeance and the uneasy weight of failure battled in his gut, and for the first time in his life, he wasn't sure what to do next to stop them.

Seven, six, five, four, three, two, one.

On one, the lights changed to green, like they always did after her twenty-three-second countdown. After only two weeks of being here, there wasn't a light in the grid of San Diego's Gaslamp Quarter Amy Murray didn't know. She'd always had an exceptional memory, and not in the "good enough to appear on *Jeopardy*" kind of way. Sure, her random general knowledge was significantly deeper than the average person, but her memory extended to the sequence of a pack of playing cards after one quick look.

She counted the seconds of a light change to relieve the boredom, and then remembered how long it had taken every time she returned to the same intersection. It was a game for her, to predict when she'd be able to ease her foot off the brake and move forward.

The I-5 had been clear as she had driven from the San Diego FBI office in the suburb of Sorrento Valley back to her home in the city. It took thirty minutes on average, but she needed to add six minutes if she left after 5:37. And she could subtract three minutes if she stayed until 6:56, as she often did.

She checked her rearview mirror as she changed lanes, and laughed as she noticed wisps of blonde hair had escaped the tight bun at the nape of her neck. How long had it been like that? Hopefully not during the long meeting she'd sat through all afternoon. Off duty, she loved her hair, which was Scandinavian blonde with a California wave. But on duty—taken together with lips that were a fraction too full and eyes she'd once been told were the color of a tropical ocean—it just added to the difficulty she had being taken seriously. Fellow agents took her looks as an invitation to hit on her. Hell, so had the criminals she'd pursued as part of the Organized Crime unit.

Which was why she'd transferred to the San Diego office last month.

Eight months of escalating advances in Atlanta from a senior-ranking agent had been as much as she'd been able to take. She'd put off filing a sexual harassment report for as long as she could because she hadn't wanted to be *that* girl. The one who caused trouble. The one who rocked the boat. The one nobody believed. And worse, she'd known that complaining would put her case at risk, the one she'd cared about with every fiber of her being. But eventually she couldn't shake off his behavior with a hot shower and glass of Chardonnay at the end of the day.

The investigation had taken six months to vindicate her. By then, the damage had been done. Her transfer had taken yet *another* half year to approve.

Six months of enduring the nudges between men, six months of evil glares from wives and girlfriends who didn't believe she'd played no role whatsoever in his behavior.

Six months during which she hadn't so much as felt like talking with a man.

Amy shook her head to clear her thoughts. She'd promised herself she'd leave all of that behind. Moving here, after all, had been about moving on.

Which included reviewing the files for the missing-women case she'd been assigned the previous week.

Missing women weren't simply her job, they were her vocation. Her calling. The thing that made her get out of bed in the morning, and the reason she'd joined the FBI. The wheels for her career decision had been set in motion decades ago, but every day was a new opportunity to bring someone home, reunite a family, or at least give a loved one a chance to grieve through the knowledge of what happened to their family member.

That she'd be working such a complex case with a wide-reaching task force ticked every box.

She pulled into the underground lot and parked in her space. The classic car parked next to her made her think of her father and the Dodge Dart he'd bought in 1970 and still drove today. She grabbed her phone and dialed.

One ring . . . two rings . . . three rings.

On eight, it kicked into her father's voicemail like it always did, and she left him a quick message.

She grabbed her files and took the stairs up to her apartment. They were a welcome break from sitting on her ass. On another day, she'd probably spend a half hour hitting the gym in her building before taking a long run down the waterfront.

But today, having a plan to go out for drinks with friends later and limited time to read about the case, she found herself sitting at the breakfast bar in her kitchen, eating leftovers from the burrito she'd bought yesterday. As she studied the images of the women on her laptop, she found herself running her fingers along the long brunette hair of Helen Foy, her heart squeezing as it always did when she placed herself in the shoes of the families.

Their hurt was something she understood. Waves of panic washed over her, as they always did when she remembered the day of her mother's disappearance. She would never forget the moment her father had hugged her so tightly that she could barely breathe as he'd told her in words a ten-year-old could understand that the police suspected someone had taken her mom away and that they were working really hard to bring her home. Then he'd cried, his tears soaking her T-shirt. Her father had never cried.

The tears had scared her more than anything that had followed. Her daddy had always been the strong one. And if he was already out of faith, then so was she.

Her mother had loved her father deeply. Amy remembered the way she'd pause and smile to herself when she talked about how the two of them had met. She remembered how they'd never left the house without telling the other that they loved them. She remembered how wonderful her house had been at Christmas, her mother's favorite holiday season, with the whole family congregating at their home—grandparents, cousins, friends. And she remembered *that* day . . . the day her mom had told her she was going to pick up some more eggnog. The bells from the enormous wreath on the front door of their Vegas home had jangled as it slammed shut—a sound Amy had associated with her mother ever since.

Amy and her father had gone through all the cycles of grief for a missing loved one. The hope in the early hours and days that followed that she'd be found. The determination in the months afterward to chase every lead and offer rewards for information. The desperation that had her father talking to mystics alleged to have found missing people. The crushing sadness that came when she'd realized that just knowing where her mom's body was would provide comfort, even if she'd never get to hug her one last time.

And, finally, as an adult, the agony of living every day feeling like you hadn't done enough to find them, hadn't followed every lead, hadn't spoken to every person. Somebody *must* have seen something, and what if there were CCTV cameras that hadn't been checked? Hoax calls had claimed her mom had been spotted in Iowa, and Ohio, and Phoenix, and Georgia—all of them turning out to be from people trying to get their grubby hands on the generous reward her father offered for information.

Amy studied the face on the screen. Helen's green eyes were lit up with a smile. Freckles dusted her nose. What had happened to her? Who had taken her, and what had they done to her? With her? Whatever pain Amy had felt when her mom disappeared had to have been nothing compared to what her mom had endured. Or Helen. Or Melanie Stokes, or Joanne Gleave, or any of the other women in the folder.

With a sigh, she closed her laptop, allowing herself to experience the feeling of loss and panic she always felt at the start of a case like this. If she didn't, it would fester, leaving her thoughts unclear, her brain fuzzy.

She caught sight of the time on her phone, and remembered her plans. Drinks with a couple of girls she'd met the previous Saturday at a local yoga class when she'd ended up in the back row with them. She, Leigh, and Penny had laughed as much as they'd meditated. That was what she needed, to go out with new friends and shake off the melancholy.

Then she'd return to the file and give these women her full attention.

They deserved nothing less.

Cabe took another sip of his beer and listened half-heartedly to Six and Mac's conversation. A year ago, his two best friends probably would have been talking about the relative hotness of every woman who walked past. Tonight they were talking about . . . billing. Friday night in San Diego's Gaslamp Quarter had always been a good time, but since Six had met Lou, and Mac had reunited with Delaney, things had definitely taken a turn toward low key. He was happy for his friends. Happy they'd found someone who'd made them has happy as he'd been with Jess.

As always, Cabe watched the crowd. A couple were quietly arguing in the back corner, all glares, folded arms, and hand gestures. He kept an eye on them. The guy was

big, but the woman was feisty and appeared to be holding her own. Something told him that she wasn't in any
danger, but he'd keep an eye on the situation. A first date
was taking place to his right. There had been an awkward-
handshake-meets-kiss-on-the-cheek moment when they'd
first met, after which she'd blushed and he'd apologized.
Now they were sitting very close, fingers entwined. The
bouncer was openly discriminating against men. By
Cabe's reckoning, he'd let in three women to every guy,
which meant the bar was filled with women dressed to the
nines.

None of whom his friends particularly seemed to notice. Since setting up Eagle Securities and dealing with
all the complications that came with running a special
ops firm, when they did have a precious few minutes outside of the office, they still ended up talking about work.

Visas, weapons shipments, overseas lawyers . . . the
list was endless.

"I've been thinking about Monday's op," Cabe said.
They'd spent the day reviewing why the op had gone
wrong, and the flaw had been their intel.

"Yeah. It's gnawing away at my gut too," Mac said.

Six nodded in agreement.

Cabe leaned toward the center of their table so he
could lower his voice. "The CIA obviously haven't tapped
into the right seam of people willing to be informants for
the kind of deal that keeps them out of prison."

"So, your suggestion is . . . ?" Six asked.

Cabe knew what he was about to suggest would take
money. Lots of money. But it was going to be essential.
"We start to build our own. Increase our investment in
intel collection. People, systems, contacts. I'm done with
relying on other people."

Mac let out a low whistle. "I hear you, but that's going to take a serious cash injection."

Cabe nodded. "I know. But I think we've got to start."

"We can increase our fees. I'm telling you, the price on the Syria contract is too low," Six said. "Increase our rate and it's pure profit. I was talking to the head of an infrastructure and engineering service out there who said they're paying fifteen percent more for their contract security than we're charging."

"We have an option to review that contract in four months, so we'll do it then," Cabe said. "But we should talk about growth. We had a plan and everything kind of exploded. We need to build a new plan. Examine the risks of running full tilt. See if we should back off expanding boots-on-the-ground operators, and increase our backroom setup."

"At least you two are consistent," Mac said, chuckling. He took a sip of his beer. "Six has never been able to find the brake, and Cabe, you could overthink a bowl of ramen. Do you remember when we set Eagle Securities up? When we were doing security-guard training to pay the bills? Did either of you really think that a year later we'd have three teams and twelve active guys?"

"Yes," Six said, slamming his pint glass onto the table. "We should fucking celebrate that."

"As starts go, it's been pretty incredible," Cabe said. "No more having to ask Louisa to borrow money so we could grow—or, for that matter, eat."

Six frowned. "Yeah, fucker. Not like I would have ever taken a penny from her that we didn't pay back." Six's fiancée was incredibly wealthy and generous, but Six had always been vigilant about making sure she was paid back. One hundred percent, plus interest. "Speaking of which, I think I'm going to go grab her from your place, Mac, and take her home."

"Well, if you're leaving, I'll walk with you. Delaney will give me shit if you show up for Lou and I stay out. We've barely seen each other this week thanks to the new article she's been working on."

Cabe shook his head. "Whipped. The pair of you," he teased, and buried the envy he felt. He'd had that once.

Had is why they were here. To distract him. Today would have been Jess's birthday, and they hadn't wanted Cabe to drown his sorrows alone. She would have turned thirty today, and he had no doubt they would have spent the day doing something adrenaline-filled, like skydiving or climbing one of the seven summits . . . something she'd always wanted to do. Something he would never have let her do alone because their adventures were the thing he loved most about their life. Together they had been unbeatable in the face of any physical challenge. But their plans had been torn apart on an Afghan roadside, destroyed by an IED while Jess had been on a routine patrol. When they'd first started dating, he'd worried about being the one killed. It had never occurred to him that he'd be the one left behind. The engagement ring he'd given her was still sitting on top of the dresser in their apartment.

They'd never gotten the chance to achieve their five-year plan. The one that involved them both leaving the military behind, the one that saw them start Eagle Securities, the one that saw them married. Fuck, they should be trying for kids right about now.

Cabe rubbed a hand across his face.

Their plan.

He just didn't have it in him to build a plan with someone else. He knew, had known from the way Jess had looked at him when he'd gotten down on one knee while on vacation in Maui, that this kind of love came around once in a lifetime.

As weeks went, this one was turning out to be a piece of shit.

Mac slapped him on the back. "You cool if we head out?"

Cabe nodded. "Yeah, thanks for the distraction."

Six hugged him. "Since meeting Lou, what happened to Jess has become much more real. I'm so sorry, man."

Cabe swallowed hard as he nodded.

He watched his best friends leave the bar to go to their women. *Goddamn.* He should probably go home, but it was the last place he wanted to be. Too many memories. Everything too close. He should move into a new apartment. He'd looked four times, even found a perfect rental in Mac's building, but when he'd sat with the contract in front of him and a black pen in his hand, he hadn't been able to make himself sign.

Anxious to chase thoughts of Jess from his head, he walked to the bar and ordered a double Macallan. He closed his eyes and took a sip. If he got drunk enough, he could probably catch a few hours' sleep.

A woman laughed, a light sound. If he'd been feeling poetic, he might have made comparisons to the tinkle of wind chimes.

"Three more margaritas, please?" The faint scent of the ocean reached him, but it was the husky voice that had him opening his eyes. A young woman with spectacular light blonde hair whom he'd noticed sitting with friends across the room earlier stood next to him. As she ordered and got her credit card from her purse, he had a moment to take in her profile. Long eyelashes almost brushed her cheeks as she blinked. Skin that had appeared unblemished at a distance looked even softer up close. So soft that he wanted to run the tip of his finger along her cheekbone and his thumb across those pillowy lips.

And while he hadn't meant to stare, from his height and the way she was leaning up against the bar, it was impossible to miss the white lace of her bra and the curve of her breast. He shook his head. It was only human of him to notice, but it was Jess's goddamn birthday. He should have a little more respect. For Jess *and* the woman standing next to him.

His phone buzzed in his pocket and he reached for it. The text was from his mom, asking how he was doing. It was the fourth one she'd sent him today, but it tugged at his heart. She'd loved Jess just as much as he had. Today was hard for her too.

Suddenly, his phone was knocked out of his hand and sent skimming along the bar as the woman next to him crashed into his side. Immediately he reached to stop her fall while holding his hand out to push the boisterous drunk who was stumbling next to them away from her. "You okay?" he asked.

She turned to face him. "I'm good. Thank you for catching me," she said, smoothing her dress before running a hand through her hair.

Cabe held her gaze and loosened his grip on her hip until he was sure she was steady, then reluctantly let go to grab his phone and slip it back into his pocket. "My apologies. I hope *I* didn't hurt you."

Now that he was looking at her straight on, he could

see that his original assessment was correct. Those lips, currently fighting a smile, were delicious.

"I think I should be apologizing for turning you into the human equivalent of a bowling pin," she replied. Blue eyes the color of aquamarine sparkled with humor and then flared in interest as she lowered them to his chest, then his arms, then back to his face.

Cabe took a sip of his whiskey. She was tall, maybe five-eight or five-nine. The red sundress she wore accentuated her waist; the cream heeled sandals, her legs. "I'm pretty sure *that* honor belongs to him," he said, nodding in the direction of the drunken idiot who was now dancing like a lunatic, all waving arms.

"I guess that makes us both bowling pins then. Which is super pathetic, because you look absolutely nothing like a bowling pin."

He couldn't help but grin. "Let me get this round."

The blonde laughed. "Amy," she said, offering him her hand.

Cabe took it, savoring the way her skin felt against his as he shook it. He loved the feel of a woman, loved the way Jess had always . . . damn. He needed to stop thinking about her. "Cabe," he said.

Guilt teased the corners of his mind. He felt disloyal talking with another woman, especially an attractive one who sparked his interest. But in the last twelve months, he'd needed . . . something. It was hard to define. He still loved Jess just as much as he always had. But he'd felt lonely. No, not quite lonely. Definitely horny—which was probably as shallow as it sounded. The first time he'd slept with someone else, he'd been out in Sierra Leone, providing security for a charity that was building wells. And during a layover in Paris on his way home, he'd met a museum curator. A flirtatious conversation about whether Van Gough or Cezanne was the better artist had turned into dinner followed by eight hours in his 7th arrondissement hotel room. But by the time he'd boarded the plane home, his body had felt tenser than ever. Guilt had a way of turning great sex into the equivalent of lactic-acid buildup.

He pulled out a couple of bills from his wallet and paid the bartender. "Why don't you drop those drinks with your friends and then come back?"

She tilted her head to one side, and if he had to guess, she was assessing his motives. "Give me one minute." Amy picked up her drink along with the others, rather than leaving it on the bar with him. Smart move.

Her hips swayed as she walked, and he was sure it wasn't deliberate or for his benefit. It was the sway of a woman who was confident in her femininity. Jess had been more reserved in the way she presented herself. Years of military conditioning to not draw unnecessary attention to herself around men. She'd been more athletic. They'd run every day together when they were home. Hell, she could beat him over eight miles.

Past tense.

Had been able to beat him over eight miles.

And today was her birthday.

Standing here in a bar trying to pick up a woman suddenly felt seedy, obvious spark or not.

Amy had just reached her table. Her friends looked in his direction, and Cabe suddenly felt like a fraud. He placed his unfinished whiskey on the bar and, as her friends turned their attention back to Amy, slipped quietly out of the bar.

CHAPTER TWO

Amy squinted in the early morning sunshine despite the sunglasses she wore as she pulled onto the I-5 and headed toward work. The three margaritas with Leigh and Penny hadn't been the best of ideas, but she'd had a lot of fun talking with the women and getting to know them. Leigh worked at the Marriott Hotel as an event coordinator, and Penny was a vet. The two of them shared an apartment a block south of her own. They'd been friends since high school, and Amy had found it entertaining that the two of them could finish each other's sentences.

It had been a fantastic evening . . . until she'd met *him*.

After the harassment had started, Amy's interest in finding a boyfriend had plummeted to zero. Friends had tried to set her up, and an old flame had gotten back in touch over Facebook to ask her if she had any interest in reconnecting after four years of being apart. But no one had sparked her interest, even after it was all over and she'd moved here.

Until last night.

Her stomach rolled, and she grimaced in embarrassment. It had taken her just a minute to bring her friends the drinks, but when she'd turned around, he was gone. Not realizing that his disappearance was permanent, she'd waited at the bar for him, assuming he'd gone to the bathroom. He'd been cute . . . no, he'd been more than cute. He'd been handsome. Dark brown hair just a touch on the messy side had framed a face with a strong jaw and a smile that had given her goose bumps. Plus, he had a very muscular physique and dwarfed her five-foot-eight, which didn't happen all that often. But when he hadn't returned fifteen minutes later, she'd given up waiting and returned to her friends where she'd then labeled him a jackass.

She'd felt a spark when he'd taken her hand. And his eyes . . . There had been something in the way he looked at her. She'd seen a playfulness there that she'd wanted to explore. His disappearance made no sense. She'd gone through all the possible explanations in her head, compassionate ones where he'd had a family emergency he didn't want to share with a stranger to ones where he was simply an asshole. A completely attractive and well-built asshole.

Amy's phone rang, the distinctive sound of Fleetwood Mac's "The Chain" filling the car through the speakers. She shook her head to clear away thoughts of the asshole and pressed the button on the wheel to answer.

"Hey, Dad."

"Amy, sweetheart. Just picked up the message about the car from yesterday. It was nice to hear your voice. And because I miss you, I wondered if you'll be coming home for Christmas." Floyd Murray was a worry-wart. And a planner. The worst possible combination. Right now, she could picture him in his bathrobe, smoking a big fat cigar, his old-school week-to-view diary in hand.

The brown leather of the nearly twenty-year-old diary cover was battered and scuffed and stained, but it had been the last gift her mother had bought him before she'd disappeared.

Amy looked at the temperature on the dash and smiled. "Dad, it's seventy-six degrees and the last day in August. I just started at my new office. Let me settle in before I request vacation."

The hiss and crackle of her father's cigar was reassuring. She'd long since given up trying to persuade him to quit. There was as much of a chance of that happening as of her becoming a Dallas Cowboys cheerleader—no matter how much she loved their white boots.

"You can't blame a man for trying to lock down a visit with his baby girl," he said gruffly.

"You know you can always come see me," she said with a laugh. It wasn't like he couldn't afford it. Floyd Murray had won eight World Series of Poker bracelets and had won the Main Event twice, beating the record of *his* father, who'd won six bracelets yet had never managed to win a Main Event. Grandpa Murray had always blamed his lack of success on "that damn Doyle Brunson." Only a handful of players had ever won as many titles as Doyle, recognized internationally as one of the greatest poker players of all times, but Grandma Murray always whispered with a wink that after his children had been born, Grandpa Murray hadn't wanted to leave home quite as often to go play.

"I might just have to do that. I had a great night at Bobby's last night," he said, referring to the exclusive high-stakes poker cash game that was played in the famous "Bobby's Room" at the Bellagio. "You want a piece of that in your Christmas stocking, you'd better be home on the twenty-fifth. Otherwise you're getting zip." Her father laughed, and the sound made her homesick.

Amy grinned as she pulled into the FBI parking lot. "I know you don't mean that and I don't need your money," she said, knowing her father was teasing. "I gotta go, Dad. I just got to work. Don't forget to follow-up with Dr. Hamill about your cholesterol test."

"Yeah, yeah. Have a good day, sweetie."

"You too, Dad."

She hurried to her desk. She'd once read a book that said the first hundred days of a new job were the most important. In practice, it felt like such a short time to build a network and create a good impression. Still on her to-do list was to find a new mentor.

The FBI had been her dream since the days and weeks that followed her mother's disappearance. Special Agent Hank Zarrados hadn't given up the search. He'd kept that file open for years, following up on every lead, no matter how implausible or small. Nobody had believed that Serena Murray had just upped and left her loving, close-knit family. Amy knew it for sure because as an adult she'd personally gone through all the publicly available sources, back to every single person and witness she could legally identify to interview them herself to make sure nothing had fallen through the cracks. They'd all confirmed that Serena Murray had loved her life, her husband . . . and her daughter.

Though she'd never been found, the FBI had given her hope during those darkest times, something she wanted to offer others. Simply being in the FBI office made her feel like she was making a difference.

"Murray." Her boss, David Cunningham, stuck his head out of his office window. "You got a sec?"

Amy dropped her purse off at her desk and grabbed a notebook and pen. She had no idea what he wanted, but whatever it was, she was determined to nail it. Heck, he could ask her to figure out how to make the world rotate in the opposite direction and she'd give it her best shot. She liked Cunningham. He was a straight-shooting kind of guy who said what was on his mind.

"What do you need?" she asked, stepping inside of his chaotic office. His sandy-colored head was down as he read something on his phone. Papers were piled up around his elbows and three coffee cups stood in a line next to his laptop.

He threw his pen down on top of the report open in front of him. "Those poker genes in your family . . . any of them get passed down to you?"

Please don't let it be a social card-game thing. Over the years, people had challenged her to games countless times. She usually won and then had to deal with the fragile egos of men who couldn't handle being beaten by a woman. Those experiences had taught her to be very honest up front about her skills.

"Yes," she said firmly. "A whole heap of them, sir. I debated going pro like my dad after college, even won a couple of tournaments, but I loved forensic psychology too much."

Cunningham placed his elbows on the desk and rested his chin on his hands. "Is it just poker?"

Just poker? Amy smiled. "Are you asking if I can play other games?"

"I am, Murray."

"Yes, sir. I can play just about all the obvious casino games from blackjack to poker and craps. But also a whole bunch of lesser-known ones . . . like fara, pai gow, and acey deucey."

Her words hung in the air. Cunningham stared at her and grinned like she was the answer to all his prayers. "Your godfather is the pit boss at Caesars Palace, right?"

Uncle Clive lived and breathed the betting floor. "He is, and he'd be happy to hear you used the term *pit boss*. He finds the PC term *pit manager* to lack a certain old-school class."

Cunningham took his glasses off and spun them by the arm. "You know where virtually all the missing women we are looking at worked."

Amy nodded. "The Lucky Seven Casino."

"Hypothetically," he said, "if we needed someone on the inside of the casino—undercover, instead of a broader team role—perhaps someone who could play, or deal even . . ."

Cunningham let his words hang. It wasn't an invitation to an after-work card game. It was an invitation to a different role in the case. The most perfect kind of role for her, because if there was one thing she knew, it was how things happened in a casino. It was also a chance to walk a mile in the shoes of the women. To find out from the inside who they befriended, to see how seriously the casino cared about the security of their women, to be . . . bait. That last part was something that wasn't directly stated, but couldn't be overlooked.

Amy sat a little straighter and tried to ignore the waves of excitement crashing in her stomach. "I'm your agent."

"The team's about to grow in size . . . there's a lot more to it than just the women. The CIA and a group of contractors they've been using suspect the Lucky Seven

Casino of money laundering. It's going to be unwieldy—
us, the CIA, and SDPD. Representatives from the NSB—
National Security Branch—and the Criminal, Cyber,
Response and Services Branch. But we all need eyes on
the ground, and one person can't cover all the bases."

The Lucky Seven, just south of Del Mar, only twenty
minutes north up the coast . . . where most of the missing women had worked. "So, we are going in as a team?"

"Yeah. Us, the CIA, and some external guns for hire.
Doesn't make me happy, but it's the only way of doing
it. You're going to need to bring your A game, Murray.
I'd have preferred someone with more experience, but
you're the best candidate to go undercover in the casino.
You think you're up to that?" Cunningham leaned toward
her and placed his elbows on the desk.

"Yes sir," Amy replied, anxious to begin.

"Well, we start on Monday," Cunningham said as he
slid a folder toward her across the desk. "And you need
to read this."

"*Vegas!*" Mac declared just as Cabe walked through
the door of the San Diego base of Eagle Securities.

"What's happening in Vegas?" Cabe asked as he
dropped his bag onto the conference room table before
grabbing a cinnamon roll. They were meeting in a few
minutes with their CIA contact, Andrew Aitken, to
talk about their ongoing project—one that had started
with the attempted abduction of Six's girlfriend and had
later been supported by evidence provided by Mac's
investigative-reporter girlfriend, Delaney. But why would
it have anything to do with Vegas?

He caught the look that passed silently between Mac
and Six. It seemed, for a fleeting moment, like concern.

Or sympathy. *Vegas.* It could only mean one thing. Six was about to do the one thing Cabe'd missed out on. The one thing the guys knew he'd wanted more than his next mission. "Wait. Are you guys getting married there?"

Six laughed, his blond hair falling in front of his eyes. "Good guess, but not quite. The three of us need to go there before November twenty-third."

"Why then?" Cabe asked.

"Because November twenty-third is one of only three days between now and Christmas that the three of us aren't scheduled to be away," Six replied. "And of those three, November twenty-third is the only day city hall had availability. At ten in the morning. Because I know that if I give Lou all day to overthink leaving the house and marrying me in a room with twenty people in it, she won't want to do it."

Joy for his friend filled Cabe. "Holy shit. Did Lou agree to this?" The differences between Six, his outgoing and fast-talking military brother, and Louisa, Six's chronically shy fiancée, were too many to list. Crowds were most definitely not her thing.

"Yeah. About that." Six topped up his coffee from the pot in the corner. "We're planning it. The wedding."

"What do you mean, *we're* planning it?" Mac asked. "She *is* down with this plan, right?"

"She is," Six replied with a grin. "She's going to take care of the dress. And that's it. You didn't see her the night I met her on that balcony before she had to just give a presentation. She was beyond freaked out. Calling caterers, booking venues, dealing with people . . . the thought of doing that would make her ill. And I don't want her to have to worry about a thing. Which means

I need you guys to do shit like taste-test cakes and whatever the hell else it is you need to do to get married right."

Cabe stared. "What on earth do we know about planning a wedding?" Jess had taken care of all of their wedding plans. He hadn't even known whom he'd needed to call to cancel after she'd died. Among other things, he'd forgotten all about the company making the wedding invitations. When he'd returned home from his tour and opened the box his mom had left on his kitchen counter, he'd unashamedly wept. While in theatre, he'd refused to think about what it meant to not have her in his life anymore, but holding those beautiful navy and cream invitations in his hands was a bitter reminder of the future he'd lost.

"Dude, we found our way out of Kunduz at night with no nav, no back-up, insurgents to the left of us and drug runners to our right, there I was, stuck in the middle with you," Six said, breaking into a mashed-up version of the Stealers Wheel song. "How hard can it be to plan a wedding?"

Mac groaned. "Okay, but I vote for roping in our moms. I'm not too much of a coward to admit I am out of my depth."

"You do realize that we're in our thirties, right?" Six said with a laugh.

Cabe shook his head. "You do realize we are completely useless at that kind of shit, right?"

Six stood and looked out into the hallway. "Too bad, because I already signed you guys up. You've had my back in more places than I can remember, and I have to tell you this is probably the scariest mission I've undertaken. I'm not going to do it without you."

As much as Cabe would rather pull his own finger-nails out with a pair of pliers than organize a wedding, the slight hitch in Six's voice reminded him they were family. "We'll figure it out," he said, his throat feeling a little dry. "We'll give you and Louisa the best wedding you could possibly have." He threw his arm over Six's shoulder and hugged him tight just as Andrew Aitken walked into the room.

"I'm not interrupting anything, am I?" he said as he put his bag down onto the table.

Cabe stepped away from Six. "Not unless you count being roped in to plan a wedding."

As Aitken congratulated Six, Mac took a seat and Cabe helped himself to a cup of coffee. Once everyone was settled, Aitken pulled out a document and began.

"We need a new formal contract for this," he started. "When you guys first came to me to ask for permission to look into that chemical theft at VNP Laboratories, the lab where Louisa North worked, I said yes more as a favor to Six than for any other reason. I mean, there were always real implications for National Security . . . but then there always are. In the current political climate, it just didn't rate high enough on our radar. But then, as you know, it grew."

"When we set out to help Louisa at the beginning of all of this, we had no idea where it would lead," Cabe said. He remembered the day Louisa had arrived at their offices looking for Six. Cabe had wanted to redirect her concerns to the police, but it had been clear from the start, despite Cabe and Mac's advice, that Six had already felt something for the shy scientist. But who would have thought that protecting Louisa would have turned into a mission to close a chemical weapons lab before it could start production. And he never could have imagined that exposing Louisa's colleague, Ivan Popov, and his grandfather, Vasilii, for selling the drug Louisa had created to Ivan's godfather, Sergei Lemtov, would have risked not only Louisa's life, but that of her mother and Cabe's colleagues. For that alone, Cabe had wanted to take Lemtov down. The fact that Lemtov was a mid-grade asshole in the syndicate with aspirations to grow his reach only added to the pleasure Cabe got from locking his ass his prison.

"And to think," Six said, with a grin on his face, "you'd said it wasn't the kind of work we like to take on."

Cabe shrugged. "Guilty. But I don't think any of us knew where it would lead, Mr. I'm Getting Married in Eleven Weeks."

Six laughed.

Aitken coughed, which Cabe suspected was an attempt to get them back on track.

"And then came the findings from Delaney's investigative piece," Cabe said, slowly turning his cup. Both alphabet agencies, the F.B.I. and C.I.A., had been embarrassed when Delaney had proven the round-robin supply route with drugs and weapons going one way and cash going the other.

Obviously tired, given the dark circles under his eyes, Aitken rubbed a hand along his temple.

Cabe placed his elbows on the table and rested his chin on his hands. "What do you need from us?"

"We have some intel that supports Ms. Shapiro's findings," Aitken said. "But as you know, we need Sokolov, Lemtov's boss. And we don't have proof of the money laundering, which we know is necessary for them to keep operating. Before this all blows up in our face because we can't close the net, we're going to close in on where we think it's happening: the Lucky Seven Casino."

Cabe nodded. It made sense. Ivan Popov had told Louisa that he was deeply in debt to the casino. They suspected that his debt was the reason he sold the formula as a chemical weapon to Lemtov, with the profits ultimately going to Sokolov, but they didn't have proof that the casino staff or owners were directly involved in any major corruption.

"The casino is owned by a private family," Aitken continued. "Faulkner Woods is the manager, and his father, Hemingway Woods is the owner. I shit you not, those *are* their names. Right now, Hemingway is off cruising the Med with wife number four on the proceeds."

Cabe smiled to himself. Someone knew their titans of American modernist literature, given that Faulkner and Hemingway had been literary rivals, though, it struck Cabe as an odd method for naming a child. He wondered if a daughter named Steinbeck was hidden away somewhere.

"Both of them walk and talk like hard-core businessmen," Aitken continued. "It's been impossible to pin anything down on them before now. We don't understand their relationship to Lemtov or his boss Sokolov, other than the latter has been seen in the casino. But these men most definitely have the connections, the clout, and the cash to front what is happening."

Six stood and began to pace. "You want us to check it out?"

Aitken nodded. "I want one of you to go undercover. It's a cross-agency task force. Technically money laundering is FBI. The Racketeer Influenced and Corrupt Organizations Act, RICO, falls under them. But you guys have been operating as one of us because of the threat to national security. You don't need to worry about the pissing match. I spent eight hours of my life and lost numerous brain cells in that battle on Friday."

"Don't envy you that," Cabe said. While deployed, he'd listened to his seniors battle plenty of times for the right to control an op.

"Thing is, when we approached them, they already had Lucky Seven in their sights. Part of an investigation into a number of missing women who they believe are linked. The only agreement we could get is that you work hand in hand with the FBI, specifically with an agent who will be working undercover as a dealer. I was going to fight it, but it turns out Special Agent Murray has a unique and distinctive skill set that should work in everyone's favor."

"Missing women" was something Cabe hadn't seen coming, and he'd prefer not to muddy the waters with two cases running simultaneously. "There's no way we can go in on our own?"

Aitken scowled. "No chance. The FBI will explain their reasons to investigate the casino themselves. I'll let them explain at the project setup on Thursday. You guys in?"

Cabe thought about the implications, including staffing. The majority of Mac's team were committed to a South American shipping company dealing with piracy. Six's team had just returned from a six-month on-and-off security detail in Syria. The guy had a wedding coming up and deserved to spend time with his wife-to-be. Which left Cabe and his team, who had a series of small jobs between now and the end of October, when they were to switch with Mac's team and head into South America for two months. "My team is the only one that could take it on."

"I'd love to argue with you," Mac said, "but I think it makes sense. If we need to, my team can keep rotating into South America until yours is ready to switch out, depending on how long the job takes."

Six nodded. "I agree. Mine needs some downtime. I know if we said they needed to do it, they'd find a way to figure it out. But really, Cabe's team is on the freshest legs."

Andrew pulled open his briefcase and pulled out some paperwork. He slid it across the table to Cabe. "Take a look at the terms. Get back to me tomorrow. Kickoff meeting is over at the feeb office," he said, referring to the Sorrento Valley FBI office. "Figured it would make them feel like they were in charge, even if we all know they're not."

Cabe grinned. It looked like Eagle was going to land right in the middle of alphabet-agency soup, whether they liked it or not.

"Hey, Amy, sweetheart, it's all set." Uncle Clive's gruff voice on her voicemail reflected the twenty-a-day habit he'd had for decades. According to Uncle Clive, Frank Sinatra had offered him his first cigarette in January 1977 when Clive had been hanging around the dressing rooms of Caesars Palace. He remembered the day, he'd said, because Frank's mom, Dolly, had died in a plane crash on her way to see him perform. "You know you can come by the casino any time. I'll set you up with Valentina."

Amy smiled, pressing her phone to her ear as she juggled the notebook, folder, and pens in her hand. Valentina was the very best dealer at Caesars Palace, and arguably on The Strip. With her faint Spanish lilt that still lingered after thirty years in the States and a memory for faces and names and preferred decks of playing cards, she managed and dealt in the private rooms, where players would leave tips in the tens of thousands of dollars. Amy couldn't think of a better person with whom to brush up her skills. When Amy had asked for help, her family had known better than to ask why she needed them. They'd simply said yes.

Relief and excitement battled in her stomach as she took the eleven steps down to the conference room. Undercover roles came with high expectations, but she knew she had what it took to live up to them. There couldn't be a more perfect intersection of her worlds. And the confidence boost she got from that was immeasurable. When she'd first moved to San Diego, she'd been nervous that her undeserved reputation would follow her. Or worse, some other dick would treat her the exact same way. But she had to give Cunningham his due. While he'd never asked her about what had happened, she knew he knew, and there had been no sign that anybody else had known when she'd arrived. There were no loaded stares, no nudging in the hallway as she walked by. Her gut told her that he believed the official statement she'd submitted. And that meant, as far as he was concerned, she had a clean slate for her professional career.

She pushed open the door to the conference room. A quick scan told her there were thirteen chairs . . . not the most auspicious number. Amy dragged one of the chairs from under the window to the table. Better to be safe than sorry.

Cunningham eyed her carefully. "Everything okay,

Amy?" He looked tired, but then he always looked a little harassed. And while his suit was always expertly pressed, his shoes looked as though he'd walked a hundred miles too far in them.

"Perfect," she said as she organized her things. "Can't wait to dig in and meet the rest of the task force." There had been murmurs about it, whispers through the hallways that shouldn't exist but always did. Plus, a boatload of CIA peeps had shown up at the building the week before.

Cunningham rubbed his forehead and offered a grim smile. "Wish I could share your enthusiasm. I have a feeling that these guys can't even spell RICO, let alone know what it means."

The Racketeer Influenced and Corrupt Organizations Act was their bread and butter. And when outside organizations tried to take a bite, the FBI snarled. But somehow, a deal to work together had already been done, or else she wouldn't be sitting in this meeting room waiting for them to arrive. By the look on Cunningham's face, the FBI had tried hard to bounce the deal but had been unsuccessful.

"Probably thought we were talking about *Puerto* Rico," Mills, a fellow agent, said. Just as she laughed, the door swung open.

Cabe.

Her stomach dropped, and her head spun. Despite everything, her heart betrayed her and skipped a beat at the sight of him. It was understandable. Her memory of him had not even begun to do him justice. He wore a navy blue suit tailored to his swimmer's frame. The jacket hung open, fitting snugly over his wide shoulders. A pale blue shirt stretched perfectly across his trim torso. She'd bet dollars to donuts that there was one of those hugely attractive six-packs beneath the soft-looking cotton.

She watched him greet one of the analysts assigned to the project, his back now to her. *Damn*, that butt.

Which she shouldn't be studying. Because the guy was a jerk. There was no other word for him.

He was joined by the men she'd seen him sitting with in the bar. One was tall, like a Nordic Viking. The other one was equally built, with chestnut hair and a broad grin. They had an easy confidence. It irked her.

Cunningham had joined Cabe and was shaking his hand. Her stomach sank even further as she realized what he was about to do. Yup, there it was. He lifted his hand in her direction, and Cabe's eyes met hers.

No freaking response. Wow.

Nothing.

A body-language expert would get absolutely zero from him.

No telltale lines of concern between his brows, no curl of a smile in recognition. No *Oh my god I am so freaking sorry for being a jerk and leaving you standing alone at the bar in front of a room full of people.*

As hard as she focused on keeping her gaze equally neutral, she knew she was failing. If her cheeks felt hot—and by her guess were likely a little pinker than normal—there was nothing she could do to control it. Her breathing was a little more erratic than normal. But she took a deep breath as Cabe walked toward her.

"Cabe Moss," he said calmly, offering her his hand. "Eagle Securities." His tone was even, not a hint of recognition. Had she been that bland, that uninteresting that he couldn't even remember her? Amy tried to clear the thought. If he truly didn't remember her, it was a good thing. It would make working with him even easier.

"Amy Murray." She reached for his hand, and memories of shaking it in the bar crashed through her. It was just as warm as she'd remembered, and large, his handshake firm and confident.

Not even a freaking blink from him. Or a wink. Or an extra squeeze of the hand. No, he just let go of her hand after a completely appropriate length of time.

Goddamn.

"Six Rapp," the blond guy said. "Also from Eagle. Looking forward to working with you on this." Cabe stepped away as she took Six's hand and found her voice.

"You, too. I'm looking forward to getting started."

"That's Malachai MacCarrick over there with your boss. Goes by Mac," Six said, tipping his head in Mac's direction. "We own Eagle and will be assisting in surveillance for the money-laundering side of the op."

"Okay, everybody, can you take a seat please?" Cunningham took his place at the head of the table. In the usual way of things, people took seats based on an unspoken hierarchy. Whoever the CIA head honcho was sat to the left of Cunningham. The assigned analysts took the chairs farthest away. Cabe took the seat directly across from Amy. Six whispered something in his ear, and Cabe grinned.

That smile was going to be the death of her. As much as he'd pissed her off, she'd still dreamed about that goddamn grin.

"Let's do a roundtable introduction," Cunningham offered. "Name, department. The usual shit. Keep it brief or this'll take all day."

Amy smiled. Blunt and brief. Quickly, Amy drew the

shape of the table in her notebook, and made a note of who sat in each corresponding seat. The simple act of documenting it helped her memorize who they were. It had always been a skill of hers. There was something about seeing things in her own handwriting that made it stick in her head. She wouldn't need to look at the piece of paper again after this meeting.

A man who introduced himself as Andrew Aitken, the CIA director of operations, fiddled with his laptop for just a moment before his slides appeared on the large screen. "While we didn't know it would end here, we began this operation over twelve months ago as part of an investigation to recover a stolen chemical formula that we believed was going to be weaponized."

Three photographs appeared on the screen. A female with brunette hair, a young male around the same age, and an older male with salt and pepper hair. "Louisa North created the formula as part of her research into a medical condition. Ivan Popov stole the formula from the lab they worked at together and passed it to Sergei Lemtov."

The next slide showed a chart of organizational hierarchy, with Popov on the bottom and a guy called Sokolov on the top. But it was difficult to remain focused when Cabe briefly gripped Six's shoulder, earning a tight nod from Six, who appeared to be grinding his teeth. Spidey senses told her that whatever had just been presented was personal to these men.

Cabe caught her glance and held it. The intensity in his eyes, the color of which split the difference between gray and green, shook her.

She wanted to look away. Wanted desperately to look to the slide currently projected on the screen.

But she couldn't.

CHAPTER THREE

Cabe tore his eyes away from Amy's.

Not because he wanted to. Not because he was interested in what the slides showed, seeing as he'd been the one to prepare them with the help of Eagle's new analyst, Ersel. But because if he didn't, he was sure as shit going to get turned on by the woman sitting opposite him.

She was beautiful, despite the unflattering pantsuit and the way her hair was secured to within an inch of its life at the nape of her neck. That hair in and of itself had been enough to make her the star of his dreams the last couple of nights. Dreams that had left him hard and achy and wracked with guilt. It had been Jess's birthday after all, and he hadn't even had enough self-control to resist flirting with a pretty woman, let alone dream about said woman getting her workout from riding him up and down and nice and slow.

No. It wasn't just her sex appeal—currently contained or not—that was distracting. Nor was it the way he'd witnessed her bite that full lower lip of hers as he spoke. It was that he now knew she had the brains to back up the beauty. And brains were the sexiest goddamn thing about a woman.

He focused on the slide on the screen as if it was the most interesting thing he'd ever seen. All the details of the way Six had met Lou were laid out bare. The failed wonder-drug turned chemical weapon. The Russian syndicate. The abduction of Louisa's mom until Louisa had been ballsy enough to allow herself to be taken in a swap.

He smiled to himself when he remembered the way he and his team had taken down the ranch-style house, saving both Louisa and her mother.

Lemtov wasn't giving anything away. He was lawyered up tight and knew that if he revealed anything, his life would be over before he even got to prison. Vasilii Popov had done a plea deal to testify that his grandson took the drug to Lemtov, his godfather, a story that differed from the testimony Louisa was going to give, one that would place the actual sale at Vasilii's feet.

Ivan Popov was still missing. Wherever he was hiding, he'd not come up for air. There had been no attempts to draw on any of the family funds, and nobody had attempted to enter either Vasilii's or Ivan's homes, despite an alleged unpaid debt to Lucky Seven casino.

Amy's eyes were still on him. He could tell. He had always been able to see without seeing, a talent he could never explain. An instructor had told him at the end of BUD/s, the hellish training all SEALs underwent to prepare for the role, that what he had was an uncanny sixth sense . . . a strange knowledge of what people would do next. It had served him well.

Which is why he also knew that Cunningham was unhappy about both the very existence of the joint task force and Eagle's participation. He probably thought the short, sharp exhalations every time Eagle was mentioned and the eye contact he'd made with his right-hand man when Aiken was speaking were subtle.

Cabe wasn't the only person the FBI didn't really want on their team. Three of the men in the room had repeatedly given away their misogyny. When Amy's role in the project was announced, one had reached for his phone and seconds later the other two had looked at their phones and had laughed as all three had looked in Amy's direction. The FBI might think they had it all covered, that they didn't need Eagle's help, but some of their operatives didn't have the first clue about keeping their emotions off their faces.

To be fair, had he known that the woman who would be going undercover as a dealer was Amy . . . well, the evening they'd met would have gone very differently.

But unlike the three jerk-wads, it had nothing to do with her gender. Hell, he'd cheered Jess's rise up the military ranks. And he'd been raised by a strong mother who had shown him repeatedly that women were often more capable than men.

It was just that had he known that the woman he'd met was going to be involved in *their* op, he certainly wouldn't have flirted with her, half-sunk in his whiskey and memories. And he wouldn't have paid so much attention to the softness of her skin. The mere act of shaking her hand at their introduction today had revved his engines. And at the moment he was cursing his uncanny ability to remember every detail in every situation, wishing he could turn off the thought of how cute her breasts had looked in that goddamn sundress.

"Cabe, do you want to take over from here?" Aitken asked, his voice cutting through Cabe's thoughts.

"Sure," he said, switching back into work mode. He took the time to explain how Delaney's investigative report had closed in on the production of the weapon and how it had led to the arrest of key players before getting down to the nuts and bolts of what was involved. "We've split the work into three key streams: intel, external surveillance, and internal surveillance. Intel will take the lead on tracing the finances, broadening the search on the perps involved. External surveillance will be responsible for the setup and monitoring of the inside op. Internal surveillance will be Agent Murray and me on the inside."

As he talked through all their respective roles, responsibilities and immediate to-dos, he made a point to get a better look at everyone, including Amy, who deliberately avoided his eyes. He knew he'd been an ass by ignoring her, but he'd had his reasons. Before they went any further, he'd have to explain them to her.

When he'd finished talking, he sat back down, wondering what it would take to thaw the atmosphere between the two of them.

Cunningham stood. "There is a final piece from our side that you may not be aware of." The images of three young women appeared on the screen, all of them attractive and young. "These three women all worked at Lucky Seven. All of them have been reported missing by their families over the last two years. When SDPD did some more digging, they learned that more women who worked there are unaccounted for but were never reported as missing."

Two more images appeared on the screen. The hairs on Cabe's neck stood on end. He needed to talk to his brother, Noah, a detective in the SDPD Special Case Squad.

"The women never provided their friends or families with any details of where they were going or who they were associating with, and the investigations ran out of leads and then steam. No witnesses, no bodies, no crime scene. The water gets muddy if we make this an additional priority, but this is why this cross-functional team is necessary. With our involvement for the missing women who we believe may have been trafficked, and Eagle's involvement for the CIA due to the egregious National Security rules overruling our ownership of RICO."

"For fuck's sake," Aitken muttered under his breath. "They are not egregious."

Even as Cabe's mind raced with the new information, he placed his hand over his mouth to hide the smirk. Cunningham was going to be a bundle of laughs to work with.

"Anyway," Cunningham continued, ignoring Aitken's glare, "it's something we need to be aware of to ensure Agent Murray's safety—and if we can find anything out to help SDPD, then we should. You got anything you want to add, Mr. Moss?"

Cabe shook his head and let Cunningham wrap up the meeting. Seeing that Eagle was on FBI turf, it made sense that the FBI have the final word, even if they didn't realize they weren't the ones steering the ship.

Amy was the first to stand and head for the exit. "Grab my shit," he muttered to Six before he jogged after her.

"Agent Murray, wait up," he said as she marched ahead of him. Even draped in an ugly black fabric, she still had a fantastic ass. It was going to be hard to switch gears from the context under which they'd met to the fact they'd be working together. He needed to be professional again.

For a moment, he thought he was going to have to break into a sprint, but she stopped suddenly and turned on the ball of her foot. Her shoulders dropped for a moment as if sighing, and then she straightened again. "What can I help you with, Mr. Moss?" Her words were bright, collegial even, but the thunderous look in her eyes told him it was an act.

There was a lot to be said for squaring up against a woman with a bit of spark. He'd take a firecracker over a mouse any day of the week. But he figured that wasn't what Amy would want to hear right now. Instead, he went for straightforward honesty. "It's Cabe, and I'm an idiot. And I want to clear the air." He could hear footsteps behind him and looked over his shoulder. The conference room was beginning to empty. Some of her colleagues, Cunningham included, were heading their way. "You keep looking at me like you want to kill me, and whoever is heading our way is going to wonder why."

She glanced over his shoulder, not taking his word for it, but the look on her face then immediately softened. "Of course. Why don't I walk you out to your car?"

They walked in silence until they were out of earshot, where Cabe then turned to face her. They were mature adults, and he was determined to act like one despite his behavior the night they'd met. Which meant ignoring that piece of hair that had fallen from her bun and resisting the urge to tuck it behind her ear. "I'm sorry. For two things. First, I'm sorry I disappeared on Friday evening. It's a long story, difficult to tell, and very personal." For a moment, he debated telling her more, but he swallowed the urge. "But I acted like a shit because of it. I regret it. And I'm sorry for acting like I didn't know you in there.

I didn't know how you'd want to play it, but I guessed bringing your personal life into the office wasn't the best bet. If I was wrong, I'll correct the impression I gave everyone else the next time we all meet."

Amy looked out toward the parking lot and sighed. "Will you tell them you were a douchebag? What you did was cruel. I felt like an idiot when I had to go back to my friends and explain that you'd disappeared on me."

"I'm sorry."

She returned her gaze to his. "As much as I'm mad, it's probably for the best anyway. We're going to be working pretty closely."

He could have sworn he heard regret. He felt a twinge of it too.

But there was nothing they could do about it. And not only because they'd be working together.

When Jess had died, it had torn him apart that he hadn't been able to keep her safe. It had never bothered him that she had a job that not only meant she wouldn't avoid trouble, but that she'd run straight into it. Until it had killed her. And given Amy's job and her spine, she'd probably be the exact same way.

He was never going down that road again.

The following day, Amy pulled off the highway into a nondescript industrial-looking complex. A haze of heat settled a foot above the tarmac. Her sat nav told her she'd reached her final destination, but she wasn't sure which building was Eagle Securities. Mac had described it to her as "an ugly gray box with no sign outside." She scanned the lot until she spotted a building at the far end of the units matching the description and drove toward the parking lot in front of it as she'd been instructed.

She parked her car and grabbed her bag off the passenger seat, but instead of getting out, she sat for a moment and stared at the building. The people inside held power over her being able to achieve her career aspirations and being able to finally dodge the whispers that had plagued her in Atlanta. And both goals rested on her ability to work with Cabe, a man who despite letting her down had at least had the courage to admit to being an ass.

Though there was nothing at all remarkable-looking about the building, it held the ability to make everything right.

With a renewed sense of excitement and optimism, she stepped out of the car and up to the front door and pushed it open. The interior was a complete contrast to the exterior. The walls were white, the floors were light wood, and there were plenty of pops of bright blue throughout— from the fabric chairs in the waiting area to the large Eagle Securities logo on the wall behind a large opaque-glass-front desk. Behind it sat a mature woman, easily in her fifties, wearing a headset and talking into a small microphone.

"I'm sorry, Mr. Moss is in meetings all morning," she said, raising one finger and flashing a smile in Amy's direction. "Can I put you through to his voicemail?" There was a pause. "Of course. Putting you through now." The woman disconnected the call.

"Good morning," she said cheerily. "I'm Leslie. How can I help you this morning?"

"I'm here for a meeting with Cabe Moss. I'm Special Agent Amy Murray."

Leslie slipped her headset off and stood. "We've been expecting you," she said warmly, sliding a visitor's pass across the desk. "If you'll follow me, I'll take you to the conference room."

Amy clipped the pass to the pocket of her jacket as they walked. Leslie used her pass to open a set of double doors leading into an office area that appeared to be a hub of activity. Men she hadn't met walked purposefully between rooms, all of them dressed casually. She suddenly felt a little overdressed. One of the men smiled at her in welcome, and she nodded in response.

"Hey, Amy," Cabe said, walking out of an office to her left. He was wearing jeans and a white T-shirt that stretched across his chest perfectly. His dark hair was still wet, as if he'd recently showered. And no, she was most definitely not going to think about Cabe showering. "You found us okay?" he asked. He held out his hand to point her in the direction of a large conference room with no windows.

"Yes. You were right about the building. It's amazing how something can almost disappear into the background."

The conference room, on the other hand, was anything *but* nondescript. It was a high-tech den of activity. The walls were white and the industrial-tile carpet gray, but they were the only boring things about the space. A bank of screens lined one wall, each one tuned to something different: a parking lot, a rural property, the exterior of the very building she stood in. A man with shorn dark hair sat in front of a large command console watching the screens. Three other men were already seated at the large table.

"Just how we wanted it," Cabe said. "As soon as we saw the place, we knew it was meant to be ours. I'll give you a tour later. But for now, let me introduce you to the team. Guys, this is Special Agent Amy Murray. The guy by the screens over there is Miller Stubs. We call him Lite. He's going to be leading the intel arm of this op."

Miller Lite. Amy grinned. Lite lifted his hand in greeting.

Cabe pointed in the direction of a guy who could easily pass for a surfer, with blond waves that just kissed his shoulders. On his head was a pair of Oakleys with tinted lenses. His T-shirt declared that he was there only in spirit. "That over there is Harley Burnham. Don't let the 'I don't give a shit' vibe put you off. When it comes to tracking, I don't know anybody better."

"I resemble that remark," Harley replied. "Nice to meet you Amy."

"You too."

"And finally, Tweedle-Dee and Tweedle-Dum over there are Bailey Franklin and Joel Budd, who we call Buddha. They are going to be our backup, managing external surveillance and, where we can, some internal surveillance. There are a couple of others who aren't here right now, Gaz and Jackson, but you'll probably see them around."

Amy smiled in greeting. She'd seen enough movies to have heard of the military penchant for nicknames and call signs. Cabe pulled out a seat near the head of the table as Six and Mac walked into the room. Once everyone was seated, Cabe recapped the background, going a little deeper than they had the previous day.

"Tell us about the missing women," Cabe ask her.

"They have all worked at Lucky Seven at some point," she replied as Cabe projected the file she had forwarded to him the previous evening. A pretty brunette with small lips and green eyes faced them. "Helen Foy. Aged twenty-six. Arrived here a week before she landed the job at Lucky Seven and worked there for two months before she disappeared. According to her boss, Johnnie Ortega, she was a good worker. But that seems to be a theme common to all the missing women. They were competent at their jobs. Helen worked in the casino by night and was working toward an online degree in psychology. Her parents reported her missing when she didn't show up back home for Thanksgiving, which was four days after she was last seen at the casino. No friends here to immediately miss her. But she seemed pretty close to her parents."

Cabe tapped his pen on the desk. "If she was so attached to her family, how did she end up here?"

"The lure of the big city. She'd been let go from her part-time job in her small hometown and thought she'd stand a better chance of managing school and maintaining employment in the city." Amy shook her head as she thought back to the interview notes from Helen's lecturers, comments about how her coursework had shown real promise and a solid grasp of all the concepts. "By all accounts, she was totally pulling that off here."

"What about the others?" Six asked before grabbing his mug and taking a large sip of coffee.

"Melanie Stokes," Amy said, turning her attention to the dark-haired woman with blue eyes and thirteen piercings along one ear. "Almost the exact same story. A year younger. Interviewed for the job on a whim while on a West Coast road trip with friends. She'd spent the previous summer as a dealer in Atlantic City and felt like a change of scene after breaking up with her boyfriend. In her case, it was the ex-boyfriend who finally reported her missing after coming here to surprise her. There was no sign of her at work, and she'd always been responsive on social media. Instagram, Facebook . . . but suddenly there were no posts and she wasn't returning anybody's messages."

Cabe was studying the face of the third woman, a blonde with cute glasses and a pixie cut. "Is Joanne Gleave the same story?"

Amy nodded. "Sadly, yes. Except the first two were dealers, and Joanne worked behind the bar. Joanne was, by all accounts, a free spirit. Traveled around the country for three years. Periodically she'd pick up bar work to rebuild her savings. She'd told her brother in Boulder, Utah, that she was going to drive there for Christmas. It was normal for them to not have contact for long periods. Joanne was at best flaky when it came to keeping in touch, according to her brother. He called SDPD to report her missing on the twenty-eighth of December, but by then she hadn't shown up at the casino for six weeks."

There was silence for a moment and then Cabe stood. "You mentioned more?"

When she'd read the files initially, her heart had raced as she'd noted the similarities. Something told her the women were connected, but there was only so much information to go off of. "When the police interviewed Joanne's coworkers, they were given the name of another girl, Alison Berry, who had previously worked at the casino and had seemingly disappeared without telling any of her coworkers she was leaving. Although in this case, Faulkner Woods was able to provide a resignation letter from her. We are keeping her details on file because even though she hasn't been reported missing, she hasn't resurfaced anywhere else. No tax filing, nothing posted on social media, no driver's license renewal in another state. Nothing. She's vanished."

"I'll start digging on all the women," Bailey said. "See if I can't find something through different channels."

Amy nodded her approval. "I'd appreciate it. I'd like to say that since SDPD and the FBI have all looked at this already, there isn't any need, but we all know how easy it is to miss a small detail. I don't think we can have too many eyes on it."

"Agreed," Cabe said. "Were they the only ones? Are we sure there aren't more?" His eyes connected with hers, and for a second she was back in the bar. There was a quick flash of interest, but it disappeared as quickly as she'd seen it.

"The person who worked this case before me was unable to secure a warrant for the casino's past and present employee list because it felt like a fishing expedition, but if there was a way around it through the access and approvals you are able to get, I'd be very grateful."

Cabe looked at Harley, the man he'd said could track anybody.

"On it," Harley said and turned around to the bank of monitors against the wall.

"I'm assuming you did some searching over the same time period for missing women in the area in general . . . and went back in time for those working at the casino?" Cabe asked.

Amy tapped her fingernails on her keyboard, though not hard enough to press any of the keys. It was just something she did when she was thinking. Then she opened the file.

Seven more names. Bringing the list to twelve.

"Holy shit," Six said.

"Look at the dates," Amy suggested. "Or better, look at them grouped with the last known sighting of each of the victims." They bundled into almost three perfect blocks.

"Each block is six months apart," Cabe said. "Which means the next block starts next month."

"That's why we think it's trafficking. It's too systematic. Transportation of victims needs setup, needs organization. The first two weeks in October are highly likely for this strike to happen again. We think at least two girls from the casino have gone the last couple of times."

"You're there as bait," Cabe said coolly.

"No. I'm there as an agent. With a rocket-high GPA and a shit ton of case experience. But yeah, let's call it what it is. I was *also* chosen because I can play, because I know my way around a casino, and because I can deal."

Cabe raised his hands and shook his head. "Wasn't challenging your credentials there, Amy. It was simply a statement."

She believed him; there was understanding in his eyes that soothed her irritation. "You're right. We both know that the girls on that screen were pretty but new in town. I'm new in town, and from the unsolicited dick pics I get on Tinder, I qualify for pretty."

If there was one thing Cabe must have understood as a former SEAL, it was the use of inappropriate humor in stressful situations. He studied her for a second longer, but it was long enough for her to forget there were other people in the room. Cabe shook his head and ran his hand over his chin. "Guess I can't argue with that," he said gruffly.

For a moment, she couldn't think of anything else to say.

"Okay," Cabe said, stretching his arms up over his head. "Is the business portion of today concluded?"

It was after seven, and only Mac, Six, Amy, and Cabe were still around.

Amy nodded and pulled the bobby pins out of her hair one by one. "I certainly hope so because I am officially toast." The hair that had been pulled into a bun at the back of her neck all day fell into a long braid.

Cabe tried not to groan. To get the job done, he needed to stop thinking about what that braid would feel like wrapped in his hand. And for his mental health, he needed to not get involved with a woman in a high-risk occupation.

But she was bait. Fucking bait. It didn't sit well in his gut. But since she was willing, he'd get with the program.

"I'm starved, and Lou is in the middle of some big experiment," Six said. "I know she'll be late tonight. Anybody want to grab pizza?"

"I'm game," Amy agreed.

"Perfect. I'll go order," Six said, standing. "I know what these two like, but any no-goes for you, Amy?"

"No tuna. Because seafood does not belong on a pizza."

"That I totally agree with," Cabe said, stacking his papers, wondering how many other things they agreed on. Small things, big things, it would be fun to figure out . . . no. He cut the train of thought off. That kind of thinking sounded a lot like the fun of dating. Getting to know the other person. And he was so not ready for that.

He looked over at Amy, who was putting her laptop away in her bag. To her left was a pile of handwritten notes, all seemingly color-coded, and meticulously organized. The way she'd communicated with them during the day had been the same. Structured and cohesive. He shook his head to clear his thoughts. "Give me a sec to go put my stuff in my office."

He placed his laptop and his papers on his desk. The unsettled feeling that had niggled him all day finally had a name. Disappointment. It was better to acknowledge the weakness than pretend it didn't exist. He was disappointed that he couldn't get to know Amy on a more personal level. The boundaries were clear and he'd honor them, but he needed a moment to get over the fact that it sucked.

"Good session, today," Mac said as he walked into Cabe's office.

Cabe nodded his head in agreement. "Knowing more about the missing women helps."

"Helps that Amy knows her shit," Six said, joining the conversation.

"That, she does," Mac agreed.

"Listen. I have an idea," Cabe said.

"What is it?" Mac asked, just as Six joined them.

Earlier that morning, as he'd been about to leave the apartment, he'd seen the slim metal case by the rest of the games and had decided to take a chance and bring it to work. "We have zero time to build a working relationship with Amy. Today was a great start. But we need to get to know each other. And I need some practice," he said. "What do you say we see if Amy will play poker with us over pizza?"

Six laughed. "For real? How many hours have we spent playing that damn game?"

Cabe grinned. "I gotta believe it's not going to be straightforward. She almost went pro."

"She's going to kick our ass," Mac said with a shrug. "But I'm game."

Now it was Cabe's turn to laugh. "Yeah. We're gonna lose. But it'll be fun." He dug the case out from behind his desk.

Mac coughed. "Can I say something without you jumping down my throat?"

Cabe stood. "That you even need to ask me that question means it's pretty much guaranteed that I am going to jump down your throat, doesn't it?"

"Okay. But you and Amy. I might be being stupid, and it's highly possible that because I love my girlfriend to death, I'm seeing love and shit, but are you two . . . is there? I don't . . . I can't say it was anything really obvious but . . ."

Cabe sighed as he leaned his ass on his desk. He needed to come clean about what had happened because secrets among teammates could be deadly, even if they seemed innocuous. "Last week, when we were at the bar, after you guys left . . . she was there. We got talking."

"Oh, for fuck's sake," Six said.

"Nothing happened," Cabe jumped in. "Hell, we didn't get past first names and some flirtation that said it could have gone exactly where your mind just did. But I bailed on her."

Mac's eyes locked on his. "You what?"

Cabe rubbed his hand over his chin and then adjusted his watch on his wrist.

"Quit stalling," Mac said and took a step closer. "You. Did. What?"

"She was cute, I hit on her, and then I felt guilty as shit that it was Jess's birthday and I was talking to another woman. So while she was taking some drinks to her friends, I ducked out the door. I spoke to her about it at the FBI meeting. Apologized. Told her I was a dick, and she agreed it was probably for the best that we didn't take it any further, given that we are going to be working together."

Since then, she'd been all business. Since then, she'd done nothing but behave professionally with him . . . except. Shit, Mac was right. There had been moments today when they'd just seemed in synch: when they'd blurted out the same proposed answer to the setup of the op; when they'd liked the same country artists; when he'd looked at her while she spoke and their eyes had locked for a millisecond.

"I don't suppose it will do any good to remind you of our fraternization policy, would it?" Six asked.

"Because you paid so much attention to it when you slept with Louisa after promising not to? And like you did, Mac, when you hooked back up with Delaney? I swear to god that policy isn't worth the paper we wrote the fucking thing on."

Mac walked to the bookshelf and picked up Cabe's copy of *Book of Five Rings*. "You seriously read this shit?"

Cabe rolled his eyes. "Miyamoto Musashi's writing on conflict and taking the advantage is nearly four hundred years old and just as valid now as it was then."

Mac replaced the book on the shelf. "I'm going to say two things, then I'm going to go get pizza. The first is don't mess this up. For her sake. My sisters will tell you how hard it is for women to be taken seriously sometimes. I gotta believe it's doubly hard in the feebs. The second . . . well—"

The buzzer to the building sounded. "That'll be the pizza," Six said, and Mac looked toward the hallway.

"The second?" Cabe asked.

"She wouldn't want you to be alone, Cabe. . . . Jess. She wasn't selfish. She'd want you to find someone else." Mac slapped him on the shoulder as he and Six left the room.

Cabe sucked in a deep breath and sat on his office chair. Mindlessly he spun it toward the window. The view was uninspiring, but he could see a stretch of sky above the building next to theirs.

She wouldn't want you to be alone.

Buried deep down inside was the knowledge Mac was right.

He took a few minutes before joining the others in the conference room. When he did, the smell of tomatoes and pepperoni hit him full in the face. His stomach rumbled as he placed the case down on the table. "While we eat," he said, opening the case of poker chips and cards, "I thought we could practice. I'll be heading into the casino after Amy starts and don't want to be rusty." Reconnaissance for evidence of money laundering was going to require every ounce of focus. It would require covert camera placement, identification of targets, and hours and hours of intelligence gathering. But he couldn't just walk around or sit at the bar. He'd need to play, and play well.

He looked straight at Amy. "Plus, I want to see just how good little Miss Spawn of the World Poker Series

Dynasty actually is." Amy narrowed her gaze playfully, and he winked in return. He liked teasing her.

Amy laughed as she waved a hand in front of her mouth. He guessed the pizza was hot. "Oh my god," she mumbled. "This spawn is seriously going to kick your ass." She swallowed the pizza and shook her head in what looked like an attempt to regain composure. "Shit, that was hot. Look, I point blank refuse to play you for money."

"What if we just said fifty bucks?" Mac said, pulling out his wallet and throwing a fifty-dollar bill down on the table.

Cabe watched Amy closely. If for a moment he thought she was truly uncomfortable, he'd tell his friends to put their money away.

"I can do chips only," Six said, but he pulled his wallet from his pocket, placing two twenties and a ten down. "But I'd rather take Mac's money."

Mac shook his head but smiled. "What makes you so sure you're taking mine? What if it's the other way around? What if I kick your ass?"

While the two of them bickered, Cabe took out his own wallet and pulled out a fifty. He held it between the tips of his fingers. "What do you say, Amy?" he asked quietly. "If it's not cool, I can tell these guys to check their egos and their money. We can just play for chips."

Amy met his gaze. The sparkle was back in her eyes, the one that had intrigued him at the bar. She placed her pizza down on her plate and brushed the crumbs from her hands. "Fine," she said, reaching for her purse. "But I want it in writing that you are not going to be a bunch of sore losers when I walk out of here with all your money in under an hour."

"Yes!" Six shouted and walked toward the glass wipe boards that had all their notes from the day on them. He reached for a pen and wrote: *We do solemnly declare that we will not be pouty bitches if we get our asses kicked by Amy Murray.*

He signed his name and offered the pen to Mac, who dutifully signed it. Cabe took the fifty out of her hand and placed it on the table with his own, then took the pen from Mac and added his own signature. "Now then," he said, holding the pack of cards in his hands, "can we play?"

Amy smiled like a woman with a plan and took the pack from him. She slid the cards out, discarded the unwanted ones, and looked at the three men sitting around the table.

"Yes," she said, then proceeded to do two-card spring flourishes, the cards going airborne between her hands, followed by a one-handed shuffle that blew his mind. And just when he'd thought it over, she laid the cards out on the table in a perfect fan, flipped them over so they were faceup, and then flipped them all back before scooping them up and completing another perfect one-handed shuffle.

Cabe grinned as Amy took in Mac's and Six's faces.

"Ready, boys?" she asked.

And he so knew they were going to get their asses handed to them.

CHAPTER FOUR

Ruby Woo better come through.

Amy tried not to laugh at her pun as she carefully applied the famously named, perfectly matte red MAC lipstick. It was rare that she was willing to put her looks front and center to get ahead, but landing the job as a dealer at Lucky Seven was crucial. If it meant the addition of an extra two cup sizes, courtesy of Victoria's Secret, then so be it. She popped the lid on the lipstick and placed it on the counter in the utilitarian all-white bathroom. It was bright, if just a bit on the small side, although the large mirror above the sink tricked the eye into thinking it was larger than it was.

When she'd transferred to San Diego, she'd barely had time to research neighborhoods before she'd hit the road with her belongings in her trunk. In a hurry to settle and get ready to start her new job, she'd opted for a simple yet airy apartment rental in Little Italy. The six-month lease was long enough for her to find her feet and decide if she wanted to put down roots. There were apartments and houses closer to work, but growing up in

Vegas had given her a love for cities. She loved the smog, the noise, the general bustle—although San Diego seemed way more chill than Sin City.

Plus, she wanted a while longer to save up for a deposit to buy her first home. Her father was wealthy, but he'd always believed that Amy should learn the value of money. Even when she was a child, he'd never spoiled her. Determined to not leave college with huge loans, she'd earned her own tuition every year by playing cards. Every vacation, she'd hit up different casinos, always with the same goal . . . enough money to comfortably last the term. Many people thought counting cards in blackjack was illegal. But it wasn't. Of course, casinos could always deny a player service if he or she was caught, but it couldn't even be considered cheating as it didn't require the help of another person or any fancy equipment. And she happened to be fan-freaking-tastic at it. She'd tried all of the strategies. The Hi-Lo, the Omega II, the Zen Count. Personally, she liked the challenge of the Halves method. She loved keeping score in her head, assigning plus scores to the low cards that benefited the house and minus scores to the cards that benefited her. Rarely did she disabuse people of their notion that everything they'd seen Raymond Babbitt do in *Rain Man* had nothing to do with the way card counting really worked.

She wandered to her bedroom and checked herself in the mirror. Her hair was curled into bouncy waves. One tease more, and it'd be heading into bouffant territory. The new white shirt pulled tight across her chest had more one button left open than she was usually comfortable with. If she leaned forward, the person sitting opposite her would get a subtle flash of white lace. She turned to the side. Yep, the black pencil skirt that fell to her knees was demure but hugged her ass tighter than Saran Wrap, and the black patent heels with a platform brought her posture into pin-straight alignment.

That morning, when she'd woken up, she'd felt queasy. It was a word she hated, yet it summed up the state of her stomach perfectly. She couldn't stumble at the first hurdle.

She looked into the mirror again for a reminder that Johnnie Ortega, pit boss of the Lucky Seven, wasn't going to know what hit him.

A quick glance at her phone told her it was time to leave. She walked into the kitchen to grab her purse, freshly filled with the hundred and fifty dollars she'd taken from Cabe and his friends, and the plastic folder sitting next to it. With the help of her godfather, she had a reference from one of the best pit bosses in Nevada. It would stand her in good stead. And even if Ortega called to confirm the reference was legitimate, there wouldn't be a problem. Uncle Clive could bullshit with the best of them. She was certain his story about losing his virginity at eighteen at a party held by Sammy Davis Jr. while Dean Martin stood guard by the bedroom door had to be an exaggeration.

Her suitcases were by the front door. She'd given the casino the address of an apartment to the west of the Gaslamp Quarter. It was a cover, the property, the car, and all her ID having been provided by the FBI in the name Amy Reynard, using her great-grandmother's maiden name. Should she get the job, the suitcases would be whisked to her new home by Cabe.

Amy took the elevator to the street and walked to the end of the block before hailing a cab. From now on, she needed to be careful. Nothing traceable. No Uber. No calling cabs to pick her up at her own front door. She needed to start acting like Amy Reynard, not Amy Murray. She needed to become invisible outside of the casino.

A few minutes from the venue, her new phone rang. "Hey, this is Amy."

"Are you on your way?" Cabe asked. His deep voice was unmistakable, as was the effect it had on her. Was it dangerous to feel a little wave of excitement at the sound of him?

"I am," she said, looking straight ahead into the rearview mirror to keep an eye on the driver.

"I'll keep it brief." Cabe's voice was low. "We got a drone over the casino, and Harley is in the parking lot to the west of the entrance. There is next to no chance anybody will pull anything in broad daylight, but it's good to be prepared just in case. Any signs of trouble, leave. But you should be golden."

"Good to know, but this isn't my first rodeo. I got this." The casino appeared to the right of the highway, and the cab took the exit, circling back around into the parking lot. She pointed the driver toward the employee entrance where she'd been instructed to arrive.

"Take care of yourself, Amy." Cabe's voice was rough, telling her he meant every word.

She allowed herself a moment to indulge in the idea that he truly cared. "I will."

Once she'd hung up and paid the driver, she approached the door and knocked on it. She was greeted by a security guard and was taken through to an area that very much reminded her of the rooms behind the guest areas at the Bellagio. A simpler red-and-gold carpet than the customer areas, less-ornate walls painted a pale lemon. Three chairs sat in the corridor against the walls. The guard politely asked her to sit there until she was called.

Amy waited until he was out of sight before she stood and began to look around. Aware that the security cameras were watching her, she acted like she had a cramp, standing and limping on her leg. She'd periodically stop to shake it out and then would resume walking again. There were two offices on her left with glass panels in the doors. One looked unused and the other was covered in wall planners. She walked to the end of the hall but saw that the door there required some sort of pass to open it. She walked back toward the chairs. The two rooms on the other side of the hall had solid doors. The third one opened just as she reached it.

"Ms. Reynard?" The man who stepped out was a good foot shorter than she was. She'd give him the benefit of the doubt, for now, that the twelve-inch height difference was the reason he stared at her chest. Score one for Victoria's Secret. He quickly brought his gaze back to hers.

"Yes," she replied. "I'm sorry," she said, continuing her act. "I just got a most annoying cramp in my leg." She rolled her ankle for good measure, drawing his attention to her legs.

"I'm Johnnie Ortega. Let's take a walk to the pit. I understand from your resume that you have experience in Las Vegas," he said as they passed through the bland corridor.

"I do. My former pit boss wrote a reference," she said, passing him Uncle Clive's comments.

He began to scan them. "What brought you back to San Diego?"

Amy laughed sadly, her rehearsed response. "I felt like I needed a little less sin in my city."

Ortega laughed, as Cabe had predicted he would when she'd run the line by him. Once they were in the pit, he gestured her to the dealer's spot, then sat down on the opposite side of the table. It was set up for play. He reached for a fresh pack of playing cards, emptied them into his hand, and discarded the jokers. He then placed them on the table.

"Ortega," said a tall man with a narrow chest, lazy gait, and a face she recognized from their intel approached them, "is this the candidate for Eve Canallis's replacement?" He ran his eyes up and down her in a way that made Amy's skin crawl, but she kept a smile plastered to her face.

"It is, Mr. Woods," Ortega said, looking back toward her. "Amy Reynard, this is the manager of the casino, Faulkner Woods."

She held out her hand. "Pleasure to meet you, Mr. Woods. You have a fantastic casino."

Woods shook her hand. "Why, thank you. I certainly hope your interview is successful so I'll have reason to show you around. We take a lot of pride in our croupiers and our dealers, and would argue they are as good as any Vegas venue. If you get through the interview, we'll make sure you get any additional training you need." His smile seemed genuine, but she couldn't trust him. She couldn't trust anyone. There were women she needed to find, and money laundering that Cabe needed to stop. It hit her suddenly that she wasn't sure, if it boiled down to it, which case took priority. Would the FBI move on the women if the money-laundering evidence wasn't in place?

Worse, would Cabe and his team move on the money without them knowing where the women were? Could they afford to hold off moving on either case while the other worked itself out?

Her thoughts shifted to her mom, and she prayed, that if it came down to it, human decency would win out and all sides would put the missing women first.

"I look forward to it," she said as she extracted her hand gently.

"Good luck, Ms. Reynard," Woods said before heading off to another table.

Ortega watched him walk away with a slight scowl on his face.

"Want me to show you why my boss was sad to see me go?" she asked, drawing Ortega's thoughts back to her and her interview. She couldn't let whatever was going on between the two men to ruin her chances of being hired. "He's really hoping I fail here so I go back."

Ortega's gaze returned to hers, and he snapped out of the funk that Woods had just put him in. "Let's play," he said with a grin that reminded her of Uncle Clive. No matter what was going on in the casino, Johnnie Ortega belonged there and loved it just as much as her uncle did. "Give them a shuffle."

"You have a preference on type here?" she asked. She began to run her fingers over the cards. "We've got the adolescent overhand or stripping shuffle," she said as she made a series of cuts into the cards. "Or I can do every poker bro's riffle." She split the pile into two and then, using her thumbs, lifted the corners and let them go into one pile before pushing them together. "Or, if you prefer, I can do the Hindu, the pile, the weave, the Mongean." One by one she illustrated each, finishing with a Zarrow shuffle, the one used by magicians to give the illusion of a shuffle even though the cards remained in the exact same order. "Ta-da!" she said with a flourish and grin.

"You know, Ms. Reynard," Ortega said with a genuine smile, "I think the two of us are going to get along grand out here in the pit."

"Bailey, can we go through the status of all the key players we know so far?" Cabe glanced at the clock on the wall and mentally kicked himself. It had been ninety minutes since he'd spoken to Amy. How long did a job interview for a dealer actually last? Ninety minutes was too long, wasn't it? Goddamn, he needed to stop this shit. Amy was a trained professional. And last he checked, the FBI didn't let unqualified people graduate from Quantico.

But the missing women had been plaguing him. While he had only one brother, he'd grown up around Six's and Mac's sisters. One summer, they'd taken Mac's little sister, Aoife, down to the beach. They'd been distracted by a group of girls from the year above them in school, and when they'd turned around, Aoife was missing. It had taken thirty minutes to find her, sitting on some rocks, enjoying an apple from their cooler, but Cabe's heart rate had raced for hours. Fear of all the possibilities that could have happened had haunted him for weeks after. Aoife had been fine, and even though she wasn't his sister, he'd personally felt responsible for not looking out for her.

When their best childhood friend, Brock, had died during a failed cliff jump—a jump Cabe had made only moments before—he'd struggled with the same feelings of uselessness, of failing to protect someone he cared about.

One of his BUD/s instructors had told him that his capacity to actually care for his team would either be his greatest asset or liability, and he'd spent his career ensuring it was always the former.

And then he'd met Jess. He'd thought she'd cured him of the need to protect. He'd never met anyone more willing to throw themselves into anything that would result in a flood of adrenaline. Nor had he met anyone more prepared for every eventuality.

"Sure thing, boss. Any particular order?"

He focused his thoughts back on the operation, rather than the operative. "I want an update on the Popovs. I want to talk to the Assistant District Attorney to see where the case against Vasilii stands. Then I want to see everything we have on Lemtov and his boss, Sokolov, again."

Cabe pulled out his phone. The signal was shit in the conference room, so he took a walk out to the front of the building. He drew a line at holding his damn cell phone in the air to see if he could increase the three bars to four.

Nothing.

Come on Ames. Where the fuck are you?

He dialed Harley.

"Boss?" Harley answered in his brusque way.

"Any sign?" There was no need to tell Harley what he was talking about. When a mission was in progress, nothing else mattered. Even when it was as simple as a routine interview.

"Hasn't come out yet. But traffic into the casino is picking up. I can see both exits from the front and rear. Buddha's got the rear by drone."

"Keep me posted." Cabe hung up the phone.

The door clicked shut behind him. "You okay?" Six asked, coming to stand by him. He was in a soaked T-shirt and shorts. The gym in the back of Eagle was a godsend for them all.

"Yeah. Just checking in."

They stood in silence for a moment. "You know the guys are on it, right?" Six said, as he stretched his quad, holding his foot to his ass.

"Yeah, I know. But tell me you don't feel a little bit weird about those missing women. It doesn't sit right that they are a secondary issue."

"Yeah. I don't like it either. But our mission is the money-laundering side of this. We have to trust Amy and the feebs and SDPD to do their part for those women. It makes sense to have clear lines of demarcation."

Six was right, as usual. "I don't know how I feel about Amy being set up like that, I guess."

"We don't know for sure she's being set up in this role," Six said, changing his stretch to the opposite leg.

The moment Cunningham had put those images on the screen, he remembered that Amy had suddenly sat straighter. This was her thing. It was what she was there for. And it was clear that it was what she was passionate about. "'Set up' is the wrong phrase. But it's crystal clear that there is a profile for these missing women. They're all young, single, and living alone or new in town. They don't have anyone obviously looking of for them. Amy fits it perfectly."

"You don't think she's up to this?" Six asked matter-of-factly.

"It's not that," Cabe said. "From what we've seen and know of her, she's more than capable. It's just . . . I don't . . . I hate the idea of a woman getting hurt in the line of duty, even if she signed up for it. And yeah, I know there's probably some place reserved for me in the feminist version of Neanderthal hell for saying that."

Six frowned and put his hand on Cabe's shoulder. "You going to be okay doing this? With what happened to Jess? I mean, it's not too late for one of us to switch out with you."

Cabe scoffed and shook his head. "Jesus. Of course I've got this." He did. Didn't he?

Shit. He'd always been an advocate for women in the Navy. He mentored them, trained with them . . . hell, he'd even been supportive of women joining the SEALs as long as they could meet the physical standards. Many men weren't, but he'd met weak men lacking in grit, and women with drive in spades. Gender wasn't a proxy for courage or strength. But for months after Jess's death, he'd had a recurring nightmare of being forced to step over the bodies of women he knew to finish an op. Sometimes a face had been Jess's. Sometimes his mother. Or even Six's and Mac's sisters. Women he'd grown up with and loved.

In his nightmare, he'd been stuck between staying with the bodies or pushing on with his mission until he'd been shot in the forehead because of his indecision.

It was just jitters. To be expected. It had been two years since Jess. And he'd meant what he'd said about Amy. From what he'd already seen of her, she was calm and levelheaded, capable. He needed to focus on that.

Cabe rubbed his hand over his jaw. "Yeah, I got this." The phone in his hand rang, the caller ID showing it was Amy. "Murray?" he said, using her surname to make it less personal. "How did it go?"

"I'm pretty certain I got the job," she said. "He wants to double-check the references, but he said I'd be a great fit."

Adrenaline flooded through him like it always did at the excitement of a new op. "Nice work. Did he say when he'd let you know?"

He heard her muffled voice give her address. "Sorry, just got into a cab. Sometime this week. He gave me the impression he was desperate. They are a couple of dealers down, and I asked when I would be able to start. Will you bring my things over? I'm making the call that this is going to be a go."

She'd given him the spare key to her apartment and instructions of what to collect. "Yeah, I'm on it. You on your way there now?"

"I am. See you in a little while."

The phone disconnected, and he looked at Six. "Looks like she's in. Need to wait for final confirmation, but they were pretty impressed."

"Nice work, Amy," Six said, admiration in his tone. "Not like it was ever in any doubt. The woman fleeced us out of a hundred and fifty bucks in forty-seven minutes. I'm no World Series of Poker champion, but I can usually hold my own. She's also got a pretty wry sense of humor that kept us all in our places last night."

Cabe nodded and smiled at the memory. "Now I just got to get myself on the inside."

"There are worse jobs than gambling with the feebs' money."

He laughed. "Yeah, I get to go play poker for a living. My life definitely doesn't suck." He checked his pocket for both his and Amy's keys. "I'm gonna go pick up Amy's stuff and drop it over at her rental. Then I'm going to work from home for the rest of the afternoon on some files Bailey is sending my way. Can you make sure he sends them through?"

Six nodded. "I'm on it. I'm going to see if we can't get a better lead on the money trail. I've got a forensic accountant willing to give us a consult."

Cabe took a minute to dive back inside to grab his laptop and then hopped in the truck to head for home. Amy's new apartment was fifteen minutes from his own, and her old one in Little Italy was on his way. After he moved the suitcases, he was going to see if his brother Noah was available for a workout at their cousin's gym, just for a change of pace.

Twenty minutes later, he pulled up in front of Amy's nine-unit apartment rental. The white building had a traditional terracotta roof and little balconies framed with stucco arches. It was cute. Many of the balconies were covered in plants and had small seating areas, and he could imagine Amy sitting at one of them, reading a book or sipping coffee. It had been a long time since he'd done that, sat on his balcony and enjoyed simple pleasures. Eagle had taken over their lives, and they'd been working nonstop. Perhaps when this job was over, he'd take a few days—hell, maybe even a week—and hop a flight to Hawaii. Surf, sleep . . . *sex*. Yeah. Maybe it was time to figure out how to savor that again too.

He let himself into the building and jogged up the two flights of stairs to her floor. He found the apartment, unlocked the door, and stepped inside. It smelled just like she did. Like warm vanilla and cinnamon. He noticed the large white candle on the counter. He dipped his nose closer, and the scent got stronger. That Amy liked candles made him smile. Despite being a badass agent, she was very much a woman.

The apartment was filled with light and plants. A row of succulents in cute little square pots sat on the window ledge. A large fern filled out an otherwise unused corner. Several orchids in whites and purples and yellows graced some side tables and a desk in the far corner of the living room. He wondered who was going to water them while she was away.

The suitcases were exactly where she'd said they'd be. Two matching black Samsonites and a small duffle carry-on. Above them on the wall was a series of framed photographs. One was of her hugging a large man in a Stetson, a cigar hanging from the corner of his mouth. That had to be her father, Floyd. There was a picture of Amy under the classic "Welcome to Las Vegas" sign. Another showed her with three girls in a shared dorm room at college. She was wearing a cropped T-shirt and high-waisted shorts. As cute as her college-age body had been, she'd definitely grown into her looks. By his reckoning, she was five years younger than his thirty-four.

While he was certain her home would tell him more about her, he didn't want to pry. As much as her job still terrified him, for the first time in a long time, someone had intrigued him enough to want to find out about her slowly.

Cabe slung the duffle over his shoulder and pulled on the door. He propped it open with his foot, grabbed the suitcases, and took them down to his truck. Well, not *his* truck. It was a vehicle provided by the FBI for him to use while on the job. Once the cases were secured, he headed south to the Gaslamp Quarter, parked in the underground parking lot, and used the spare key he'd been given to enter Amy's new apartment.

He put down her luggage in the hall and looked around. The apartment was very different from the one she'd chosen for herself. For a start, there were no plants. No greenery. It was a modern space, much like his own, but the open-plan space was stark and lacked character. A cream sofa and small coffee table sat at one end of the white-walled living room and a round glass table with four gray chairs sat at the other. Generic artwork that wouldn't have looked out of place in an Olive Garden graced the walls. The kitchenette ran along one wall. Basic sink and fridge, with a four-burner stove.

A key rattled in the lock, and the door burst open just as he went to open it.

Amy stumbled over the threshold, and he reached out to stop her fall. "Holy shit, Cabe," she said, putting her hand to her chest. "I didn't think you'd be here yet."

He wanted to respond. He really did. But his mouth went dry at the sight of her. She looked hot. No, even that seemed a tepid word. She looked like an old-school siren. Her hair fell in vintage waves, and that red lipstick had him thinking all kinds of dirty thoughts, especially as his hand slid around her waist to stop her momentum.

Amy put her hand on his chest. Her touch seared him. "We've got to stop bumping in to each other like this," she said with a grin, then stepped away.

Just like he had in the bar, he felt the loss of contact.

"Oh my word, that feels so good," she said as she slipped off her heels, circling her ankles and moaning in such obvious relief that his dick perked up at the sound.

"Sorry," he said, regaining some sense of composure.

"Thought you'd want your stuff as soon as you got here. Great job on nailing the interview. I'm sure you made quite the impression."

"Well, I certainly didn't fall on Ortega like I did you, but I think he'll remember me. And thanks," she said as she bent down to pick up her shoes. The already-fitted skirt stretched even tighter across her ass. Since no good was going to come out of taking the time to appreciate it, Cabe wandered to the sofa and took a seat. Amy followed him and sat at the other end.

"Tell me about it. How did it go?" Cabe asked, keeping his gaze firmly fixed on hers, not on that pretty glimpse of lace peeking out from her shirt.

"Piece of cake," she said with a grin. "To be honest, if I didn't know all of the stuff that is really going on, I'd say it was a great place to work. Ortega was friendly. He runs a tight ship in the pit. I met Woods and he seemed pleasant enough but definitely skeevy around the edges. The interview was to test basic skills, but I think I'm going to need to be great if I'm going to stand out."

"Going to stand out" meant being targeted.

Her safety was not his job, though. He was supposed to focus on the money-laundering side of the case.

But "standing out" would put her straight in the line of fire.

Which meant there was only one place for him.

And that was in front of her.

CHAPTER FIVE

There was nothing quite like the high of nailing something important. And this was big. As soon as she'd heard about those missing women, she realized exactly why she was involved.

So why the hell did it mean so much that Cabe was proud of her? That he was certain she'd made a great impression. Of course she had. And she'd done it all on her own. Pulled up her big-girl panties and made it happen. But there was a look in his eye that she couldn't quite identify. Recognition for a job well done, pride that she'd pulled it off, maybe, and that damn spark that she'd felt between them from the very first time they'd met.

His proximity on the sofa was driving her just a little bit crazy. He sat with his arms folded across his chest, which made those biceps of his stretch the sleeves of his navy blue polo. The collar was a little rumpled at the back, and she fought the urge to lean in and fix it.

He was close enough that she could smell something clean and fresh, like maybe his shower gel. The size of the goddamn couch was going to be the death of her.

She turned her mind away from how warm his skin would feel if she reached out and touched it and put it back on the case. It had been agreed that a dealer with the background she'd created would prefer to be right in the bustling downtown neighborhood. It also made it easier for her to make it onto someone's list for abduction. A young girl in a new place without anybody worrying about her would be an easy target.

She'd focus on that, not on the thickness of his thigh muscles and the way the denim he wore hugged them. His knees were close to hers, which made her feel just how she had at age twelve when boyishly handsome Lincoln Stoddard had been assigned to be her lab partner and sat down on the stool next to her.

But Lincoln Stoddard couldn't hold a candle to the man to her left, and she was spending too much time admiring the reasons why.

"We need to run a search of Eve Canallis. That's who I'm replacing. I just want to be certain that a disappearance hasn't taken place a little earlier than the usual pattern."

Cabe faced her. "Did something tip you off?"

Amy shook her head. "I could be totally wrong, looking for something where there isn't a problem. But I'd rather be hyper-vigilant than miss something because I wasn't looking hard enough."

"Fair enough," Cabe agreed. "We can sort that out through SDPD, see if she's been reported missing first. My brother is a detective. I can give him a call."

"Do you guys have a floor plan for the casino? I can mark up some of the things I've already noticed. Where passes are required, security cameras, what offices are where."

He grinned. "Started the job already?" he asked.

Usually, comments about her work ethic irritated her. Boyfriends in the past had been frustrated by her commitment to her job, but there was no hint of judgment in Cabe's tone. If anything, there was a hint of admiration. "You know the key to this will be moving quickly."

Cabe stood. "Let me get my bag out of my truck, and we can go though it together. I'll give Noah a ring while I'm walking down. Eve Canallis you said, right?"

Amy nodded. "Yes. While you do that, I'm going to get changed out of this," she said, gesturing up and down at the outfit that felt like it was cutting her intestines in half. She watched him leave and took a deep breath as the door closed behind him. She stood and grabbed the suitcase she knew contained her toiletries and casual clothes and wheeled it into the bedroom. It smacked her ankle has she heaved it onto the bed, making her wince. Between the platform heels and luggage accidents, her feet were never going to forgive her.

Amy caught a glimpse in the mirror opposite the bed and almost didn't recognize herself. Bright red lipstick had never really been her thing, and she couldn't wait to take the heavy makeup off. She unzipped the suitcase and rummaged until she found her toiletry bag and headed to the bathroom. It was darker than the bathroom in her own place, dingy even. But if they all worked hard, they could pull the op off quickly and she could be back in her own white bathroom before Christmas. Once her hair was off her face, she washed it clean. Finally, she felt as though her skin could breathe. The scent of her moisturizer made her feel better immediately, as did the quick flick of mascara and a little pink lip gloss.

Amy stared hard at her reflection. What were the

chances she'd finally met a man she felt an attraction to, a man who had already shown the capacity to accept her and her job, a man who had already shown a level of personal interest, only for their work to make it difficult to explore things further?

With a sigh, she stripped off her clothes, tossing them into the laundry basket by the closet as she walked through to the bedroom. As she dug around in her case for her white capris, a thought flitted through her brain. They wouldn't be on the op forever. And perhaps . . . maybe . . . there would be an opportunity down the line to date. All she needed to do was resist the urge to rip off that damn fine polo shirt to see exactly what was underneath until they were finished.

She pulled on a black V-neck made from the softest cotton and whipped her hair into a simple fishtail braid. One look in the mirror reassured her that she now looked much more like her usual self. As she walked back to the living room, she heard the door click shut.

"Noah is running a search on Eve Canallis, and I've got the floor plans on my laptop," Cabe said. "But talk to me about money laundering. I want to pick your brain. We've been doing research on our end, but from an FBI perspective, how does it really happen? What are we looking for?"

Amy sat back down on the sofa, and Cabe joined her. He pulled his computer out of his bag and placed it on the low coffee table in front of them. "Okay," she said, "that's a long conversation. But basically, it boils down to a couple of things. Casinos in the U.S. that generate over a million in annual gaming revenues are required to report certain currency transactions to help expose money laundering. Basically, any transaction of ten thousand dollars or higher needs to be reported to help FinCEN, the Financial Crimes Enforcement Network of the U.S. Treasury."

"That's different from Title Thirty-One, right?" Cabe asked, referring to the Bank Secrecy Act that was designed to prevent money laundering through the banking industry. He'd obviously already done some research.

"Yeah. This is specifically aimed at large transactions through slot machines and gaming tables. Even automatic change machines. Money launderers have been known to stand in front of those suckers for an hour feeding in ten-dollar bills and converting them to fresh dollar bills—or worse, coins that they then convert back into hundred-dollar bills at the cashier cages."

Cabe rested his elbows on his knees. "Playing devil's advocate here, but if all this is supposed to be regulated, how does money laundering still happen?"

Amy lifted her foot and tucked it underneath her opposite knee as she turned to face him. "Within any twenty-four hour period, a person can't exchange more than ten thousand dollars without filling out a currency transaction report. And if casino staff see individuals changing large sums in a suspicious manner, they are required to complete a report—in our lingo, a FinCEN form 114. But there are four ways around all the security measures, and they rely on the casino being vigilant to spot it."

"What are they?" Cabe asked.

"The first is structuring. Easy enough. Break the ten thousand into a handful of smaller amounts. Some casinos record transactions above three thousand dollars, just to make sure they don't see multiple trips from the same person to different cashiers to try to wash through larger amounts."

"We'd need to find out what Lucky Seven does, right?" Cabe said, making a quick note on his laptop.

"Yeah. It's on my list to get close to some of the cage staff to ask about the missing women," Amy said. "The women all share the same locker room, so there is plenty opportunity for that. I'll see what I can find out for you too."

Cabe made another note. "I can add it to my list of things to do too. I'll try each variant. Exchange the ten thousand to see if they follow the basics of the law, then split up some into smaller amounts and see what their cutoff point is. We're going to need to determine whether the casino is involved, or whether it is specific individuals, as quickly as possible. I'm assuming that with organized crime, this could be happening with or without the casino's consent—although with Sokolov having been witnessed at the casino, it's not too much of a stretch to assume Lucky Seven is complicit."

Amy nodded. "I don't think we should just look for intel that proves only that, though. We might miss something if we focus on that too hard."

"Fair point. What is number two?"

"Smurfing."

Cabe laughed. "For real? What the hell is smurfing? Like the little blue people?"

"Believe it or not, that's where the term comes from. Smurfs worked like a collective. Smurfing is taking a big transaction and breaking it down across several people, sometimes referred to by casinos as *agents*."

"I prefer smurfs," Cabe said.

This time Amy laughed. "Yeah. Me too. There are, of course, also some legit reasons for breaking down a large transaction. Like a husband and wife who each get chips.

He goes to play poker, she goes to blackjack, and they get back together at the end of the night and cash in the chips. Not everyone who splits up transactions is a bad guy."

"Okay. What's number three?" Cabe leaned back in the sofa.

"Minimal gaming. Say you have twenty grand you need to get rid of. Maybe they are marked bank notes. You go to a high-value slot machine. Like a thousand-dollars-a-spin kind of machine. You load all the bills in, press the button once, maybe twice, and then cash out. If you win, then yay for you. If you lose, it's a small loss to get clean cash. Those machines tend to pay out in slot tickets that you take to the cage to get clean bills."

"And number four?"

"As you said earlier, complicit employees—which may or may not be synonymous with complicit casinos. It's not unheard of to buy off a cashier, or even plant a cashier. Someone who ignores the smurfing or smaller transactions. Someone who turns a blind eye to the same person returning four times over the course of the day."

As Cabe made another note, she leaned over to see what he was writing. It brought her close to his shoulder. He turned to look at her. His mouth was close to hers. She noticed his gaze drop to her lips and then immediately back to her eyes. "Didn't anyone ever tell you it's rude to read over someone's shoulder?" His voice had dropped an octave, and it made her shiver.

"I take in details," she whispered. "It's what I do."

He held her gaze for a moment, and at first she thought he was going to kiss her. With a sigh she could feel brush against her skin, he leaned back. "I was making a note to ask one of my team members to play near the slots as opposed to the tables. And to ask one of our tech guys if we can hack the camera feed so we can do our own assessment of who is showing up at the cages and whether any staff are letting the rules slide." His voice had returned to normal, and the moment passed.

"This is going to be a long assignment, isn't it?" Cabe asked, his dark eyes fixed on hers.

Her insides flipped a little as it dawned on her exactly what he meant. He didn't mean literal days and weeks, he meant moments, time spent together trying to fight whatever it was that was between them.

"Yes."

When he was younger, Cabe's sex life had been fulfilling enough, but none of the women he'd dated had gone on to become longer-lasting relationships. Then he'd met Jess at a charity event, a muddy ten-kilometer obstacle course. They'd been placed on the same four-person team. By kilometer three, her fitness level had impressed him. By kilometer six, it was her endurance. By kilometer eight, it was a motivational speech she'd yelled while halfway up a rope cargo net that had given them all the push they needed to finish first.

It was only when he'd picked her up later for dinner that he noticed how fantastic she looked in her skinny jeans.

After a dinner that had gone on for five hours, he realized that time spent in the company of a smart woman revved his engines. That *Jess*, and everything she was, did it for him.

He loved intelligent women.

He loved women who knew shit. Random shit. Honestly, they could talk about anything they were passionate and knowledgeable about. Six had always laughed at the way Cabe had found women's IQs way more interesting than their bra sizes.

But listening to Amy explain money laundering was having the same affect.

When she'd walked in, all red pout and doe eyes, he'd let his prurient fantasies run riot, but he preferred her like this. Soft pink lips on a smart mouth..

And then he'd let his concern slip out: *This is going to be a long assignment, isn't it?*

He didn't mean that literally. The assignment was straightforward. He meant being around her, every day, until it was over. Staring into those blue eyes, holding that gaze, shouldn't be this easy, should it? It was scary how normal it felt.

"I'm sorry," Cabe said. "You know what . . . I should probably go. Coming to your apartment was a bad idea."

He stood to go, but Amy put her hand on his arm. "Just sit down," she said quietly. "We should talk. Perhaps talking about this"—she gestured between the two of them—"will help clear the air."

This was way out of his comfort zone.

Amy looked up at him. "You want a glass of wine?"

Cabe shook his head. "Not sure alcohol is the best idea. Looser inhibitions are the last thing I need."

"Yeah, well, I need one to tell you what I'm about to."

He watched as she walked over to the fridge that had been stocked for her. She pulled out the bottle of white and cracked the screw top before grabbing a large glass from the cabinet. "You sure?" she said, holding the glass in his direction.

"I'm sure."

Amy poured it and took a sip before placing the bottle

and glass on the kitchen island. "We have to work together. We have to trust each other. So I'm going to trust you with something I wasn't going to tell anybody."

Her tone was not quite sad, more like resigned. He wanted her to trust him. In spite of all his mixed emotions, he deeply did.

"I was sexually harassed before I moved here. By an agent. It's why I moved."

"Holy shit, Amy. That's . . . that's fucked up." He thought about some of the shit Jess had had to deal with as she'd worked her way through the ranks. Men who commented on her body. Men who doubted her capabilities. Men who questioned her commitment. Wives of men questioning whether she would lead their husbands astray.

Amy nodded. "That's one way of describing it. He was a senior agent on a case I was working who also happened to be married. At first, it was hard to put a finger on what made me feel uncomfortable around him. Sometimes I'd catch him looking at me in the hallway. I don't know. It just felt creepy."

Cabe walked toward her and took a seat on the stool on the other side of the island.

Amy took another sip of wine. "It's always a risk as a woman to call out a man. It's too easy to be labeled as the one who couldn't handle herself, the one who couldn't take a joke. The one who needed others to solve her problems. But that isn't what stopped me. He didn't care about the women we were looking for. There were five missing prostitutes and he didn't feel they were worth our resources. I knew if I reported him, the old boys network would close in and I'd be the one reassigned. And if I left the case, I knew it would turn into a cold case because he really couldn't give a shit if we found those women. Every night, I'd lie in bed, wondering if he was making anyone else feel the same way he made me feel. But those missing women had no one speaking for them, no one was advocating for them. I couldn't let them down. So I ignored his stares and just tried to stay out of his way."

It shouldn't make him feel warm inside that she was trusting him, but it did. "He didn't get the message, right?" he asked.

She walked around the counter and sat on the stool next to his. She was close enough that their knees touched. "The first time he brushed his hand across my ass was in a crowded conference room. . . . 'Sorry. Too little space for too many people,' he said as he shrugged. I knew it was deliberate. And I knew I'd get laughed at if I tried to say he'd grabbed my ass in a packed room. So I learned to walk down the opposite side of the room when I saw him coming. I employed the usual girl-code strategies to avoid him. On days we were both in the office, I'd get one of my girlfriends to meet me at my desk to go for lunch. And I know—I even knew then—that I was modifying my behavior to stay away from a predator instead of confronting him, but sometimes that's the only option women have."

"What a douchebag," Cabe said. "Wasn't there anyone you could trust? Someone else in the department who could have spoken to him? Someone more senior who might have listened to you?"

Amy shook her head. "You know, I thought through all those options, but they all felt like too much of a risk first to the chance of finding those women, and second, to my career." She sighed. "And then, at our Christmas party, he cornered me in the hall on my way to the bathroom and asked me whether my breasts were real or fake. I called him on his behavior. Told him to back off. I said it had gone too far and that I was going to report him, but he said there weren't any witnesses. And, of course, there weren't. In the end, I stopped going to company events all together because the time I would spend dreading any interaction with the guy far outweighed any enjoyment I got out of actually attending."

"That's so awful you had to go through all that. And I'm sorry you had to handle that alone. Is he still with the FBI?"

Amy shook her head. "He got fired."

Her words sunk in and Cabe smiled. "You called him out? Good for you."

Amy laughed sardonically. "Sort of. He forced my hand. I got home from work one Friday and had run a bath. I was supposed to go out for drinks with a girlfriend for her birthday. When someone rang the bell, I thought it was Kadia, since we were going to get ready to go out together. Stupidly, I didn't check the peephole. And it was him. He'd told his wife that he was away working for the weekend, so we could spend time together. I slammed the door and called the police. Then I called my boss. And HR."

By the way her shoulders slumped forward, and given that she was currently in San Diego instead of Atlanta, he figured that wasn't the end of the story. "How did you end up here?"

"Well, somewhere between those phone calls and him getting fired, my complaints were challenged, my reputation torn apart. At first I was accused of making it up. That was his immediate defense. He told the police that we were having an affair, and that I had only called the police because I was mad that he wouldn't leave his wife. Because there were no witnesses to any of his other abusive actions, it was my word against his. Then he had the audacity to claim that I'd promised him sexual favors in return for mentoring and promotion and he'd just gotten carried away." Amy pursed her mouth and swallowed deeply. She shook her head quickly and pushed her hair over her shoulders. "Anyway," she said breezily, "back to us working together. I'll be honest and say I liked you in the bar. I'd seen you with your friends when I walked in. I was mad when you left. Madder still when I saw you again. But now . . . I'm sad and just a little frustrated because I like who you are, and I don't think that's going to go away. But I can't act on it, no matter how much it might seem like a good idea. I can't give anyone an opportunity to think I moved here and hooked up with another more senior guy in a different office. I can't allow my actions now to lead those people back in Atlanta to believe they were right all along. That this is how I operate."

Unnamed emotions bounced around in Cabe's mind. It was hard to process them all. Each was like a kernel of corn in a popcorn maker, exploding in front of his eyes but then disappearing into a pile in front of him. She liked him. That was first. She'd been treated badly, and he wanted to kick someone's ass. Guilt. For being a douchebag when they'd first met. And the same frustration she probably felt at being denied the opportunity of being together. Because of her job, he wasn't sure there'd ever be a future in it for them.

He considered telling her about Jess and explaining his reasons for having walked away that night. But he wasn't certain that it wouldn't come out more like *Well, if you don't want me, I don't want you either.* Which wasn't what he would mean. After listening to her and getting to know her, *not* falling fast and deep into a relationship with her felt like the absolute wrong thing to do. But the right thing to do was to respect her wishes, because he understood them as much as they disappointed him.

She placed her hand on top of his and let her fingers fall in between his. He looked down at their tanned hands entwined. The image of their legs tangled in white sheets sprung to mind, but he buried it deep.

He moved his gaze to her eyes, the depth of the blue catching him off guard as it often did. "I'd be lying if I said I hadn't thought about where this could go. You're a pretty awesome woman, Amy, and it's complete shit what you've had to go through. I understand you need some distance from that before you consider anything else."

Goddamn, the look in her eyes, the heat they held just for him made him want to throw everything he'd just said out of the window and press his lips to hers, but for both of their sakes, he knew he needed to do the opposite. He stood. "I'm gonna go. Not because of the line you just drew underneath this, but because I agree with what you just said."

"But why go?" she asked. "We could work some more."

Cabe sighed and gave into the urge to place his palm on her cheek and let his thumb run gently along her lower lip. The sigh she emitted would be, he was sure, the very memory he would jerk off to in the shower later. "We both need this to settle between us," he said. "And if I don't leave, we both know I'm going to kiss you."

CHAPTER SIX

Amy looked at the report on the Sokolov family finances one last time and then slammed the lid down on her laptop. "There's got to be a way in to the financial paper trail," she said to Six, who was still staring at the copy on his own computer.

"Working on it," he said, rolling his neck from left to right.

They'd been at it for most of the day. Mac was in the corner with Lite working on a plan to set up better tracking of Sokolov. Cabe was poring over schematics of the casino.

When her phone rang, she reached for it, but then realized it wasn't her work phone ringing. It was her burner. "Quiet!" she shouted, and the room fell silent.

Six stood and walked to the door, she assumed to keep anyone from running in.

She grabbed the phone on the fourth ring. "Hello," she answered calmly, if not a little flightily. That was the persona she'd created. A voice a couple of notes higher than normal, a tone that sounded just a fraction away from laughter.

"Amy, it's Johnnie Ortega. Do you have a couple of minutes?"

Amy grinned. This time it wasn't part of the act. She was certain from the tone of his voice that she knew what he was going to say, but she played along. "Sure thing, Mr. Ortega. What can I help you with?" She could feel Cabe's eyes on her and she gave in to the urge to turn and look at him. The anticipation in the room was palpable.

"The job is yours, if you want it. Forty hours over five shifts. Salary at the rate we discussed. I brought in cover for this weekend, but I'd love for you to start on Monday if you can. The casino is a little quieter Monday through Wednesday, so it'll be easier for you to get the lay of the land before the crowds rush in at the weekend."

For a moment, she thought about offering to come in sooner and making a counter-argument against delaying, but deep down she knew the best thing to do was accept the conditions he'd laid down and use the rest of the time preparing. "Thank you, Mr. Ortega. You've made my day."

She spent a couple of more moments on the phone clarifying the details of her shift, how and when she'd get paid, and when she should swing by to collect her uniform. And of course, she spent a few minutes gushing to Johnnie Ortega about how pleased she was, and how excited she was, and yes, how grateful she was.

When she finally hung up the phone, there was a momentary silence, and then a whoop came from behind her as Six patted her on the back. "Nice work, Murray."

Cabe held her gaze and grinned. "You did good. Really

good. We should celebrate with something better than this tepid coffee," he said, lifting his cup up in the air.

"I have Scotch in my drawer," Six said. "Just one shot though, given we're all driving later." He walked past them to, she assumed, go get it . . . and hopefully some cups too, because there was no way she was doing that swig-from-the-bottle-and-then-wipe-it-on-your-sleeve thing.

Her stomach flip-flopped as excitement and nervous adrenaline began to build.

She was in.

It was a big deal. A huge freaking deal.

"When do you start?" Cabe asked. "We should refine our plans based on that. Figure out which G-men will be joining us."

Amy snapped out of her excitement and focused. "Monday. I'll call Cunningham." His use of the slang term for an FBI agent—Government Man—told her Cabe wasn't happy with the additional FBI support in the casino. Only this morning, she'd overheard Cabe point out to her boss that the men who had sat in the room with them on the first day had an abject lack of poker face. Cabe had pushed to have his own team there, but in the silence that followed, she was certain that Cunningham had reminded Cabe it was a joint op and had refused to budge.

The sound of a cell phone ringing cut through the conference room. This time Cabe reached into his pocket and pulled out his phone, grinning when he looked at the screen before answering it. "What's up, Noah?"

Noah. Wasn't that his brother? The one with SDPD?

It had been two days since Cabe had asked his brother for help in finding Eve Canallis. She had begun to regret the decision to rely on the police and not go straight to the FBI. Hopefully he had news.

Six walked back into the room with a bottle of whiskey, some red plastic cups, and a large white cake box. Her stomach grumbled at the sight of it, but she was distracted by Cabe flipping his laptop open.

"Mmm-hmm." Cabe said. "How long ago was that?"

There was another pause, long enough for Six to open the cake box and pull out a platter with different types of cake on it. He waved a fork in her direction. She looked over at Cabe one last time as he continued to study whatever was on the screen. He ran his fingers along his jaw. "Did you check it out yet?"

"What is this?" she asked Six quietly, knowing that Cabe would fill her in once he was done.

"Wedding cake. Me and Lou are getting married in two months, and we need to pick a cake. Now you're part of the team, you can give me your opinion."

Amy took a piece of a vanilla sponge cake. It burst with lemon icing when she popped it in her mouth. "That's so good," she mumbled, pointing her fork in the direction of the cake she'd tried. "But shouldn't Lou be part of this process?"

"Long story. I have the least-weddingy wife-to-be. If there is an opposite of bridezilla, that's Lou." Six actually looked proud of that. "She's a genius in a medical laboratory but needs . . . well . . . she has an issue being around people."

"Except you?"

Six laughed. "Yeah. Except me. She's taking care of her dress. I'm taking care of everything else. And as long as I get to be married to her for the rest of our lives, it feels like a fair fucking deal to me."

Cabe stood and walked toward them. "Yeah, okay. No, this is great. Thanks. . . . Definitely. Bye." He hung up the phone and then faced her. "Is eating cake part of the job description now?" Cabe teased.

She couldn't help smiling at his playfulness. "If it's not, we should make it a part of it," she replied.

He grabbed a fork and dove straight into the red velvet cake. "This one for sure," he said to Six.

Six grinned. "Always the red velvet."

"Don't mess with perfection," Cabe said.

"You know, Amy," Six said, "Cabe was the only kid who had a tiered red velvet cake for his birthday every year."

Amy tried a bit of the red velvet, and it was divine, melting perfectly against her tongue. "That seems a bit overkill, but this *is* good. How did you know you were going to like this cake best?"

Cabe reached over and turned the box around so she could see the name of the side—*Moss Patisserie*. She looked straight at him. "A family member, I'm guessing."

"His mom," Six said. "She cried when I picked up the samples earlier, by the way."

Cabe grinned. "Of course she did. You and Mac are as much her sons as I am."

Amy helped herself to a forkful of chocolate cake. "How long have you guys known each other?" she asked before popping the cake in her mouth. She had to stop herself from groaning. It was perfectly chocolate, but not sickly sweet.

"Since kindergarten. Earlier really, as we all grew up close to each other," Cabe answered. "Our moms were and still are friends."

Her heart warmed at the idea of these lifelong friends

still being so close. It must have been such big deal for Cabe's mom to be asked by Six to make his wedding cake. "I think they all taste good, but I like the chocolate best."

"Even if I order a six-tier chocolate cake, his mom will still send a little red velvet cake on the side for her boy," Six said, his voice turning babyish toward the end.

"Fuck off," Cabe said good-naturedly. "Although he's right. She will."

"Did I miss the cake?" Mac said, crashing into the room. "Did she send my favorite?"

Cabe caught Amy's eye and grinned. "The chocolate, like you," he said, pointing to the side of her mouth. "You have some there." Before either of them realized, he'd reached across and rubbed the pad of his thumb along the side of her lips.

It was such a cliché to feel like time had stopped, but she could have sworn it had.

She was going to combust.

And Mac was staring.

Cabe moved his hand quickly and busied himself getting more red velvet cake. "Turns out you have the best instincts. Eve Canallis disappeared. The SDPD went over to her apartment. To get her neighbors to talk, the detectives made up a story that Eve's identity had been stolen online."

"I like it," Amy said. It was a short and simple lie. Stolen identity was something everyone needed to worry about.

"They told everyone on the block where she lived that they needed to talk to her urgently or she might lose everything. At first, nothing bubbled to the surface, not a whisper. But they got the landlord to let them into her rental, which had been pseudo-emptied. The majority of her clothes were gone, some books, her car and keys."

"Damn. So, she's a ghost, just like the others?" Disappointment rushed through her.

Cabe shook his head. "No. She left behind her laptop. She'd given it to a friend who lived two floors away. Told him she was having some problems with it, and the guy is a tech geek. She was supposed to pick it up from him on Tuesday but never showed.

"She didn't just run." The disappointment evaporated as quickly as it had come.

"No, she didn't," Cabe said. "And Noah has her laptop."

"When you said you had all this covered, I guess I should have believed you," Cabe said as the gold limousine whisked them from McCarran Airport the following day. Crystal decanters sat in custom-built cabinetry, and if this had been a vacation, he'd have been tempted to pour himself a couple of fingers of whiskey and sit back and enjoy the ride. Instead, he was focused on the woman who sat opposite him.

She wore red a lot, he'd noticed. This time a fitted dress the color of ripe cherries with a low V-neck that revealed a tantalizing glimpse of her cleavage. He should know. They'd sat next to each other on the plane. On her feet were nude heels that made her legs look as though they went on for days and revealed toenails that matched her dress. On the plane, she'd worn a fitted denim jacket with the cuffs turned up, but it was now slung over her large cream purse on the seat next to her.

Amy looked as if she belonged in the limo, in this lifestyle to which she was obviously accustomed. She grinned at him. "You haven't seen anything yet. When I told Uncle Clive we were coming, he got so excited. Normally when I go home, I stay with my dad. He was beside himself when I said we were coming into town and needed hotel rooms."

The sun had long since dropped below the horizon, and the bright lights of the Strip began to come into view.

"You never mention your mom. Is there a reason for that and can I ask why?" Cabe asked.

Amy sighed and smiled sadly. "My mom went missing when I was ten years old." She ran a fingertip along the edge of the window. "She decided we needed more eggnog, which we didn't, because a week after she'd gone, when my Dad emptied the fridge, we had four liters, and who needs four liters of eggnog?"

Suddenly, so much about Amy made sense. Her commitment to their op, the unique skills Aitken had mentioned when he'd first brought up that they'd work along a federal agent. "I'm sorry, Amy. I take it she was never found."

Amy shook her head then looked at him. "No, she wasn't. I haven't stopped looking, but the leads dried up long ago."

A part of him was glad he knew, the other part was mad he'd upset her. That hadn't been his intention. "Tell me about Uncle Clive," he said in a bid to bring the conversation back to someone alive and well.

Amy uncrossed and crossed her legs. He didn't see anything untoward, just the long lines of tan legs and a hint of thigh, but it was enough to bring the inappropriate thoughts he'd had of her legs wrapped around his waist bubbling to the surface.

"I suppose the easiest way to describe him is a bit of a legend and a bit of a relic." She laughed at her own description. "He'd love the former and detest the latter. But both are true. He's worked on the Strip since before child labor laws were actually a thing. And he's the last remaining employee who worked at Caesars Palace since the day it opened. At one time, he was a runner for the first Caesars Palace pit boss—paid under the table to quite literally run information to wherever it needed to go. To a guest room, to the telegram operators. Whatever was needed. He's full of stories. One year on my birthday, I get a call from Uncle Clive. He tells me he has someone there to sing happy birthday to me, and sure enough Frank Sinatra and Dean Martin jump on the call and start singing in two-part harmony. Last year it was Celine Dion. And he's a relic because he hates how nobody dresses up to play in the casino anymore. And he hates the noise of the slot machines."

It was clear just how much Amy loved Clive. He wondered if she realized how between details, she'd sometimes smiled to herself as if remembering more stories in her head that she considered sharing but didn't.

"Well, I thought to bring a jacket. Remind me to put it on before we go meet him." Uncertain of what they were actually going to get up to in Vegas beyond practicing for the roles they were going to play, he'd packed for both ends of the dress-code spectrum.

The limo pulled up in front of the hotel, and staff suddenly swarmed them. Someone opened his door while another man opened the trunk and retrieved the suitcases. Cabe waited and offered Amy his hand to assist her getting out of the car. Her grip was firm as she accepted his help. For a moment, he realized it would have given him great pride to be walking into the hotel with his arm around her. There was a quiet confidence in the way she carried herself, and a whole lot to watch as her hips swayed when she walked in those shoes. He noticed a group of four men standing in the lobby watch her as she walked by, and he had to stop himself from marching up to her to throw an arm over her shoulder.

"There's my darling goddaughter."

At first glance, Cabe thought Al Pacino was headed toward them. The man had a lightly gnarled face, dark black hair with gray at the temples, eyebrows darker than Cabe thought natural, and a sharp pinstripe suit with those two-tone shoes that gangsters had worn in the twenties.

Amy's face lit up when she turned and saw him. "Uncle Clive," she squealed and hugged him.

"It's been too long since you were last in town," Clive grumbled.

She stepped back and playfully slapped Clive on the arm. "It's only been five weeks, you old bat."

"Yeah, well when you get to my age, you don't know how many blocks of five weeks you've got left. Now. Where is this young man of yours?"

Amy looked over toward Cabe and grinned. "He's not mine, but Cabe Moss is standing right behind you."

Clive turned and looked at his chest, then up at Cabe. "You might be tall, but I know all the best places to bury a body in this town. If you keep your hands where I can see them, which means at least a foot and a half from my goddaughter at all times, you and I are going to get along great."

Cabe looked over at Amy, who had her hand pressed across her mouth. The shaking through her shoulders told him she was laughing. "It's a deal," he said, offering Clive his hand.

An hour later, he found himself waiting for Amy in the bar. She'd gone off with Clive to catch up with a couple of friends. Their training wasn't due to begin until the next day, so as the sun went down over the Strip, he'd caved and ordered a beer. It was long and cold. Utterly perfect. Just like the woman who was walking toward him.

She'd changed her shoes, the tall heels replaced with white Converse that gave the dress a much more casual feel.

"I have a great idea. Have you ever seen the Neon Boneyard?" she asked.

Cabe shook his head. "Can't say that I have."

She held out her hand, and he took it, allowing her the pretense of pulling him to his feet. "Oh, my god, it's one of my most favorite places on earth. Let's go."

Twenty minutes later, after a brief cab ride and a phone call during which Amy had made arrangements to join a tour of some sort, he stood in the midst of huge illuminated neon signs from some of the old, torn-down casinos along the strip. Some of them were lit up, the heat from them almost as strong as the sun had been earlier in the day. Others sat unlit on the ground.

He turned to Amy. "This is incredible." It sucked that they had to join a tour instead of wandering their own way through the boneyard, but they lingered near the back, Amy providing him with his very own tour.

"It is, isn't it?" she said as they studied the giant Stardust casino sign. "This is from 1958, and it was salvaged before they blew up the Stardust in 2006. It was the Bellagio of its day. A favorite of Sinatra's. The epicenter of organized crime."

There was something a little eerie and wonderfully

nostalgic about all the signs. "I guess it was such a different time back then." He moved to stand next to Amy, and she linked her arm through his. It was platonic, or maybe not. But he wasn't going to remove it. It felt good to be here with her. To pretend they had normal jobs and were two normal people on a normal date.

"Yes. It was. You need to come see this sign to understand just how different."

They walked arm in arm until she stopped them in front of the sign from the front of the old Moulin Rouge Hotel casino.

"This," she said, slipping her arm from his and gesturing with both hands toward the sign, "is probably the most important sign here and the most important casino in Vegas history."

Cabe tried to come up with the reason but couldn't. "Want to give me a clue as to why?"

She turned to face him. "Until the nineteen fifties, segregation ruled in Vegas. People of color couldn't stay here, not even stars like Sammy Davis Jr. or Nat King Cole, who were allowed to perform here but never allowed to sleep here. The Moulin Rouge was the first-ever desegregated hotel."

That he would never have guessed. "That *is* cool."

"The sign was also designed by Betty Willis, who not only drew the whole thing by hand because she couldn't find a font she loved, but also designed the iconic 'Welcome to Fabulous Las Vegas' sign. There weren't many female sign makers."

He'd visited Las Vegas over the years. Bachelor parties and the like. But he'd never given much thought to the people lived here. Who worked here. People who were entrenched in its history. He turned to face Amy and, unable to resist, tucked a loose strand of hair behind her ear. "Thank you for bringing me here."

"You're welcome," she said quietly.

They'd lost the rest of their group, and the residual chatter faded farther and farther into the distance. Amy's eyes held his, and for a moment he saw a flash of a future.

While on a mission, there were often times when he could see his team's destination in the distance but had no fucking clue how he was going to get them there. Enemy snipers would hold them in their position. Aerial assaults would threaten them where they stood. Their own minds would play tricks on them, attempting to convince them they were on a suicide mission. But through it all, Cabe never, not once, lost sight of the end goal.

Was a relationship between the two of them the end goal? Would they be able to overcome all the obstacles? Amy's attempt to outrun an asshole in a senior position? His memory of Jess? Their immediate op? Their career choices? And as much as he wanted to slip his hands to those cheeks of hers and kiss her senseless for realizing an evening spent gambling or trapped inside a theater would so not have been his thing, he stepped away and broke the contact.

"I don't know about you, but I'm hungry . . . for food," he clarified.

Even if his body was hungry for something completely different.

CHAPTER SEVEN

Amy glanced out of the window of her Caesars Palace suite and looked up at the sky. It was brilliant blue, the sun bright and clear yet still low in the sky. The Strip was pretty empty, but then it was only seven thirty in the morning, and Vegas was the ultimate party town. Most revelers were probably still tucked up in their beds, and even those few who ventured from their rooms had probably only gotten as far as the all-you-could-eat buffet.

She threw her napkin down on her half-eaten super-human-sized bowl of yogurt and granola and berries, and tried not think about what Cabe was doing in the suite across the hall. The previous evening, after the trip to the Neon Boneyard, they'd grabbed some food at a steak restaurant over at The Venetian. They'd talked about everything from the conflict in Syria to the construction of the Bellagio fountains. He'd been an easy dinner date.

Date.

It hadn't been a date.

At least, that was what she'd repeated to herself every time he'd tilted his head ever so slightly to the left and smiled at her. Or when he'd raised his hands above his head in a stretch, just as they'd left the table, to reveal three delectable inches of the hardest abs she'd ever seen.

They'd walked down the hallway together in a silence that became more and more potent the closer they'd gotten to their opposing doors. Tension built with every footstep until there was an awkward moment as she pulled her keycard from her purse and Cabe had reached for his wallet for his.

"Well," she'd said lamely, without even looking at him. "Have a great evening."

"You too," he'd replied.

She'd let herself in and closed the door, resting her back against it until her heart rate settled. It had been another minute before she heard his door close, and she wondered if he'd simply been staring at her door, as confused as she was about what to do with their growing feelings.

It didn't take long for her to pull on some shorts and a pale pink T-shirt. She put her hair up into a messy bun and applied a quick slick of lip gloss. A quick glance at her watch told her it was time to go and begin her lessons with Valentina. With one last look at her bed, which had been heavenly to sleep in and in which she could have spent at least another hour, she sighed and headed for the pit.

"Amy, my beautiful girl," Valentina said when she saw her enter the private room set up for her practice. She rolled her *r*'s in the wonderful way Amy had tried to practice when she was younger.

"And you don't look a day older since the last time I saw you, Valentina," she said, hugging her small frame tightly. "How is Matias?" Matias had moved as a young man from Quebec to Las Vegas to perform in the Cirque du Soleil show, *O*, when it had opened in the Bellagio in the late nineties. But his body and constant injuries had finally told him it was time to retire.

"Frustrated," Valentina replied honestly. "I encourage him to find something new he loves."

Amy couldn't imagine what it must be like to have to give up a career you adored. She loved working for the FBI, and she loved the problems she had to solve on a daily basis. She loved the way it helped her feel connected to her mom, but would it crush her if she had to give it up for some reason? She wasn't sure.

"Anyway," Valentina said with a wave of her hand at if she were physically pushing the problem away, "I need to turn you into a dealer, today, *si*?"

Amy grinned. "Yes, you do. I already know the basics, but I don't know how to be the greatest like you are."

Now it was Valentina's turn to smile. "We will never make you as great as I am in a day, but I will get you pretty darn close." Valentina pulled a tray of chips from beneath the table she was standing next to. It was full of all the different colors, everything from the blue-and-white dollar chip to the black-and-white hundred-dollar chip. Even the rare pink one, which was occasionally used for the three-to-two payoff in blackjack. There was a stopwatch on top of the tray, which Valentina put to one side before upending the chips into a huge pile into the middle of the table. She leaned in and spread them around, making sure they were completely mixed. "First we will work on your basics." She stood and reached for the stopwatch. "The goal of a good dealer is to minimize the length of time the table is out of play. This is for two reasons. One, it is obvious that the casino will make more money if more hands are played in twenty-four hours. But two, and personally the one I think is *most* important, is that you do not want to disrupt the players' flow. Regardless of whether they are on a hot streak and don't want to break it, or whether they are on a cold one and *want* to break it, every disruption to the game can throw them off. I've always believed my goal is to help them enjoy their experience—while I take their money, of course." Valentina gestured to the pile in the middle of the table. "At the end of the hand, or a turn, the table can be full of chips. And it is important for you to be able to clear it as quickly as possible to keep everyone in play and to stop anyone from walking away because of the time it is taking you to clear the chips. I want you to show me how quickly you can sort and stack the chip tray."

She'd been around chips her entire life, could stack them and shuffle them until they were interlaced. But she'd never timed herself.

"Go!" Valentina shouted.

Amy scanned the table, working as quickly she could to find the blue-and-white ones. When she had stacked as many as were obvious, she moved to the pink ones, and then repeated switching colors each time she felt her options were running low until finally the table was clear and the tray full. "How did I do?" she asked Amy, hopefully.

Valentina rolled her eyes. "I am too ashamed to tell you the time," she said, shaking her head playfully. "But I promise you that within the next hour you will halve it."

By the time lunchtime came around, Amy had not only successfully halved her time but had gotten it to within fifteen seconds of Valentina's. She'd also received a refresher on the rules of all the games played at the Lucky Seven. As a dealer, she'd need to handle all the casino table games, not just the ones she played frequently.

"Where are you hiding my baby girl?" a large voice boomed from the hallway.

Valentina nodded her head in the direction of the doorway. "You should go find him before he disrupts any of the private tables," she said with a smile.

Amy wandered to the door and found her Stetson-clad father looking into one of the rooms. "I'm right here, Dad," she said as she hurried to him and hugged him in the hallway. He smelled of leather and cigar smoke. Maybe it was because she'd lost her mother so many years ago, but it was impossible to explain the feeling of safety that washed over her when she was fortunate enough to spend time around her father.

"Let me look at you," he said, taking a step away from her. He studied her face. "Humph. San Diego appears to agree with you. I was kinda hoping it wouldn't."

"It does. And while you know I can't talk about what I'm working on, the job does too." Over her father's shoulder, she saw Cabe walking toward them with Uncle Clive. She smiled when she noticed that Cabe was wearing a black jacket that fit him to perfection. He'd remembered. "Dad, let me introduce you to Cabe Moss."

Her father turned and offered Cabe his hand. "Well, aren't you one big son of a bitch? If you're the guy who has my little girl's back, I feel better already."

Cabe's face broke into a grin. "My pleasure, sir."

"Sir. I like manners in a man. Military?"

"A SEAL, sir." Cabe said.

"Well, let's see if we can't teach you a thing or two. Which room are we in, Clive?"

As Uncle Clive led her father farther down the hallway, she turned and noticed Cabe's eyes were on her legs. Her bare legs. "Eyes up here, soldier," she said, humor in her tone. It made her feel warm inside that he was looking.

"It's sailor," he said with a wink. "They're good-looking legs, and I'm only human."

It was wrong to let him flirt, it was wrong for her to respond, but for a moment, she wanted to pretend the rules didn't apply. She reached forward and brushed a piece of lint off the shoulder of his jacket, then smoothed down his lapels. It was an intimate thing to do, she knew. And a risk, given the requirement to stay focused on the job. But hell, a piece of her had always believed in the what-happens-in-Vegas slogan. Here, in the middle of Caesars Palace, the real world didn't truly exist. "You look good in a suit, *sailor*."

Cabe placed his hands on top of hers and squeezed them gently. "You're killing me, Ames."

The heat of his fingers burned her inside. Made her want things she had no business wanting from a man she had no business wanting them from. "Why *Ames*?"

He shrugged. "I don't know. I just like it. It's catchy. Makes you sound like one of those TV cop heroines from the seventies."

Amy looked at their joined hands for just a millisecond longer before pulling them away. "You should go and start practicing," she said. "If I'm going to work my way into the Lucky Seven Casino's inner circle, I'd feel better if you were there too."

"I'll be there. But rest assured, even if I'm not invited, I'll find a way to cover your back." Cabe placed his hand around the back of her neck and pulled her forward gently to place a chaste kiss on her forehead. "I'll be there, even if you can't see me. I promise."

"That," Cabe said, pushing his plate into the center of the table to resist the urge to scoop another morsel onto his plate, "was the best food I have had in forever."

And it was true. The yellowtail with jalapeño had provided the perfect kick, the rock shrimp tempura had been cooked to perfection, and the Japanese wagyu beef was so melt-in-the-mouth tender that he'd dream about it for weeks to come.

But part of him wanted to keep eating just to prolong the time he could spend talking with Amy, who sat opposite him in the booth of Nobu in Caesars Palace, wearing a pretty cream dress and a content look on her face that surely matched his own. "I want to eat the rest of that vanilla miso tart," she said with a groan. "But I worry that if I do, I might not fit back into my uniform next week. Or my stomach might explode."

When Amy had floated the idea that they return to her Las Vegas home to perfect their skills before assuming their undercover roles, he'd been skeptical. But when she'd told him she would take care of the details for their trip, he hadn't imagined the luxury he'd spent the day in. He'd pictured crashing at her father's place and practicing his poker skills over a kitchen table. Most definitely not a day spent in a private room with some poker legends where he'd at least doubled his skill set, dinner at one of the best restaurants on the Strip, and a suite upstairs with a kick-ass bed just waiting for him to fall into. Even if he'd be falling into it alone.

The last mouthful of wine sloshed against the side of Amy's glass as she swirled it softly. Not that it had been any old bottle of white. It was a Coche-Dury Corton-Charlemagne Grand Cru, according to the label, and nearly two and a half thousand dollars a bottle according to the wine list. He'd never been more relieved to not be paying the bill in his life. Somewhere between Uncle Clive and Floyd Murray, the whole thing had been comped. He'd been surprised the two men had been able to call in such big favors, but then he'd seen the way Clive was treated by customers when he was in the pit . . . like some kind of poker star royalty who shook players' hands, greeted them by name, and remembered some little detail about the person's life story from his or her previous trip to the casino three years before. Cabe appreciated that level of recall.

And Floyd. Well, the fact that he'd changed a quarter of a million into chips once Cabe's training had finished without so much as batting an eye told him that Floyd was likely one of the casino's legendary high rollers.

Amy finished her wine and then ran her tongue along her lower lip as she placed the glass back on the table. The simple gesture made his heart race a little faster. It was wrong to think about her in any other way than as his colleague, but somehow that message had yet to reach his dick. The simplest thing to do would be to head back to his room.

"Tell me some more about what you learned today," Cabe said, leaning back into the booth instead.

She tapped her fingers on the table as she thought. They were long and slender, her nails perfectly squared off and unpainted. Practical, like she was. "It's the details. Like I had no idea that there was a serial number on the wheel and the bowl of a roulette wheel and that they have to match. And there is a skill to sorting a large stack of chips. Valentina had me sort and stack over and over again until I was fast enough. I'm going to have to practice at home, though. I had to card count every black-jack hand, just as if I was playing, and she'd challenge me. The first time she asked what my count was, I said "minus seven." She told me it was minus six . . . and I dithered. Then she said I was right and that I shouldn't allow myself to be put off. I had to act like I knew best, have confidence in myself, you know? And that I should always stand by my first count because the odds were I was right."

"Explain it to me. How do you card count?"

Amy grinned, reached into her purse, and pulled out a pack of cards. "It's pretty easy. Let's do the basic Hi-Lo method. High cards are good for the player. Ten, jack, queen, king, ace. They get assigned a minus-one count. A minus because as the number of them in the deck gets depleted, your advantage as a player goes down. The opposite is true for the low cards. Two through six are good for the dealer, so they get a plus-one count. As these cards are depleted, the players' advantage goes up because there are fewer low cards left in the deck to hurt them. Seven through nines are neutral, so they have no value."

She dealt them both a pair of cards, faceup. Her fingers lingered near her cards, and Cabe wondered how she'd feel if he lifted her hand to his mouth and brushed his lips across her tanned skin.

"Ace, three," she said. "That's a minus one and a plus one. You got a zero. I got a queen, jack. Lucky me."

"Which is a complete fix, by the way," Cabe said as he grinned. "Must be your lousy shuffle."

Amy tilted her head and laughed. Her hair fell over her shoulder, revealing the smooth skin of her neck and shoulder. And god, now he was thinking of pressing his lips there too. He probably should have stopped with the wine a glass ago because when she looked at him the way she was looking at him now, it was easy to forget they had a job to do.

"Hey, I have a great shuffle game according to Ortega," she said, tapping her own cards. "But what's my score?"

Two high cards, minus one plus minus one. Easy. "Minus two. And I don't believe Ortega. You're a cheat!"

She laughed. "Most definitely not. But now the running count is minus two. Because that's what my score plus your score equals." Amy dealt another two hands.

Cabe checked the cards. All low. "Four low cards, all plus one, making the hand plus four."

Amy placed her hand on top of his, and Cabe relished the warmth. They both leaned into the table, their heads closer. "Yes! But the running count for the entire blackjack game is the minus two from the first hand and the plus four from this hand, which means it is plus two."

This close, he could see how pink her lips were. For heaven's sake, he was going to need a cold shower when he got back to his room.

"So you keep a running count of the game, and the lower the count, the less you bet, the higher the count, the more you bet?" Cabe asked.

"Nearly. You have to convert that to a true count because there are up to five packs of cards in play, each with all the high and low cards. It's simple math. You take the running count and divide it by the number of packs of cards left. For example, a count of nine with four and a half decks left leaves you with a true count of two."

Amy gathered the cards up and slipped them back into her purse.

"Jesus, that's a lot of math on the fly for every hand." Noticing the restaurant was starting to empty, Cabe looked at his watch. How was it suddenly after midnight?

"It is. And you have to do it all in your head while holding conversations with other players around you so the casino can't tell you're card counting."

Cabe stood and offered Amy his hand to assist her from the seat. It was the gentlemanly thing to do, plus he just wanted to touch her once more. Her fingers gripped his, and for a moment, he thought she was going to keep hold. The sigh followed by the slight frown told him she was grappling with the two of them just as much as he was, and she let go of his hand.

He led them to the elevator that would take them to their rooms. The Nobu tower elevator required him to scan his room pass before entering, and Amy's room was just across the hall from his own. The doors slid open, and unable to resist, he placed a hand on Amy's lower back to guide her inside, where they stood with their backs to the rear wall, almost shoulder to shoulder, but not quite touching. The elevator was devoid of people but filled with the same kind of tension that always ignited when they were alone. The door slid shut painfully slowly, enclosing them in the small space. He could feel the heat of her skin close to his, and the nearness made the hairs on his arms stand on end as truly as if he were standing in the middle of an electrical storm.

He tried to focus on the reasons why she shouldn't have the effect on him that she did, but he couldn't list even one. His mind and his senses were filled with only her.

"Do you feel that?" he asked hoarsely. Surely he couldn't be the only one who felt it.

After a momentary pause that felt like an hour but was likely shorter than the span of a heartbeat, Amy sighed. "I wish I could say I didn't, but I do."

He looked at the numbers, willing them to get to their floor before he did something stupid. But they took too damn long, and he couldn't help himself. He turned to face her, placed one hand on the wall behind her head, and placed the palm of the other against her cheek, cupping it softly. "Tell me no and I won't," he whispered. Perhaps she could be strong enough for the two of them. Perhaps she could see through the heat of the moment, see what it would mean for the op if they gave in to feeling instead of thinking.

"We shouldn't," she said, turning her gaze to his. Her eyes were wide, and she ran that damn tongue of hers along her lower lip. "But I'd be lying if I said I didn't want to know what it would feel like."

He pressed his forehead to hers, heard her gasp of breath, and took a deep one of his own. But the feeling didn't pass. It kept building, the heat cycling between the two of them, growing, burning, until it was all Cabe could do to hold her gaze. They had to be sure.

One second ticked by. Then another.

Just when he felt as though he might be able to rein in his emotions, Amy tilted her head, the warmth of her breath tickling his skin. She was so close, he was certain that if he so much as opened his mouth to speak, his lips would brush hers.

"Kiss me, Cabe," she breathed.

And he did. Slowly at first. She was a woman who deserved to be savored first and devoured later. Hopefully there would be time for both. He pressed his lips to hers as her arms reached for his waist and pulled him into the cradle of her body. His imagination hadn't done the moment justice. He'd not expected to feel the rush of blood . . . to his head and his cock. He hadn't expected to feel this way about a woman ever again, let alone about a single kiss.

She tugged at him in a way he couldn't explain but was determined to show. His trailed his tongue along the seam of her lips, groaning as she opened for him.

The elevator pinged and came to a halt.

Amy put her hand on his chest.

Fuck.

He moved away from her as the door slid open.

"I'm glad I know," Amy said as she stepped out into the hallway. Her cheeks were flushed, her lips even pinker than they had been at dinner.

"Know what?" he asked gruffly as he discreetly rearranged himself, taking her hand.

The smile she gave him was cute as all hell. "What it will be like when this is all over."

His heart dropped, realizing what she meant a fraction before his brain did. "You aren't saying what I think you are, are you?"

Amy backed away from him toward their rooms. Their fingers fell away from each other. "If you're thinking that we can't do this while we work together, you're right. I shouldn't have encouraged you. And I'm sorry for that, but I guess I just needed to know what it was going to be like when this is all over and you take me out on a date."

"A date?" *A date.*

Slowly, she ran her fingertips across her lips. And deep down, he knew she wasn't doing it to tease him, she was reliving that singular moment of perfection they'd fallen into during the elevator ride. "Yes. A date. Ask me out when this is over, and I promise you it's a definite yes."

Cabe sighed, but it wasn't one of frustration. She was right to put the brakes on. While he was certain that spending the night with Amy would have redefined the term "sin city," he didn't want there to be any regrets the morning after. And she was uncertain . . . not of their growing feelings, but of their timing. As was he.

"Fine, Ames. Put a note in your calendar for the night after the op is over. Hell, make it thirty-six hours long. I'm a guy with plans."

Amy laughed. "So noted. And I'm a girl who needs a cold shower. Good night, Cabe." With that, Amy turned down the corridor, that cute ass of hers swaying side to side.

Cabe stood exactly where he was until he saw the door to her room click shut. For a smart guy who was well read in just about every form of literature, he couldn't think of a word to say.

CHAPTER EIGHT

The count at the blackjack table was plus two, and Amy, back at her table in San Diego, was relieved it was dropping steadily from the plus nine it had been only twenty minutes earlier. A run of picture cards had thankfully been put into the hands of amateur players who didn't know whether to ask for more cards when the two in their hands added up to fourteen. Fourteen felt like such a long way from twenty-one, that they never realized that asking for another card only ever gave them a fifty-fifty chance of not going over. Most of the time they looked shocked when they did. Thankfully, the players had gotten greedy and asked for extra cards, landing a run of tens and nines.

It was the last hand she was going to deal that night, and she was ready to get home. Vegas had been a lot of fun, but thinking about the flight home yesterday, sitting so close to Cabe, had her wound up tighter than a banjo string. Occasionally, her hand would brush against his, or his knee would touch hers, all of which had left her frustrated. Sleep had taken a long time to come around last night.

Amy risked another glance toward the cage. It was her first day, and nobody was expecting her to solve the op in one shift. This was the long game. Her main goals were to fit in and get to know people, especially those who were familiar with the ins and outs of how the casino was run. Johnnie Ortega, the man who had interviewed her and the current pit boss, caught her eye and cast a reassuring look in her direction. During her break, he'd caught her lingering in the hallway near the main offices as she'd watched the comings and goings while pretending to sip a cup of coffee. She'd played it off as needing to stretch her legs, and Johnnie, who knew firsthand how hard it was to stand still as a dealer for hours on end, had been fine with it. He'd even taken a moment to let her know that he thought she was doing a great job and would be an asset to the casino.

"Hit me with another," the gentleman in the ball cap said.

She looked at his cards. A four, a two, and a five. No matter what card was dealt, he wouldn't go bust. Not on that hand. Quickly, she slid another card in his direction. A three. She grimaced internally. Valentina had warned her about amateur blackjack players chasing the Five Card Charlie and then expecting something incredible to happen once they got it—a reward only offered on online betting sites, where bonuses were paid out for staying under twenty-one with five cards. According to Valentina, amateur gamblers were the most likely to claim they were getting screwed when the casino didn't come through.

The house had stuck at nineteen.

Woods, the manager, approached Ortega. Woods was tall and lean, with a slight slouch that made him appear shorter than he was. He placed his hand firmly on Ortega's shoulder and leaned forward to whisper in his ear. Whatever he said made Ortega blanch. Woods tilted his head to one side and glared at Ortega, who nodded.

"I'll take another," the gentleman said, bringing her thoughts back to the table. Of course he would. She knew the card would take him over, though, before she even turned it to face him. "Nine of clubs," she said, "brings you to twenty-three. House wins."

"Darn it," he said. "That was meant to be my lucky last bet before I fly home tomorrow." He grinned at her as he flipped a five-dollar chip onto the table. "Thank you."

"You're welcome, sir."

As Valentina had taught her, she cleared the chips quickly. It was one o'clock, according to the small clock under the table. The casino didn't close until two, but tables began to close toward the early hours as both patrons and card stacks dwindled. There were spaces at other tables that didn't warrant her pulling another card stack together. Plus, it was always better to have lots of players at the same table. People tended to be more risk averse when they were alone with the dealer, even though they appreciated the one-on-one attention. When a group of men play against one another instead of against a pretty dealer for the house, ego always took over. Valentina had said that after all these years, she could smell the testosterone when it kicked in.

Amy ensured the players at her table settled themselves elsewhere, cleaned everything down, and made sure her chip tray was accounted for.

She made her way to the ladies' changing room, where a number of girls were in various stages of getting ready to leave: dealers in the black-skirt-and-white-blouse uniform, bar staff in all black, and servers in black-with-gold vests. A small group sat chatting in the corner. Two women stood by their lockers, minding their own business, intent on getting out as quickly as possible.

As much as she naturally wanted to talk, introduce herself, and get to know these women, she didn't engage in conversation. The women who were missing had been good at what they did, but hadn't been the most popular, and had often kept to themselves.

She grabbed her sports bag from her locker. Many of the girls were simply changing out of their heels and into flats or sneakers, but since Amy was fully aware that the girls who had gone missing had *worked* here, she was not going down in a restrictive pencil skirt and an unnecessarily sexy white shirt if someone put her in his sights.

Since they had no idea what had happened to these women once they were abducted, she had to assume the worst. She changed into boyfriend jeans, which allowed her to move but were way more difficult to remove than yoga pants. On top, she went for workout attire: sports bra, T-shirt, and hoodie. Last, she put on sturdy sneakers in case she needed to run.

Because security insisted on checking their bags as they came in and went out to ensure that there was no criminal behavior such as theft of chips or having devices that could be used to commit fraud, it was impossible to bring in her firearm or any other weapon of significance. Fortunately, they'd allowed her to bring mace, which she now pulled from her bag before stuffing her uniform into it.

"Are you Amy?" asked a woman in a black suit and bright red heels. She appeared to be in her early fifties.

"I am," Amy said, offering her hand.

The woman shook it. "I'm Elaine Dumont. I'm one of the day-shift pit bosses here at the casino, but the evening-shift assistant called in sick, so I offered to stay and provide cover. We're thrilled to have you join us. Why don't you let me introduce you to some of the other girls?"

If she was going to meet the girls, it was better that someone more senior in the organization introduce her rather than seeking it out herself.

"Oh, are you the new girl who left Vegas . . . why on earth would you do that to come here?" asked a young woman with a sharp bob in a bright red color.

Amy couldn't help but smile. There were days she asked herself the same question.

"That's Tanya, one of more recent hires. She's been here four months," Elaine said, rolling her eyes like a tired mom with a hyperactive child. "I thought we'd finally have a full roster, but then Eve Canallis left suddenly and we were back to being shorthanded."

Lines appeared on Tanya's brow. "I don't get it," she said. "She was a natural in the pit. Made good tips. And I get that she missed home, talked about her family and Cleveland like it was the center of the universe instead of The Mistake on the Lake, but seriously, why the disappearing act?"

Amy decided to play dumb and curious. "Disappearing act?"

"She just didn't show up for work the Friday before last," Tanya offered helpfully. "No call, nothing."

Another woman joined them. An older woman with thinning peroxide-blonde hair pulled up in a shellacked beehive got up from the bench she'd been sitting on. She was wearing a server's uniform. "That girl just went home. Enough with the drama. I swear you watch too many mysteries, Tanya," the woman said in a deep husky voice that suggested a lifelong smoking habit. She offered Amy her hand, and Amy took it. "Pleasure to meet you. I'm Edie." Edie turned to face Tanya. "That girl followed that good-for-nothing boyfriend of hers here, but as soon as he took off, all she wanted to do was to save enough to get back to Cleveland. I'm happy for her."

Amy wanted to ask so many questions. Who was the boyfriend? Where did he take off to? What was the nature of their falling out? But she didn't want to draw attention to herself on her very first shift. Not if she was going to be here for the long term. She needed to play it cool despite the urgency tugging away at her mind.

She wondered where the police were at with searching through Eve's laptop. If Eve was on social media, she would have posted something online as soon as she'd made plans to leave. It would be a simple matter to check her name, find her parents' address, and see if she'd arrived back home. Surely the SDPD could let them know if she'd been reported missing. Maybe they could get ahead of the investigation if the girl was missing but nobody had reported it yet.

There were at least two traits Eve shared with the missing women. The first was being new-ish to town with no immediate support network. It was easier to take a person when nobody was looking out for them. Which was yet one *more* reason she couldn't get involved with Cabe or even write it into the script. Even if they tried to hide it, there was always a risk someone would see them together. She was a great undercover operative, but as a woman, would she really be able to hide any developing feelings from those around her? As soon as anybody even suspected she had a boyfriend, the kind of boyfriend who would report a girl missing within hours of a disappearance, her potential as a target disappeared.

The second trait was homesickness. It was easy enough for anybody to imagine a super-homesick person leaving to go back. And if that person had been pretty isolated, with few new friends, nobody would think to call the police because the obvious explanation for the woman's disappearance would seem to be that she'd simply left. Playing into it, Amy came up with a plan. "I guess I understand why Eve left then," she said to Edie. "I miss my family back in Vegas." It was the truth. After seeing them over the weekend, she missed them even more. "I'm sorry Eve left you in the lurch, but this vacancy really saved my bacon," she said as she picked her sports bag up and threw it over her shoulder. "Eve's loss is my rent."

She took the few steps out of the casino, and counted the seconds until she could get on the phone, ask for an update on the data search of Eve Canallis's laptop, and begin to look for Eve's boyfriend.

"Well, don't you look all *GQ*," Six said as Cabe walked into the conference room two days later.

"Ha fucking ha," Cabe responded, pulling his white shirt cuffs so they showed a little under the edges of the sleeves of his black jacket. He spun the compass rim of his watch that Jess had bought and hidden from him before both of them left on tour. Discovering it nearly a year to the day after her death, when he'd finally decided to clear out her side of the closet, had reduced him to a shell. Clearly, she'd meant it to be his wedding present. He'd gone to work, put one foot in front of the other, but he had no recollection of that time other than the gaping hollow feeling in his gut. At night, he'd held the watch in his hand, spinning it around and around, pausing every now and then to look at the inscription: *To Cabe. IOU forever. Jess x.*

It was one of those things she'd always said. He'd fixed the dripping faucet in her apartment when they'd first started dating, and she'd told him that she would owe him forever because she could finally have a good night's sleep. When he'd showed up with his friend's tow truck on the day her car broke down twenty miles outside of San Diego on the way back from a girls' weekend in L.A., she'd again said, "I owe you forever"—this time with a smile and a glint in her eye that said she'd thank him in bed later. And when he'd proposed, she'd said she didn't have an engagement gift for him, that she'd just have to owe him forever instead.

"Ignore Six. You brush up well, dude," Mac said just as floor plans were projected onto the wall.

In truth, for all the years he'd worn a uniform, he liked wearing civilian clothes. Dressier ones than the usual jeans and polo shirt. It was nice to dig them out of the closet and have a reason to wear them. Plus, it felt like a disguise. They'd decided that although Amy would have a fake identity, Cabe would keep his own, because it was possible that somebody from the military base would recognize Cabe in the casino. Thanks to Mac's multimillionaire brother Lochlan, Cabe's bank account had been temporarily padded, Between the FBI and CIA, he'd been provided cash to bankroll his gambling, but not the kind of money that would secure him a place at Sokolov's table, should that ever become an option. Now, thanks to a significant loan from Lochlan, should anybody choose to check if he could afford to gamble with the big boys, he'd pass with flying colors.

Plus, there was no risk that Eagle's government contracts would be uncovered. They were completely sealed.

The only difficult part was that they'd decided he should pretend to be disenchanted with the military, and even, if necessary, support and perpetuate the allegations of Russian interference with the current military and political regime. The rest he'd play by ear.

"Harley and Lite are in the casino, sitting by the bar having a beer. Lite's got an eye on Amy's current position, which is here," Mac said, pointing to a table not too far away from the cage. "He's lost her a couple of times when she's gone into the staff-only area for her break."

It had bothered him to have to listen to what was going on up until now instead of actually being there, but they'd decided as a team that he shouldn't make himself known at the casino on Amy's first day. The live-stream video from the hidden cameras the guys carried wasn't the best. It was often jerky, always moving, and at one point he'd begun to feel motion sickness watching them.

But he needed to know that place inside out before he stepped in there. "Harley's completed a full three-sixty walk-around, taking in every point of entry and exit. Places to hide, places to fade into the background," Six said.

Thanks to that effort, Cabe felt like he'd already been inside.

Now he couldn't wait to get started, his usual patience feeling sorely stretched. But Mac had pointed out that arriving too early in the evening would have smacked of being a tourist or a gambling lightweight. He needed to play later, with the big boys.

His lessons with Amy's father were about to be put to the test.

"You know the key guys," Six said, going through photographs pinned to the wall of the main targets. "Pit boss, Johnnie Ortega. Casino manager, Faulkner Woods. His father Hemingway Woods is *still* moored in Monte Carlo on a yacht that is *still* bigger than my house."

Cabe listened intently as Six went through the names. Repetition was the key to remembering, and he wasn't going to take it for granted that he'd remember everything. There was a first time for his memory to let him down, and he didn't want this case to be it.

"I'll call just before I head in. Get an update," he said, grabbing the keys to his rental car. Knowing where Amy was, knowing Lite's eyes were on her for now, would help him resist the temptation to look for her so that he could focus on his own role. Which was the money, not the women. Although those lines of demarcation were starting to make him itch, just like the tape holding the wires of his microphone to his chest. They'd decided to wait on his wearing an earpiece until Cabe was officially on the inside, so for now he'd be able to record information, but not be able to receive it. The feebs were taking care of hacking into the feed from the existing cameras installed in the casino, which of course heavily focused on the gaming floor, but the behind-the-scenes areas were still very much a mystery. And they needed a better sense of what happened back there from Amy before Eagle could break into the casino and place cameras where they needed them.

A small pen camera, held strategically in place in Cabe's top pocket, was all they could rely on for now. It was small, discreet, and actually worked as a pen should anybody try it.

"I'll check in after I've been there a few hours," he said, heading out of the door.

As Cabe neared the casino, large lights appeared alongside the highway along with billboards declaring that a wild night of fun was just around the corner. He ran through his key objectives: to determine how and where the laundering was taking place; and to identify what, if any, involvement Faulkner Woods had in the illegal activity. There was a chance the man could just be running a shoddy ship, in which case his actions, while still illegal, were not criminal with intent. However, if there was a chance he was in on it and profiting from it, Faulkner Woods was going to end up in a world of hurt.

Cabe parked his car in the lot in front of the casino. Given the later hour, there were still an ungodly number of cars there. As he walked up to the front entrance, he took another look at the external security setup. There were cameras all over the front lot and aimed at the main entrance. Anybody who tried to sneak in through the front would be caught in a heartbeat.

The intel he'd been given claimed that the back door had only twenty percent of the coverage of the front, but he now wished he'd taken an extra moment to drive around the rear to confirm it.

The double doors opened automatically, and he stepped inside. The rhythmic, mind-numbing repetition of the slot machines hit him first. He pushed past his gut reaction to the grating noise and forced himself to settle into a place of stillness, a place of calm that allowed him to rise above the problem he was facing to see it from all angles. Knowing that even his entry could be traced back

on video if he was to make his way into Woods and Sokolov's inner circle, he made a show of looking around
as if deciding where to go play. Days of studying floor
plans and watching video from the rest of the team meant
that he knew even minutia about the space—there was a
floor vent twenty steps to his left and an ATM forty to
his right. But it was important, for character and appear-
ances, for this to seem as though it was his first visit.

He grabbed a beer at the bar, his first port of call.
Though he had no real intention of drinking, the location was prime real estate, and from his position up
against the solid wood, he could see the cage, check . . .
the manager, check . . . and, there she was. His eyes
glanced over to Amy at her table but went right back to
looking at his beer.

Faulkner Woods, the casino manager, walked by with
a purposeful stride. Staff asked him questions as he
passed their stations. His answers were short at best and
abrupt and curt at worst. It took two minutes to decide
he didn't like the guy. Five minutes after that he'd
doubled-down on that opinion when he saw how Woods
got handsy with the female staff. He slipped a hand
around the waist of a server asking him a question and
leaned his lips so close to the ears of both a dealer and a
bartender when he spoke to them that he could swear
there must be contact. Cabe noticed a couple of the
women sidestep Woods, and Cabe wished he was there
on a day off so he could teach the guy how you worked
professionally alongside women.

Which was ironic, given he'd kissed Amy.

But she'd wanted him to.

And he'd wanted to.

And it was everything he'd expected.

No.

It was *more* than everything he'd expected.

But now he had a job to do.

Woods walked over to the back corner of the bar where three men were sitting in a booth. The lights were a little darker back there, casting it in shadows. Ten, fifteen, and then thirty minutes went by, Woods's head seeming permanently tilted in deference the longer he sat there, his shoulders becoming ever more rounded. When he finally walked away, his face had the ashen hue of a man used to subservience.

When Woods was finally out of his line of sight, Cabe was able to make a positive ID on Sokolov as one of the men in the booth. Certain that he couldn't spend much longer in a casino bar without actually playing a game or doing *something* as a cover, and hoping to hear what the men were saying, he contemplated approaching a pretty woman in a simple black dress who sat at the round wooden table in front of the booth, her back to Sokolov, and using the old chestnut, "Is this seat taken?"

He had a flicker of doubt about the strategy, but his sense of duty was stronger. If Amy happened to look up and see him, she'd realize it was his cover. Wouldn't she? Either way, he needed to park his thoughts of the two of them. They were only muddying his concentration. Now it was time to do what was best for the op.

As Cabe was about to stand, Woods returned to the bar, heading straight toward him. "Anthony," he said, leaning over the bar toward the bartender, "please set up Mr. Sokolov's usual tray and have it sent to the Como private gaming room."

Cabe ran through the Italian-named private suites that he'd reviewed from the floor plans and seen from the

three-sixty video. They ran in alphabetical order. Amalfi
and Bergamo to the left, Florence and Genoa to the right.
"Private suite" was a bit of a misnomer. Though the
general public wasn't supposed to wander back to them,
they were really just open-fronted booths partitioned
from the casino by glass walls. He quickly made his way
to the cage and requested fifty thousand dollars of
chips, and made inquiries about where he might bet in
a less public setting. Once he'd filled out the appropriate paperwork and the transaction had been cleared, he
walked toward the private area and looked around for a
moment, hoping to appear as if he had no clue what he
was doing.

"Mr. Moss," Woods said, hurrying up behind him.
He'd outright ignored Cabe at the bar, but Cabe assumed
he'd been now made aware of his sizable stack of chips.
"I'm Faulkner Woods, manager of the casino. I understand you require a private table this evening."

"I do," Cabe said. "I'd like that one," he said, pointing
to Florence, right next door to Como.

Because watching was what he did best.

"Amy," Six yelled, popping his head around the door of
his office as she walked along the corridor to the conference room. "I need your opinion."

She'd worked at the casino four out of the past five
nights. She would be there again tomorrow, Saturday, but
she wasn't scheduled to be on tonight, for which she was
eternally grateful. The late nights and long days were
already catching up with her, and she was looking forward to a solid night's sleep. Plus, Saturday was the peak
night at the casino, which meant more customers she
needed to get to know.

She was also more than thirty minutes early to meet Cabe.

"Sure thing," she said. She liked the high energy that followed Six. It was the complete opposite of Cabe's steady strength. "What do you need?"

Six spun his monitor. "Which of these do you like best?"

Incredibly, there were images of three small handheld bouquets on the screen. "Erm . . . these are for the wedding, right?"

"Yep, can't decide which Lou will like best."

"Well, shouldn't you ask her? I mean . . . what color is her dress?"

Six looked confused. "White, right?"

Amy sat down on the chair opposite him. In so many ways, she admired the way he was taking responsibility for arranging the wedding, but she really wanted to meet his elusive bride-to-be. She'd done a little snooping about Louisa North, and from what she'd read, the extremely wealthy woman was a research prodigy whose drive to find a cure for Huntington's disease had been fueled by her father's death from it. "She could wear any color she wants. What's her favorite color?"

"She wears a lot of that blue color, the same shade as that fancy jeweler."

"Tiffany blue?" Amy asked.

Six put her words into the search bar on his computer and looked at the images. "Yeah. That color. She has clothes, and Chucks, and jewelry, and other shit in that color."

Amy ran through all the things she'd consider if she was picking her own colors. "Is she having a bridesmaid? A maid or matron of honor?"

"Mac?" Six yelled, almost deafening her.

Mac wandered into Six's office hugging a cup of coffee. "Do you have to be so loud?"

"Did Lou ask Delaney to get a specific-color dress for the wedding?"

Mac's frown burrowed. "She probably mentioned it, but . . . you know . . ." He gestured something going in one ear and out the other.

"Can you check?" Six asked.

"For fuck's sake," Mac said, rolling his eyes. "Is this our life between now and November twenty-third? Inane questions about weddings? Is there any reason you can't ask Lou? Never mind, I'll call Delaney."

He pulled out his phone. "Hey, Buttons, sorry to wake you." Mac smiled as he listened to whatever she said. "Yeah, sweetheart, I'd have liked that too, but I had to be here early."

Amy blushed at the suggestive tone of his voice.

"Listen, what color dress did Louisa tell you to get for the wedding?"

There was a pause.

"Got it. Thanks, babe. Go back to sleep." Mac hung up the phone and slipped it back into his jeans pocket. "Black, with a Tiffany blue sash or ribbon or something around her waist."

"Thanks, bro." Six turned back to the flowers as Mac left the room. "None of these are Tiffany blue," he said, looking to Amy.

"No," she said, leaning forward. "They aren't. But, see that white bouquet there? I bet the florist could add a ribbon around the stems in Tiffany blue. You could get a large one for Louisa, a smaller one for . . ." She searched for Mac's girlfriend's name but couldn't think of it. "Buttons."

Six laughed. "Delaney."

"Yes, Delaney. Then have boutonnieres made for the men with a small ribbon the same color."

"Shit. Do I have to wear those flower things in the buttonhole?"

Amy laughed. "It's your wedding. I don't think you have to do anything you don't want to."

Six looked across the desk, straight at her. His stare was oddly compelling, the whole Scandinavian god thing working for him. But he wasn't Cabe. "You're right. I don't need to deal with this shit if I don't want to. I was just going to wear a suit. I guess I should wear black."

Amy nodded. "And if I can suggest, a Tiffany blue tie or pocket square or something."

"Pocket square?"

"The handkerchief square that goes in the top left pocket of your jacket," Cabe said from behind her. She'd recognize his voice anywhere. And it sent shivers through her. Cabe placed a hand on her shoulder and left it there for the briefest moment, but she felt the heat of it for much longer. "Morning, Ames."

Ames. She loved the familiarity of it.

"For your apartment," he said, placing a little cactus in an eggshell blue ceramic pot in front of her. She looked at it, then at Cabe. He'd noticed she had no plants in her new apartment and had done something about it. Her heart tripped over with happiness.

"Thank you," she said, hoping her eyes conveyed the rest.

"You're welcome." He sat down in the chair next to hers. "Wedding stuff?"

Six nodded. "*Ames* was just helping me figure out bouquets."

Cabe eyed Six as if his humor wearied him. "Good. One less thing I have to help you figure out. And yes, for the record, the Hotel del Coronado can do a wedding brunch for twenty on November twenty-third. I booked it with my credit card for now, so don't change your mind."

Six leaned back in his chair and grinned. "You know what, Cabe?" he said, placing his hands behind his head, a move that showed just how big his biceps were. "I'd be lost without you. I can't help but think it's going a little too smoothly. I'm beginning to worry we are forgetting something important."

"You are so lucky it's going so well. My cousin turned into a total bridezilla. She uninvited her maid of honor when she found out she'd be seven months pregnant on the day of her wedding," Amy said. "Told her it would ruin the aesthetic of the wedding pictures."

"Shit, we need a photographer," Six said, and quickly made a note in his phone. "Lou's going to hate that."

"What if you just had a couple of candid photographers?" Amy suggested. "Nothing formal, just people who could capture moments as they unfold? Sometimes those shots can be better than anything staged. Those would be the kind of shots *I'd* prefer."

She looked at Cabe, whom she could have sworn was studying her. She wondered what kind of wedding he would want. Not that they were anywhere even remotely close to that kind of conversation.

Six grinned. "That sounds perfect."

"Let me take care of organizing that," Cabe said. "We'll just get whoever we hire to capture candids when Lou isn't even looking. And if I deal with the photographer, it means the girly shit of decorating the room gets to be Mac's job."

Amy couldn't help but laugh.

"I have news," Cabe said finally. "About Eve Canallis. Noah sent me the SDPD report—with all the appropriate approvals of course."

Six closed his laptop, and Amy leaned in his direction. "And?"

"There was a bunch of crap in there," Cabe said as he continued to stare at her. "Her friend was right. She did have multiple viruses. But they managed to get it cleaned up while retaining much of the original data. And I think we have a lead."

"What? Is there something on there about her plans?"

Cabe rubbed his fingers across his jaw. "Sort of. You have to triangulate, but it's pretty clear. The first thing was, she'd been researching seasickness cures. Natural and chemical solutions. Plus, she'd placed an order for a pair of travel-sickness pressure-point bracelets."

Amy leaned forward. "Did she have travel plans? Was she taking a cruise? Is she on vacation and just out of signal range?"

"According to the Department of Homeland Security, she hasn't traveled anywhere on her passport, even though it was missing from her apartment."

"Just spit it out," Six said. He turned to Amy. "He's been like this since we were little. He likes to lead into something, make it sound mysterious, then rain down some epic ending to the story so it sounds even more amazing than it really is."

Cabe grabbed a paperclip off Six's desk and threw it at him, hitting him square in the temple. "Okay, here's the thing. Outside of cures for seasickness, she'd googled one other thing before she disappeared." Cabe took his phone from his pocket and pulled something up on it.

"She looked up whether offshore gambling was illegal, whether gambling in international water is legal, and whether card rules changed in international water. Are you catching a theme here?"

Amy's pulse raced. Oh, my god. She was going offshore to gamble. "Who the hell was organizing that? Lucky Seven? Faulkner Woods? Sokolov?"

Cabe shook his head. "That's something we are going to have to find out. But let's play this out for a second. If there is an illegal syndicate gambling out on international waters, it's the perfect foil for drug running, money laundering, or sex trafficking."

"I hate the idea that sex trafficking is the reason women are going missing, but it's the only explanation. If this was a serial killer, we'd have found a body by now. Their modus operandi is show-and-tell for the most part. Also, there is too much precision to the timing. Serial killers escalate. The duration between victims decreases. Plus, the fact that all the women are still missing says something." Amy ran her fingers through her ponytail and gripped it tightly. It cleared her head.

"It's a workable hypothesis that the women were handpicked to join the cruise and were invited to deal or serve there." Cabe paused for a moment as the reality set in for both of them. "Perhaps they were promised extra shifts or extra money. Maybe they even worked their shift on the boat as normal but were never allowed to return home."

Eve's face and those of the other women flashed into Amy's mind. "If there are offshore gambling games, I need to get picked to check them out. I need to be on the next boat."

"In that case, so do I," Cabe said.

CHAPTER NINE

By the way Woods was marching around in a mood that was as dark as his slate gray suit, something was happening in the casino—something important. Amy made a point to maintain eye contact with her guests, do her job, and maintain her count at the blackjack table, but when she could, she looked around, filing away critical pieces of information.

Like why had Edie, the server she'd met on her first night, taken a silver tray loaded with bottles of spirits through the employee door? At first, she'd considered the possibility of overstock, but then Edie had been followed by another server with mixers, and a third with bar snacks. People were convening behind the scenes, and she needed to know who.

There was a slim possibility that the drinks had been for some high rollers in private rooms, but then why would have Edie taken the circuitous route that involved locked doorways and corridors and passes when she could just as easily have taken them around the customer floor and walked straight in?

It was hard to believe that it had been only a week ago that she had started there. In that time, she'd managed to create and maintain the persona of a newcomer who was isolated and homesick. She'd also made about eight hundred dollars in tips, which she intended to donate to a missing persons charity or maybe to a private effort to raise a reward for information if the FBI would let her. While she was still new, she should be able to get away with playing dumb and pretending to be a girl with no sense of direction. She intended to make the most of it.

In cultivating that part of her persona, she had started small, pretending to head in the wrong direction to the employee room, only to have Ortega turn her around and point her the other way. When she saw someone she'd gotten to know, she'd point in the direction in which she was walking and then ask the person if she was taking the right route to something she knew was at the other end of the casino. Word was getting around that the new kid couldn't find her way out of a paper bag, and that suited her just fine.

First, however, she needed a reason to step off the floor. She began with a subtle, casual flapping of the collar of her uniform and a small sigh. After a while, she pressed the back of her hand to her forehead as if checking her own temperature. Then for effect, she gripped the edge of the poker table with both hands and allowed her head to drop forward.

"Are you okay, Amy?" Ortega asked.

She shook her head and tried for a wobbly smile. She leaned toward Ortega's ear, as if embarrassed by what she had to say. "I feel dizzy," she whispered. "It's my own fault. I was running late, so I skipped dinner."

Ortega called for Vanessa and asked her to take Amy's

place. "You," he said, "go take a minute. Get some water. Swing by the kitchen and grab a snack. Do you need me to walk with you?"

"No, I got this. I'm so sorry." Amy felt shitty lying to Ortega—an odd emotion, she knew, to feel, given that he could be, well, one of the bad guys. But he just didn't *feel* to her like a bad guy.

Using her pass, she let herself back into the employee area. While the customer-accessible areas of the casino were richly decorated, saturated in hues of deep red and gold, the employee areas were much more subdued and had the user-friendliness of a rabbit burrow with corridors running in all directions from the offices where the finance and HR teams were situated to the kitchens and storage areas.

If this had been her permanent place of employment, Amy would have been tempted to suggest that some simple signage on the walls might make life a little easier for everybody. But it wasn't—and the lack of signage would be her excuse if she was discovered here. While there were cameras in these back areas, they were not as prevalent as they were in the rest of the casino. What few existed were heavily focused on the obvious areas: the vaults, the liquor storage areas, the employee locker rooms.

Staying in character, she painted a pained look on her face and filled a plastic cup with cold water from the water fountain. She put the back of her palm to her forehead and walked toward the exit that led to the staff parking lot.

Two security team members stood by the open door. One turned and looked at her. "Can I help you?"

Amy shook her head. "I felt a little faint. Mr. Ortega

suggested I just come back here and get some water and a little air."

"You need a chair or something?"

"Please," she said as pathetically as she could muster and smiled when he led her behind the security desk to a chair pushed into the corner. She wouldn't be fully hidden, but would be spotted only if someone approached the desk directly.

Through the gap between the two men, she could see cars in the employee parking area that were way outside the pay scale of the majority of the employees. The guard shook hands with two men and let them in through the employee entrance without passes or name badges.

A long limousine pulled up, and Faulkner Woods strode down the corridor to it, presumably to welcome the woman who was being helped out of the vehicle by the driver. Where inside were all these people going, and why?

If it was simply a high roller service they were attending, the casino should probably do some work on the back of the place. Coming in through a half-lit doorway couldn't hold a candle to the secret rear entrance of the MGM hotel that led to The Mansion. Ninety-nine percent of visitors to Vegas didn't even know the boutique hotel existed, let alone housed the entrance to the VIP high roller welcome suite.

But they weren't heading toward the private suites.

The security guards closed the door and resumed their seats at the security monitors. Amy waited for a few more moments before standing. "I'm going to grab some more water," she said.

Amy made a show of heading toward the kitchen but paused at a narrow hallway that ran to the left of the jan-

itorial area. Though the jangling noise of the slot machines that lay on the other side of the wall made it hard
to hear anything else, she could have sworn she heard the
murmur of voices coming from the door at the end of the
hall.

There was no valid reason for her to go down there. It
clearly wasn't the way to food, the exit, the gaming floor,
or any employee area.

"Lost?" a voice said from behind her, and she felt a
hand on her shoulder. She jumped a bit in her shoes.

Her heart raced as she turned to find Faulkner Woods
staring at her. A quick search of his body language said
she had nothing to fear. But then she looked into his eyes.
They were cold, dead almost. Realizing her hand was
still splayed on her chest, she patted over her heart and
pasted a smile on her face. "Oh my gosh, Mr. Woods," she
said, scrambling for something to say, "you scared
the bejesus out of me. I'm so sorry. I felt a little ill.
Mr. Ortega suggested coming back here for a moment to
get some water. And food. And . . . air."

Woods looked over his shoulder, then placed a hand
on her lower back, guiding her away from the door. "This
is a very long way away from any of those things. Didn't
you realize that?"

"I did. A couple of minutes ago. I'm so sorry. I promise I'll make the time up. I tried to backtrack, and now
I'm even more lost. I should have left a trail of bread-
crumbs to follow . . . or something."

He studied her face. "Fairy tales," he said eventually.
"How very intriguing."

Babbling felt like something her character would do.
"It's been a joke ever since I was a child. My dad used to
say I couldn't find my way out of a paper bag without

instructions. I have zero sense of direction. There was this one time I went on spring break, and I got so lost in the Orlando airport that I missed my flight."

Woods smiled. "Ortega told me that finding your way around is probably the only thing you can't do in a casino. He speaks very highly of you."

"I'm glad to hear it. I'm really enjoying it here. The rest of the girls have been really nice, and I haven't had any trouble with any of the clients."

Woods looked up and down the hallway and moved closer to her, the tightness in her chest growing in direct correlation to his proximity. "I think you should let me help you back to the employee area."

She took a step back. What she wanted to do was kick him in the balls before he completely ended up in her personal space. But what she *needed* to do was play along. "Thank you," she said and tilted her head to one side, looking up at him through her eyelashes. She was safe from abduction while they were in the casino. But harassment, she knew, could happen anywhere.

The door at the end of the corridor opened, and the woman she'd seen arrive earlier slipped through it. There was a temporary bar set up, a white tablecloth thrown over a table. "I'm sorry, I'm taking you away from. . . ." She deliberately left the sentence hanging, in the hope that Woods would fill in the blank.

Woods looked toward the door, then back at her. He stepped back, his eyes suddenly warm. "I want to help you get ahead here, Amy. You've got a lot of potential. The transition from where you are to becoming a pit manager can be a long one, and I think you could do it with some hard work. But you are going to need more training, perhaps a broader set of responsibilities once your trial period is over, a clear mentor. Ortega really respects you, so that would work."

Confused by the sudden switch in mood, she played along. "Thank you, Mr. Woods. I'd like that."

Woods sighed. "Now isn't the perfect time for a career conversation, but you are going to need to put in some serious hours. Hours the casino may not always be able to provide. But if I could get some additional dealer work for you, private work to bump your hours up," he said, encouraging her to move down the hallway, "would you be interested? Off the clock, but good money."

The pressure that had been building in her chest was replaced with a flood of adrenaline. "Yes, I would. I have loans. And I'd love to make the trip home for the holidays if I can afford it."

They were now walking so fast that Amy had to jog the occasional step to keep up.

The quiet chuckle he emitted scratched its way along her spine like nails down a chalkboard. "I'll see what I can do to make that happen. And, listen, I can't do this for everyone. Just people like yourself. So you're going to need to show a certain amount of discretion. Understood?"

Amy nodded, because internally she felt like she was making a deal with the devil.

"The exit to the floor is that way." As he let go of her elbow, which was pinned close to her side, he brushed her breast.

She flinched. Disgust flooded her as a wry smile dominated his face. He leaned his lips to her ear. "I'll find you later to pick up this conversation."

What the fuck?

From his spot at the bar, Cabe could see straight

through the employee door, and right now, he'd got a clear line of sight on Woods, who stood way too close to Amy for his liking.

Woods looked over his shoulder, as if only just noticing the open door, and quickly stepped away from Amy.

Hands slapped the bar next to Cabe. The noise made him jump internally; externally he didn't move a muscle. "I have seen you in the private gaming area, no?"

Sokolov.

"Mmm-hmm," Cabe said. "It's no Wynn baccarat salon, but it'll do."

Sokolov huffed. "I tell the manager, Woods, that he could turn this into so much more with some modest investment."

Cabe nodded non-committedly, one eye still on Woods through the open doorway. If he laid a finger on Amy, Cabe was going to march through that door and—

"Konstantin Sokolov," he said gruffly, offering his hand.

Cabe took his eye away from Amy for a moment and shook it firmly. "Cabe Moss."

"What is it that you do, Mr. Moss?" Sokolov reached for the vodka that had been placed in front of him without him having to order it. Condensation was already forming on the outside of the glass.

"I'm a security specialist," Cabe replied, knowing he needed to focus on his target, not Amy. As the door drifted closed, Amy leaned back against the wall and took a deep breath. When the door opened only a moment later, and Amy walked to the table where she was supposed to be dealing, her eyes found his for the briefest second. It secretly thrilled him that she'd needed to know he was there. "I arrange for all manner of security. For people, organizations, buildings. And yourself?"

While he wanted nothing more than to head to her table to play with her as dealer so she could be reassured that he was there—that he'd seen, that she wasn't on her own—he needed to return to his mission.

"Ah. I run a number of local enterprises, predominantly imports and exports. Are you formerly military?"

"Yes, sir," he said. "But happy to be a civilian again."

"And why is that?"

"Honestly? Being deployed to fight battles we shouldn't be in and couldn't win," Cabe said. He swallowed the feeling of betrayal as he said the words. Given the list of illegal enterprises Sokolov was involved in, he was never going to befriend a law-abiding military man. And even though it was only a role Cabe was playing, a part of him ached to defend his career. He was proud of the things he'd been able to achieve with his brothers. He knew that not everybody agreed with war, but he was more than happy with the legacy of his career. "It's a shit-show of underpaid and undertrained men heading out into battle without the proper provisions, and there was no way I was shipping out again."

"I have never understood the American war machine," Sokolov said before taking a sip. "It has always seemed so . . . what is the American word for this . . . jingoistic."

Cabe played along. "Extreme patriotism, extreme foreign policy, extreme religion all fill other people's pockets, but it's the common man and woman who pay the price."

Sokolov laughed before downing the rest of his shot. "We all pay the price for those decisions eventually.

Perhaps we will get the chance to play together in the future," he said, placing the glass back on the bar.

Two meatheads in badly fitting leather jackets stood five feet to the left of the bar making lewd gestures behind the back of a young woman waiting to be served. Sokolov's stooges. He wondered if Sokolov realized just how ineffective they'd be if anyone with any real training came at him. They'd rarely looked up to check on Sokolov since they'd started talking.

"I'd like that," Cabe said as Sokolov turned to walk away.

He'd need to be ready to go play with Sokolov whenever he was asked, because while Amy might be the expert at card counting, he was getting pretty adept at it, and he looked forward to kicking Sokolov's ass. He'd practiced it every night he'd come to the casino, always biding his time until the dealer stack was replenished so he could keep the true count straight in his head. So far, on his fifty-thousand-dollar chip outlay, he was up seven and a half grand.

Stooge One was bulkier than Stooge Two, but not by much. Just a thicker neck and stockier build. He didn't understand why more people didn't do research when finding a bodyguard. Sure, in a gunfight you could probably hide behind meatheads and body builders to avoid being shot, but really, in a foot chase their cardio sucked balls. Not to mention that someone who could think fast on their feet in a dangerous situation, someone who had personal experience of combat, was priceless in a tense situation.

Over Sokolov's shoulder, he caught sight of a man approaching the cashier. Cabe recognized him from the first night he'd visited the casino. Jet black floppy hair, patchy stubble, and jeans with a rip more than was cool. The guy pulled a thick pile of notes out of his jacket pocket and went to the same cashier as before, an equally dark-haired woman in the end booth.

Cabe wandered to an empty table that overlooked the cashier and watched as his suspect walked over to the slot machines and played just a handful of games, using some cash from his pocket, before heading to the roulette table and placing one fifty-dollar chip on black twenty-eight.

The ball rattled around the wheel. Cabe couldn't hear it over the base-level drone of the casino, but he could see the ball bounce around the wooden wheelhead until it landed in a pocket. By that time the guy had already walked away from table without having even seen where it settled, as if resigned to losing.

He returned to the cashier, who was in the process now of shutting down her booth. She pulled a stack of notes that appeared to be pre-counted and placed them onto the counter before shuffling through the chips as if to confirm the amount she suspected she needed to pay out.

When her counting was complete, she handed the man the money without making any notes, and he left without further comment.

Leaving his drink sitting on the table, Cabe gave one last glance to Amy, who appeared to also be packing up her table, and followed the man outside. The brightly lit customer parking area didn't allow for completely covert trailing, but . . .

Cabe felt eyes on him, and he wasn't sure where they were, but when the hairs on the back of his neck stood on end, he knew better than to ignore them. And until he was certain where, or even more important, *who,* the eyes were, it would be reckless to follow his target beyond his current position.

Instead, he stepped back into the shadows and made a show of checking his phone.

Fortunately, the target he'd been following didn't go far, climbing into a waiting red Ford, and Cabe made a mental note of the license plate. They'd arranged for a drone to be airborne whenever they were in the casino. "Buddha," he whispered into his mic. "I'm tagged. You need to follow that red sedan," He hated relying on the fact that his backup team could hear him through his mic without getting a positive confirmation in return. It frustrated him that he wasn't wearing an earpiece, but it would be too visible to someone sitting next to him at a poker or blackjack table.

A text came through on his temporary phone.

On it.

He kept the phone in his hand, using it at as a distraction while he looked around. The cameras were still oriented in the direction they had been during his earlier surveillance of the front of the building. The tinted doors of the casino made it difficult to completely see inside beyond the outline of bulkier figures. And without his night-vision goggles, he couldn't see into any of the parked vehicles, especially those parked out of the glare of the parking lot's lights.

But still, something niggled around in his brain.

He looked down at his watch. It was only ten more minutes until closing, so it would look odd for Cabe to walk back inside now. He texted the license plate of the vehicle and debated hanging around the rear entrance to ensure Amy got safely to her car but he couldn't do that now. Not that he needed to, given that Harley was back there in a black truck registered to a person who didn't exist. He was Amy's backup. If all else failed, Harley would follow Amy if she ended up in difficulty. But still he wished he could be the one to check on her.

Sokolov's meatheads exited the casino and he wondered if they were the eyes he'd felt on him. Perhaps they'd been watching through the door. Perhaps they'd not been looking for *him*, just looking in general. Sokolov came up behind them, and Cabe moved farther back into the shadows. Hide and observe. Hide and observe. Sitting back was often the best course of action. While Six was always ready to jump in with both feet, Cabe had always been more measured.

"Get the car," Sokolov said to the larger of the two men and shook his head as if disappointed that he needed to ask them to do the obvious.

They really were dumb and dumber. The other man stepped to one side and reached inside his jacket to withdraw a packet of cigarettes, the action revealing a gun strapped to his ribs in a holster. Which was where Cabe's firearm should be.

Fuck it. He was going to carry from now on, no matter what the feebs suggested.

Three young men came out of the casino, goofing around with one another. They seemed drunk, but something about them looked off—like they *wanted* to appear drunk. All three were watching Sokolov. They veered a little to the right and then quickly corrected course so they were headed straight for Sokolov.

When they collided with him, Sokolov stumbled forward but remained on his feet. He cursed loudly in Russian.

Meathead turned around and threw off one of the

men, who raised his hand in apology. The second did the same as the third man began to walk quickly away from the building, something in his hand. They'd stolen Sokolov's wallet. Realizing an opportunity to build his relationship with Sokolov had fallen into his lap, Cabe broke into a run.

He heard Sokolov yell again behind him and then the sound of fighting and the pounding of another pair of footsteps, but Cabe was certain the guy he was chasing was the one who was holding the wallet they had lifted. He sprinted around the rear of the casino, his shirt flapping, with Cabe following and gaining ground, grateful he'd refused to wear dress shoes and was instead wearing his black sneaker-style footwear.

When he was within arm's reach, Cabe launched himself at the guy's back, taking them both to the ground. Even though the target softened the blow, the slam of his chest to the ground took his breath away. Stuffed with bills, Sokolov's wallet went skittering across the asphalt of the lot.

"Let me go, you dick," the guy said as Cabe grabbed both arms behind the guy's back. He didn't have cable ties or anything he could use to secure the target, so he held on until Sokolov and Stooge Two appeared.

"You really should get better security," Cabe said, breathing deeply.

Sokolov eyed the guy on the floor, then Stooge Two. "You may be right," he said sourly. "And it appears I am now in your debt."

It felt as though Woods was watching her. Her skin prickled with the knowledge that his grope earlier hadn't been accidental. But with the op in play, it was imperative that she continue to do her job. She couldn't go around making accusations about him if she wanted to remain employed.

And she'd never get invited to those after-hours events he'd promised if she didn't play nice. But just how *nice* was she prepared to play for the sake of this case? How far would she have hoped someone would have gone to find out information about her own mom?

She dealt the last of the cards from the stack of five packs to the men at her table and continued smiling, counting, and watching. But her hackles were raised when it came to Woods. Was he involved in the women's disappearances? Was he grooming her for something? Or was he just sleazy around the edges?

Plus, she had a beast of a headache brewing. Something about the slot machines was driving her a little crazy, their constant noise and the flashing lights she could see out of the corner of her eyes getting on her last nerve. Which was unusual for her. It had never happened in Vegas.

"You're off when the pack is burned," Ortega said over her shoulder, and she nodded. She couldn't wait to get home and take a shower. It felt as though Woods had left a stain on her skin, and she couldn't wait to wash it off.

Cabe had played on the table two down from her, making good money it seemed by the stack of chips he'd had in front of him when the game ended. The FBI might just end up in a cash-positive situation after the op if Cabe won enough big hands. The idea made her smile, and the smile loosened the tension in her jaw.

"House wins," she said after studying the cards. She leaned forward and collected all the chips. "Thank you so much, gentlemen. It's been a pleasure dealing for you all tonight."

"You really gotta go, honey?" one of the men asked. He wore a Marine Corps T-shirt that had seen better days. "I could buy you a drink."

"That's very kind of you, but I'm going to have to decline."

"Oh, come on, sugar. What does a guy have to do to get you to say yes?"

Amy pasted a smile onto her face. "If I said yes, I'd get fired. And you don't want me to end up out of work, do you?" she said sweetly. It hurt her tongue to have to explain herself to him. A woman should be able to say no and mean it.

The man pouted. "That's too bad, sugar, but I'll be over at the bar grabbing a nightcap if you change your mind." He flipped her a dollar chip. *Wow, big spender.* He'd been at her table for a good hour. The other men followed suit and she grabbed her tips and her chip tray, allowing for the table to be cleaned while she took them to be counted and converted.

When she got to the women's locker room, she sighed and leaned her back against the wall. Standing on her feet in tall heels was killing her lower back. She slipped off her shoes and groaned as her arches met with the floor. Her skirt quickly followed, and she pulled on a pair of jeans. They felt like heaven around her waist. Finally, she unbuttoned her vest and shirt and replaced them both with a soft peach T-shirt.

What she needed now was a large glass of Merlot and the book on international art theft she'd begun to read before this assignment took over.

Thankful that the changing room was empty, Amy

hurried to stuff her clothes and shoes into her tote bag and slip on a pair of sneakers before anyone could come in and want to make conversation. After grabbing her purse, she headed out of the room and toward the exit. Cabe had left not long ago, and though she'd wished she could have waved or at least met his eyes, she'd ignored his exit, as it was important for their roles that they didn't act familiar.

The sky was the color of dark blue ink, casting the staff parking lot into darkness as she headed for her car. The front of the building and the side that could be seen from the highway were lit up like the fourth of July, but back here it was like a bad horror movie. Bushes and trees crowded the edge of the property line, and the area didn't have many cameras, though she'd deliberately parked in full view of one of the few.

"Amy, wait. I was hoping I'd catch you." The voice made the hairs stand up on the back of her neck. She heard the staff door click shut.

Faulkner Woods.

Though her heart raced, she turned calmly to face him. She made sure she was in a solid stance—feet hip-width apart, her right foot a little farther back than her left. She'd taken down bigger and more-prepared men than him in basic training and wouldn't have any qualms doing it again if he tried anything extremely stupid.

"Was there something you needed, Mr. Woods?"

He stayed a foot away from her and smiled. "I just wanted to wrap up the conversation we started earlier. There's never a quiet moment in there." He tilted his head in the direction of the casino.

Woods had lost his tie and had undone the top button

of his shirt. If she looked at him objectively for a moment, ignoring his behavior, he was a reasonably attractive man. His voice was smooth. Too smooth. Plenty of girls had probably fallen for it before her. She stepped back out of reach and resumed her stance. Her car was still another ten feet away. "I'd appreciate a conversation about my career, but could it wait until I am back at work?"

"My car's just over there behind yours. Why don't we go get a drink together? I'd like to discuss some of the other opportunities that might be available to you." He raised his eyebrows once, then twice.

Play nice, Amy. Play nice. "I'm sorry, Mr. Woods. But there's a no-fraternization policy between employees."

Woods smiled. She shivered inside as she glanced over her shoulder to her car.

"Technically, I don't work for the company. I own it. But this isn't anything untoward. Ortega tells me that you are incredible and I want to see what we can do with that."

She took another step back. Enough small ones and she would be at her car. "Those are semantics that you can get away with but I can't. The policy most definitely applies to me, and I really need to keep this job, so if you don't—"

"Amy. I'm serious. This is a professional conversation. I'm trying to show you this is important. We can talk about how things are going. And wouldn't you like to learn how to become one of the more senior dealers quickly?"

The control she'd felt earlier was beginning to slip. She took another step back, and then another and another, all the while feeling behind her for the door. When she grasped the metal with her fingers, she took a deep breath.

"You know, I'd like to," she said, "but I have the mother of all headaches. Could we do this another time? Tomorrow, maybe? Or Wednesday?"

Woods placed his hand on the roof of the car, inches from her head, and grinned. The noise echoed in the darkness. She looked around. Nobody else was in the parking lot, even though she'd been told Harley was on surveillance that evening. Clinging to the confidence that she knew enough self-defense and fighting techniques to break free of him, she tried to quell her panic.

If she defended herself, she could get fired, and then she'd never make it into the secret gambling ring. She could lose what was possibly their only lead to the missing women. Could she live with the weight of that on her conscience? But how much of Woods's attentions could she deal with to ensure no other woman would be taken because Amy wasn't around as first choice? Women like her mom, who deserved better.

He placed his nose in the crook of her neck. "You are an attractive woman," he whispered against her skin. She swallowed deeply. "And it would be my pleasure to spend an hour with you, talking this through. Come on," he said, reaching for her arm. "Why don't you get in my car and we can talk on the way?"

No amount of training had prepared her for the revulsion and panic that slithered through her as Woods's lips brushed her ear. Her breath came a little quicker than normal, adrenaline making her hand shake a little as she carefully placed it against his chest to push him away. It was foolish to expect him to budge, but she wanted to give him every chance to step back before she had to do something that could get her fired. Though she loved her job, there was no way in hell she was performing sexual favors as part of it.

He placed his cool, clammy palm against the back of her hand. She pulled it away and used both arms to try to shove him back. "I want to talk with you, *Mr.* Woods. I just . . . Please, not tonight. I don't feel so good," she said as he grabbed her hip.

"Everything cool, guys?" The voice came from behind her, but she knew who it was in a heartbeat.

Cabe.

His voice was the greatest sound she'd ever heard and the worst thing that could possibly happen. If she was going to get fired, they couldn't afford for Cabe to be banned from the casino too.

"This is company business," Woods said as he looked over her shoulder while increasing the tight grip he still had on her hip. "Why don't the two of you step inside and ask Anthony to get you a round on me?"

She gasped in pain as Cabe walked into her peripheral vision. With him, bizarrely, was Sokolov.

"Look, I get it. She's cute 'n' all. But this is the kinda shit that gets a guy into trouble." Cabe's tone was almost jocular, but she could see the muscle twitch in his jaw. She'd thought he'd come out swinging.

She wanted him to look her way so she could let him know she was fine, but he didn't.

"I've got this," she said, hoping Cabe would take the hint and back away enough that she knew she was covered while she extricated herself. She didn't want to shut

the conversation down permanently . . . she just wanted
to meet with him on her own terms.

"You heard the lady," Woods said.

Cabe stepped forward, and Amy held her breath,
uncertain whether his next move would ruin everything.

"Woods," Sokolov barked. His tone was agitated.

"Why don't the three of us go have a drink?" Cabe
said to Woods coolly, as if he hadn't been just about to
step up to Woods's personal space.

Amy shivered but then forced herself to breathe. If she
didn't know Cabe better, she would have sworn he didn't
give a shit about what he'd just witnessed. But there
was something about his stance, the way his shoulders
were a little too high, his legs in a position that would
keep him balanced if he needed to fight, that reminded
her that he did. And she knew him. She reminded herself of the detailed conversations they'd had while setting up the op, the way Six and Mac had teased him
over his thoughtful process of planning. He wasn't the
guy to lose his head.

"You need to go, drive home," Cabe said to her calmly,
never taking his eyes off Woods.

"Mr. Woods," she said, her voice more controlled than
she felt inside. "I'm grateful you think so highly of my
skills, and I'd love to carry on our conversation at a more
appropriate moment."

Woods turned his gaze to hers and nodded stiffly.
"Good night, Amy. I'm sorry if my exuberance and interest in your talent was misconstrued in any way."

What was going to happen to Cabe the moment she
pulled out of the parking lot? What if Sokolov and Woods
turned on him? He could—

"Good night!" Cabe said, his voice clipped.

If she stuck around much longer, one of them would blow their cover. Resisting the urge to stay, she stepped to the car door and slipped inside. She watched the three men in her rearview mirror as she drove away until they disappeared in the darkness.

CHAPTER TEN

The cold fury racing through him wouldn't abate. It poured through him like a waterfall, powerful and fast flowing. It gave him strength and clarity, especially as he heard the engine of Amy's car fade into the distance.

Adrenaline surged through him as he considered what could have happened had serendipity not led him around the back of the casino in time to see Woods leaning on Amy.

He looked at Woods, whom he wanted to pound into the fucking pavement. If she ever found out, his mom would be pissed he hadn't taught the guy that respect was spelled with two fists and a kick to the balls so hard Woods would be singing soprano.

Thoughts of Amy flashed through his mind. He'd not been able to hear much of what had been said, but he could tell from the body language that something wasn't right. While Amy's upper body was all tension, her lower body was in perfect fighting stance.

"Let's go back inside," Cabe instructed.

"I don't know what you think you just interrupted, but

it was nothing more than me offering to mentor a talented dealer," Woods said.

Cabe had to give him credit for a ballsy response. "Listen. I've seen her in the casino. Good-looking woman and good at what she does. But she's your employee, dude."

"Faulkner, Cabe is right," Sokolov said through clenched teeth. "You do not need a lawsuit from a young woman saying you sexually harassed her."

That got Woods's attention. He straightened as he stared at Amy's taillights leaving the parking lot. "I didn't sexually harass her."

"Let's go," Cabe said, pointing in the direction of the staff entrance. His blood was still boiling. Whichever way he looked at it, Woods was a dick. If he was being a handsy boss, then he was a dick. And if he was grooming Amy, he was a dick . . . even if he was a dick that might give them a lead.

An hour later, with the situation under control and a whiskey he didn't want lining his stomach, Cabe called a cab. He needed to see Amy. Needed to see how she was. In the heat of watching Woods with his hands on her, his only thought had been how best to extract her, an elemental need to get her to safety. But now, with the streetlights racing by as the cab sped down the highway, he could acknowledge that his actions had also been driven by the most primitive of feelings. Possessiveness. And a need to protect her from another guy who felt she was public property.

His phone rang. "Cabe," he said, gruffly.

"Boss," Harley said. "With respect, what the fuck was that?"

Cabe ran his hand over his face. There was no value

in pretending he didn't know what Harley was talking about. "I took care of it. I had it covered."

"And so did I. It's what you pay me for, remember? Only I wouldn't have been the one risking my cover."

A moment after Cabe had intervened he'd realized that. "Fair comment. Look, can we talk about this tomorrow?"

There was a sigh at the end of the phone. "Sure thing. For what it's worth, I get why you had the death stare going on. You have more restraint than I do because I might well be up on assault charge if I'd had to go in there." And with that, Harley hung up.

When Cabe reached Amy's neighborhood, he got the driver to drop him a couple of blocks away. His heart was still racing, and no amount of slow and steady breathing was going to still it. The streets were quiet, the tourists having long since gone back to their hotels when the bars and restaurants had begun to close down for the night. Only a handful of stragglers remained.

Using his key, he let himself into the building and took the elevator to her floor. When the elevator opened, he walked to her door but refrained from unlocking it, even though she'd told him it was okay to use the key he'd been given at the beginning of the op. Instead, he knocked, wanting to give her time to compose herself and decide whether she even wanted to see him tonight.

A shadow ghosted the peephole.

Smart woman.

He heard the telltale rattle of the chain and slide of the deadbolt before the door opened.

"Are you okay?" she asked before he had a chance to speak. Her hair was damp from the shower and she was no longer in her uniform. Her pale pink tank was so thin he couldn't help but notice her erect nipples. Her navy blue sleep shorts were loose and covered in flamingos. But it was her eyes, wide and bright, that held his attention. She was worried about him, and the thought warmed him in places the whiskey hadn't reached.

"I should be asking *you* that. Did he hurt you?"

The shrill whistle of the kettle distracted them both, and Amy hurried to the kitchen to turn it off. "I'm fine," she said, although her voice faintly wavered. "Do you think we blew it?" She shook her head and sighed before opening the cupboard to get two mugs. "I should have gone with him."

What the hell? "Can I look at you?" he gestured to her side.

Amy sighed and nodded.

He took a step toward her and gently lifted the hem of her tank that had risen as she'd reached for the mugs. A series of bruises ran up her hip, and his fingertips almost matched them perfectly. "Son of a bitch," he cursed. "He left marks on you."

"They'll fade," Amy said with a shrug. But the wariness in her eyes told him that Woods had both scared and hurt her. "What happened after I left? And what were you doing with Sokolov?"

Cabe took her hands, then her wrists, and then her arms, turning them carefully to look for injuries. Her skin was soft and warm, which made it even harder to accept that some asshole had held her so tightly that he'd left purple and red marks behind. "I drank a watered-down whiskey and told him he was lucky you didn't call the police. He now thinks he owes me one."

"And Sokolov?"

"You wouldn't believe me if I told you, but suffice it to say he now owes me one too. I'll tell you the whole thing tomorrow, but for now let me look after you."

Her hands began to shake in his. "We almost blew it tonight. You shouldn't have been around the back of that building. There was no reason for you to be there."

"Amy, keeping you safe is my priority." Gently, he put his arms around her and held her close.

"Your priority is those women and the money laundering," she said, her words muffled against his shirt. "I can take care of myself."

In spite of the situation, he felt the corner of his lip twitch. Her ability to stay focused on their goals was stronger than his own. And he wondered when he had become so affected by her that he'd lost his usual concentration. He brushed his lips to the top of her head as his body absorbed the fact that she was pressed up against him.

Her arms slid around his waist and held him tightly, and his hand trailed to the base of her back.

"I know," he said, quietly. "But did you honestly think I could leave you with him?"

Amy leaned back a little but thankfully didn't step out of his arms. He hadn't realized until they were holding on to each other that he needed the reassurance that she was okay as much as he wanted to provide comfort. "It's part of the job, it's part of being in deep cover. Shitty things happen. Sometimes you have to be the one doing them to belong, to get the information you need. Sometimes you need to be on the receiving end. You know this."

Cabe sighed. "I do. But it's killing me."

"Because I'm a woman?"

Cabe looked down at her fresh face scrubbed clean of makeup. She had no idea how vulnerable she looked, how sweet her pink lips were wiped clean of the vixen red she'd worn. "No, Amy. Because it's you. I hate to see the people I care about get hurt."

Amy ran her hand to his face and cupped his jaw. "You're a good man, Cabe Moss," she whispered.

He tugged her close, then repeated her actions until *his* palm cupped *her* cheek. They did nothing but gaze at each other, and Cabe knew they were at a turning point. He wasn't strong enough to walk away, but it needed to be Amy who made that decision. Instead, he stood and savored the way her body lined up flush against his, the way her breasts pressed firmly against her chest, the way his hand rested on the sweet curve of her ass.

"I don't think I can keep pushing you away, Cabe," she said quietly.

Cabe pressed a kiss to the top of her head and pulled her closer. There was tremendous comfort in the way her head lay against his chest. "I don't know that I can spend months wondering what it could be like between us, either."

Minutes passed by, or it could have been mere moments, but Cabe allowed his heart rate to settle now that he knew that in spite of the bruises, she was actually okay. Lazily, he ran his hand up and down her back.

Her hands began to move, exploring his biceps, down his ribs. The movements shifted from quiet curiosity to a sexual teasing that began to drive him crazy. It tickled as she dragged the tip of her finger around his waist, dipping an inch below the waistband of his jeans.

"Maybe one time would take the edge off," she murmured.

With a firm grip, he lifted her face toward his and gazed at her intently. "Be certain," he growled.

"I am," she replied, lifting to her toes.

Cabe claimed her lips with his own, savoring their softness. Sensations flooded him. The minty taste of her toothpaste, the soft moan that escaped her throat, the way her hands gripped his skin suddenly as if she needed his strength and support to remain standing.

The thought that she needed him fueled his already rising lust. Without a thought, he lifted her into his arms. As much as he was dying to simply give in to baser urges and take her where they stood, he wanted their first time together to mean something. Because it would be the first of more. Even though he had baggage to work through, he knew this wasn't a one-night stand.

She wrapped her legs around his waist and he ran his hands along her thighs until he was able to cup her ass. Not once did they break the kiss. His tongue found hers before they reached the bedroom, and he pressed her against the hallway wall, taking a moment to drive them both wild. His dick was hard and lined up perfectly against her warm heat. Knowing there was nothing between them except a layer of denim and soft cotton sent sparks of excitement running down his spine.

"Goddamn, Amy," he groaned. "I want you in the worst possible way."

Amy placed her hands on either side of his face. "And for tonight you have me."

For tonight.

The words sounded ominous, but he would deal with them in the morning. Right now, there was no coming back from the ledge they were standing on. He took her weight in his arms again and walked the remaining distance to the bedroom before laying her gently down on the bed. The room was small, the bed smaller and made of wrought-iron, which meant it was likely to squeak like a motherfucker. But disturbing the neighbors was the least of his concerns.

Especially when Amy's white-blonde hair spilled out across the pillow as she bit down on her lip. "You seem to have way too many clothes on for what we have in mind."

Cabe reached for the buttons of his shirt. Despite the fact he very easily could have pulled it open, sending buttons skittering across the floor, he wanted to prolong the moment. It would be too easy to strip naked and be inside her in record time. But they both deserved more. They deserved the anticipation that came before great sex. From the way Amy's eyes flared as she watched his fingers undo each button, he knew he'd made the right decision.

He pulled his arms out of the sleeves and draped the shirt over the chair next to the bed. Before he took off his jeans, he needed to see more of her. To touch her and taste her before his own desires got the better of him. Gently, he placed his hands on either side of her head and kissed her again, his mouth moving over hers as he devoured her sweetness. Cabe knelt between her thighs and reached for the hem of her tank.

Amy lifted gently as he slid his hands along her ribs, his thumbs brushing the taut nipples that had been teasing him since the moment he had walked into her apartment.

When she lay back down, he took a moment to take her in.

"You're beautiful, Amy," he said.

Cabe leaned forward and kissed his way along her jaw, down her neck, and along her shoulder. The action made her shiver, made the hair stand up on the back of her neck as she squirmed beneath him, his body as aroused and turned on as her own.

"Please," she gasped as he covered her nipple and sucked it deep into his mouth. Her back arched off the bed as her hands slid into his hair, holding him exactly where she wanted him. God, the way his tongue moved against her, over her, swirling around her.

Cabe lifted his head for a moment. "I love how sensitive, how responsive you are," he said roughly.

But she wanted more. She writhed as he replaced his mouth with his hand and shifted to her other breast, repeating the action of swirling his tongue around her taut nipple before sucking firmly until she cried out his name.

Cabe kissed his way along her stomach until he reached the waistband of her shorts. Raising himself up on his arms, he looked into her gaze. His eyes were heavy, darkened with the same desire swirling through her. "We still good, Ames?"

She loved that he'd asked. That he'd given her a moment to cool things down, to tell him to stop. But she didn't. "We're good, Cabe."

To show him just how good they were, she raised her hips to enable him to lower her shorts, and being the gentleman he was, he slipped them down her thighs. Amy glanced down at his erection. Dear Lord, his jeans had to be cutting his dick in half.

"Naked may be your best look, Ames. I love your smooth skin, and the curve of your breasts, and the flat of your stomach, and even this narrow strip of hair." He removed her shorts from around her ankles and then settled in between her legs, easing her thighs over his shoulders as he pressed his lips to the crease of her hip.

Her hips arched from the bed the moment he ran his tongue along her core. She was already wet, desperate for him, wanting him to fill her and take her outside of herself, if only for tonight.

Cabe circled her clit, deliberately avoiding the very place she ached. He placed his hand on her mound, holding her still while adding his thumb to maximize her pleasure.

"Cabe," she gasped, shocked at the breathy sound of his name coming from her mouth. "Please."

He looked up and studied her with those dark eyes, and intuitively she knew he understood what she wanted. But he held out, deliberately let the moment build between them. When he dragged his tongue straight up her center, flicking her clit before sucking it into his mouth, she cried out, the sensations too much. Ruthlessly, he added his finger, sliding it deep inside her before easing it out to add another.

"You taste so good, Amy," he said, taking a moment to watch his fingers slide out of her core. He curled them upward as he pushed back inside her, reaching for the place guaranteed to get her off. "I can't wait to see you come, can't wait to taste you, can't wait to feel you come apart in my arms."

Amy began to shake beneath him. She teetered on the edge of orgasm, the glorious moment just before the fall that she tried to hold on to for as long as she could, savoring it before rushing over. "Oh, god, Cabe. I'm so close," she gasped, her head turning from left to right on the pillow as she stepped closer to the edge.

"I've got you," he said, before he rapid-fire flicked his tongue across her clit.

It bore down on her and she felt the shaking intensify, felt the orgasm explode.

Lights flashed behind her eyelids as her orgasm took over. There was no sense of time or place. No scent or smell or sound. Just an inordinate pleasure that came from being so deeply in touch with her own body that nothing else on earth mattered.

Cabe softened the strokes of his tongue. They were less urgent, less desperate, more forgiving, savoring instead of dominating her.

She lifted onto her elbows and looked down at him, his dark eyes catching hers as his tongue flicked the top of her clit. She couldn't help but to gasp.

"For the record," he said, before running his tongue over his lips. "I intend to do that as many times as you'll let me." His voice was gruff and deep. "Because you taste delicious. But right now, I just need to be inside you." He stood and pulled his wallet out of his back pocket, reaching inside it to pull out a condom that he placed on the bedside table before returning to the foot of the bed.

Amy crawled to meet him there, sitting at the end of her bed. She reached for him, pulling him closer so that she could undo the buckle of his belt. She could see the outline of his erection. There was no doubt Cabe was well endowed, but she wasn't some naive virgin worried about whether it would fit. Her only thought was how would she emotionally survive what they were about to do.

Once the buckle was open, she looked up and met

Cabe's gaze. It was dark, potent. Like a storm cloud, revealing just a hint of the power of which it was capable. When she ran a fingertip along his length, Cabe muttered a curse but never took his eyes from hers.

Amy unbuttoned his jeans and pulled down the zipper. As her thoughts turned to lowering his jeans, Cabe stepped back and kicked off his shoes. "Fuck this," he said and slid down both his jeans and underwear, catching his socks as he pulled them off his legs. "Sorry." He grinned as he crawled back up the bed, taking her with him. "I couldn't wait any longer. And if you'd touched my cock one more time, this would have been over before it started."

The sight of Cabe's incredible naked body leaning over her, resting on his arms, had her tongue-tied. She knew she should say something. Or smile. Or move. But emotions caught in her throat. She wasn't sure what she was in that moment, other than his.

Cabe's face suddenly was lined with concern. "Are you okay, Ames?" he asked, brushing her hair from her forehead.

Amy swallowed deeply and then nodded. "Overwhelmed, in a good way."

When his lips brushed gently against hers, she knew he understood what she was trying to say. As he reached over to the side table and grabbed the condom he'd dropped there, she took a deep breath. Quickly, he ripped the packet open and pulled the condom on.

He settled back between her thighs, his weight over hers solid and true. He kissed her again, this time with more force, more pressure that quickly had her moving beneath him. Oh, god. She needed this, she wanted him, no matter how bad the idea was for their careers and the

operation at hand. There was no room in her mind for
that now, though, because it was filled with him. Filled
with the vision of him standing at the foot of the bed,
those ridiculous abs of his for which he must work so
hard rippling as she'd run her fingers along his erection.
Filled with the way his warm skin currently pressed up
against hers in a way that made her feel vital, needed
and . . . safe.

Amy ran her fingers across his broad shoulders and
down his back, feeling the muscles move beneath his
skin. "I want you," she whispered against his ear.

"Well, that's a good thing," Cabe said as his hand
slipped between the two of them. "Because I happen to
want you too."

The feel of his head against her entrance made her
sigh. He didn't press in straightaway as she'd expected.
Instead, he slid against her, the sensation of him rubbing
against her clit almost having her come again. "Cabe,"
she groaned.

Cabe continued to rock against her. "Just imagine how
incredible it's gonna feel when I slide deep inside you, if
it feels this good now."

He tucked his arm under her knee and lifted it, opening her to him. She felt exposed and vulnerable, but one
look in Cabe's eyes told her she didn't have to worry. He'd
take care of her, she knew he would. Just like he'd done
today. At the risk of everything else, he'd put her first.

This time when he slid back and then pushed forward
again, he entered her. "Amy," he gasped, pressed his lips
to hers. "Fuck, Ames, you feel so good."

Dear god. She'd known he was large, but he stretched
her.

Cabe pulled back, and eased himself back into her, to

the hilt. This time it was her turn to cry out, to gasp against his lips, to suck in air as if she were going to die if she didn't take her next breath. She could feel Cabe twitching deep inside, not coming, but pulsing in contrast to the rest of his body that was tense. "Jesus, Ames." He pressed his forehead next to her on the pillow. "Is it crass to tell you that you have the most perfect pussy? I need a minute."

Amy felt the power that she'd laid squarely at his feet drift back into her as she realized *she* was doing this to him. She was the one making him weak. She was the one who had him turned on to the point that he could barely move. And she began to move. Gently undulating her hips, just moving a fraction back and forth until *she* was the one who needed more. Until *she* was the one who needed the pressure on her clit.

For a minute, Cabe remained stationary. Then he lifted his forehead and eyed her. "You call that giving a guy a minute?" he asked, but the grin on his face told her he was onto her, and he began to move with her. Pulling out and sliding deep, over and over. Hitting her in the places she needed it.

He slid his hands beneath her butt and she felt him lift her, move her until he was moving at such a pace that she could barely draw breath.

This was so much more than sex. It was a claiming, an owning on a level she had never known before. "Oh, yes. Just like that," she gasped as he tilted her hips so he was driving upwards, not just back and forth. It wouldn't be the first time she'd ever come twice, but it was a rare occurrence and one that hadn't ever happened during her early encounters with a new man. It had only happened once a lover had got to know her and had gotten to know the things she liked and wanted.

But with Cabe, everything was different. It was like he knew, somehow, exactly what she needed. How she wanted it to get off.

She lowered her hands to his butt, relishing the way the taut skin and tight muscles flexed beneath her hands as he pounded into her.

Amy kissed his neck, and he found her lips.

She tightened her grip, and he raised her hips.

Their bodies moved together as if they'd been made for each other. For this very moment.

She closed her eyes and felt the orgasm begin to build.

"Yeah, Ames," he growled. "I can feel that." His words came in breathless grunts. "Chase it with me."

Oh, god.

She needed to come. Which was incredible, seeing she already had that evening, but she knew she could get there. Knew she *would* get there with him again.

And soon.

Cabe pressed his lips to hers. It was fierce, and reckless, and she wanted more. Wanted *everything*.

"Oh, yes," she cried out when the dizzying sensation, that first tremor of sparks, began deep in her core. At some point, she stopped breathing, stopped worrying about anything else as the sensations took over.

"Ames. God. I'm right with you," Cabe gasped against her lips.

His eyes met hers as they came together.

And for that moment, there was nowhere else she wanted to be.

CHAPTER ELEVEN

The sun crept its way beneath the heavy bedroom curtains, a thin line of light in an otherwise dark room. The slow drone of the air-conditioning as it clicked on and off was monotonous but necessary. It was warm despite the cool air coming through the vents.

Amy was pressed up against him, her thigh over his leg, her head on his chest, that blonde hair obscuring her face. At least twice during the night, he'd attempted to brush it from her face, but it had stayed put all of ten minutes before it ended up back the same way. It had made him smile, made him wonder if she was simply so used to it being there that she didn't even notice.

Cabe ran his fingertip gently down Amy's arm, careful not to wake her. Sleep was the one thing she needed more than him right now, no matter how much his dick protested the idea. When he'd followed her home after dealing with Woods, it had purely been out of concern for her safety. And when he'd seen the marks on her body, he'd been furious, wishing he'd taken more extreme action. A switch had been flipped inside him as he'd taken care of her, and he'd been unable to stop himself from acting on his feelings. But he couldn't put his finger on the exact moment it had happened. Maybe it had been as simple as the moment she'd appeared at the door in those damn pajamas. He was only human after all.

But a hot woman in cute shorts wasn't enough to override his self-control. After all, women often walked around San Dog in not much more than that, and he certainly wasn't thinking about jumping all over them. It was the woman inside the outfit who had him standing at attention.

Perhaps it was the moment she'd reminded him of his operational priorities when he'd attempted to put her first.

Perhaps it was the moment silence and comfort had filled him when she'd stood in his arms.

Now that they'd slept together, he couldn't imagine it having played out any other way. He knew he should probably leave. They were going to have to be careful with their interactions at the casino or write their fledgling relationship into the script. Flirting with Amy at the casino would take very little effort on his part because it would require zero acting. And they needed to make a call before the meeting they were both supposed to attend later that morning.

As carefully as his large body would let him, he disentangled their limbs, grabbed his jeans, and wandered into the hallway, where he slipped them on but didn't bother zipping them up. First, he'd make them breakfast, and then he was going to seduce her one more time before he left. He poked his head in the fridge and noticed the fixings for omelets and toast—easy enough to make. He began the search for a bowl and pan in which to whisk and cook the eggs and a cutting board to chop the veggies on.

He pulled out a stack of nesting mixing bowls, sorting through them to grab the smallest. In the bottom of the next smallest was her FBI badge.

The sight of it was like having to stare at those damn hoses they'd used on him during Hell Week in the middle of the night. SEAL training was not for the fainthearted— but it didn't come close to the reminder of what she did for a living and how, on a daily basis, she put her life on the line. Fuck. Cabe ran his thumb over the lettering. Federal Bureau of Investigation. He took a deep breath. His thoughts ran to Woods. What he'd done. What he *could* have done, had Cabe not intervened. Would Amy have gotten away? Would Woods have forced himself on her? Would he have raped her? The thought got stuck in the back of his throat.

Then he thought of his call with Harley. *I wouldn't have been the one risking my cover.*

Cabe stood, placing his hands on the counter. Images bombarded him, and he, the iceman of just about any raid they'd ever had to do, fell back on basic box breathing just to calm down. It wasn't too late to back out. He could let one of the other guys on his team be the feet on the ground. Harley could do it.

But then he looked in the direction of the bedroom where Amy was sleeping and realized it would kill him to not be there to help her if something went down.

This was what had happened to Six and to Mac. And he'd accused both of them at one point or another of jeopardizing their mission because of their torn loyalties to their op and the women involved in them.

He should talk to one of them. To both of them. He

knew better than to keep secrets, but when it came to Amy, all bets were off. A wash of disloyalty to Amy flowed over him at the thought of sharing her secrets. Which meant he was going to have to deal with his feelings about Jess and the need to protect Amy if they were going to finish their op successfully.

He replaced the badge in the bowl and returned it to the cupboard. It had been a smart move on her part to put it there. If anyone broke into her apartment, she needed it to look like a dealer, not an FBI agent, lived here. There would be no way for her to pass that off as a fake ID, and if the right person—or in this case, the wrong person—saw it, she could end up in a world of hurt. But she'd thought of that.

Because she's smart.

And a good agent.

But Jess had been a great soldier.

Shit, he had to stop that loop somehow.

Cabe reached into the fridge and pulled out peppers, onions, and cheese, and started chopping. The mindless act gave him something to focus on.

"What are you doing out here?" Amy came to a stop near the entrance to the hallway and leaned against the wall, wrapping both arms around her middle. She wore a soft gray robe made of jersey, and he imagined how one pull on those ties would open it to reveal a perfectly naked body. But he needed to stop that line of thinking before he blew off the idea of breakfast and simply snacked on her instead.

"Thought I'd make you some breakfast, or *us* some breakfast, before we go in and face the music," he said. He placed the knife down on the chopping board and stepped toward her. Her hair was up in a messy bun, but her face still had that sleepy morning look. Soft cheeks, sweet pout. All welcoming warmth. He put his arms around her, but she froze before stepping into his embrace.

She didn't move her hands to put them around him. In fact, she didn't seem to want him in her space. He stepped away immediately. "What's going on, Ames?"

She sighed as she walked by him to the stool under the kitchen island and pulled it out before sitting down, taking a moment to make sure her robe covered her thighs. "What happened last night after I left?"

Okay. She was going to dodge the question, and he was going to let her. For a minute or two. "I told you last night. I took Woods back into the casino and he bought me a whiskey. It's quite possible I gave him a lecture on how to treat a woman. When I left to go home, he told me he owed me one. And I intend to cash in that chip, pun intended." Saying it out loud now, he was relieved his training had overridden the urge to beat the crap out of the guy. Now he had Woods on his side.

"While you were patting yourself on your back, did it occur to you that he could be the reason the women are missing?" Amy asked. She placed her hands on her hips. "I'm not going to be stupid and say I wasn't a bit scared, but we blew it. What if he'd talked those girls into going home with him, told them to keep their pending hookup quiet, and then killed them?"

He knew she had a point. He'd come to the same conclusion himself. There was *every* chance Woods was the reason the girls were missing. But there was no way he was going to stand back and watch the same thing happen to Amy. "Follow that through in your head, Ames. What if that was exactly Woods's MO? You could be dead. So, yeah, maybe I should have let you go then followed you because there was no way I would have let you go off with only Harley watching your back. But then I would have had to explain to Sokolov why I ran off and got into Harley's car. And, yes, perhaps I should have called for backup instead of weighing my ability to deal with a single untrained antagonist, but how on earth was I meant to make that call with Sokolov breathing down my neck? I didn't go in blindly, Ames."

"Don't call me Ames," Amy said, tugging her robe more tightly around her mid-section. "Don't make this any more personal than it already is. And Harley's a professional. He would have known to follow me, right?"

Cabe reached for her hand, but she folded her arms in front of her chest. "Hate to break it to you, sweetheart, but last night was as personal as it can get. The genie is out of *that* bottle, and there's no forcing him back in. And yes, just so you know, Harley is also pissed I didn't leave it up to him."

"Listen. I'm as guilty for what happened last night. I should have played it different with Woods. And I shouldn't have opened the door to this . . . to us. You gave me an out, and I didn't take it. I get that this is on me. But I'm professional enough and smart enough to know when I made a dumb call. This . . . the two of us . . . feels like something that should wait because it obviously affects our thinking. I should have stuck to my guns instead of folding. I need some space. . . . I'm going to need you to leave."

Cabe shook his head. "This feels like something we should talk through."

Amy shook her head. "There's nothing to say. We

need to stop this before we make another stupid mistake on the case."

He wanted to fight, to convince her that she was wrong, but the look in her eyes told him he should leave it. "Fine. For now. But we should talk about this after the briefing. And we need to get our stories straight."

"Simple. We tell them a version of the truth, everything that happened exactly as it happened in the parking lot, and that you came to check I was okay. We say I was a little freaked out, and that you crashed on the sofa. But that's where we end it."

Anger was starting to bubble inside, and he wasn't sure who it was aimed at. "Okay," he said, even though it wasn't okay at all. Pinning down his emotions was difficult when Amy stood against the wall, looking as desolate as he felt.

"I'm going to shower," she said as she walked to the bathroom. "And I'd prefer it if you were gone by the time I got out."

"What were you thinking?" both their bosses said at the same time.

Which meant they were in trouble—Dolby-surround-sound style, like at the movies.

Amy had avoided any meaningful eye contact with Cabe since entering the room. She wasn't ready to dissect all the things that had happened in the last fifteen hours with him, even if he'd made it hard by being caring and considerate when he'd come in. *You okay, Ames?* he'd asked her quietly, a passing whisper, and she'd nodded without tearing her glance from the landscaped grounds at the front of the building. She'd even waited for him to sit down and then turned and took her own seat away from him.

"I was thinking it was not okay for Agent Murray to be potentially sexually assaulted in the parking lot when there was something I could do about it," Cabe replied. Sitting back in the chair, his long arm reached out over the back of the empty seat next to him, he looked cool and calm. Meanwhile, her insides were churned up so badly that she wondered if she shouldn't grab some indigestion tablets from the drugstore.

"You okay, Murray?" Cunningham asked her.

She nodded. "Perfectly fine, sir. Although I'll admit it's not really something I want to repeat. We're in agreement that unless my life is threatened, Cabe won't intervene again. Right, Cabe?"

Now she met Cabe's eyes. He still looked as cool and calm, but there was something she couldn't put her finger on telling her that beneath the still-lake exterior was a raging waterfall. "That's right," he said easily, holding her gaze for a moment before he looked to Aitken. "Plus, I now have an 'in' with Woods. He owes me one. While things could have gone a little differently, I think it brings us to the same place in the end. We're getting in."

Amy looked across the table at Cabe and wondered if he realized that he held so much of the power in their messed-up dynamic. She wondered if he realized that this would end way worse for her than it would for him if word got out about their relationship. Their op was in jeopardy because of their relationship, their growing feelings making Cabe go off plan to protect her instead of focusing on his own goals. From the look on Cunningham's face and the fact that his skin had taken on a mottled look, she knew he wasn't happy with how things had gone down. He was probably questioning just how far she was really willing to go when she was undercover. For the sake of her career, she needed him to know that she was willing to do whatever it took.

But, to be honest with herself, she wasn't sure that was true.

And what if the men she worked with found out about what had happened between her and Cabe? Would they then believe that what happened in Atlanta was her fault, if they even knew about it? Would they take it as carte blanche to hit on her, or to ask not to be partnered with her? Or both?

Cabe, on the other hand, even though he was about to get his ass kicked, would at the end of the day only suffer from a little hurt pride over her asking him to leave after the best sex of her life.

The very best.

The kind that made her press her knees together under the table.

The kind that made her forget for a millisecond that they were in a world of hurt.

"You," Aitken said, pointing at Cabe, "know better than this."

"Not going to disagree with that," Cabe replied.

"But you're not going to apologize, are you?" Cunningham asked.

Cabe shook his head. "No, sir. I had a call to make. I felt it was too early in this op to risk Agent Murray."

Amy's ire rose. "It wasn't your call to make," she said, forcefully. "You don't get the final say in what happens to me and how it gets handled."

Cabe looked across the table, his eyes narrowed. "I only—"

"I don't need you to figure out my role. Did I like Woods's handsy moves yesterday? No. But would I have been able to get myself out of them if I really needed to? Yes. And could I have done it all without blowing cover? Yes. If he crosses a line I can't live with, I'll fight my way out of it and pretend I take Krav Maga classes at the Y."

"We haven't determined pattern of life yet; we don't know enough about how these people, Woods especially, operate day to day. The drone was being used to follow a money-laundering suspect, so we couldn't have it follow you too," Cabe replied.

Amy took a deep breath. Cabe's only saving grace was that he was coming from a place of caring about her. She wished deeply that someone had been looking out for her mom the same way Cabe looked out for her. But his protective act nearly jeopardized the case, and that she couldn't live with. "Harley could have. *You* could have. And anyway, I had no intention of going anywhere with him."

Cunningham looked between the two of them. "Okay then, Murray. From your perspective, what the hell happened?"

She'd practiced her answer to this over and over in the bathroom mirror before she'd left the apartment. "I'm sorry, sir. I didn't feel it was in the best interests of the FBI, CIA, or myself to go off with the casino owner without anybody being aware of my whereabouts. I couldn't be sure that Cabe would know because he'd left earlier than I did. But I do agree with him that the way it was eventually handled has given us an advantage with Woods. But, it may have come at the cost of my being

selected for the private games. I don't know how Woods
will handle things with me after Cabe's intervention."

"Listen, as for tracking Agent Murray, that's what her
GPS is for." Cunningham looked at Aitken, who tapped
his pen against his notebook. "Sort this out, the two of
you. It's beginning to sound like amateur hour. Now tell
us about Sokolov."

Amy listened as Cabe told them some improvements
he wanted to see, such as insisting they get their own
cameras set up. The team wanted an opportunity to go
in under darkness that evening to set it up. Cabe hated
they were flying blind on intel, something with which
Amy agreed. After a little back-and-forth, they got their
go-ahead.

When they were done, Aitken stood and left the room,
and Cunningham followed. At least they'd done Amy and
Cabe the courtesy of reaming them a new one in private.

Her heart raced, grateful that this was as far as it had
gone and that neither of them had questioned Cabe's excuse of staying over at her home to ensure Woods didn't
look up her address in the employee records and decide
to stop by. It was most definitely a stretch, but way better
than admitting the real reason.

"You okay, Ames?" Cabe asked from the other side
of the table once the room was empty. "Won't be the first
time you get your ass kicked, won't be the last."

"The ass-kicking I can handle. But I need to know
whether you can handle what needs to be done to see this
through. You can't repeat what happened last night, and
if you can't manage that, I'm going to ask that you're removed from this investigation."

Cabe didn't react . . . or not in a way that most people
would catch. But having been around poker players for-

ever, she took in the way he reached down to his wrist and straightened his watch and knew something was happening inside him. It was a funny tell, it gave away his real emotions. She supposed he thought he gave off the impression of boredom, of looking down at the time as if to say *How much more of this do I have to deal with?* But she'd noticed he did it when he was mad. Or under pressure.

For all his calm demeanor, she knew that what she'd said had hit a nerve.

And despite, or possibly even *in* spite of, her own feelings for him, she knew it had to be said.

"Ames," he began.

She loved and hated the name equally. Loved it because a man she'd developed feelings for was calling her something she hadn't been called before. Hated it because it hinted at the relationship they were missing out on.

The women who had disappeared needed her help though, assuming any of them were still alive. Doing anything that jeopardized her role on this case went against everything she held dear. She was smart enough to know that she wasn't the only one who could solve the case of the missing women, but there wasn't anybody who cared more or would work harder than she would.

"Don't call me that," she said. "I asked you this morning to stop."

Cabe got up and walked to her side of the table. He pulled out the chair next to hers, but instead of sitting on it, he perched his butt on the table and crossed his arms and his ankles. "Let's get a couple of things crystal clear," he said, his eyes pinning her to her seat in a way that shouldn't turn her on—but, like everything about him, did. Even those arms. "There are reasons, really good fucking reasons, why you and I should keep our distance. There is shit you don't know about me, about my past. And there's this case. And there's everything that happened to you in Atlanta. It feels like a lot. And yeah, I get it feels insurmountable, because I find myself wondering why the hell I'm even considering you and me."

He took a moment and looked out of the window, up toward the sky.

"But?" she whispered.

"But doesn't it feel worth it, Ames?" he said quietly.

The employee door was the only way to get into the casino undetected, and they were going to come at it through the woods. Six and Ryder had done a detailed surveillance around the casino earlier that day. They'd found a route whereby they could park the van with all of their equipment on property away from the casino. Property that didn't have security cameras or patrolling guards. They'd also figured a route to the casino from the parking lot that wouldn't fall in the range of any CCTV camera, enabling them to disappear like ghosts.

And it was close enough that if the plan went to shit, they could sprint from the back of the building to their transport in less than thirty seconds and be on their way back to Eagle HQ before anyone had time to call the police.

In their night gear and goggles, nobody would be able to ID them anyway.

Lite, Buddha, and Harley were hidden on the other side of the lot with the required tech equipment: the digital kit to hack the entrance, the pass they'd cloned from Amy's employee pass to open doors, and the laptop to create copies of the video surveillance before they entered so it could be used to wipe the footage when they arrived.

Next to Cabe, Six lay on his stomach, hidden in the safety of the trees, with his favorite .300 Win Mag stretched out in front of him. He'd get one shot. The silencer would minimize but not completely eradicate noise. Cabe breathed slowly as Six took his time figuring out wind speed and direction. Cabe didn't have an ounce of doubt that Six would do what was required.

But not yet. The pattern of life they'd constructed for the casino over the previous evenings revealed a security team would do a drive-by in a white van at approximately three thirty, which was four minutes away, and wouldn't return for another hour.

Mac crouched beside Cabe and blocked his own mic. "Want to tell me why you spent the night at Agent Murray's house?" he whispered.

"Relevance?" Cabe asked as he stared straight at the building, completely unmoving.

"You got to be fucking kidding me." Mac said, although the humor in his voice was evident. "This isn't like you. You could have blown the op."

"Do we need to talk about this now?" Cabe sighed and shook his head. For once, he didn't have an answer. "What do you want me to say?"

"Careful, Cabe," Six said, without taking his finger off the trigger or his eyes off his target. "The next thing you know, Mac'll pull the fraternization policy that none of us really give a shit about out of his ass and rub you down with it."

He didn't want to lie to his friends, but he'd promised Amy his confidence. He felt torn, and ambushed. "There's nothing to tell. After I went to check on her, she was bruised up. I didn't think she should be alone after something like that, but she isn't in the kind of situation where she could call up a girlfriend to come over."

"Since when do you do the whole comfort thing?" Mac asked.

Cabe rolled his eyes. "I'd have done the same for either of your sisters. Would you have wanted me to just drive off and leave one of them alone?"

"Fair point," Mac said.

He didn't want to tell them that Amy had pretty much kicked him out of her apartment after the most mind-blowing sex he'd ever had. It was bad enough that he had a feeling he'd relive the stunned look on her face when she'd come in his arms, those pretty blue eyes of hers going wide before flickering shut, every night when he fell asleep and every morning when he woke up with a raging hard-on. "Can we just let it drop?"

The white van pulled into the lot, silencing them all. According to the intel they'd collected, the men never got out. They slowed until they were crawling around the rear of the building. And as per the intel, the men gave scant attention to what was happening around them. The beam of a flashlight pierced the darkness, its light aimed at the rear doors for a few seconds before it was switched off.

It was Breaking and Entering 101. Close the door behind you once you are in, leave the place as undisturbed as possible. Shining a freaking light to check that a door was still sealed was as useless as . . . well, hiring a dumb-ass security company.

Finally, the van pulled out of view, and a black sedan

picked up the van's trail. While their intel said the van would return in another sixty minutes, Gaz and Jackson, two Eagle operatives, were going to follow them as a precaution and report in when the van was far enough away to give Cabe and the team time to get in and out.

Thirty minutes would have to be enough for them to do what they needed to do. As long as Lite could hack into the internal cameras quickly. They needed him to loop the previous thirty minutes of internal camera footage to cover footage that would show them actually being inside.

With the careful squeeze of the trigger and a silent pop, the camera on top of the large pillar exploded.

Then they waited.

They waited to see if Gaz and Jackson would instruct them to stay hidden, to tell them that the security van had been given instructions to return to the casino.

They waited for a security team to come running out from the shut-down building.

But the van was never notified, and nobody ever came out. As they'd thought, the building was empty.

Silence fell between them until the comm lines crackled to life. "You're clear," was all Jackson said.

Grateful that the rear of the casino was bordered by woodland, they hurried the short distance across the parking lot. Dressed in black from head to toe, they blended seamlessly with the night, their footsteps silent as they hit the asphalt.

As Buddha began working the mechanical locks, Mac began working the electrical ones. Cabe kept watch until he heard the click that told him they were in. Silently, they crept into the building, and Lite immediately sat behind the security monitors. He cracked open his laptop and went to work. Within two minutes, he looked up and gave the okay.

Everyone had his plan. Lite was on security cameras, and Buddha was putting the entry panel back together so they could leave quickly. Mac and Harley were finding a way to put a camera near the vault, while Six and Cabe would put one in Woods's office along with a listening device on his desk. When they were finished on the employee side of the casino, the needed to hit the main floor with a focus on the cashier's cage.

Cabe's heart raced. Flawless execution was required to pull this off. Everybody had to do his part. Leave no trace—that was the goal. Or, more accurately, leave no trace of what they left behind.

Cabe and Six took the stairs together to Woods's office. It took Cabe less than twenty seconds to pick the locked door. Wordlessly, they set about their tasks, Six finding a place to plant the camera, Cabe finding a place to plant the bug. Given that they'd have one chance to place it, Cabe wanted to put it somewhere it would last. And somewhere it could pick up the most sound. It was a cliché, but he hid it in the lamp fitting.

Thanks to DCSNet, the Digital Collection System Network, they didn't need to tap Woods's phone. The FBI had already done that with the touch of a button, but the tap had revealed very little. They could only assume that Woods and Sokolov either used burner phones or held their conversations in person at the casino.

"We've got company." Buddha's voice crackled through the comms unit.

"Jackson?" Cabe called out.

"Security car is still ten miles out."

"Who the fuck is it?" Six mumbled, pressing his body against the wall alongside the window. Thanks to their night vision goggles, they hadn't needed to turn on any light. "Another white van, a second one from the security company," he whispered. "We must have triggered something."

"Entry panel is reassembled. Door closed," Buddha said.

"We . . . wn in . . . hear . . . at." The voice was clearly Mac's, but Cabe he couldn't tell what he was saying. He wondered if the vault was protected by poured concrete. It would definitely interfere with the efficacy of his comms unit.

"Shit. If we can't hear him, he probably can't hear us." Cabe planted the second bug on the underside of Woods's two-story letter inbox.

The security guard got out of the van and looked up at the building before saying something into a radio. There was no way he could see them, the interior way too dark. Maybe they'd still have time to plant the cameras on the gaming floor.

"The guys we were following just ran to their van," Jackson said. There was a pause. "They're heading back in your direction at speed."

"We need to get out of here," Six said.

Cabe watched the security guard look between the van and the building. "Wait. He's scared. Doesn't know what to do."

The guard walked back to his van. "He's going to do a loop around the building. Everybody out. Buddha, make sure Mac knows to get out."

Six and Cabe ran down the hallway, Cabe's heart racing in the adrenaline-filled way it used to when he was on a mission. Mac, Harley, and Buddha came pounding down the hallway behind them. Cabe stopped, letting them run ahead.

Last out was Lite, as he made a minor adjustment to the security recording before packing up his laptop.

Buddha stood by the door, ready to close both the mechanical and electronic locks as Cabe and Lite ran from the building.

At the far end of the lot, a beam of headlights appeared along the side of the building.

"He's turning into the lot in three seconds. Move your ass, Buddha."

"On it," he whispered.

Lite took off toward the dense tree line.

The van began to turn.

Shit, please let the guy be nearsighted.

"Buddha?" Cabe warned.

"Easy," Buddha said, and the two of them sprinted after the rest of the team.

"Little more hustle next time, okay?" Cabe said with a grin on his face as they disappeared unnoticed into the trees.

CHAPTER TWELVE

"I want twenty-four-seven surveillance of that unit," Cabe said, relieved they finally had a lead. The target they'd suspected of laundering money had led them to an address they were familiar with. A target they had followed when they were protecting Louisa had led them back to a dated rental unit in San Ysidro. The shakedown had led to a number of petty crime arrests, mostly minor firearm and drug offenses. Carrying without a permit and a few baggies of marijuana weren't going to lead to any major time in prison, unless those arrested happened to have histories with law enforcement.

"On it." Six's voice sounded tinny inside Cabe's rental car. He'd arranged for a sedan on the booking form, but when he'd arrived at the airport, all that had been available was a car with less legroom than the church pews his mom had made him sit in as a kid. "It can't be a coincidence that he ended up in that apartment block in San Ysidro."

Cabe slowed as he drove over Memorial Bridge and headed down to the white marble entrance of Arlington

National Cemetery. "Agreed. These guys run in very tight circles. Let's see if we can't get a list of tenants in that building. And when I get back tonight, let's head on over there and put a GPS on the vehicle."

"You know anyone of the team can do that," Six said.

He did. There wasn't a guy on the team he wouldn't trust with his life. But this op had gotten under his skin. And he wanted . . . no, he *needed* to do more.

"I know. But where is the fun in that? What about you and me go do it for old times' sake?"

Six laughed. Despite being opposites in every way, they'd been the best of friends since kindergarten, and for some reason, having Six around would help Cabe focus. "Fine. I'll set it up. What time do you want to go?"

"Let's plan for midnight, but I'll keep you posted on travel."

"Sounds good."

"In the meantime, can you get one of the guys working on a full history on the target, and let's probe any existing relationship between our target and those arrested during our takedown last year."

"Will do. You there yet?" Six asked.

His early morning flight to D.C. had been painless. What hadn't? Evading telling Amy the truth. He'd simply explained that he had an important meeting in Washington, which was true. The anniversary of Jess's death had thankfully fallen on Amy's day off. He'd wanted to sit down and talk to Amy, but after what had happened earlier on in the week, it didn't feel like the right time.

The semicircular building with the view of Arlington House high on the hill behind it was as imposing as it was beautiful. He pulled into the visitor's parking lot and switched off the rental car's engine. "Yeah. Just pulled in. Gotta go."

"Take care of yourself, brother," Six said, and the phone connection died.

For a moment, he simply sat there and cleared his mind of the case. Instead, he thought about how Jess must have felt that morning.

The night before she'd died, the stars had aligned for the two of them to talk. Looking back, he couldn't remember so much of what they'd said, only what he'd felt. That he was the luckiest man on the face of the planet.

He got out of the car, uncertain of what he was actually going to say when he reached her grave. The day they'd buried her had been bitterly cold. Though she'd died in late September, by the time forensics in Germany had finished their investigation and her body had been flown home, there had been a two-month wait before a slot for burial would be available at Arlington. Knowing she was lying alone in cold storage had driven him crazy all those months, but then he'd realized that lying in the cold Washington dirt wasn't going to be any more comfortable.

The temperature was significantly warmer than it had been on the morning of her mid-December burial. As he walked to the spot where Jess was buried in the shade of one of the large trees close to the nine-eleven Pentagon Burial Marker, he pictured the caisson being pulled up the hill and remembered the horses' hooves clipping on the path, the only sounds to break the quiet blanketing the cemetery.

The silver United States Air Force Memorial glinted in the sunlight as Cabe made his way through the white headstones. He thanked each one as he passed until he reached the one he wanted.

His heart flipped at the sight of her name.

Jessica Ann Price.

Tears stung his eyes as he sat and then lay next to her. "Hey, Jess," he said quietly. A jogger ran by along the path but was too far away to hear anything. Cabe brushed his fingertips over the meticulously mowed lawn of Arlington Cemetery in the same way he used to run his fingers along the length of Jess's spine after they'd made love. She'd had those perfect dimples at the base of her spine and would giggle and squirm as he circled his fingers around them.

But secretly she'd loved it. He'd known. Just as much as she'd loved him.

His army brat.

God, he'd missed her.

"There's so much to tell you. So much is changing." He looked up at the leaves in the tree above him. They were still clinging to summer's green, but he knew within a month they'd be turning brown and falling to the ground. Another season, another circle. "I'm envious of them, Jess," he said. "It's wrong, isn't it, that I'm jealous of my best friends?"

Brilliant white clouds scudded across a sky so blue it looked fake. Like a child's painting. There had been many days during his deployments when he'd yearned for a sky exactly like the one above him. At night, when he'd lain in bed, unable to sleep for the perpetual noise that always existed on a deployed military base, he'd imagine the sky over Encinitas. A sky under which he'd skateboarded down E Street with Six or played football on the beach with Mac. Thirty years of friendship meant he should be happy for them, right?

From his spot lying flat on his back in front of her headstone, he imagined Jess responding. She'd place her hand on his shoulder blade and run it in circles. Hair the color of sable would fall over her face as she tilted her head to one side, pondering his question. Then she'd smile, the perfect dimple in her left cheek teasing him. "No," she'd say. "It's not wrong, it's normal. You're only human, Cabe. When are you going to learn that?"

You're only human.

Only human.

A faint breeze messed with the ends of his too-long hair, but the sun warmed his skin.

Jess had loved the sun.

Hell, she'd even loved the dustbowls and the sand-storms. It was why she'd signed up for her third and final tour. She wasn't going to re-enlist again, she'd promised, even though she'd never pressed him to do the same. Time had come for her to focus on them, she'd said, and the idea of growing their family.

He rolled onto his side to look at her headstone.

"Six finally got down on one knee and proposed to Louisa. I was certain they'd elope. Go off on vacation one day and come back married since there was absolutely no way Louisa would want a big wedding." Cabe grinned. He was grateful that running away and coming back hitched wasn't in the cards, though, because as much as he would have understood, he didn't want to miss the day his oldest friend was felled officially by the love of a good woman. "You would love her, Jess. She's shy as shit, the complete opposite of you, but she's gold

inside. Believe it or not, Six is doing most of the arranging so she doesn't get too overwhelmed. And he's roped
in me and Mac. The only thing she's picking out is her
dress, which I know would have driven you crazy."

He wondered what Jess would have looked like in *her*
wedding dress. He swallowed tightly at the memory of
having gone to the bridal store to cancel her order. They'd
already received it, they'd said, but had offered to return
it. Though it had been a stupid idea, he'd asked if he could
see it. A teary sales assistant had gone into the back room
and then called him to join her about five minutes later.
She'd put it on a headless mannequin, but he'd fallen to
his knees as his mind took over and put her firmly in it.

Jess would have looked stunning. He'd have been
proud to stand at the top of the church aisle to wait for
her to reach him.

He wondered if she would have been proud of him, of
what he'd accomplished since her death.

Cabe coughed.

"Eagle is doing great. I wish you could see us. Me,
Mac, and Six have offices. Freaking offices with
professional-looking furniture.

"And Mac and Delaney are so loved up they may as
well be married already. I wish you could meet Delaney
too."

But Jess never would. She'd never get the chance to
meet the growing families his brothers were creating.

As suddenly as he'd thought this, the image of Amy
laughing at something Six had said flashed into his mind.

Guilt flushed his cheeks, thinking of her as he sat by
Jess's grave. The first twelve months after Jess's death,
he'd done nothing. Literally nothing. He'd returned to his
deployment after her funeral and hadn't spoken a word

about her. He'd known Six was worried. The man had gone on at him like an old lady, desperate to hear Cabe spill his emotions all over his military-grade bedding. Mac had given him pep talks about bottling stuff up and kept reminding him that he was only a bunk away.

But in the last year, he'd needed . . . something. It was hard to define. He still loved Jess just as much as he always had. But he'd felt lonely. Lying here next to Jess, he suddenly felt ashamed.

"I'm sorry, Jess," he said quietly. "I feel so lonely without you. *Felt* so lonely. I don't know what to do."

Cabe sat up, rested his elbows on his knees, and buried his head in his hands. He suddenly felt disloyal to Amy. He wasn't with her because he was lonely. He was with her because she was becoming as vital as the air he breathed.

His heart thumped in his chest.

"I'm scared, Jess. Scared I'm getting feelings for someone else," he admitted. Silence surrounded him. A brilliant blue and white butterfly fluttered around him and landed on her headstone. "If that's supposed to be some kind of sign, Jess," he said, "you're going to need to be a little more specific."

The butterfly fluttered its wings and pulled them together, sitting still as a statue—something Jess would do when she had a problem that needed solving, when she was listening. Fuck. Was he really going to talk to a goddamn butterfly?

He shook his head. And then . . .

"Her name is Amy," he began.

"Amy," Ortega said as she stepped onto the casino floor on Friday. "I need to talk to you. Just give me a second," he said before turning back to Siv, a grad student from Norway who had successfully landed a part-time dealer position.

Ortega is going to fire me.

She knew it might happen, of course. There was no way that Woods would let what happened on Tuesday go unanswered. Wednesday had been her night off. On Thursday Woods had been out of town. But now he was back.

Ortega finished talking with Siv and turned to her. "Mr. Woods asked to see you as soon as you got in today. He's in his office."

"Okay, I'll head straight there," she said, her heart racing. How could she dissuade him? Promise to meet him for dinner? Drinks? The idea turned her stomach, but not as much as the idea of being fired. She turned and pressed her pass to get off the employee floor, but before she could take a step, Ortega reached for her elbow.

"Amy, wait," he said, following her into the hallway and letting the door click shut behind them, deadening the incessant noise from the slot machines. The corridors were empty, but that didn't stop Ortega from looking up and down to make sure they were alone. "Listen. I heard a rumor. From the guys in security. I know Mr. Woods was . . . well, I heard he was inappropriate toward you."

She hadn't been expecting Ortega to lead with that and wasn't entirely certain what to say. "Thank you," was all she could think of. "I guess I'm going to get fired."

"I doubt it," Ortega said with a grim smile. "Listen, it isn't my place to say this, but Mr. Woods . . . well, he isn't going to do anything without Mr. Sokolov's say so."

It took her a moment to process what Ortega was saying. "But Sokolov was there. He saw everything." There was a line between revealing too much to Ortega and playing the role of Amy Reynard, a young woman who needed her job as a dealer.

Ortega sighed, pursing his lips for a moment. "Amy," he said, "listen to me carefully. There are things . . . that happen. . . . Hell, I'm just supposing, projecting even, but I think the two of them have an agreement. About the casino. I'm not entirely sure. But my guess is that they want to know if you reported this to the police, and if not, if there is a way to avoid you doing that."

Maybe Ortega was one of the good guys. He could be lying, setting her up, but her radar for those things was usually pretty accurate. "You think they're worried about what might happen if I did?" she asked, her voice deliberately going up at the end in what she hoped sounded like surprise.

"Listen. I don't know. I started working here when Hemingway Woods ran it. I love my job. I keep my head down. But you remind me of my niece, and I'd hope someone would look out for her. So, I just wanted to give you a heads-up that Mr. Sokolov *is* there. Upstairs with Mr. Woods." Ortega tipped his head in the direction of the management offices.

Amy nodded. "Thank you for looking out for me."

Ortega nodded and walked back out onto the floor.

She watched him disappear before heading in the direction Ortega had been looking, in slow motion and with a sick feeling.

The office door was closed when she reached it. She knocked and waited for a response.

"Come in," came a voice from inside the room.

She reached for the cold silver knob and turned it, slowly pushing the door open. The office was plush to the point of gauche. Too much red and gold in the drapes and carpet. A huge wooden desk stood in the middle of the room, and even to her untrained eye, it was a complete reproduction, along with the Tiffany-style lamp on the corner that was as fake as the gel nails she'd had applied to look the part.

Two doors on the left wall led to who knew where. They were closed tight.

Faulkner Woods was behind the desk working on his laptop, and the room was otherwise empty. Odd, since Ortega had been adamant about Sokolov being here.

"Mr. Ortega said you were looking for me."

Woods looked up. "Close the door, would you?"

Amy paused. Should she play along—close the door and walk up to the desk? There was some logic to that. She knew there was a bug in the lamp on the table. But a smart young woman in that situation wouldn't in real life. "I'd rather not," she said, remaining in her spot by the door.

Woods sighed and closed his laptop. "I suppose I deserve that." Slowly, he made his way around to the front of his desk and popped his hip on the edge.

She looked around the room as if taking in the decor, making sure nobody else was in the large room with them.

"I'm sorry, Amy. Contrary to current evidence, I'm not an asshole. I spoke to Mr. Moss and Mr. Sokolov, who witnessed my lack of grace. But you are the first real talent I've seen come through here in a long time. I want to build the reputation of this casino to be as great as any you could find in Las Vegas. If I was over-exuberant in my articulation of that, I apologize. If you would like to leave, for reasons that are completely understandable, I would be willing to give you a severance pay by way of apology." He looked suitably contrite with slightly rounded shoulders and sad eyes.

Amy had to bite her tongue. Hush money. A payoff. A way to get a broke girl out of his hair without any real impact to himself. She didn't believe the words he was saying any more than the fake smile.

"Or?" she asked.

"You can continue to work here, of course. Mr. Ortega agrees with me that you are an asset to the casino. I'm hoping you'll consider staying."

If only he knew that she had no real choice in the matter. In real life, there was no way she could consider his offer. In fact, he wouldn't have had the opportunity to make it because she would have quit that night in the parking lot. But for the op, she needed to at least make a show of considering it. "I'm not certain . . . Could I have some time to think—"

"What would make it better for you to stay?" Woods asked, cutting her off, something that inherently annoyed her.

Amy considered it for a moment and then it hit her, a suggestion that would solve two of her problems. "I hear the women who work the private gaming areas make significantly more money in tips. Could you wave the probationary period and let me work in that area of the casino?" She raised her voice at the end, determined to make herself sound insecure. Like she could be bought, or convinced.

Woods grimaced. "That may be tricky because a couple of the other girls who joined before you are also in their probationary period."

He was such a weasel.

A creaking sound came from the other side of one of the two doors and it was difficult to not be distracted by it. Obviously someone was there. She couldn't help but wonder if it was Sokolov. "Oh, I thought you said I had potential," she said, doing her best to sound disappointed. She didn't add anything more. One of the things she learned early in life was if you left a gap of silence, invariably somebody felt the urge to fill it.

Woods picked an imaginary bit of lint off his houndstooth suit trousers. He looked up at her. "Fine. I will clear it with Ortega. But I would still very much like to have that conversation with you about your career. If you are amenable."

Internally, Amy grinned like a Cheshire cat, but she simply nodded her head. "Of course, Mr. Woods."

Woods nodded and then glanced in the direction of one of the closed doors. A shadow moved in the light that escaped underneath it. "That will be all, Ms. Murray," he said.

Amy left, wishing she could run to Cabe and tell him immediately what had happened. It meant progress in her accessibility to the suspects, it meant progress in the op.

And for now, she'd avoid answering the question as to why she felt the need to run and share her news with Cabe.

Cabe knew his mic was secure. He'd taped those damn wires himself, after all, and gotten Six to double-check them. The last thing he needed was for the thing to come loose. Everything would be lost. This time he was armed, and the thought warmed him like an aluminized thermal blanket on a freezing night. It might only be a small pistol in an ankle holster, but now that he knew how lax security was, it was a risk well worth taking.

He'd traveled by taxi, which he'd picked up outside the Marriott, but carried keys belonging to a car the FBI had provided that was parked at the side of the casino should he need to make a quick exit for any reason.

An unsettled feeling drifted over him. Amy was giving him the cold shoulder. Well, not at work, where she acted like the consummate professional. There, she was fully in control and fully present . . . but when she looked at him, it was as if a glacier stood between them. And he should know what that felt like, because he'd scaled a couple of those in his time.

The jury was still out on how Sokolov was going to respond to his intervention, but he was going to force the issue by seeking Amy out where Sokolov could see. He wasn't sure of the nature of the relationship between Woods and Sokolov, but it was definitely beyond casino owner and customer. They still didn't know whether Woods was complicit or even receiving a cut of the laundered money. And if he *did* know about what was going on, was he somehow being threatened into complying?

Walking the line of treating a target as suspect or a victim was something he was used to. When they'd go on raids, they'd often pass men and women with their hands in the air and have to make a split decision about whether they were a threat or not, and make decisions about whether to apprehend or move on. For now, he was treating Woods as hostile.

Amy was out on the floor talking to Ortega. Perfect for the interaction he had in mind and for what was going to follow.

"Hey, we didn't get introduced the other night. I'm Cabe," he said, offering her his hand. "Are you okay?" he asked. It took effort to push aside how good her hand felt in his, and he had to force himself to let go.

Amy looked to Ortega, who stepped away, though not far enough that he couldn't hear. "I'm Amy. And thank you, but I'm good. It's all been taken care of. I just met with my boss a couple of minutes ago."

She had?

What the hell had happened? What had he said? He guessed by the way she was still on the floor wearing her badge that she hadn't been fired. "Well, I'm glad. If you ever need someone to walk you out . . ."

Amy smiled, and it was a genuine one. He loved the way the corners of her eyes crinkled. "I'm sure I'll be fine, but you'll be the first person I ask if I'm ever uncertain. You'll have to excuse me, Cabe. I'm working over in the private rooms this evening," she said as she walked away. His gaze followed her. *The private rooms.* The guy had basically promoted her to keep her quiet.

Fucking asshole.

Luckily, he was an asshole who'd just played into their hands by allowing her to deal in the area of the casino where Sokolov played.

Good work, Ames.

Cabe wanted a drink, a real one, to take the edge off the need to march to wherever Woods was hiding his ass and beat him into a pulp. But he wasn't going to do that.

Someone bumped into him.

"Shit. Sorry," Harley exclaimed. Cabe stumbled until he was pressed up against an empty poker table. Harley reached out his hand to stabilize himself on the rail of the table.

"Watch where you are going," Cabe said gruffly as he pushed Harley away.

Harley raised his hands. "Sorry again. Didn't see you there."

The two of them separated, Harley heading toward the bathrooms, Cabe toward the bar, neither of them looking back to confirm the location of the pinhole camera Harley had stuck on the table leg, facing the cashier's cage from an angle the casino cameras didn't cover.

"Wait, sir," Ortega shouted. "You dropped something."

Cabe could barely breathe. Had the adhesive not secured the camera into the crease of the poker table leg? He turned as if he had nothing better to do, as if he had all the time in the world. Perhaps he could slow Ortega enough that Harley could get out of the casino before security arrived.

"Here," Ortega said, handing him his receipt for the taxi that he'd thought he'd shoved in his pocket.

Relieved, he smiled. "Thank you. Those damn expense receipts get everywhere. My accountant hates me," he said, folding the paper and putting it in his pocket.

Ortega grinned. "You need every deductible possible."

At the bar, Cabe grabbed an ivory cream leather seat and looked out over the gaming floor. When the waitress arrived, he ordered a tonic water with lime. He wasn't particularly a fan, but he wanted to drink something that could pass for alcohol. The way Sokolov and his friends had thrown back vodka, he knew they'd be unimpressed if he wasn't drinking.

When his drink arrived, he sipped and waited.

Which was par for the course on this assignment. Hurry up and wait. Hurry up and wait. Six and Ryder were currently trailing the man they'd followed from the casino on Monday, but he'd done nothing more exciting than pick up a case of beer then drop it on the asphalt by the trunk of his car. Six had sent Cabe a photo of it with ten laughing emojis.

It should have been funny, but Cabe struggled to laugh. Dissatisfaction with their progress sat like rocks in his gut. This kind of internal dissatisfaction was disconcerting. It was unfamiliar. It reeked of failure.

Their night foray to place a GPS had been simple enough. A budget rental unit in a less than stellar neighborhood was never going to have CCTV coverage. It was simply a matter of biding their time until the coast was clear and placing the GPS inside the wheel arch of the car. It was simple, but after the emotional wringer of explaining to Jess about Amy, he'd needed some night air, a hit of adrenaline, and a couple of hours with Six.

But it hadn't led anywhere . . . yet.

A group of men stood at the bar, laughing loudly. Chinos and pressed shirts, early thirties just like him. Three women walked in, and while he was focused on the relationship between him and Amy, he would have had to be blind to not take note of their great figures. If he'd been pushed to guess, he'd have said fitness models. One of the men made a joke, obviously at the women's expense, as they walked by. A second slid his wedding ring off his finger.

Maybe he was just in a foul mood, but it seemed the world was full of assholes today. A part of Cabe wanted to get up from his seat, march over there, and explain to the dick just how much he would have loved to be wearing Jess's wedding ring. But then the wash of disloyalty toward Jess because of his growing feelings for Amy flowed through him. It suddenly didn't feel right to compare the world around him and where he was at in his life to Jess any more.

That thought unsettled him.

In the reflection of the mirror behind the bar, he saw Sokolov arrive, but he didn't move or turn around to acknowledge him. Instead, he waited for Sokolov to take a seat and get his first drink in his system. Once he'd done so, Cabe stood and wandered over to his table. The two meatheads were new. Leaner, stronger. They stepped forward. One of them placed a baseball-mitt-sized hand onto Cabe's chest to stop him from progressing farther.

Strike three for assholes today.

He looked the meathead in the eye. "Take your hand off me."

It was a good old-fashioned game of chicken to see who'd move first, and it sure as shit wouldn't be Cabe.

"Let him through," Sokolov growled.

The meathead scowled as he removed his hand, a vein pulsing in the side of his head. Given the guy was already silently fuming, it was wrong to goad him, but Cabe couldn't help himself and winked.

"Mr. Moss," Sokolov said, gesturing to the leather seat opposite his own. "What can I do for you?"

"I trust you haven't gotten yourself into any more trouble since I saw you last," Cabe said.

"You have a funny way with words," Sokolov said in a tone that said he found Cabe decidedly *un*funny.

"Did the casino help you out on Monday? Were the men who tried to rob you arrested?" Cabe asked, knowing full well already that they hadn't been. His brother had already notified him that there had been no report filed.

Sokolov held his gaze. "Yes, they were taken care of."

The unspoken implication was clear. Yes, they'd been taken care of, but not by the American legal system. "Sometimes it's necessary to take care of business on your own," Cabe said.

Sokolov scoffed. "And what do you know about that?"

"Three tours and a whole bunch of shit that isn't covered by the Geneva Convention." By not offering more, he made certain that Sokolov would ask.

At first Sokolov played it nonplussed. He leaned forward and grabbed his glass of vodka, taking a sip. "You didn't enjoy your military service?" he asked eventually.

"Parts of it, no. Parts of it, yes. Not everything in life is palatable, but those seemed to be the things I was best at."

Sokolov turned to look at him. "I think you and I may well end up getting along."

Cabe smiled. "I think so too."

"I'm going to a private room to play momentarily. The buy-in is one hundred thousand dollars. Would this in any way interest you, Mr. Moss?"

Excitement and adrenaline combined in Cabe's gut, and he reveled in the sensation. "I think it would."

CHAPTER THIRTEEN

"Ames," Cabe said as he pushed the door open to her apartment. For a moment, she wondered why she'd told him to just let himself in with the key he'd held since the day he'd moved her suitcases, but deep down, she liked that she could almost pretend this was normal. That it was Friday night and he'd just finished work for the day and was racing home to see her.

She should have told him not to come when he'd texted her to say he was on his way. Her feelings for him grew every time she was around him. When she saw the good and fair man he was. When she witnessed his usually measured responses. It made sense that the safest way to survive the op in one piece was to spend as little time with him as possible, even though her heart hated the idea. But she'd wanted to tell him how her meeting with Woods and Sokolov had gone. About the apology she'd received. How she was still an employee of the Lucky Seven Casino. To explain the hint she'd given him before hitting the private rooms, where she'd made a killing in tips, even though she'd been distracted by Sokolov and Cabe in the room next door.

"I'll be right there," she said, hurrying to apply body lotion to her arms. She'd needed the shower, finding great comfort in taking the mask of the casino off at the end of the day. She might be Amy Reynard during the working hours, but at night, tucked up in bed, she wanted to sleep as Amy Murray. Once she was finished, she slipped the peach satin robe over her shoulders, allowing herself to luxuriate in the feel of it against her skin.

It probably wasn't the smartest thing to wear while talking to Cabe, but a part of her hated that they were in this mess, and her robe was the closest she could get to the feel of his fingers against her skin.

She walked down the hall to find him sitting on the stool, his back pressed up against the kitchen island, one foot on the bar of the stool, the other flat on the floor. His arms were crossed against his chest, making the sinful lines of his biceps pop. But the one thing more spectacular than his arms tonight was his smile. "Woods made things right with you?" he asked, offering his hand.

She shouldn't take it, but somehow, in the safety of the apartment that wasn't even her own, she found it impossible to resist. As soon as their fingers met, he tugged her closer until her thighs were brushing his knees as he pulled her between them.

Amy nodded. "He did," she said, finding it hard to focus on the question at hand instead of the way the heat of his legs burned through her thin satin robe. "He apologized, offered me a cash settlement if I wanted to leave, but invited me to stay because I was good for the casino."

Cabe's other hand landed on her waist, then slid down

her hip until his fingertips grazed her butt. She could see the moment Cabe realized she wasn't wearing anything under the robe, his eyes going wide and flipping to hers.

"Sokolov was pretty quiet while we played," Cabe said, his fingers stroking her skin through her robe.

Her pulse began to race, and there was a telltale tightening between her thighs. Would he slip his hand beneath the silk and slide his finger between her already wet folds? "What did he say?" she asked, trying to keep her voice normal.

"Small stuff. Boring stuff about his businesses. Why he prefers Vegas. How he hates Atlantic City. Nothing big."

Excitement raced through her. Would he slide the robe off her shoulders and suck her nipple into his mouth? "But you made contact with him, which is good. Right?" she asked, but the word "right" came out on a hitch. She coughed to clear her throat. "That's . . . you know . . . when you appeared with him the night you handled Woods, I was convinced this was over, but you were right. It *was* a good thing."

Cabe wrapped his arms around her. "I'm right about all kinds of things, Ames," he said as their chests pressed up together. His fingers began to curl the hem of her robe higher and higher until it was skimming the bottom of her ass. Certainly he could feel how hot her body was becoming. Surely there was the telltale flush of her chest that always happened when she got aroused. There was no way he couldn't tell what he was doing to her body.

God, she knew she should step out of his arms, but like Icarus, there was no way she could stay away from her sun. From him.

She placed her hands on his shoulders and allowed

them to drift down his arms, along the fluid lines of his muscles, along the length of the veins that stood proud on his forearms. A sigh escaped, and she turned her eyes to him.

"I should leave," Cabe said before allowing his lips to brush her cheek, the corner of her lips. The whisper of his touch made her shiver. "Cold, Ames?" he asked gruffly.

Amy turned her head a fraction so her lips lined up with his. "I don't think I can wait any longer," she whispered.

Cabe pressed his forehead against hers. "You know, I think I can stand waiting, but I don't think I can handle another false start. Be certain this isn't what that is, please. I know this is difficult for you, and I respect that. I just don't want to feel the way I did the other day when you asked me to leave. I'd rather wait until you are certain. I need to know you want me, not just *something*."

Was it what this was? Was it a whole bunch of adrenaline and excitement from the op turning around leaving her needy and desperate for something to take the edge off? Or did she need something only Cabe could give her? Would she regret her decision tomorrow?

Something this good couldn't be fleeting. Not wanting to wait a moment longer to start their relationship, she placed her hands on either side of his face, his rough stubble tickling her palms. "It's not a false start, Cabe. It's so hard to resist this. I don't know how to stop it any more than you do," she said honestly.

All rational thought escaped her as Cabe's hand slid beneath her robe and cupped her butt, pulling her tight up against him, his erection pressing against her hip bone. All thoughts of implications unraveled as quickly as the sash of her robe did. One tug, and she was under Cabe's spell completely.

"Thank god for that," Cabe said as he moved his lips to hers.

It felt so right to be in his arms, to feel his lips against hers, that her heart raced. She couldn't close her eyes, didn't want to look away from him for a moment. As his tongue gently met hers, she ran her fingers into his hair and smiled at his groan.

His hands slipped inside the folds of her robe, sliding the peach silk off her shoulders. "I was lost the moment I realized you weren't wearing anything under this," Cabe murmured against her lips.

Amy did smile then. "I was lost the moment you realized it. All I could think about was what you were going to do about it."

"Did I do this in those thoughts of yours?" he asked, fulfilling her fantasy of him sucking her nipple into his mouth. His tongue circled and laved, and she pressed his head firmly against her. "Oh, god, yes," she cried out.

Cabe released her breast with a pop. "I'd hate to be predictable," he said with a grin. He slid the gown down her forearms and let it slither to the ground and pool by her feet. For a moment, he leaned back against the counter and studied her, his eyes taking a lazy journey down her body. Seconds ticked by as he held her gaze, then studied her lips, her shoulders, her breasts, down the flat of her stomach to the juncture of her thighs.

A part of her wanted to cover her body, to shield it from him as nerves crept in. But under his gaze, she could feel her body come alive. Nerve endings she didn't know she had vibrated in excitement without a single touch.

"We're going slow, Ames," he said, gruffly, his eyes

finding her again. "I rushed getting to know you last time, but tonight, I'm going to learn everything there is." He reached for her wrist and she struggled to respond, her mouth too dry. Cabe placed a kiss on the inside of her wrist before sliding his lips along her skin to the crease of her elbow. The move tickled, and she squirmed, earning a stern look from Cabe. And dear mother of god, if that didn't turn her on even more.

She was a smart woman, but damn, the idea of him looking at her like a hungry man stared at a steak dinner definitely flipped her switch.

Cabe continued his journey up her arm, kissing her shoulder, her clavicle, the sweet spot behind her ear. "You smell like flowers," he said as he pressed his lips to her neck.

Shouldn't she have words? Shouldn't she be a more active participant in this? But her legs were only just holding her up, and her brain had turned to mush. She should—

"Ames," Cabe said, cupping her cheek gently. "Stop thinking. Stop worrying. You are perfect. I'm not here for the woman you *think* you should be. I'm here for the woman you are. Okay?"

A weight lifted from her chest, one that should never have been there. "This all just feels like . . . more. I don't know how to describe it."

Cabe took her hands and placed them on the buttons on his shirt, undoing the first one to indicate he wanted her to do the rest. "I think 'more' is a good word to describe us."

Amy took over the buttons, undoing them one at a time, savoring the reveal of Cabe's fine body. A dusting of hair on his chest, and abs for days . . . her favorite combination. She tugged the hem from inside his jeans and began to unbuckle his belt under his steady gaze. When she unzipped his jeans, her knuckles running along his hard length, Cabe let out a soft grunt. The tip of his head was visible above the waistband of his navy boxer briefs.

Copying Cabe's actions, she took his hand and kissed the inside of his wrist, making her way up to his neck. But instead of moving to his lips, she made her way down the lines of his chest, across his defined pecs, down the ridge between his abs, smiling as they flexed beneath her, until her lips hovered an inch from his erection. It glistened, his arousal as obvious as her own.

Her eyes moved to his, holding the anticipation for a moment before running her tongue along his tip. She didn't touch him with her hands, didn't move his briefs to reveal more of him. She simply ran her tongue along the narrow band of flesh that had been revealed.

She heard Cabe's fist hit the counter. "Goddamn, Ames. I already liked that mouth of yours . . ."

"Well, if you want more of it, you'd better follow me," she said as she headed toward the bedroom.

He wasn't sure which part of her was going to be the death of him. The ass currently sashaying away from him? The eyes currently looking over her shoulder to see if he followed? Or the mouth that had just nearly rocked his world in 2.3 seconds? Either way, he was going to die a happy man.

He gave himself a second before he stood to follow her, not because he couldn't wait to bury himself deep inside her, but because if he did, right now, after that perfect tongue had circled his dick all of four times, it'd be over faster than the time it took to go from zero to a hundred in his truck—6.3 seconds to be precise.

Amy turned into the bedroom, and Cabe took the time to kick off his boots and socks, pull off his shirt, and remove his belt. His mind was full of all the things he wanted to do to her, all the ways he wanted to experience this with her.

Barefoot, he walked to her room. When he got there, she was on the bed, lying on top of the duvet. He was relieved to see she hadn't covered herself. The still-damp hair from her shower that had been up in a messy bun when he arrived was now down. "You ready for this, Ames?" he said, pulling a condom out of his wallet and throwing both items down on the bedside table.

"'Ready' doesn't begin to describe how I feel right now," she replied, her voice husky. She opened her legs slightly and slid her hand between them, her fingers exploring the places he wanted to be, her actions surprising the hell out of him.

Watching as she teased him, he slid his jeans and briefs down and kicked them off before crawling onto the bed between her thighs, pushing them wider. "That's really fucking hot, but for the rest of tonight, this pussy is mine," he said as he lifted her hand, sucking her fingers into his mouth. She tasted like heaven. Sweet. Tangy.

"Cabe," she said, her eyes searching his. "I know you said slow, and explore, and I am so down with all that— eventually. But really, right now, I need you inside me. Can we do slow later?"

Cabe grinned and reached for the condom, sheathing himself. "Ames, we can do whatever you want." He moved back a little and flipped her over. Amy squealed and then giggled, turning to look over her shoulder at him. Cabe couldn't help but grin. This was the view that had been occupying his thoughts in the early hours of the morning. The curve of her ass, the flawless straight line of her back, all that hair available for him to grab a fistful. He ran a trail of kisses up her spine until he reached her ear. "I'm going to fuck you now, Ames. You might want to hold on to that headboard."

Placing his knees either side of her thighs, he ran his hands over her ass, the perfect handful of smooth skin. Slowly, he ran a finger down the crack between her cheeks, farther until he could feel her wet heat. Using his other hand, he eased his cock toward her and, biting a gasp when he reached her entrance, pushed inside. In this position, she was so tight and so wet. He had no chance in hell of making it last. All he could hope for was that she was as ready for him as she had said. That she was as close to exploding as he was.

"Oh my . . . yes," Amy groaned, pressing her face into her pillow and raising her ass off the bed an inch or two, just enough to give him the room he needed to sink deep inside.

This time they both groaned, and Cabe had a strange feeling wash over him. He couldn't pin it down, but in Amy's words, it felt like . . . *more*.

More than sex, more than just any woman, more than temporary.

Just "more."

Cabe began to move, looking down at the place where he could watch himself stretch her, watch how his cock was becoming covered with her juices, watch the way goose bumps began to cover her skin. And damn, if that didn't make him harder, make him needier. He leaned forward, covering her with his body. He fisted a handful of her hair, and Amy turned to look at him, her eyes wide.

God, had he ever felt this connected? This *in* someone, and not just physically, but emotionally? She didn't speak, just gasped, those perfect lips in an equally perfect O. Yet he could swear her heard her. Begging him to take her, telling him how good she felt. And he hoped she could hear him too. Hear that this was everything. That this was "more."

Amy moved beneath him, though he had her pinned between his legs, underneath his chest. The feeling of dominating her was dwarfed by the feeling that she was dominating him in every way there was.

"Cabe," she whispered, those eyes of hers telling him everything he needed to know. She was there, right there with him. Her body told him the rest, the way she tightened around his cock in a way that just drove him crazy. A way that jacked him so hard and fast, he was about to fall over the edge.

But not without her.

The moment was too perfect to experience it alone.

He slid his hand beneath her, and finding her clit, already wet with her own excitement, began to circle it.

Amy cried out. The gasp was so pure and raw that he groaned in response. He pressed his lips to hers, connected in every way possible, and pounded into her. He rode her hard, desperately, his body giving name to the emotions building up inside him.

Cabe felt it the moment Amy began to come. Her body lost its rhythm as she tightened around him, squeezing him so hard it felt as though an electric current was flowing straight down his spine.

"Cabe," she whispered, as if that was all she had the energy for, and he thundered over the edge with her.

Gasping, he kept his weight on his hands and his lips to her temple. His dick pulsed in the moments after release, aftershocks of pleasure as his body stood down from what had been the best sex of his life.

He kissed the back of Amy's neck in the silence that existed just beyond their heavy breathing.

Her hand slid down from the headboard and gripped his. He opened his hands and let their fingers join. It was a simple action, but in the half light of the bedroom, it was almost more intimate than what they'd just shared.

Cabe slid out of her and rolled onto his side so he faced her. Her features were soft, sweet. Gently, he pressed his lips to hers.

"That was definitely *more*," she whispered.

He placed his arm across her waist. "Can't argue with that, Ames." She had a small scar under her chin, he noticed, and wondered what the story behind it was. Was it from work, or had she always had a risky streak and gotten it as a six-year-old?

Amy reached out and ran a finger along his jaw. It tickled, making him smile. "The day I saw you at the FBI office, you said you'd left the bar for a reason. A long story, you said. Can you tell me why?"

Cabe's heart jolted as memories of Jess flooded in. But the shame he usually felt when he thought about her after sleeping with another woman wasn't there. It felt unfair to discuss another woman while in Amy's bed, but she'd asked. And he owed her an answer. He stalled for a moment, removing the condom and tying it up before dropping it on the floor.

"Two years ago, my fiancée was killed in action," he

said, waiting for the sting of loss that usually hit when he told the story of Jess. Tonight it didn't come.

Amy eyes went wide and shined with unshed tears. "Oh, Cabe. I'm so sorry."

Cabe rolled onto his back, and tugged Amy under his arm so she rested her head on his chest. He wanted her close, yet needed space. Instead of staring into her eyes, eyes that threatened to undo him, he stared at the long crack in the ceiling. "The day I met you was her birthday. That was why I was out with the guys. They knew it was a tough day for me."

Amy's finger drew circles on his chest, and he reached for her hand, holding it flat against his heart. There was probably some symbolism in that. The very reason it was beating right now was Amy, and he wanted her to know that Jess was easing into the past. Not in a way that meant she'd be forgotten, but in a way that would enable him to build a new future instead of lamenting the one he'd lost. But somehow the words wouldn't come.

"That must have been hard for you," Amy said, her breath whispering against his chest, reminding him that right now there were only the two of them in the room.

Cabe swallowed deeply and shrugged. "When I flew out this week, I flew to Arlington to visit her grave. That was the two-year anniversary of her death. I'm sorry I didn't explain that to you."

Silence reclaimed the room, and he wondered what Amy was thinking. What questions might be rattling around in that brain of hers.

"Are you . . . I mean . . . have you . . . shit. Never mind. I'm sorry," Amy muttered.

Filled with the need to reassure her, he turned to face her. "Ask it, Ames. Say whatever is on your mind." If what was happening between them was to go anywhere, they needed to be honest with each other.

"Are you in a good place? To start something new?" Her hand tightened around his. "You asked me if this was a false start. But I didn't ask you the same question. This isn't something you still need to work through, is it?"

Cabe took a breath and let the question settle. A month ago, before he met Amy, he would have answered that it was. But now? "There are things I am certain of and things I'm uncertain of." He reached for a lock of her hair, now dry, and let it slip through his fingers. "I'm certain that Jess will always be a part of my past and my present. I'm still friends with her parents, with her brothers. But since meeting you . . . I don't know. I can't explain what happened, but you've given me hope that I still have a chance to find the type of relationship I thought I would get only one chance at. I thought I'd lost that when Jess died. You aren't a rebound. You aren't a replacement. And I'm here for this. For you. For us. If that makes any sense."

Amy nodded. "It does. But what are you uncertain of?"

Christ, he could write a fucking list. He was uncertain whether his heart was capable of going all in again. Or whether he could handle a relationship with a woman who would perpetually be placed in danger. He was uncertain about his own skills to keep her safe, to keep her alive.

He kissed her, this time with the churned-up urgency he suddenly felt inside. "I'm a work in progress, Ames. I'm uncertain about everything except the connection between the two of us. Don't doubt that for a second."

CHAPTER FOURTEEN

A noise drilled into Cabe's head. It was loud, and suddenly wherever he was felt a little too bright.

There were open curtains. And too much daylight.

His hands stroked the soft skin of a woman's back.

And he grinned.

Amy.

Shit. That was his phone ringing. He tried to reach out his arm to grab it, but it wasn't there. Instead, his fingers brushed the container of the little cactus he'd bought her. The cactus Six had given him shit over.

"It's on the counter," Amy said, throwing the covers back and hurrying out of bed.

Cabe followed her ass as it disappeared through the doorway. Then, as quickly as she'd disappeared, she reappeared, and damn, if he wasn't momentarily distracted by the way her breasts bounced when she entered the room—so much so that he fumbled the phone when she handed it to him.

"It's Six," she said, before disappearing into the bathroom.

Before Amy, it had been a long time since he'd allowed himself the simple luxury of waking up in a woman's bed, with her in his arms. He liked it—more than he probably should.

"Yo," he said as he answered.

"We got a break on the target we followed from the casino. Want to meet up at the office before you guys head into the casino tonight?"

"Sure thing. What time were you thinking?"

Six laughed. "Honestly, I've lost my wife-to-be to that lab of hers. They're on the edge of some big break, which means I'm not going to see her today and could pretty much do any time you want, even though it's Saturday."

Cabe envisioned Six making frozen dinners and eating them from a tray all alone in his house while his wife was busting her ass saving the world, one disease at a time.

"We'll swing by around three. What's the thirty-second overview?"

"We have the relationship between the target and the cashier."

Amy returned to the bedroom, and he winked at her as she climbed back under the covers. "Do we have a name yet?" He ran his palm over her breast and mouthed *shh*, even though she probably understood the need to be quiet. She placed her hand over his and squeezed, and damn, if his dick didn't respond.

"We do. Shit, Lou's on the other line. See you at three. Later."

"Okay. Later, bro."

He switched his phone off and placed it on the bedside table. Then, in one swift motion, he grabbed her and positioned her so she was sitting over him. "I need more of you, and then I need some serious food," he said, knowing he was grinning like the Cheshire cat. He couldn't help it. She did that to him.

"I need a shower." She reached up and piled her hair on top of her head. She had to know full well that her arched back made her breasts stand to full attention. Kind of like his dick was. "Plus, my hair takes a while to dry."

Cabe sat up quickly and kissed her. "Wet hair suits you," he said, and grinned, thinking of how her hair had still been damp when he'd taken her from behind the previous evening.

Amy began to grind over his dick, and he groaned. "Keep that up, Ames, and this is going to be over before it's even started."

She leaned forward and kissed him, her breath minty fresh. Someone had brushed her teeth when she'd snuck away to the bathroom. "Well, if it's over quickly, it just means we'll have time to do it again before we leave."

Five hours later, Cabe found himself pulling into the Eagle Securities' parking lot. Amy's car was already there, and he felt an unexpected jolt of excitement at the thought of seeing her again. Which was ludicrous. Wasn't he too old to be getting lost in his feelings? Wasn't it too soon? But those thoughts slipped away as he studied the building, knowing Amy was inside it.

He used his pass to let himself into the office and his thumbprint to open the second doors they'd had installed. He could hear Amy's laughter coming from somewhere down the hallway, and he let out a deep breath. There was a peace that came from knowing she was currently in the safest place she could be.

"So," he heard Six say, humor ripe in his tone, "Cabe

had to wait over half an hour with his head stuck between the railings until the firefighters could come cut him out."

More laughter.

Asshole.

"Keep feeding her stories," Cabe said as he entered the room, "and I'll tell her about that incident in Alaska."

Six stopped laughing and eyed him dangerously. "You wouldn't dare."

Cabe folded his arms in front of his chest. "Try me," he said, before looking at Amy, who sat primly upright in her chair. Her hair was styled into a sleek ponytail, and her makeup reminded him a little of an old-school screen goddess from the black-and-white movie era. His breath caught in his throat.

"Fine," Six said, but he looked between Cabe and Amy curiously. "Let's get started."

It felt strange, but Cabe sat down on the opposite side of the table from her. Partly because he could steal the occasional glance, but also because he knew himself well enough to know that if he sat next to her, he'd spend the whole meeting resisting the urge to slide his palm along her thigh, or perhaps under her skirt to see if he could make her as wet as she was when—

"You ready, Cabe?" Six asked, bringing him back to the present.

A smile threatened to break through his poker face, and he bit it back. Literally. His teeth dug into the inside of his lip.

When Amy glanced up, Cabe caught her eye, but he revealed nothing.

"We followed the target from the casino," Six said as video footage from the drone played on the white wall of the conference room.

Amy snapped her attention to the screen. And even though he'd of course known it all along, it really struck him that she was a goddamn FBI agent. In their moments together, he'd finally managed to forget that she had a career that would consistently put her in danger. Hell, she was bait in the casino, constantly striving to figure out how to become the next victim.

And he hated it.

Hated it so bad that he struggled to focus on the information Six was showing them.

"The person you spotted in the casino is a very distant relative of Sokolov. It's his cousin's grandson . . . I don't even think that kind of family connection has a name. Third cousin, maybe? Anyway . . . if you play the Kevin Bacon degrees of separation, it could be a coincidence that they are related at all."

"Have the police spoken to him?" Amy asked.

Cabe stood and poured himself a cup of coffee before sitting back down. Maybe it would clear his head.

Six shook his head. "No. They haven't. They're waiting on us to decide if we want to. The camera feeds from the casino show him doing exactly what Cabe said. But the thing is, it would be super simple for him to provide an excuse, like he intended to play big, then got sick and felt the need to cash out, or some other impossible-to-disprove statement."

Amy sighed. "Okay. Who has their eyes on him?"

"Right now, your guys," Six replied.

"What do we know?" Cabe asked before taking a sip of the coffee. It was fresh and steaming hot but, more important, strong, just how he liked it.

"He left the casino and headed straight back to San Ysidro. The apartment building we already visited." Six threw up a map that showed an aerial view of the apartment complex. "These were the buildings the SDPD raided looking for Kovalenko," he said, pointing to two on the lower lever where they'd attempted to find the man who'd carried out the abduction attempt of Louisa. "But this is where the target lives. His name is Phillip Shevchenko. Age twenty-seven. Works for a family-run scrap-metal firm. He came straight back here. Yesterday morning he left and went to this house in Little Italy." The image of a small home painted white appeared on the wall.

Cabe looked at Amy. "Here's where he tells us who lives there and drops his mic," he whispered.

Amy laughed as he'd intended, just as Six put a picture of the casino cashier on the wall.

"*This* is who he went to see."

The Lucky Seven cashier.

"CIA wants to move now," Six added.

"That's because they're desperate to find the cash, as we all are. But if we pick up two grunts, they'll be dead before we get them to trial. Nobody will take any ownership of them, and the two of them, half terrified that they are going to be assassinated, will probably argue that it was just them anyhow."

Amy nodded. "Plus, we get two people for money laundering, but that doesn't necessarily have anything to do with or prove anything in regard to the missing women."

"What else?" Cabe asked, knowing there must be more intel for Six to have dragged them into the office.

"From the camera feed, the photos taken in San Ysidro yesterday, and the use of some facial recognition software, Harley was able to give us three other suspects for the smurfing ring—which still remains the most stupid name, by the way."

Three faces appeared on the screen, and Cabe immediately recognized two of them. "I've seen the two guys on the left. We need to get the FBI and SDPD to help stake these guys out, find out who they are talking to, who is giving them their instructions, where they're getting the money from."

A fresh lead always gave everybody a renewed boost of motivation. New intel, new direction, new hope. But the feeling of futility returned for reasons he couldn't explain, and he hated the sensation. It was like an itch, one he couldn't scratch. In all the years he'd been deployed overseas, even in battles that had raged for decades, he'd never felt as though the situation was out of control. But this one . . .

Cabe looked across the table and saw Amy completely engrossed in what Six was telling them. She ran the ends of her hair through her fingers as she listened.

He hated the feeling that sand was trickling through his fingers.

And he wondered if she wasn't the very reason why.

It was getting close to the end of her shift, and Amy felt antsy as she dealt poker. She couldn't put her finger on what had her so . . . unfocused. It certainly wasn't because the flop she'd just dealt had provided a pair of tens—the spade and heart—and a nine of spades. Nor was it because there was nobody playing the private rooms right now, so she'd been asked to deal on the main floor.

Ever since the meeting earlier, Cabe had been at best ultra-focused, and at worst distant. Cool even. And she couldn't determine what on earth had changed since they'd woken up in each other's arms. She knew their relationship was on the down low in public at her request, but a part of her couldn't help but wonder why the issue was so big of a deal that it would have killed him to at least have taken hold of her hand and squeezed, if only in passing.

But instead he'd given her a few words of no substance or meaningfulness.

Just like she'd asked.

God, even *she* could tell she was being irrational.

The betting continued. A woman in a simple black shift dress and intricate updo giving off an Audrey Hepburn vibe fidgeted on her seat. Amy would bet the pot that she had at least one of the other tens in the deck. Poker face was a thing.

Her thoughts drifted back to Cabe's underwhelming send-off from Eagle—a nod of the head. A quick, "Take care and see you later." Weak farewells left her unsettled. After all, on the day her mom had gone out for eggnog, their goodbye had been quick, both of them assuming they'd have time to chat over dinner. If only Amy could go back in time and switch off the damn *Stuart Little* movie she'd been so engrossed in and go with her mom to the store like she'd asked. It wasn't as if she hadn't already seen it a hundred and fifty times already. But her mom had been in a hurry, and Amy had still been in her pajamas and couldn't be bothered. Not even the lure of people singing carols in the strip mall parking lot and the promise of a hot chocolate from Starbucks had persuaded her to move. Over the years, she'd tried to let go of the idea that had she been with her mom, her mom wouldn't have been taken. But she couldn't let go of not being able to remember what shoes her mom had been wearing. Amy hadn't even turned away from her movie for a millisecond to say goodbye to her mom properly. She'd give anything to have that one last memory of her mom's face now.

Going off to do what they did without that last connection to Cabe felt . . . empty. When had he become so vital to her?

"Hit us up, sweetheart," a man in a Duke University T-shirt said playfully. The turn provided a four of clubs.

Damn, she needed to focus. Make it through the last few hands before she switched out with another dealer. Then she could go home and sleep because Sunday was her night off. She had plans for an at-home spa evening and catching up on *Outlander*. Or any other thing she could do to put Cabe's behavior out of mind until she had a chance to sit down with him and discuss it. The last thing she needed was to be distracted.

With all the bets in place, she turned the final card and the river provided a six of clubs. By the bouncing around, the woman was showing that the card had provided her with what she felt was a winning hand. Amateurs always got excited at hands without picture cards.

The woman's disappointment was palpable when, after making a performance of placing her pair of tens to make a four of a kind, the man in the Duke hat showed a seven and eight of spades, giving him a straight flush, which beats a four of a kind.

"Hey, sweetheart," the man said, obviously aware that he'd just stolen her hand. "Will you let me get you a drink to make up for that?" The woman grinned and nodded as she grabbed her remaining chips.

Amy collected the chips thrown her way as tips and set about cleaning down her table. Ortega walked toward her, watching the couple leave. "You know how many people I've seen arrive at a poker table as strangers and leave it together, only to come back years later to celebrate their wedding anniversary by playing at the table where they first met?"

Amy laughed, unable to help herself. "I didn't take you for a romantic, Mr. Ortega."

Ortega shuddered. "Divorced. Twice. Never doing it again. What about you?"

"Oh, most definitely single," she said, even though the words rippled through her uneasily.

There was a crash over by the bar, and Amy looked over just in time to see Cabe hitting a man in the face. "Oh, my god," she whispered, as cries of "Knife!" sounded around them.

Security was running to the scene, and Sokolov, to whom she assumed Cabe had been speaking, was on his feet to wave them over. The two henchmen who usually trailed behind Sokolov grabbed the man, one under each arm, and took him outside. Cabe shook his hand and wiggled his fingers. Without overthinking it, Amy hurried to the bar, grabbed a linen napkin, and reached over the bar for the shovel in the ice tray. She scooped up ice cubes and dropped them into the napkin before twisting the ends to stop them from escaping.

She headed to Cabe. His eyes were dark, and from the way his chest stretched on every exhalation, she could tell he was breathing deeply. His jaw was set as she took his hand in hers and placed the ice on top of it. "You helped me the other night," she said, just loudly enough for Sokolov to hear. "I guess this makes us even."

She took his hand in one of hers and placed the ice against his knuckles with the other.

"Thank you. It's Amy, isn't it?" he asked gruffly.

"Yes," she said.

Cabe slid his hand over hers, his thumb brushing her wrist, until he had hold of the napkin.

His eyes held hers a fraction longer. "Thank you, Amy. There's a knife over here somewhere. You'll be safer over there," he said, nodding in the direction of her table. "Go."

As much as she understood the adherence to character, she hated the dismissal, the lack of warmth in his tone. She headed back to Ortega, who decided to let her go a few minutes early.

Though she knew it was a risk, once she'd changed she drove to Cabe's place. They were practically neighbors, with only two blocks separating her rental from his. There was no point heading inside because she had no idea of his floor or unit, so she walked to a nearby coffee shop to grab a latte while she waited by the entrance. She didn't have to wait long.

"What are you doing here?" Cabe asked, walking toward her. She appreciated how he never took a cab all the way home or, for that matter, to any destination, just in case he was followed.

Amy took his now-bandaged knuckles in hers. "I was worried about you," she answered honestly. "What happened?"

Cabe looked over her shoulder and then over his own, and she knew he was making sure that nobody was watching them. "You should go, Amy. This isn't a good idea."

"Can we at least step inside, off the street?"

He didn't answer, but the way Cabe gripped his watch told her everything she needed to know. She placed her hand over his. "That's your tell, you know."

"What is?"

"Your watch. When you have something on your mind, you fiddle with it."

Cabe immediately let go of it, and her hand fell away. "I'm sorry."

She wasn't sure what he meant the apology for. The watch, or the chill that had settled between them. "Don't be. Just talk to me. I'd prefer that to an apology every time."

He looked at his watch, and she noticed it was midnight. "You don't have to be in tomorrow night, right?"

Amy nodded.

"Can we go somewhere?" he asked. "Somewhere away from all this."

"Away" was probably a good idea, and she trusted Cabe to not put them at risk. Softly, she nodded.

"One sec." Cabe pulled his phone out of his pocket and dialed a number. Whoever he was calling took a while to answer—she guessed it was because of the late hour. "I know it's late, Nikki, but you got any rooms free for tonight? . . . yeah. Two . . . shut the fuck up . . . this time of night, twenty, twenty-five minutes . . . will do." Cabe hung up and slipped the phone back into his pocket. "Grab your bag from the back of your car. I'm going to get *my* truck. Meet you back here in a couple," he said before disappearing into the building.

Amy did as he said and a handful of minutes later, she heard the steady drone of a throaty engine as Cabe's black truck appeared from the underground lot. He leaned across the seat and pushed the door open.

"Come on, Ames. I won't bite, despite my current appearance."

They drove the coastal road north in silence. Part of her wanted to fill the air, to drag whatever was bothering Cabe out of him. But for now maybe he just needed some time to clear his head. She'd rather hear what he had to say after he'd thought through it.

A little less than thirty minutes later, they pulled into the beach resort of Encinitas, continuing north until they hit Beacon's Beach and a hip-looking motel, all cedar wood and white paint with SURFHOUSE written on the side.

Cabe opened his door. "Let's get inside." He grabbed both of their bags and entered the pin code into a blue-gray door that had a large number one painted on it in white and BEACON on a small plaque under the light fitting.

The stylish motel room had wood flooring the soft color of driftwood and was decorated in soothing beige and white. A sliding barn door painted a soothing aqua hid what was obviously the bathroom. A large TV hung on the wall opposite a queen bed. And on the unit next to the sink was a metal bucket with a couple of cold beers and water. She walked to the counter to read the note. *Thought you could use these, Nikki.*

"What are we doing here, Cabe?"

This time, *he* reached for *her*. "I'm being a dick. I know I am. And I'm still figuring out why. But I thought we'd come here, as Cabe and Amy. As civilians, as . . . I don't know. I guess boyfriend and girlfriend. Test this out between us. And talk."

Amy yawned, she couldn't help it. "Oh god. I'm so sorry."

Cabe looked at his watch. "It's late. We've both had

an exciting night and need some sleep. I promise we'll talk in the morning and I'll tell you everything." He reached for the zipper on her sweatshirt and tugged it down.

"I'm awake," she said, forcing her eyes wide. "You can at least tell me about how this happened." She reached for his hand and kissed his bandaged knuckles.

"No," Cabe said softly, pressing the softest whisper of a kiss to her lips. "First we sleep. Then we talk. Get into bed, Ames, before I change my mind and fuck you as a way of apology."

"What if I want that?" she asked as she slipped out of her clothes and slid under the covers in just her panties.

Cabe followed suit and spooned up behind her. He kissed behind her ear and then nipped her lobe. "Then you'll *still* have to wait until morning."

Amy searched for a response to the way his words heated her body but fell asleep before she had the chance to say them.

Surely there wasn't a better combination to wake up to. The feel of Amy's body pressed up against his and the sound of waves crashing onto Beacon's Beach just outside the bedroom window.

Amy burrowed closer, her leg over his thigh, her hand on his stomach, her head tucked into the crook of his arm. Peace filled the room and settled someplace deep in his chest. Moments of beauty had been few and far between since Jess's death. Hell, even before that. But there was something almost magical about the quiet he'd found with Amy.

Cabe ran his free hand, the one that wasn't cupping Amy's delicious ass, over his face and yawned. By the light creeping in around the edges of the curtains, it was likely a little after nine. He'd slipped his watch off and put it on the table.

Gently, so as not to wake Amy up, he turned to look at it. In the half light, he could make out the inscription he knew by heart.

IOU forever.

Forever.

Even with Amy in his arms, he'd expected a wave of guilt, sadness . . . something to wash over him, but it didn't. The same feelings of comfort and happiness he'd felt earlier stayed with him, and he tightened his hold on Amy.

"What's got you sighing?" she said on a whisper.

He looked down and saw her blink as she struggled to keep her eyes open. Her eyes were clear, her cheeks pink with sleep, and her lips . . . goddamn, as rich and full as he'd ever seen them. Thoughts of them wrapped around his cock had him hardening below. For once, he ignored it. They needed to talk.

"I'm out of synch, Ames," he said. "I can't explain it better than that. I've been through tougher mental conditions. This case is a walk in the park compared to some of the shit I've seen, but with you at the epicenter of this . . . I don't know. I can't think clearly. The op seems fuzzy." Joni Mitchell's "Help Me" began to play somewhere out in the parking lot, a perfect lazy morning kind of song.

Amy pushed up onto her elbow. "Then break it down with me, each thing that feels fuzzy. I'll see if I can help."

"I was listening to Six talk about the new leads, and normally I'd be all over that shit. But then I look across the table and I see you, and I know these waves of missing women are coming again in just a few days. And instead of being relieved that we have more intel, I panic because I don't think I have enough time to wrestle the leads down, which leaves you at risk. And I don't like the idea of you at more risk than is necessary. The best way I know how to handle that is to do the work. Work harder. Work faster. No distractions."

Amy pressed her lips to his, left them lingering there for just a moment. "Let's put aside the fact I've done this job successfully for a number of years and am as capable as you are," she said, a smile gracing her lips that didn't quite reach her eyes. "You said "I" a lot in that sentence. *I* don't have time. . . . The thing is, you don't have to. The FBI has my back, Eagle has my back, and I have my back."

Cabe rolled his neck from left to right, trying to loosen some of the tension. "Last night, some idiot pulled a knife on Sokolov over a bad debt."

"Is that what the fight was about?" she asked, reaching for his hand and then checking his knuckles, which were bruised. She placed a kiss on them, and the gesture warmed his heart.

"Yeah. But all I could think was what would I have done if you'd got caught in the middle of it?"

"You would have done *your* job, not my job, or Six's job, or anyone else on the team's job. It's not all on you. It's not on you to find the evidence, to place the cameras, to find the money, to keep me safe, to arrest Sokolov. We're a team. I know that sounds harsh, but one thing I guarantee I will always do in our relationship is call you on your shit. Just like you should call me on mine. So, what's next?"

Cabe lay there stunned. It was the kind of advice he'd

give one of his men. And just like his men, they both had a job to do. Just like his men, she was trained and she was capable. As much as the alpha male in him wanted her to be his and his alone to protect, she was right. There was a team.

Nothing was going to happen to her.

He turned onto his side, tugging her thigh higher over his leg, opening her up to him as he did. "Did I ever tell you that I find your brain just as sexy as this?" he asked as he slid his hand between the two of them, teasing her through her white panties.

Amy grinned and ran her fingers through his hair. "No, but I'm all ears," she said, and then gasped as he slid a finger beneath the white cotton.

"Well," Cabe said, his voice dropping to a whisper as he placed his lips near her ear, "sometimes I get hard just listening to you, especially when I'm watching those words fall from that sweet mouth of yours. Especially when those words are ones I need to hear. And I get equally hard when you are wet like this. Both things at the same time means you are going to get doubly fucked."

"We didn't finish our conversation," she mumbled into the pillow as she turned her head to give him better access.

Cabe rubbed his finger along her folds, which were so wet that he wished he could just screw the consequences and take her raw as they were right now. And goddamn, if the idea of having kids with Amy wasn't a beautiful one. It hit him, full in the chest like someone was doing jumping jacks on it. Love, a proposal, a wedding, kids. He could have all that with Amy. And it wasn't simply a replacement for the plans he'd once had. Something new and different and fucking incredible. It was something more.

IOU forever.

That's what his watch said. But he owed *himself* forever. His eyes and nose stung, and he bit down on the very idea of tears by removing his hand from Amy's softness to pull her tight against him.

Christ, it would hurt if something happened to Amy. He wasn't sure his body could recover. But the idea of pushing her away, of trying to find someone else, hurt more.

Amy's arms slid around him, her face tucked in tight against his neck as he rolled onto his back, taking her with him so her thighs were on either side of his legs, her chest pressed tight up against his own. Cabe fisted her hair in his hand and pressed tightly against her lower back, decreasing the gap between them.

Words formed in his brain, but he couldn't quite say them. Words about feelings and emotions, words he hadn't said in over two years, words he never thought he'd say to another woman.

A ringing cut through the silence—her phone. Her burner phone. "Hold that thought," Amy said, jumping off him and running to the small table to grab it.

"Hello," she said casually, all traces of arousal gone from her tone. Cabe slid his hand beneath the white sheet and rearranged his dick, which was rock hard and needy. Amy glared at him and then grinned before she turned back to the wall.

"Of course, Mr. Woods. When? . . . And where would it take place?"

All thoughts of his dick dropped from his mind at the

idea of her meeting Woods *anywhere* other than the casino. He sat up in bed.

"I can. Okay . . . Thank you for thinking of me . . . goodbye."

Amy hung up and placed the burner phone back on the unit, but for a moment she didn't turn around. Cabe's heart felt as if it had fallen off the top of a tall building.

"What is it, Ames?"

"Mr. Woods asked if I'd like to deal for a private party Sokolov is having at his home."

"When?" Though he asked the question, from the look on her face he already knew the answer. "It's tonight, isn't it? That's why they gave you a weekend night off when they're usually the busiest ones at the casino."

Amy nodded. "It's tonight, and I guess so. I have to drive to a meet-up point and the address will be given to me when I get there. But I think for the purposes of planning we have to assume the address I get sent to will be Sokolov's home."

Cabe jumped out of bed and tugged some clean clothes out of his gym bag. "We need to get back to Eagle and set this up."

Amy nodded. "I'll call Cunningham and get my team organized. I just need a minute to get cleaned up," she said, and he noticed that her underwear was still askew.

He offered her his hand and smiled when she went to him without question. With a single finger, he straightened the waistband of her underwear before facing her. "I know we aren't finished with our conversation, and now isn't the time. But I promise you, Ames, we'll come back to it. We'll finish it. But until then, you have me in every way you need me. No matter what goes down today, don't doubt that for a millisecond. If it comes down to what I feel about you and the op, I'm picking you."

She lifted her eyes to his. "I know, Cabe. It's the thing I'm most certain about."

Cabe lowered his mouth to hers and kissed her in a way he hoped relayed everything he was feeling. It was deep, torturous, and did absolutely nothing to help the ache in his dick. He pulled her closer, holding her tight against him, hopefully giving her as much comfort as she was giving him. It was perfect. And it had to stop because they had to get dressed and begin to plan.

On the ride to Eagle, they each made calls. Her to the FBI, him to Mac and Cabe to rally their teams. Thankfully, with their collective experience, they were used to calls at the last minute asking them to drop their lives and go wherever they were needed. Within the hour, they had a fully functioning war room.

Within two hours, Buddha had an eye on the building via drone, Harley had found the architectural drawings for the house so they at least had a sense of the layout, and the FBI were listening in on conversations, something they'd never in a million years admit to doing without the proper authorization.

By hour three, they'd figured out how to provide cover to the back of the home, which looked onto a ravine, and the front, which was set back off the road. Discreetly, out of Amy's earshot, he'd kicked his own ass into gear and talked with Buddha and Mac offline about how to keep an eye on Amy if they tried to bundle her out of the house somehow, and about what provisions they would need if she didn't come out of the house at all. Once they had a plan that involved thermal-imaging drones and a borderline-Cinderella plan that had her emerging from the house between games at midnight under the premise of getting air, they ran her through the plans.

They'd agreed she wouldn't be able to take a firearm in with her. Woods had told Amy that her belongings would be searched when she arrived and that it was nothing to worry about.

Nothing to worry about.

Cabe looked over to the table Amy was sitting at with two agents from the FBI.

She was *everything* to fucking worry about.

Goddamn the op. He wished he'd ignored the call and pushed her back onto the bed, wrapping her in his arms where he could keep her safe. Where they could pretend that nobody had the capacity to hurt her. Yet years of training kicked in to make the op the priority in spite of his thoughts.

He reached for his SIG just for the comfort of knowing it was there. Right now, she needed the SEAL, not the lover, no matter how willing he was to be both.

CHAPTER FIFTEEN

Cabe's fingers were warm against her cheek. He'd asked her for a private word, and she'd followed him to Eagle's med room, where he'd promptly locked the door and pressed her back up against it. Without a doubt, she'd need to fix her lipstick again, but with his erection resting against her thigh, it was hard to focus.

She knew he was grappling with what she was about to do, but she didn't know how to reassure him without bringing up Jess. And the last thing she needed was to elevate her concern and his stress levels.

"We'll have every entrance and exit covered. And Buddha and Harley will have two drones with thermal-imaging cameras attached to them. We'll be able to see who is coming and going. We've got eyes on all the major roads out, and we've got—"

"Cabe," she interrupted, putting her hands on his and stilling them. "We've got this."

Cabe sighed and took her hands in his, allowing their fingers to link. Then he looked at her with so many unspoken words in his eyes.

"I mean it," she repeated firmly. "We've thought through every single outcome."

"I know we have, and I know you do," he said, finally. "I spent most of the day going through scenarios, and there wasn't a one that we didn't have covered. But it's you, Ames. And I'd be lying if I said I was cool with what you are about to do. Don't misunderstand me, I have no doubt you can handle this, can handle yourself. But it just . . . I don't know. I feel sick down to my boots."

Amy pressed up onto her toes and pressed her lips gently to his. "I love that you're concerned about me, Cabe. And I know the kind of man you are. I trust you to get me out of there if shit goes wrong."

He nodded his head once, then pulled her into a hug she knew she'd feel all evening. She'd wear the strength of it like a shield. Amy could still feel the warmth of his arms after he'd let her go and waited as she fixed her lipstick. Her FBI colleagues' day passes wouldn't let them this far back into the building—she knew that much—but certainly there would be Eagle employees milling about when they stepped outside.

But she couldn't allow herself to worry about that now.

Because now she was headed into an unknown. A place where normal laws and security and rules did not apply.

As they left the room, he squeezed her hand one last time, giving her a feeling of security she'd take with her, giving her a goodbye she could hold onto. Thinking briefly of her final farewell with her mom, she glanced at his shoes. Black sneakers. She'd remember those too.

An hour later, Amy pulled up at the address she'd been given. Sokolov's home was as imposing as the images they'd studied earlier that day had suggested. "You got this, Ames," she said to no one in particular, although she smiled when she realized she'd called herself by Cabe's sweet nickname for her. For some reason it stabilized her, brought her pulse down to some kind of normal.

She parked the car, switched from her driving flats to her heels, and walked up to the huge double door painted an imposing black with ornate gold fixings. It was pulled open by Faulkner Woods, who stepped out onto the porch and closed the door behind him.

"Mr. Woods," she said, caught off guard. "I had no idea you'd be here tonight."

"Off duty you can call me Faulkner. You'll get paid the negotiated rate at the end of the evening, and the players often provide tips in the form of chips. The casino will honor them and provide the tips to you on Monday. You'll just need to come and see me. Your job is simply to keep the game in play. The same rules regarding the fraternization policy at the casino apply, and chances are you won't be privy to the conversations because they'll mainly be in Russian."

"I just need the extra money," she said. "I don't need a date," she added primly.

Woods laughed, a vicious bark. "You'll do well to remember that being nice to Mr. Sokolov is very good for the casino, and for us."

"Why is that?" Amy asked.

Woods shook his head. "Don't worry about that right now. This is a great opportunity for you. There is big money to be made in off-the-books gaming. The visitors you saw come to the rear of the casino the other night, they were high-rolling customers who wanted to hold a private game at the casino. If this goes well, there will be more of these kinds of opportunities for you. Let's get you inside and set up. They'll be ready to begin in an hour."

Amy followed him into Sokolov's home. A black carpet ran up the large central staircase that dominated the hallway, a sharp contrast to the white walls. A gold chandelier that appeared to be bigger than her kitchen was suspended from the vaulted ceiling. She'd seen the floor plans, as Cabe had walked her through them, but even the outrageously large footprint hadn't prepared her for the overwhelmingly expensive yet tacky interior.

Two men approached them, neither acknowledging Woods. They were dressed in jeans and almost identical black T-shirts, but it was their features she attempted to memorize. Both had black hair; one was a good few inches taller. Both men had easy-to-distinguish tattoos. One had a series of what looked like paw prints making their way up his forearm. The other had four sets of numbers, all roman numerals.

They patted her down and checked inside her purse. She was relieved that her team had made the decision to send her in without a wire, but was eternally grateful that she had her GPS on her.

"There is a staff area back here," Woods said, nudging her in the direction of a long hallway. They reached a butler's pantry where catering staff were busy unwrapping trays of food. "You can leave your belongings over there," he said, pointing to a bench with coat hooks above it.

Amy removed her jacket and hung up her purse, which contained nothing more than her car keys, lip gloss, and a brand-new phone. Knowing it would take an expert less than a minute to hack her password, the phone was a burner with no contacts in it just in case someone used the opportunity to snoop through her history.

Faulkner tilted his head toward the door, and she followed him through the house.

It was hard to believe that anybody actually lived there. Despite the poor taste, it was immaculate. Not a thing out of place. Faulkner opened a door on the ground floor that led into a large games room. The walls were painted a deep green, and heavy gold damask drapes ran along one wall that, if her memory served her correctly, hid glass doors that led out to the side garden. The musty smell of old cigar smoke filled the air, likely having seeped into the curtains and fabrics. There was a pool table at one end of the room, a bar along one wall, and an impressive full-sized card table at the other end.

Woods's phone rang. "I'll go and let the others know you are here."

Amy walked to the curtains and opened them a little. Small lanterns lit steps down to a rock garden. Cabe was out there in the darkness, and she drew comfort from that.

Sokolov entered the room, and nodded in her direction. "You have a beautiful home, Mr. Sokolov," she said politely, stepping away from the drapes and leaving them open a fraction. Maybe Cabe's team could use the gap to get even the smallest look into the room.

"Thank you, Ms. Reynard, and I'm very glad you can join us this evening." Without any further comment, he turned to the seven other men who had followed him into the room. The first she immediately identified as Ivan Popov, who had disappeared after the fire that had broken out when Cabe and his team had laid siege to the place where Six's fiancée, Louisa, was being held. She wondered how the team would respond to the positive ID—especially Six, who she had learned had a fiercely protective streak when it came to Louisa.

The trays of chips were under the table, so she crouched down to count them, taking a moment to ensure her composure.

She didn't know the other six men, but after she stood again, she made a point to study each one.

"Very pretty, Woods," one of the men said, looking straight at her.

"And a fantastic dealer. I think you'll be very happy," Woods said, beaming at her like a proud father—the creepiest thing to happen so far that evening.

There were no introductions, and in many ways, she was treated as if she were invisible. The conversation flitted between Russian and English until Sokolov stood. "Gentlemen, if you would pass your buy-in into the game to Mr. Woods, we can get started."

The men retrieved envelopes from jackets and pockets and passed them to the end of the table, where Woods stood with a note counter. From her earlier review, it looked as though there was at least one hundred thousand dollars in chips on the trays. Woods ran the stack of notes from the first envelope through the counter and nodded to her, which she took as a signal to provide the first gambler, a short stocky man with thinning black hair, with his chips. They repeated the process seven more times, with Sokolov being the last to receive his chips.

Two men at the end of the table looked at her as they spoke to each other in Russian. One laughed at something the other had said, and they both looked at her chest. Amy resisted the urge to fasten an extra button or pull the gap closed. Instead, she focused on opening the five packets of cards to be used in the first game. "Mr. Woods?" she asked. "Which style of poker are we playing tonight?"

"We could play liquor and poker," one of the men said—emphasizing the syllables to make it sound like "lick her and poke her"—and the rest of them laughed. She refused to let the men see any response from her. It was an old joke, and she wondered if Sister Whiskey had realized how annoying their album title was when they'd named it.

"Texas hold 'em," Woods replied, and inwardly she scoffed. Of course, they were playing the most obvious version of the game. "The small blind is a hundred dollars, the big blind two hundred. It will increase to five hundred and a thousand at midnight."

She shuffled all the packs, asking the men to cut the deck until everyone was satisfied the cards were ready for play. Just as she was about to deal each man one card to decide which player would be the first to lay down a blind, Sokolov put his hand on hers. "Ms. Reynard, please deal to Mr. Yeltsin first." He nodded in the direction of the man who'd made the liquor and poker joke. It was unconventional, and debatably unfair, but she did as he said. Plus, it kind of served the asshole right.

After ninety minutes of play that made it crystal clear the men were rich amateurs, they broke for the food that had been laid out for them in the formal dining room. "Mr. Sokolov, if I could trouble you to direct me to the bathroom," Amy said, deliberately standing by the gap she'd opened in the curtains so that the men watching could see she was still okay.

"Of course, Ms. Reynard. Allow me," he said offering

her his elbow. It became clear that he'd been about to
direct her to a powder room on the same floor but the
two men who had made lecherous comments had
beaten them to it. Sokolov sighed. "There is another."
He pointed to the stairwell. "On the second floor. Turn
left at the top, the third door on the right."

Amy jogged up the stairs, the plush black carpet sinking beneath her feet. Even her heels took on the feel of
sneakers. Careful to survey the property as she walked,
she looked for cameras. There were motions sensors for
the alarm system, the little red dots flashing as she walked
by, but no cameras. Sokolov obviously felt his exterior security was enough to keep people away. Walking slowly,
she made her way down the hallway, pausing to look into
rooms that had doors ajar. A bedroom in a gaudy lilac
scheme, a playroom with a huge castle scene painted on
the walls. In the midst of preparing, she'd almost forgotten that Sokolov had a wife and two children. She wondered where they were.

The door on the opposite side of the hallway opened
into a room that on the floor plan had been described as
a den. But the large desk with the monitor and laptop
on it said otherwise. The cognac brown leather sofa
and chunky glass ashtray on the side table gave the impression it was a man's office. With a glance over her
shoulder to the staircase, Amy stepped inside. An over-
sized window opened out onto a manicured garden with a
large fountain, water pouring from the open mouths of
sculpted fish.

The room was dark, the only light coming from the
hallway. A pile of papers was neatly stacked on one side,
and the laptop was turned off. There was no point in attempting to open it, as she was no password hacker. A

floorboard creaked in the hallway and Amy stopped, waiting for a footstep, movement. But none came.

She quickly looked through the papers. A power bill, a cell-phone contract, a marina fee . . . *a marina fee*. For a private marina just north of the city, registered to an Ekaterina Petrov.

Two male voices sounded in the hallway. Amy sucked in a breath and, as the voices came closer, crawled beneath the desk. Her heart raced as her temples pulsed. There was no way of explaining why she was hidden where she was if she was found. Her mind went through plausible excuses but it came up blank. She should have stuck with the plan, but if she was lucky enough to make it out of there, they had a lead on a boat.

The door to the den creaked as one of the men pushed it open. He said something to the other in Russian, and both men laughed.

Amy closed her eyes and took a silent breath as the conversation continued, until the voices disappeared in the opposite direction down the hallway. Air escaped Amy in a whoosh. Quietly, she crawled from beneath the desk and tiptoed to the doorway. When she was certain the coast was clear, she hurried into the bathroom on the other side of the hall and locked the door, taking three large gulps of air.

Searching the office had not been a part of the plan, but Cabe had been right when he'd talked about new leads.

It *was* a rush.

One she realized she loved.

Cabe threw back the covers of his bed, a bed that felt painfully empty without Amy in it, and wondered whether he was pissed because of that, or still pissed because of her reckless actions ninety hours earlier, or pissed because it was only five a.m. and it felt as though fire ants were crawling up and down his arms.

Much as it had when he'd watched Amy through his binoculars and the scope of his M4 as she'd dealt cards for men he was coming to hate more and more. There was an old lesson about not making war personal, but right now this op felt as personal as it got.

Calming Six down when they'd realized Ivan Popov was in the room had made for a difficult situation. And Cabe never been more ready to pull the trigger than in the moments the two men they now knew as guys who ran Sokolov's imports and exports had overstepped their boundaries. The way they'd watched Amy when they thought she wasn't looking sickened Cabe. They found reasons to brush up against her between games. And they'd also followed her upstairs.

Up-fucking-stairs.

He'd felt as though he were having a heart attack as he'd learned there were *armed* men poised in the doorway to the office.

That was what kept his temper bubbling . . . a mental replay of Six's comm message that he had sight of Amy in a room on the second floor. With the curtains open and the light behind her from the hallway, apparently her hair had been unmistakable, so Harley and Lite had kept their weapons trained on the two members of Sokolov's security team patrolling the grounds in case they looked up and saw her too, while Six kept his weapon trained on the space to left of Amy's shoulder to take out anyone he needed to.

Which he hadn't.

But still.

And Cabe had committed the cardinal sin . . . he'd taken his eye off his own targets to look through his scope at Amy. Even though he was humble enough to admit Six was the superior sniper, he'd felt the need to add his own weapon to those already protecting her.

And the whole time, Cabe had had to keep his shit together because he hadn't come clean to the guys about the nature of their relationship. And the guys hadn't asked. Which meant it was either painfully fucking obvious or they had no clue. He guessed it was the former.

Lifting his arms overhead, he stood and full body stretched before pulling on a pair of shorts. He wandered into the open-plan living space. It had large balcony doors on one end, a bright kitchen on the other, and the comfiest huge sofa they'd been able to find in between. Jess had insisted on a bright kitchen. The day they'd seen this apartment, she'd leapt into his arms before even getting as far as the bedrooms and bathrooms, declaring it was the one.

He popped a capsule into the Keurig and set it to brew.

Once this was all over, he wanted to invite Amy over to stay. He surveyed his place with the eye of a guy bringing his lover home.

He reached into the fridge to grab milk for his coffee and saw the picture of him and Jess from New Year's Eve a few years before, her holding up a mustache on a stick, him wearing a pair of Elton-John-circa-1970 glasses. Carefully, he pulled the picture off the fridge and put it on the counter before adding milk to his coffee. As he drank, he sifted through the other random things attached to the fridge. The note she'd left him to remind the landlord to fix the balcony door lock, a picture of them at one of the many military balls they'd attended together, one of the few occasions Jess would bother to wear a dress or makeup.

When he was done, there were two piles on the counter. Things to toss, and things to put in a box of memories for now.

Grabbing his cup, he went to the living room and surveyed the mantel over the fireplace. Photographs. More memories. He pulled down the one of them celebrating climbing Mount Fuji, another of them hanging out by the pool at his mom's place, a third at some restaurant he couldn't remember where they were both drinking giant margaritas with upturned bottles of Corona in them. One by one, he took them all down. Even, finally, the one of him on one knee before a giant waterfall, Jess grinning as she realized he was proposing. He ran his finger on the glass along her cheek and sighed. "I'm sorry, Jess, but I need to move on."

Light suddenly flooded the apartment as the sun made its way over the building in front of his. It hit the cleared expanse of the fridge. It felt like a sign. A sign that a couple of months ago he wouldn't have believed in or perhaps he simply wouldn't have noticed. "Thank you, Jess," he said, knowing the love he had felt for her was now something nebulous and nostalgic rather than tangible and real.

An hour later, Cabe arrived at the FBI office with his team. Amy was already seated on the other side of the table, and even though he'd woken up still frustrated by her recklessness, he couldn't help but smile at her. For a moment, she looked confused, as if she didn't know what he was doing, and then she smiled back.

"Okay, folks," Cunningham said once they were all seated. "Who's going to lead this update?"

Cabe sat forward. "I am." He nodded toward the screen where Six had launched their presentation.

"We believe we have identified the smurf ring," he began, before explaining how they'd found their lead and identified two other men who had exhibited similar behavior in the casino. Names, images, histories appeared on the screen, along with copies of the file that would be distributed at the end. "What we haven't identified is where they are getting the cash, so each member is being trailed until we know their source. Because they only just did a run, we anticipate it being another week before they do another drop. There is only one cashier involved. Whether she has Woods's approval will be hard to prove, but we know that those transactions appear to be being entered in one lump sum. So unless he isn't checking his sheets daily, he *must* be turning a blind eye to it. It's easier to track her now that we know who she is."

There were murmured comments, generally of approval.

"I'm going to hand over to Agent Murray to update on the women," Cabe said.

Amy looked up at him, as if surprised by the chance to lead the update. It was only fair she got the opportunity to lead a part of the meeting.

"With regards to the missing women. We have reason to believe there is an offshore gaming ring that the women are trafficked through," she said, her voice clear and confident. "First, we have the search history of the latest victim. In all these cases, the victims' apartments were made to look as though the victim had moved on, taking her most significant possessions. None of these women lived in places with CCTV, so we haven't found any footage of them leaving. But in this latest case, the victim had left her laptop with a tech friend to remove a virus. We found that she'd been researching international waters gaming rules and methods to combat seasickness. And it appears Woods is grooming the candidates. With me, he's always made it seem as though what he is setting up is doing me a favor, helping me with my career. That he sees potential in me and wants to help me get ahead."

Cabe shuddered at the assessment.

"Do you have any idea where this offshore gaming is happening?" Cunningham asked.

"Not yet," Amy answered. "But I found an invoice at Sokolov's home for a marina."

"I've not had a chance to update Agent Murray, but we connected some of the dots this morning. The invoice she found was in the name of Ekaterina Petrov, which is Sokolov's mother's maiden name."

Amy barely moved, but her eyes met his and positively fucking sparkled. A look that he wanted to put on her face every day if he could. But they hadn't had conversations that ran that way yet.

Six coughed loudly next to him, snapping his gaze away from Amy.

"We are going in tonight to put surveillance on their boat. Amy's belief is that the casino chips and cash from the private party at Sokolov's will now be rotated through the casino by Woods, but we're awaiting confirmation of that too. Amy and my team have been watching for that. It hasn't happened through the front of the house, so it can only be happening behind the scenes, which would support our working theory that Woods is more than simply complicit. He's an active participant in the money laundering. We're running histories of Woods and Sokolov again to see if we can't get our arms around the relationship between these two. Something is niggling me about it. How did it start? Who initiated it? What is the power dynamic?"

"We got enough to go now," one of the agents focused on the enforcement of RICO said. "We have video footage of smurfing, enough to get a warrant and go in and search. Why are we waiting for this?"

"Because," Amy said, her tone deadly, "there are missing women involved, and if we move on the laundering before we understand where these women are, we'll never get our leads on them." She turned to Cunningham. "Let's follow up on the marina, follow the leads that make us think there is offshore gambling. These two cases are so inextricably linked that we can't move on one until we are fully ready to move on the other. And we are still a week or two away from what we think will be the next roundup of women. The evidence we have won't go away, and we have eyes on all the key players. Unless they get spooked, they aren't going anywhere."

Cunningham looked at the agent who had spoken and then at Aitken. "I agree with Agent Murray. Patience will be the only thing that gets us all the answers."

"For what it's worth," Cabe said, "Agent Murray has our support on that too. She has done a fantastic job at ingratiating herself into Woods's and Sokolov's company. If there is an illegal offshore gaming ring that could possibly be linked to the missing women, we need her to get on the boat."

Tapping his fingers on the table, Cunningham studied Amy, and she held his gaze.

As if satisfied with what he saw there, Cunningham nodded. "Agreed. Two more weeks, but if anything changes during that time, we reconvene and review. Nobody does anything without my authorization."

There were a few more discussions before the meeting wrapped up and the room emptied. "We should go," said Six, looking between Cabe and Amy.

"I just need to talk to Amy real quick. I'll see you at your truck in five."

Six nodded and left the two of them to the low hum of the air-conditioning.

"You found the boat?" Amy asked as soon as Six left.

Cabe smiled at her across the table and wondered if he'd always feel the pull to stand next to her, to touch her, to just be with her. "No. *You* found the boat. I just followed up on your lead. And I need to say something to you that has been festering. Well, two things. As your colleague, it was a ballsy move to go into the office, and it paid off, but it could have gone to shit. Next time, for all of our sakes, let's talk through all the scenarios ahead of time so we can have your back in a way that's planned, not on the fly."

"Fair point and understood," she said.

"No disagreement?"

Amy shook her head. "You were right. It was reckless. I was only thinking about people who could find me inside the house. I didn't think of security being able to see in the window, so yes, it was stupid. It could have ruined what we've been trying to do."

Shit. If he wasn't falling in love with her before, he was now. She hadn't made any excuses and had stepped up to accept a mistake.

"What was the second?" she asked.

"As your boyfriend, please don't give me a fucking heart attack like that. I'm growing attached to that pretty face of yours, and I really don't want it to get damaged. Are we clear? Because next time I'm coming in after you, Ames. Neither hell nor high water will be able to stop me."

This time she grinned. "Are we going steady, Captain Moss?" she whispered, checking outside the conference room windows for anybody lingering in the hallway.

It turned him on that she'd used his former title, even though he no longer did. "You'd be shocked if you knew my thoughts about you, *Agent* Murray. Hopefully it won't be too much longer before I can show you."

"I look forward to the day we are as simple as that. I just . . . I hate to say we need to keep us a secret. It feels so juvenile. But we do. Just know I'm thinking about you too."

He knew her other concerns still existed about people finding out about the two of them, and he would do just about anything to protect her from that. So, for now, he'd give her the secrecy she needed.

And he'd wait for the day it was no longer needed.

CHAPTER SIXTEEN

Amy could smell the mouthwatering scent of apples and cinnamon and vanilla and some other delicious baking smells that she couldn't quite put her finger on from the street. But what else had she expected from the woman who was to make Six and Louisa's wedding cake?

When Cabe had invited her to join them for a family barbecue, she'd jumped at the chance. The opportunity to experience him off duty, around friends and family, was the closest she'd come to going on a date with him since their *non-date* dinner in Vegas. Their previous attempt, the overnight at Beacon's Beach, had been a dud after her phone call from Woods. But this, hanging out with him in his childhood home, was perfect.

And discreet.

Not wanting to blow their cover, they'd driven out of the city separately, Cabe's truck shadowing her car along the highway. When she'd looked in her rearview mirror and caught a glance of him, she hadn't been able to stop smiling. He'd looked so capable driving, his dark hair blowing around thanks to the open windows, his aviator shades glinting occasionally in the sun.

She parked behind him and waited as Cabe got out of the truck and walked over to her, opening her door like the gentleman he was.

"Did I tell you how pretty you look today?" he asked, taking his hand in hers. The light breeze tousled the ends of his hair.

"Not since this morning when I got dressed," she replied, unable to contain her grin.

She was about to rise on her toes to kiss him when a cop she recognized from the SDPD walked from the side of the house to a car farther down the street. Cabe followed the direction she was looking. "I guess my brother invited some of his friends."

Amy sighed, the realization that today wouldn't be the day they got to be themselves throbbed like a bad tooth. "Is it wrong that I just wanted to be . . . you know . . . us . . . for the afternoon?"

Cabe squeezed her hand then released it. "No," he replied. "I completely know what you mean. I wanted the chance to introduce you to my family quietly. They are used to me being . . . well . . . Jess was a part of the family for them too. I wanted to give them time to adjust to the idea of us."

She wanted to reach for him, to hold him, to tell him that she understood. But as she did so, the cop raised his hand in their direction and they both stepped away and waved back.

"Discreet it is then," Amy said.

"We'll get our time, Ames. I promise you." Cabe led them up the porch and through the front door.

"Cabe, is that you?" a voice shouted from the kitchen.

"Yeah, Mom," Cabe replied from over Amy's shoulder. "I brought a guest."

Amy turned quickly. "You didn't tell her I was coming?"

He shrugged. "I didn't want to turn it into a big deal," he whispered as his mother came into view. She was the same height as Amy, with dark hair like her son's clipped back from her face and a welcoming smile. But it was hard to miss the questioning look in her eyes. "Mom, this is Agent Amy Murray. We work together. Amy, this is my mom, Deandra, but everyone calls her Dee."

"Agent Murray." Not "girlfriend." He was giving her exactly what they'd discussed only moments before on the curb, wasn't he? He wasn't touching her. In fact, the gap between them had grown since his mom had entered the room. But the distance felt like an ocean. And for a fleeting moment, she felt a whisper of jealousy. That another woman had stood where Amy was standing right now, and she wondered if Cabe was feeling a little displaced like she was.

Amy offered his mom her hand, ingrained manners and poker face kicking in to mask the sinking feeling in her stomach. "Pleased to meet you, Dee."

Cabe's mom took her hand and pulled her into a hug. "I'm very pleased to meet you, Amy," she said. "Come out back. Everyone is out on the deck." Dee took Amy's hand and led them outside. "Hey, everybody, Cabe brought a *friend*. This is Amy."

The silence didn't quite descend to the point where tumbleweed blew across the deck, but it was pretty damn close. A man she immediately identified as Cabe's father stood. They had the same muscular build and dark eyes. Mac seemed surprised to see her. Six didn't . . . at all. In fact, he turned and murmured something to the woman she assumed was Louisa, who abruptly looked up from beneath long bangs.

"Leave her alone, Mom," Cabe said, stepping out onto the deck behind her. "You know Mac." His breath brushed the back of her neck as he spoke. "That's his girlfriend, Delaney, sitting next to him. In the corner is Six's fiancée, Louisa. Both women deserve medals for putting up with the two of them."

Delaney waved, and Louisa smiled.

"Over by the pool are Mac's and Six's parents. And in it is my brother Noah and two of his friends from SDPD, Mike Purchall and you already saw Ermano Rivera." Cabe grabbed two beers from the cooler and offered one in her direction. Amy nodded and he opened it before handing it to her, at which point he jogged down the steps to talk to his brother.

"Are you with the FBI?" Dee asked. "The agent title kind of gave it away."

Amy nodded, returning her attention to his mom. "I am. You have a beautiful yard," she said, attempting to ignore the fact that Cabe had just slid his shirt over his head. The muscles in his back flexed as he gestured something to Noah.

Dee looked in the direction of Amy's gaze and smiled. "Thank you. It's been a work in progress for years. How long have you known Cabe?"

It irked Amy that Cabe had just abandoned her to his mom, who hadn't even known to expect her. It wasn't like she was the clingy girlfriend who needed to be glued to his side. But a couple more minutes of running interference and making sure she was cool before he headed off might have been helpful. "Oh, only five weeks or so.

We're working together at the moment. Whatever you
have baking in there smells delicious. Do you need a
hand?"

"You can come help me frost some cupcakes if you
like."

Amy smiled. "I'd love that." Her mom had loved to
bake. Pies, cakes, bread. Their Vegas home had always
smelled amazing on a Sunday afternoon. One of her favorite memories was dipping her fingers into the bowl of
lemon drizzle or the cream cheese frosting for her mom's
secret-recipe carrot cake.

Nearly two hours later, Amy had iced cupcakes;
helped Dee bring the food out to the patio for the barbecue; discussed the validity of digital currency with Mac's
father; and gotten to know Delaney, who was hilarious
and irreverent, and Louisa, who was as shy as she'd been
billed, but smarter than just about anybody she knew.
What she hadn't done was talk to Cabe. Or sit with Cabe.
Or swim with Cabe.

Despite the fact that she was overwhelmed by how
friendly everybody was being, she got the distinct feeling she wasn't supposed to be there . . . or even worse,
that Cabe was regretting bringing her. He'd barely looked
her way that afternoon beyond a single heated stare when
she'd removed her T-shirt to reveal her favorite aqua-and-
white-striped bikini.

And she was being petty. Being completely ridiculous.
We'll get our time, Ames. I promise you.

She knew he'd meant those words. But something had
changed in the time she'd spent with Cabe's family. They
were good, honest people. And she felt like a fraud, sitting on the deck pretending she and Cabe weren't something . . . more. It felt deceptive. And though it was the

right thing to do, she was beginning to feel uncomfortable. It felt like an undercover role that didn't fit.

She sat and finished her burger and fries, which were beyond good, and made plans to leave. Six took a seat on the deck steps next to her, holding his bottle of beer by the neck between his fingers. "You doing okay, Amy?"

"Mmm," she answered, chewing the last mouthful of her burger. "It's been great. Nice to do something not work related for a change. But on that note, I think I'm going to head out before it gets dark and do some work."

Six looked up at the sky and laughed. "You know it's not getting dark for another two hours, right?"

Amy smiled. "Yes, I do, but . . ."

He raised an eyebrow. "But what?"

She couldn't explain to Six what she was feeling. How once she'd gotten here and Cabe had left her to her own devices as they'd discussed, she hadn't felt quite so certain of herself—which as a card-carrying feminist irked her something chronic. She didn't need a man to know her place or value, but . . .

Damn. There was that "but" again. She wiped her hands on her napkin and stood to take her plate to the garbage.

"Hey, Cabe," Six shouted across the yard to the pool. "You better come say goodbye. Your woman's going home because you ignored her for the last few hours, you douchebag."

Amy's head spun as she took in the shock on everyone's faces. Mac came barreling down the stairs so that he stood between Six and Cabe. She could hear Dee's gasp behind her.

Her face was flaming red, she was sure of it. There was no other reason for her cheeks to feel so hot. And the dizziness she was feeling wasn't from spending too much time in the sun.

Cabe looked absolutely furious as he drew himself up out of the pool using just his arms. He was menacing as he walked toward Six without sparing her a glance. Mac stepped up to Cabe and braced his hands on Cabe's chest. "You know he runs his mouth off."

Six was grinning as he raised his hands in surrender. "Don't know why you're getting pissed with me, big guy," he said. "Tell me what I said that isn't true. You said you were leaving, right, Amy?"

No matter how badly she didn't want to be drawn into this, she had no choice. "I did," she said.

"And you did ignore her for the last few hours, right?" Six continued. "We all saw it."

Cabe's chest heaved as he breathed deeply, in and out. "You don't understand. Amy has reasons she doesn't want this broadcast everywhere."

Six took a step closer, a risky move given the mood Cabe appeared to be in. "But she *is* your woman, right?"

The words stopped Cabe in his tracks. He looked to her before knocking Mac's hands away as if they were nothing. Instead of approaching Six, he headed for her, walking up the steps of the deck until they were face-to-face.

"Is he right?" Cabe asked, quietly. "Because we talked about this."

"Now isn't the time," Amy replied, attempting to put a smile on her face, to diffuse the situation Six had created.

"Now is as good a time as any," Cabe said, and she was grateful that even though people could see them, they couldn't hear them.

"It's stupid of me to be upset by something I asked for. But being this close to you, yet not feeling like I belong here, or that you even want me here, really hurts. Even though . . . I hope . . . it's an act."

"You know it's an act. You have no idea how hard it's been to stay away from you."

Everyone was watching, the scene as public as it could get. "What do we do?" she whispered.

"Can I touch you? Because I really need to, Ames."

Amy nodded, knowing the move would remove any shred of uncertainty about the status of their relationship.

Cabe took another step up and placed his hands on her hips. "Ames. I come with baggage. And so do you. You told me that nobody could know about us. So I didn't tell them, although it appears that dick over there figured it out," he said, tilting his head in the direction of Six, who was now slipping his arm around Louisa. "I didn't tell my mom that I'd met a woman because I knew she'd make a bigger deal out of it than you'd be comfortable with, even though it's a really big fucking deal for me— and for my family. They've seen how I've been the last two years. They've urged me to move on. It's been painful to stay away from you all day . . . but I don't think I can be next to you and not do this, anymore."

He placed his palms on her cheeks and cupped her face gently before pressing his lips to hers. Immediately forgetting where they were and who they were with, she slid her hands around his waist. As the cool water on his chest soaked through her bikini top, she ignored the cheers and hoots and hollers. Her heart raced as she processed the fact that he'd been thinking of her even when she hadn't been thinking about herself. And she loved him for it. A part of her wanted to tell him as much, but here wasn't the place.

"Do you still need to leave?" he said, grinning as he slid a hand up her back, sliding it deliciously under the strap of her bikini.

Amy looked down at his arm, suddenly overwhelmed by a wave of shyness she didn't normally experience. "No. Do I get play in the pool with you?"

"Ames," he said, bending suddenly to throw her over the shoulder. "You can play with me wherever you want."

Even though she was still wearing her shorts, Cabe jumped into the pool. When they surfaced, he reached for her and pulled her to him.

And kissed her again in front of every single person who mattered.

Bodies were everywhere, and he was violently sick at the sight.

They were lined up like railroad ties on an old track with just enough room between them for him to place his feet as he walked over them.

It was an old dream, one he hadn't had in a while, but Cabe couldn't force himself to wake up. It felt too real. Too much. And he needed to know how it ended.

Sokolov was at the end of the hallway, sitting on a throne, and the bodies were screaming and writhing in agony, their limbs bloodied, their clothes torn.

But it was their faces, wide eyed and in pain, that terrified him the most.

Because he knew every single person. The first few—members of his old SEAL team, Mac, Six, warriors who went into battle knowing the possible outcomes but did so anyway—he forced himself to step over. In the throes of death, they encouraged him to carry on, to finish the mission. Some were draped with American flags, like they had been when they'd taken that final flight home. He could force himself to leave them behind for now, though it killed him inside. Brock, his childhood friend who'd died while they were cliff-jumping reached out his arms toward Cabe and began to vomit seaweed and water. Another person he hadn't been able to save. The next was his mom, and then Delaney, whose hair had all been shaved off. And then there was Lou, who was screaming out Six's name in a voice so hoarse it brought tears to his eyes. He crouched by her and she gripped his arm, digging her nails into his skin. "Where is Six?" she gasped. "Why didn't he come for me?"

There were two more bodies. One to the left of the throne, and one to the right.

As he got closer, he realized that one was Jess and the other Amy.

He had to choose.

Jess reached out to him. Amy remained still. His feet wouldn't move. His brain couldn't calculate the risk, figure out the odds. But his heart suddenly pounded in his chest, a sound so loud that Sokolov began to laugh.

Cabe stepped in Amy's direction just as Sokolov pulled out Cabe's favorite SIG and pointed it directly at Jess's chest before pulling the trigger. Cabe ran toward Amy until his lungs burned and his chest ached, but she kept moving farther and farther away.

"*You* killed her," Sokolov shouted. "Remember that, Cabe."

Remember that.

He sat upright in bed, taking the covers with him, gasping for breath, and searching for her with his hand.

Latching gently onto Amy's calf, he steadied himself. The clock said 3:01 and they were in Amy's old apartment. Jesus Christ. The dream.

You killed her.

Sweat clung to his skin, leaving him chilled to the bone.

He felt Amy stir, and was surprised when she took to her knees, one on either side of his thighs, and pressed her naked chest against his back. Usually that would be enough to snap him out of any funk, but the nightmare had gotten its claws into him and he couldn't shake it.

Her lips pressed to his shoulder as her arms slipped around him. "What was it about?"

"I'm sorry," he said, his voice rough. "I didn't mean to wake you."

"There's no need to be sorry for that," she said. "You were tossing and turning. I didn't know what to do. You called out my name . . . and Jess's."

He placed his hand over hers and pressed her palm to his chest so she could feel how his heart raced. He knew it was all confusion, just the rewiring of his brain as he changed and adapted to his relationship with Amy, but the dream had felt so real. "Sokolov had you. Had you both. And a hundred other people that I know. He had hurt you, all of you. And in the end, he expected me to pick between you and Jess."

They sat in silence, the occasional sound of the air-conditioning clicking on and off. "That must have been an impossible choice," Amy said finally, running a trail of kisses along his shoulder.

Not *Who did you pick?* Or *Did you choose me?* Or worse, *Did you choose her?*

She was just caring for him, and for a few moments of silence, he let her.

"I have nightmares occasionally," she said softly. "About Mom. I see her in a crowded street, but she's fading out of focus, and there are too many people for me to catch up to her. I know how brutal they can be."

"Yeah, they can." He needed her to know that he'd moved on. "Do you know what I started to do on Thursday?" He ran his palms along her thighs.

Amy rested her chin on his shoulder so their cheeks were close. "No. Tell me?"

"I started to deal with some things in my apartment so that when this is done, you can come sleep over."

"That's sweet of you, but I'm sure you didn't need to—"

"I packed up stuff to do with Jess. It started while I was drinking coffee and thinking of you and how amazing it's going to be when this is over, and I suddenly saw my place through your eyes." Cabe turned to face her, meeting her in the middle of the bed on his knees. "It was a sickening dream, Ames," he said, sliding his hand around the back of her neck, "but it wasn't a difficult choice. I never thought I'd find what I had with Jess with anyone else. I never imagined I would find something . . . more."

"'More' is a good word for us," she said.

The tenderness with which she said the words filled his heart. "'Love' is another good word," he said, taking a chance to lay his true feelings at her knees. "I love you, Ames."

Her eyes fluttered shut, and a soft smile graced her features as she sighed. "When we talked on the steps at your mom's, I thought then that I loved you for thinking of me, for protecting me that way. I love you too, Cabe."

God, he wasn't sure what he'd done to deserve a second chance at love in his life, but he was eternally fucking grateful. Gently, he nudged Amy back onto the bed and kissed her. Kissed her slowly, and deeply, with kisses that made his own head swim and his balls tighten as she moved and groaned beneath him.

"Tell me you have condoms," he said as he kissed a trail of kisses along her neck, knowing he'd used the one in his wallet with her when they'd first arrived here, a decision they'd made on the way home. It was their safe haven, away from the op, the one place they were simply Cabe and Amy.

"In the drawer," she replied, pointing to the table at the side of the bed.

"Thank God." If she'd said no, he'd have been in his shorts and sneakers looking for an open CVS.

Amy ran her fingers through his hair as he settled in the soft cradle of her thighs. There was no better place to be on this earth. He loved her, and by some miracle she loved him. He felt like he was exactly where he was meant to be. The thought gave him pause. He wanted to slow down and make love to Amy thoroughly.

He kissed her collarbone, where she still smelled of chlorine from the pool. They been so anxious to get naked that they hadn't stopped to shower. He kissed the top of his shoulder, strong with muscles. And he kissed the soft valley between her breasts. Worshipping her body was the only way he could think of to convince her that she was everything.

There had been no choice.

He'd wanted her.

He'd picked her.

– Gently, he slid a hand along the curve of her waist as he ran his lips along the tanned skin of her stomach. Devour her. That's what he wanted to do. He knelt between her legs and pushed her thighs wide with his palms while she stared at him with nothing in her eyes but a love he wasn't even sure he deserved.

When he placed his thumb gently over her clit, rubbing softly back and forth, Amy sighed. He studied the way her lips turned pink and began to swell, watched the first signs of wetness appear, and ignored the fact that his cock was hard and ready, lying heavy between his thighs.

Tonight was for savoring.

Tonight was to put a stamp on who they were together.

Tonight was about her.

"You're beautiful, Ames." His voice was gruff, his emotions heavy in his chest. Their only connection was his thumb on her clit, yet he could feel her in every cell of his body. The muscles in her stomach clenched occasionally until eventually her back arched, her eyes closed, and she gasped. "Could I get you off like this, I wonder?"

"Cabe, please." Amy opened her eyes, her mouth still open, a perfect O.

"What do you want, sweetheart? You want my fingers sliding in and out of you, reaching for the place you love so much? Or this?" He reached down and took hold of his cock, stroking it long and hard. "Because I want to give you everything you want, everything you need, everything you deserve. Nothing you can ask of me is too much. Do you understand that?"

Amy nodded, too in the moment to speak.

He bent forward and replaced his thumb with his mouth, lapping her slowly, then circling her clit in fast hard strokes until he traced straight over the swollen bud. God, he loved the taste of her. Loved the way she moved beneath him, the way she opened for him.

"Oh, God. Yes. Just like that," she said, threading her fingers through his hair and holding him where she wanted.

When he added a finger, he could feel the telltale tightening. He could tell when her mind lost control and her body took over.

But he wanted to be buried deep inside her when she finally came. He wanted to be in her, and on her, and with her, as close as one human could be to another. Because the dream had only been about one thing and he knew it. He couldn't lose her.

"No, Cabe, I was so close," she cried out when he withdrew his finger from her and sucked it into his mouth.

"I know, Ames," he said, reaching for the condoms in the drawer. After he slid one on, he lowered his body back over her and guided himself into her. Fuck, he was so turned on, so ready. Desperate to make it last, he stopped for a moment and framed her face with his hands, pushing her hair back so he could see her clearly. So he could take in eyes bluer than any water he'd ever dived into. "Call me a greedy man, but I wanted to feel you come around my cock."

He slid one of his hands beneath her and gripped her ass, opening her to him even more. Then he began to move, a slow and steady lovemaking that took the two of them deeper and deeper until he was nothing but the sensation of where they were connected, until they came together.

And while his heart still raced, and her breath came fast, "I love you" took on a whole different meaning.

CHAPTER SEVENTEEN

Cabe studied the layout of the hundred-and-fourteen-foot yacht that lay on Eagle Securities' conference room table. The ship was registered in Sokolov's mom's name, but seeing that Ekaterina Petrov was currently in Rostov-on-Don, part of the East European Plain of Russia, Cabe was pretty sure the yacht wasn't actually hers.

"You going to kick my ass if I come in?" Six asked.

It was hard to remain mad, not when his mom had kissed him and told him how happy she was that he was finally moving on and told him that Amy was an amazing woman. He'd drawn the line when she'd offered a six-tier red velvet wedding cake, only vaguely hearing a comment about grandchildren that had caused Amy to cover her mouth to hide the laughter.

He'd tried to scowl at Amy, but he got why they were all happy. Because *he* was. Happy to be himself with Amy.

But during all that, Six had made his escape with Louisa. And the air between the two of them wasn't completely clear. Because while the outcome had ended up being positive, Six had been out of line.

On the drive home, it had dawned on Cabe that he was the only person who hadn't believed he was entitled to his own happily ever after.

"You're lucky Mac got to me before I got to you yesterday," he said, sliding his hands into his pockets.

"Yeah. I get that. But it was hurting my stone-cold heart watching the two of you act like you barely knew each other."

Cabe battled his indecision. To trust his friend, like he always had, or keep Amy's secrets for her. He allowed silence to settle around him and listened to his gut. "Amy suffered sexual harassment at the hands of a senior agent in Atlanta. It's why she moved here."

"No shit," Six said, and pulled out a chair. "That's rough."

"Yeah." Cabe sat too. "At first she wasn't believed, then some thought she'd asked for it. Me and her, this op, me technically senior to her. She's worried about perception. About the optics of us dating. And Noah's buddies from the SDPD were there yesterday."

"Fuck. You guys were just on the down low because of optics. Man, I'm sorry. I'll apologize to Amy when I see her."

"Luckily for you, we're good. And Noah talked it through with his friends. He trusts them to keep it quiet. It was a dick move to out us like that, though. When did you figure it out?"

Six ran his hand through his hair. "That bullshit you fed us when we were breaking into the casino. I don't know. The way you talked about her spoke volumes. And

I'm gonna give you permission to kick my ass for even saying this, but you've been happy. I remember that day you came back to our tour after Jess's funeral and you became a machine, a robot. And sure, you've loosened up in recent months, but . . . You've seemed more like Cabe, the little shit I sat next to on our first day of Junior Kindergarten."

Cabe swallowed, then nodded. It was impossible to stay mad at his friend after his honest words. "I'm just counting down the days until this is over so we can go public instead of having to hide."

"Lou really liked her, for what it's worth, as did Delaney. And your mom. You know she called my mom this morning to ask if she knew which wedding shop Lou got her dress from, just in case Amy asks her to go dress shopping, given that it's just Amy and her dad."

Cabe rubbed his face and grinned. "I want to be mad at her, but for some reason . . ."

Six laughed. "You're sunk."

"*If* I end up marrying Amy, there is only one place she'll want it to happen. Caesars Palace. If it doesn't, I'm seriously concerned her uncle Clive will get an old-school hit man to take my ass out."

"Well, when this is over, and we go there before my wedding, I look forward to meeting him!" Six stood, yanked Cabe out of his chair, and pulled him into a hug, the kind they rarely shared. "I'm happy for you," he said gruffly, then let go before facing the scaled drawing of the yacht. "It's a good-looking boat."

It was. Chrome-effect paint on the fiberglass hull reflected the water, making it look like the upper levels hovered in the air. "Yeah," Cabe agreed. "If this guy is doing what we think he's doing, it's ironic that he thinks nothing about selling women into the sex trade, but named his boat *Katie* because he loves his momma."

Six shook his head. "That's totally fucked-up."

"We need a place to put the beacon." They were going in tonight to put it on the ship, since there was a high probability that whatever was going down was happening there.

Mac and Harley had gone out to do basic intel on the boat and the harbor. Buddha and Bailey were looking at local ordinance maps to find ways into the water that didn't include walking in through the main entrance or swimming the shipping lanes.

Hours later, after he'd called Amy on her way to the latest shift at the casino and long after the sun had gone down, he found himself dressed in his dive gear, rebreather set at the ready, in a draining channel. They'd studied the plans for the marina over and over, but this was definitely the most covert way. And it stunk like shit. Through his night goggles, he could see firsthand how the warm weather had caused the slow-moving water to stagnate. Smelly or not, slow and steady was the only way in. Mac and Six followed him. Maybe it was because he'd read way too many adventure stories as a kid, but he'd always gotten a kick out of doing missions with his best friends.

The ripples of water around their ankles sloshed despite their efforts to remain silent, but in the pitch of night they wouldn't be seen. Dressed from head to toe in their wetsuits, they would blend into the darkness. Six carried a rolled caving ladder, and Cabe carried a telescopic pole. The drainage channel opened out into the marina, and

Cabe went first, popping the mouthpiece of the rebreather unit into his mouth before dropping himself silently into the shallows.

They'd decide to use the closed-circuit rebreathers rather than the open-circuit scuba gear to conceal their dive. Bubbles were underwater stealth work's nemesis, and the last thing they needed was somebody on the *Katie* or a neighboring boat spotting the bubbles and trying to figure out what they were coming from.

The water was dark but became clearer once they moved away from the drainage channel. The three of them had been members of the same swim team once upon a time, and later their life as SEALs had trained them to be both powerful and silent under the water. As they swam around the top of the first dock, Mac signaled three with his fingers, reminding Cabe to swim beneath three of the berths.

Cabe took his dive a little deeper, silently gliding under the hull of the first large yacht. There was obviously a loud party on board, the dull thud of music sounding like it was coming through a chamber filled with cotton wool. They steered clear of the engine, staying close to the bow and away from the stern.

One boat, two boats. When they got to the third hull, Mac, the strongest swimmer of the three, swam beneath the water to the other side of the dock and hid in the shadows. Cabe could no longer see him, but knew he was going to quietly go above water and assess whether it was safe for Cabe to surface.

When Mac returned, he pointed to the hull and showed a fist. No fingers meant no people.

As silently as they'd entered the water, they raised

their heads above it. Cabe let go of his mouthpiece, letting it drop to his chest. He extended the pole and hooked it on the top rung of the caving ladder. As Cabe pushed the hooks at the top of the ladder higher, it unraveled. With little effort, he was able to get the ladder hooked over the side of the boat.

It would have been easier to simply hoist themselves onto the back of the boat and find somewhere to hide the beacon, but it would have been impossible to clean the deck of the water from their wetsuits, and an eager deckhand tasked with cleaning down the boat daily would certainly have noticed the wet tracks or semi-dried footprints that would have led to wherever they hid the beacon.

"Where are you taking me?" a female voice said with a giggle.

Cabe looked onto the dock and listened for footsteps, for more voices, for anything that would give him clues as to what to do next. Six made a play to take the pole Cabe was holding to lower the ladder, but Cabe put his hand on Six's arm.

"Somewhere a little more private," the male voice replied. It sounded young. Cabe guessed that if they just ducked back into the water, the couple would be too wrapped up in each other to question a chain ladder on the side of a boat. He slipped his mouthpiece back between his lips, as did Six, who quietly collapsed the pole and disappeared beneath the surface.

"You know I want to go with you, but we can't. My dad will come looking for us."

"Babe, I just want to touch you, you know."

"I want to touch you too," she said, her laughter ringing out through the air.

Cabe felt their pain. There were moments he felt the exact same way about Amy, and despite being in cold water waiting for cock-blocked teens to figure their shit out, he smiled around his mouthpiece.

The footsteps soon led back to the party boat, and Cabe began to climb. The moment he cleared the water, he stood still and allowed the water to drip off him as he looped his arm around the next rung and cleared the chamber of his gun by cocking it slightly, just until he could see the round. Water dripping sounded like a five-bell alarm in the quiet of the night, and he was grateful for the music coming from the boat. He held his breath, waiting for someone to hear or come rushing to see what was happening.

But nobody did.

He climbed the final rungs until he could lean over the edge of the deck and reach for the door of a small storage locker built into the side of the fiberglass hull. Once it was open, he ripped the waterproof package from his belt and released the beacon into his palm. Careful not to drip onto the deck or allow the ladder to touch the side of the boat, which would disturb the natural dew that was settling on the white hull, he reached into the locker and felt around for the perfect spot. He slid the GPS beacon into the gap, pushing it in until it was secure.

When he was certain it was, he closed the door to the narrow locker and crept back down the ladder, slipping silently into the water.

Six raised the pole and lowered the ladder, wincing as the metal clanged against itself.

"Hey, you?" a second male voice shouted. "What are you doing out here?" It was louder, gruffer.

Was the voice calling to them? He wasn't certain, but he remained calm.

The sound of three quick cracks of gunfire echoed through the air, as the same number of bullets hit the water three feet to the left of Cabe's head.

Cabe put his mouthpiece back in, grabbed the end of the ladder, and dove beneath the water, keeping it taut. The breather units were only good to six meters, after which there was a risk of oxygen toxicity levels rising quickly.

Six submerged with the end of the ladder and the two of them moved beneath the safety of the boat. Cabe began to roll the ladder as Six collapsed the pole. They still had plenty of air, but they needed a plan of escape. Cabe pointed toward the dock, dipping his hand to suggest they go under it.

Six nodded.

As they began to move, two more bullets hit the water, then the rumbling thunder of feet running down the dock. Which potentially meant more guns, with hopefully equally lousy aim.

Cabe took the lead, swimming under the dock, and beneath the yacht moored on the other side. Mac, always such a strong underwater swimmer, pulled up alongside them.

Beams from a flashlight illuminated the water close to where they were hiding before moving farther away. Cabe signaled them into deeper water, where, in the shadow of the last docked boat, he raised his head above the waterline. The idiots were only checking around the original berth.

Submerging once more, Cabe led the three of them to the point where they'd entered the water.

And then, as silently as they'd arrived, they left the marina.

Exhaustion was an awful thing to battle in high heels, Amy thought as she dealt her final cards of the night.

The hours were starting to build. The job at the casino filled her forty-hour-a-week quotient. But layered on top of that were the hours spent at Eagle and FBI headquarters. And then there were the reports and the updates.

And the sex.

She couldn't help the smile that escaped as she thought of the sex, and the love, and the raw side of Cabe she'd witnessed the previous evening. That side of Cabe had made love to her and after only a matter of moments had taken her again as if his very life had depended on it.

His dream had scared her at first, but she'd thought a lot about what it must be like to be a widow. To be single not because love had disappeared, but because the person you were in love with had. There had been moments since Cabe had told her about Jess that she'd wondered whether she would ever measure up, ever be enough to capture Cabe's full heart instead of just the bit he'd managed to wrench away from Jess.

But now she knew deep down inside and with complete and utter certainty that Cabe was hers. It was a wonderful feeling. At least, it would be if Cabe wasn't currently in the marina putting a beacon on the boat. She glanced across to the bar were Sokolov was sitting with three of his associates. Just because he was in the casino, didn't mean Cabe was safe. Sokolov had a vast reach and likely protected his assets.

Ortega approached her table. "Mr. Woods would like to see you in his office. Tanya is going to take over the table for you."

Amy's heart stuttered as she ran through all the reasons Woods might want to see her. It had been a week since she'd attended the private gambling event at Mr. Sokolov's home. A week since she'd been slipped an envelope with ten thousand dollars in it. When she'd tried to protest, Sokolov had run his knuckle along her cheek and told her she was worth every penny. Woods had whispered to her conspiratorially that Sokolov was in fact a cheapskate and should have tipped her five percent.

She'd wanted to use it to help support crowd-funded activities to find missing loved ones but had been told to hand it over to the FBI along with any tips she'd earned. Amy knew that the financial reward for information her father still promised to honor for news of her mother had brought in more wild-goose chases than anything else. But it had also helped add some clarity to her mom's last steps. And the knowledge that those nuggets of information might one day lead to them knowing the truth of what happened to her mom made it worth it. With the ten thousand dollars, there was a chance she could help another family feel the same way, and it burned not to be allowed to.

She understood why Cabe had been pissed. When he'd pointed out the danger she'd put them *all* in, the glaring mistake she'd made in her decision to enter Sokolov's office, she'd understood why. Something about this case— her desperation to find the missing women—had made her reckless.

But then again Cabe wouldn't be in the murky waters

of a marina right now putting a beacon on a vessel without what she'd done.

Why would Woods, who'd deliberately ignored her for the best part of her week, want to see her now? Had someone seen her go upstairs after all? When Cabe had asked if she'd noticed cameras on the ceiling, she'd truthfully said that she hadn't, but she hadn't looked carefully for them either.

Breaking what she was sure was protocol, she looked over to where Harley and Lite, who had replaced Cabe's cover, were seated in the bar area. She caught Lite's eye before she turned to leave the floor, hoping he would get the message that something odd was up, and didn't wait for any acknowledgment.

It was the sixth of October, and she'd heard the date of the tenth mentioned at the game. She wasn't even sure the tenth was in any way linked to offshore gaming, but on the off-chance it was, it was imperative she didn't take unnecessary risks with her safety. There was a GPS in the sole of her shoe that was permanently on and another in the wristwatch she wore. Both were checked constantly by someone on Cabe's team.

When she arrived at Woods's door, it was open. "Mr. Ortega said you wanted to see me, Mr. Woods."

Woods stood quickly, ushering her inside. "Yes. Yes. Come in, Amy." His face gave nothing away. No interest, no excitement, no anger. Nothing readable.

Amy kept her ground by the door, taking only a couple of steps inside, reluctant to put herself in reaching distance of his grabby hands. He'd kept them to himself while they'd been at Sokolov's house, but that didn't make him a changed man.

"You did very well at Mr. Sokolov's home," he said quietly. "Very well, indeed."

"Thank you," Amy replied. As always, she knew it was better to say nothing than too much. Don't fill the silence. Let the other person fill it for you.

He took a step closer, reaching his hand toward her hair and then pulling it back as though having second thoughts. "Do you remember the conversation we had when we met in the hallway?"

Her stomach turned. Was he expecting her to pay him back now? There was no way she could do what he'd expect of her. Her knees began to shake but she unclenched her jaw and forced herself to relax. She wasn't out of her depth . . . yet. And she had backup. "I do."

"I'm afraid you're going to have to trust me if you want to know how can you can make ten times the amount you made last week, Amy. I have the power to make you quite wealthy . . . if you'll let me. But I'll have to ask for you to sign a non-disclosure agreement before I can tell you any more."

A non-disclosure wasn't really worth the paper it was written on in cases like this, so of course she'd sign. She needed to know what happened next. But she also needed Woods to work for it.

Amy pursed her lips as though thinking about what he'd suggested. "Okay, I'm interested."

"Well, you're going to need to come all the way in and close the door. This is not for everyone's ears."

The door clicked shut as she did as he asked. When she was seated in the chair in front of him, he handed her the piece of paper, a copy of *Casino Management* magazine to lean it on, and a pen. Her name was already in place at the top of the page, a contract between herself and Faulkner Woods.

She'd done enough business classes to give the contract a cursory review. It explained that she was going to be told something but that she was not allowed to share it with anyone else. The language was deliberately intimidating and threatening. She could imagine a less confident, less capable, more desperate woman feeling terrified or out of options. With a flourish, she signed the document, remembering at the last moment to sign her surname as Reynard, not Murray.

"Mr. Sokolov will be entertaining a very exclusive group of friends on Friday. The venue will be a private yacht. He would very much like for you to be the dealer for the event. The guests wish to maintain their anonymity, hence the need for the non-disclosure."

Her heart leapt and fell in the space of a second. The boat. They'd been right. That was how it went down. And Mac was there now, ensuring the boat would be easily tracked. Dear God, in less than a week she'd be getting on that boat and relying on Cabe, and Eagle, and the FBI, the Coast Guard, and whomever goddamn else to get her off it again. Her life would be in their hands. In Cabe's hands. There was no way in hell he'd leave her in danger.

"It's not illegal, is it?" she asked, trying to think of the kinds of questions someone in her position would ask—the type of things Eve Canallis had searched for on her computer.

Woods leaned forward and placed his hand on her leg. The move made her squirm inside, but she acted as though his fingers weren't reaching for the soft skin behind her knee. "My dear Amy. While a little gambling between friends on a private boat *should* be legal, as long as it occurs in territorial waters, it isn't unless you have a license. Yet this causes harm to no one. These gentlemen are wealthy and private. If you agree, you'll be given a meet-up point two hours before the boat departs to ensure you have plenty of time to get there. The boat will sail at nine in the evening and will cruise for a little while before the games begin. There are worse ways to spend the evening than sailing the California coastline in a private yacht, but in case that isn't enough of an incentive, the salary for the evening is twenty thousand dollars excluding tips, which will be extensive."

Jesus Christ. No wonder the women signed on for this. No wonder there were so many. For a young woman with student debt, or wanderlust, or a need to be home for Thanksgiving, it would be impossible to turn down that kind of money.

Unless. . . . She looked at Woods's hand still on her knee and inwardly blanched. It made her ill. But maybe if someone else had been a little braver, a little stronger, more committed, her mom would be home in Vegas drinking martinis with her father.

You can do this. Amy repeated the words over and over until they sounded meaningless in her head.

"I'll be there."

CHAPTER EIGHTEEN

Cabe grabbed Amy as she collapsed onto his chest, breathless and spent, just like he was. Watching her ride him, watching her take what she needed, had brought him to the point where he'd detonated deep inside her, making him wish they didn't need condoms. He wanted to feel the sensation of her coming around him without any barriers. But conversations about testing and birth control would have to be added to the things-we'll-do-when-this-is-over list.

He knew they shouldn't be in her apartment, but the idea of her getting hooked up at Eagle with her security kit and heading out on that damn boat without him seeing her one more time alone was unbearable. When she'd agreed to his meeting her here before they went in, he'd been thrilled. Plus hard. All the time fucking hard for her, like he'd never had sex before. She only needed to look at him out of the corner of her eye and he would remember her looking at him the exact same way when he'd taken her from behind.

"Just when I think it can't get any better," Amy muttered against his shoulder, and he laughed as he rubbed his palms up and down her back.

"I was just thinking the same thing," he said as he turned to kiss the damp skin by her temple.

Amy raised her chin to face him. "I love this. I love being with you. But I'm also looking forward to being able to go outside, to walk to the market holding hands, or take a hike or a trip, maybe."

She sounded hopeful, a little wistful, and—Cabe realized—a little uncertain. A line creased between her eyebrows, and he hated seeing it there. Maybe the wait-until-it's-over-list couldn't wait.

"You know there *is* an after, right. After all this? Where we do all that? Where we argue over where we are going to spend Christmas, and make love on a tropical beach, and forget to put the toilet seat down, and decide to get tested and forgo contraception so I can do all of this all over again and feel skin on skin," he said as he pushed inside, making them both groan. He kissed her gently, then more deeply, until he could feel his cock start to harden again. Only they didn't have time to have sex again.

"Vegas," Amy said with a grin.

"Vegas, what?" He rolled them onto their sides so he could slide out of her.

"Is where we'll be spending Christmas this year."

Cabe grinned. "I already promised Mom I'd be home. And I seem to recall your dad telling me that he wanted you home but that you'd already told him you might not be able to make it."

Amy scoffed, her eyes bright. "Only because I didn't want him to get his hopes up if work called. But of course

I want to go and see him, and Uncle Clive, and Valentina."

God, she really was . . . something. "Pretty" was too girlish, "beautiful" too . . . staid. "Hot" minimized her to something sexual. Amy. She was Amy. And she was his. And he was more than happy to hold her naked body up against his as they debated the logistics of Christmas.

"Here's my suggestion," he said, kissing the tip of her nose. "Let's plan for when you finally get off the boat . . . tonight, tomorrow, whenever that may be, we'll get some sleep and then go on a date. Brunch. Somewhere we can open a bottle of wine. Near the surf. And we'll make a list. Pros and cons."

Amy smiled. "I look forward to debating this issue with you, Captain Moss."

"The same, Agent Murray. Although if I were you, I would expect to lose."

He thought about their conversation four hours later, when, for the forty-second time that week, he was running through every possible way to keep Amy from getting on that boat.

They could stop the men in port, but they would have no proof of wrongdoing if the women were boarding voluntarily.

They could try running the op without Amy on it, but without a dealer there might not be any gambling. And they couldn't be certain there was a backup dealer. Plus, Amy had balked at that. She was most definitely not down with the idea that someone else, someone less trained, would take her place.

His third idea was that if he was unable to prevent her climbing on board, he should climb on board too—sneak on and hide somewhere. Except there was nowhere to hide on a serviced yacht that was being prepped for a big game.

It had also occurred to him on more than one occasion that he should pack her up into the back of his truck and drive off somewhere safe until this was all over. As if she'd let him.

By now Eagle was a hub of activity. Members of the FBI, the Coast Guard, and the Navy were all involved with plans that ensured coverage for the three miles of U.S. waters off shore, and the twelve miles of territorial waters beyond that. Different rules for engagement were required for each. Even though they had been planning for days, they were still trying to iron out the last-minute details. Everyone's best guess was that the boat would leave the harbor and go south, heading straight down the coast to Mexico. The sooner the boat hit Mexican water, the harder it would become for the team to do anything without creating a political incident.

Plus, as the representative from the Coast Guard had said, despite the current president's claims, all the deadliest stuff headed south from the United States to Mexico. Weapons and sex-traded women.

Six was on the phone to his contact over on Coronado, who was currently watching the twenty-eight-foot-long, rigid-hulled inflatable they were going to use to trail the boat.

Their airborne intel showed that the boat, *Katie*, was a hive of activity, being readied for the night's event.

Amy slipped out of the room, and Cabe looked at the clock. She was going to get changed, having spent the afternoon in jeans and a blue hoodie she'd stolen from him that simply said Navy in white letters. It had made it even more impossible to stay away from her, but it was nondescript enough so no one need know it was his. Except Six and Mac, who'd hidden their smirks when Amy had arrived in it ten minutes after Cabe had made his entrance.

He checked his phone, hoping he'd get a call from Sokolov to join the game, but it appeared he'd failed to build a strong enough relationship with the guy to make it into his inner circle. Cabe pushed away the feeling of failure and gave her a minute to get ahead of him before he grabbed her security kit and followed. He heard the patter of her footsteps across the concrete floors of the main training space. She must be headed for the medical room, where she'd laid out her clothes.

After she disappeared inside, he looked over his shoulder to make sure nobody saw him, then dipped into the room after her, closing the door behind him and locking it in one swift move. His heart calmed at the smile she sent him. It reached her eyes, eyes that told him she was pleased to see him without her having to utter a word, and the panic that had cycled through him periodically throughout the day stilled.

Without saying a word, he slipped his arms around her waist and pulled her to him. "I like you in my hoodie."

"It smells of you, of your detergent," she said, bringing the cuff to her nose and inhaling deeply.

Trying to ignore his fear at the thought of her leaving, he leaned in and kissed her. "We need to get you ready."

Amy stepped away and smiled. "Did you volunteer?"

Cabe raised an eyebrow in humor. "You wanted one of the other guys to see you semi-naked while they strapped you up?"

She slapped his arm playfully. "Of course not," she

said as she slipped his hoodie over her head to reveal a white lace bra.

It would take nothing to slide the strap down her arm, reveal those perfectly pink nipples of hers and—

"You going to tape my GPS on?" Amy asked with her hands on her hips. Both of her eyebrows were raised, but she grinned.

"Does that mean I have to stop thinking about how good those breasts of yours would feel in my hands right about now?"

Her mouth opened. "Cabe," she gasped.

He laughed and began the process of taping the credit-card-sized GPS to her hip. When he was satisfied that there was no way anybody would feel it, even if they patted her down, he slipped a second device into the cup of her bra. The skin above the lace flashed with goose bumps, and he ran his fingertips across her skin. "Be careful, Ames. Don't go looking for trouble."

Amy placed her hands on his wrist and gripped tightly, the action grounding him. "I have three tracking devices on me . . . and I know whatever happens you'll find me."

Cabe sighed. "I need you alive when I do, Ames. I need . . ." Doubt crowded his mind. He hadn't been fast enough to save Brock, his childhood friend, from drowning. He hadn't been able to save Jess. The thought of losing Amy was—

"We've got this," Amy said resolutely.

Taking courage from her words, he kissed her. Kissed her like it was the first time. Kissed her like it was the last time. Kissed her . . . until he felt strong enough to stop. And when he was done kissing her, when her lips were red from their moment of intimacy, he held her while their heartbeats slowed.

Hours later, sitting in the foggy water off the coast of Coronado with six of his team members, listening to Buddha's update, he had an uneasy feeling. There was something they hadn't considered, a piece they hadn't planned for. But he didn't know what it was.

On his phone, he watched the live feed of Amy leaving the building and driving to the meet-up point. Every twist and turn she took once she left the highway took her farther away from him, an extra mile from his reach, but he pushed back against the negative thoughts creeping in.

There was a car and a van, lights on, in the parking lot as she pulled in. A woman stepped out of the car as Amy came to a stop. Cabe recognized the hair . . . she looked familiar, but he couldn't quite place her.

"You seeing this, Noah?" Cabe asked through his comms unit. The SDPD were patched into the feed. "Who is she?"

The woman smiled at Amy, and the two of them shook hands. From her body language, Amy didn't seem to be in any kind of distress.

"We've captured her face, running it through the system now," Noah replied. "But, bro, I got news you're going to like."

"What is it?"

"You were right. There *is* a link between Woods and Sokolov. But it's deeper than you know. Woods Senior divorced his first wife, Woods Junior's mom, because she had an affair . . . with Sokolov's father."

That snapped Cabe's attention into focus. "They're related? Tell me they're brothers."

"Not that we can tell. Birth certificates claim different, but we're trying to find the first wife now to confirm.

But there was a period from the age of eight until the age of ten, when Woods Junior would have spent time with Sokolov."

Fuck.

The knowledge yielded three times more questions than it answered, but he tucked the information away for when the night was over.

Faulkner Woods stepped out of the van and waved to the women. Two men followed him. *Damn.* What he wouldn't give to be able to hear what they were saying. But a bug on Amy had been too risky, they were too bulky. Thank fuck for the GPS and the emergency beacon which were well hidden. Otherwise, he'd lose his mind.

Amy and the woman each handed something over to Woods, their car keys most likely. Woods handed them to the men who then walked toward the two cars.

If they were abducting the women, they'd need to get rid of the vehicles. Thankfully, Amy's car was tagged. "Buddha, you've got to tell us where those cars go," Cabe instructed.

"The GPS is active," Buddha responded.

"We can get SDPD vehicles mobile immediately," Noah added.

Cabe breathed deeply.

They had everything covered. He needed to chill out. Years of practice had him exhaling as he rolled his neck from left to right. "Keep the drone on the car with Agent Murray in it," he told Buddha.

"You know we've got this," said Mac from the opposite side of the twenty-eight-foot rigid inflatable. They'd picked it for its seventy-knot top speed, which could easily catch the *Katie*'s thirty-knot maximum.

Cabe nodded curtly as he watched the van pull out of the parking lot. Any minute now she'd be on her way to the harbor and . . . damn it. Something was off. He looked at the screen as the van pulled toward the exit onto the highway.

"We've got a problem," Cabe said, his voice cold and calm.

"What is it?" Mac replied.

"They've headed north. They aren't going to the marina."

"Can you believe we get to do this?" Sonya, a leggy brunette who'd started work in hospitality on the casino day shift two weeks previously, said as the van headed out of the city. She applied her lip gloss in a small mirror before dropping it back into her purse.

Amy forced a smile on to her face, but it was an almost impossible feat, given they should have headed south on the I-5 but were now heading north. There was no way this path led to the *Katie*. She reminded herself that Cabe knew where she was and that she had three GPS trackers on her. Well, two that were active now plus the personal locator beacon tucked into her bra. "I know, right? It should be a lot of fun."

Sonya leaned toward her while glancing forward to the front of the car. When she slid her long hair behind her ear, Amy caught a better look at her. Up close, she looked much younger than the makeup and clothing would suggest. "I only moved here a month ago. My mom said I was stupid to try and make this work, and I only had enough savings for a few months. I thought I'd lucked out getting a job at the casino, but this kind of money will definitely help me stay here."

Amy was torn. She needed to keep up the act—
excitement, energy, enthusiasm, and curiosity a young
woman offered a large sum of money would have. But
she couldn't. She knew Sonya'd be crushed to find out
when this was over that there wasn't going to be a single
cent paid out, but hopefully what they'd saved her *from*
would more than make up for it.

Woods sat in the front with a driver she didn't recognize. In the rear of the van were two large leather overnight bags. They were filled to capacity, their zippers
stretched by what was inside. Everyone was acting completely normally. No sideways glances, no body language
that signaled lying and subterfuge.

Her hands rested steady in her lap while her heart
raced and thoughts rushed through her brain. Had they
drawn the right conclusions from the information they
had? Did they have the strongest plan in place? Would
the backup plans be effective? Details they'd spent hours
poring over started to slip away from her.

She took a deep breath.

They were fine. *She* was fine.

After twenty minutes, the car pulled off the highway
and entered a private marina where a large boat of
similar size to the *Katie* was waiting. When she opened
the car door, the cool damp air hit her. Though the
midnight blue water was smooth as glass, there was a
soft sound of ripples lapping the edges of the boat. The
lights of the lower deck were off, but the upper deck
was fully illuminated and a handful of people milled
about. Two men stood guard on the dock, one of whom
she could see was blatantly armed with what looked
horrifyingly like an M16. No wonder the boat was in a
private dock.

She so badly wanted to look up to confirm that the drone was still above her or search back along the coastline to find a second pair of headlights, but she didn't. Not least because Cabe's men were experts and wouldn't leave headlights on to draw any attention.

Two men hurried over to the vehicle. "Mr. Woods," one of them said. "We'll be leaving shortly and should get you and the ladies on board." They grabbed the bags from the back and carried them toward the boat.

Amy plastered a smile on her face. "It's a beautiful yacht. Is it Mr. Sokolov's?"

Woods turned to her. "It isn't. This is a last-minute replacement. His usual boat was incapacitated. Engine problems or something."

They stepped onto the wooden deck and were submitted to a pat-down. Woods first, then Sonya, whose purse they also checked. The excitement that had been so apparent in Sonya's eyes in the van had been replaced with apprehension. On autopilot, Amy formulated a joke to ease Sonya's obvious fear, something about how there had been no mention of guns and pat-downs in the non-disclosure, but then kept it to herself. If she was closer, she'd reach for Sonya's hand. Amy's heart raced, and she thought about the flat beacon taped to her hip. What if they found it? What would she do?

Again, she forced herself to breathe.

A large bald man with heavy-set eyes motioned for her to step forward, and she did as he requested, opening her arms out to her sides as if passing through airport security. The man's hands were rough, paying too much attention to the flat of her stomach. His palms, closed in prayer, slid between her breasts. She prayed the device in her bra stayed exactly where it was. He had the audacity to wink at her when he was done, and she bit down on the urge to jab three fingers into his throat.

A chill wrapped around her the way the low fog crawled through the reeds opposite the dock.

Voices sounded from the deck above as they walked into the main lounge. It was opulent. She'd expected it to be gaudy like Sokolov's home, but the ivory leather and soft gray fabrics furnishings were classy. Splashes of teal in the form of cushions and modern art paintings brightened the space. Carefully, she watched Woods's reactions. There seemed to be an air of uncertainty she couldn't quite put her finger on. His eyes had scanned the room to find the poker table. If she had to guess, they usually used the *Katie*, and this was a new boat for him too.

She didn't believe the engine-failure excuse. Cabe and the team had been fired at. That meant Sokolov knew the boat had been made. It made sense that they'd switch. It had always been a risk for the op. And Sokolov was a savvy criminal.

But she knew, with all the surveillance eyes on her, that they knew where she was.

"Sonya," he said, pointing over to the contemporary bar area with a bowl of lemons and limes on the counter. "Please go and set yourself up. I'm sure our guests are getting thirsty."

Something felt off. If they were there to provide hospitality, why would the guests arrive before the staff? And why was food still being brought on board? How long ago had they decided to make the switch in boats? Perhaps that was why things were still being set up.

"Okay," Woods said. "Let's get the table set up, Ms. Reynard."

Maybe it was from her jitters about the op, or maybe

her senses were on the fritz, but the way he drew out her last name felt ominous.

Within another thirty minutes, the boat lifted its anchor and the steady drone of the engine kicked in as they steered out of the harbor. Amy watched from her position by the table, trying to keep herself oriented in the dark and fog as to which direction the boat was heading, but it was impossible.

Woods lifted one of the bags from the car onto the table. "Does it need to be explained to you, Ms. Reynard, that this isn't completely legal?"

Amy shook her head. "The non-disclosure and paycheck made it pretty obvious."

Woods slid his finger down the side of her face, and nodded before opening the bag to reveal it was filled with cash, stacks of money she could only assume had come from the casino. He tugged on a pair of cotton gloves before he began to pull the pre-bundled hundred-dollar bills onto the table.

Men began to filter into the room. She recognized two of them, from the night at Sokolov's; the other four she didn't. One carried an equally large bag and handed it Sokolov, who opened it and began to speak in Russian. She had no idea what they were saying, but it was obviously something positive by the way the men would in turn slap each other on the back and cheer. Sokolov handed each of the men a bundle of bills from the bag and then gestured to Amy.

"You are going to count them," Woods said. "Verify the amount, and then I will replace those bills with these bills."

Amy looked away from Sokolov quickly to face Woods. This was how they were doing it. Bringing in dirty money and using Woods's access to clean funds to switch them out. She had questions, a million of them. Was Woods being forced into this? Did his father know? Was Woods receiving a cut?

By the time she had finished counting, over one and a half million dollars had passed through her hands. No wonder the men were so happy. She wondered why Sokolov and Woods didn't just trade the bills and then have Sokolov hand out clean ones, but then she realized counting the bills in both bags was necessary to ensure that neither Sokolov nor Woods had screwed each other. While Amy had worked, Sonya had provided the men drinks and a woman in a fitted black dress had brought around hors d'oeuvres that had smelled good at first, but soon left her feeling ill.

She was disoriented and was no longer certain of their direction. With the boat swaying gently in the night breeze, Amy dealt the first hand of blackjack.

Focus on the details, Ames.

Calling herself Cabe's nickname grounded her. It was as if she could hear his voice in her head. She looked around the room, searching for things she could use as a weapon, but her options were limited to bottles of alcohol and lamps she wasn't completely sure weren't bolted to the furniture they stood on.

She made a point to take in every detail of the men around her who talked in Russian and consumed too much vodka. Eye color, a tattoo, a scar. The make of watch, a wedding ring, an ear piercing. Names and locations mentioned . . . words she could pick up among the Russian. All while keeping the count of the table.

The details were necessary. Things could go wrong. People could get away. She couldn't necessarily rely on

Cabe and his team to save her. Despite every best effort, nobody had been able to save her mom, and while she had faith in Cabe and his men, she needed a plan of her own if things went down that way.

After the first hour, they switched from blackjack to tournament-style poker.

"Gentlemen," Sokolov said, clinking the side of his glass with a pearl-handled caviar spoon when the table was down to the last three players. He placed it down on the table and removed a handgun from his inside pocket before nodding at the man who had searched her when she boarded the boat.

Amy heart raced. She considered her exits, even overboard. How long could she last in open water? In the dark? Would her beacon even work in water? Then she remembered Cabe telling her it was waterproof.

"Our handover is a little premature," he said, continuing in English and looking straight at her. Out of the corner of her eye, she could see the man who'd searched her making his way over.

Shit. "Handover"? Of what? How long had they been sailing? Definitely under two hours. How far out had Cabe said the contiguous zone was, the boundary to international waters? Twenty-four nautical miles. The boat had a top speed of thirty knots, but it hadn't been cruising that fast. She'd have felt it. They must be closing in on the meet-up.

"We have some preparation to do, so we need to pause for a moment." Sokolov walked toward her and smiled. "You have done well tonight, Ms. Reynard. I believe you'll bring a good price." He lifted her shirt roughly and ripped off the patch that held the sensor to her side. She gasped as his fingers dug into her bicep.

Her heart beat so quickly that she began to see stars in her peripheral vision. "A good price?" she asked, attempting to remain in character while her mouth completely dried up.

Sokolov laughed, handing her GPS to one of his henchmen. She watched as he walked outside and tossed it over the stern. "You can cut the crap, Agent Murray."

Any control she had over her pulse evaporated at his words, and her ability to form sentences disappeared. The threats she wanted to yell wouldn't come.

Sonya screamed, and Amy turned to see her dragged away and carried down the stairs, still attempting to kick and punch.

A click by her ear gained her full attention. She'd been around guns enough to know the sound. Cool metal pressed against her temple. All she could hope was that while she stalled Sokolov, Cabe and the team would somehow realize she was in distress.

Woods reached into the bag that had held the money. He pulled out the *Casino Management* magazine she'd seen on his desk. It was open to page four. There was a candid photo, one she hadn't realized was being taken, of her father grinning at her after his last tour win.

"Take her downstairs," Sokolov said as the boat began to speed up. Her gut told her they were making their break for international water.

The man who'd disappeared with Sonya reappeared with another man who was armed with a small rifle. While part of her was ready to fight in panic, her brain kicked in long enough to know that was a bad idea. She was unarmed, and outmanned.

Bastards.

They led her down the stairs onto the lower level. Dim

lighting revealed a long corridor flanked by cabin doors. A man stood guard by the third door on the port side. He offered the thug behind her a cable tie, which he used to secure her hands in front of her.

Finally, a break. Cable ties were a rookie mistake, and easy to get out of. She made a token gesture of resistance while they checked that the tie was tight. The door was yanked open, and she was thrown inside, the impact reverberating through her spine as her knees hit the floor. The door closed behind her, thrusting her into darkness.

"Hello?" she whispered as she blinked rapidly, hoping her eyes would adjust to the darkness quickly. "Sonya?"

"Amy," she sobbed. "What are they going to do to us?"

"They're going to kill us," a second voice said.

"Or sell us," a third said quietly.

More women.

Not while I'm still breathing.

She processed where they were. As her eyes adjusted to the darkness, she saw a bed with dark linens. Climbing to her feet, Amy made sure the locking feature of the cable tie was in the middle of her two hands and, using her teeth, tightened it. It was counterintuitive, but the tighter the clasp, the easier it was to snap. She raised her hands into the air, remembering what her instructor had told her. *It's like making a chicken wing, Murray.* She yanked her hands down, pulling them to either side of her waist, snapping the cable tie. Escape 101 that so few people knew about. And given Sokolov's propensity for surrounding himself with thugs, they probably had no clue they could be broken so easily. Now they needed light, but not enough to alert the man in the corridor.

She ripped the dark pillowcase off the pillow and

threw it over the lamp before she turned it on, dimming the brightness. Sonya sat at the foot of the bed. There were two women sitting on the floor, their backs to the wall opposite the doorway. *Eve Canallis and Alison Berry.*

"I'm Agent Murray with the FBI," Amy whispered. "Everybody up." Once they were on their feet, she proceeded to show them how she had snapped the cable ties and waited for them to execute the move. She curled her finger at Sonya, gesturing for her to take the spot next to the lamp. "Can you do this? Can you use the lamp to make an SOS that can be seen outside the ship?" she whispered as she used the switch to turn the lamp on and off three times quickly, three times slowly, then three times quickly. Dot, dot, dot . . . dash, dash, dash . . . dot, dot, dot.

The Morse code SOS. Totally old school. It felt like something Cabe would understand.

She could only hope Cabe was watching.

But in case he wasn't, she needed to find a way to get the women out herself.

"What do you mean one of her trackers stopped moving?" Cabe shouted through his comms unit as the rigid inflatable raced through the water. The ice-cold spray stung his face like a thousand bees as they chased the yacht that had suddenly sped up after eighty-two minutes of lingering on anchor. There was a swell, and the G-force had him holding on for dear life as they smashed through the waves.

"Exactly what I said," Buddha shouted, though it was almost impossible to hear him over the racing engines on

the back of the boat. "One of her GPS trackers is stationary; the other two are still moving."

"I want the fucking Coast Guard airborne now to
check the stationary GPS."

For the first time in his life, he felt nauseated on a boat.
Truth be told, he'd felt ill since the car had gone north
instead of south, leading them to an unnamed vessel in
an unnamed dock, but when he'd realized what was happening, he'd locked his feelings down tight. They were
gaining on the boat. Thanks to Amy's GPS, they'd known
exactly where it was heading.

"On it." Buddha would make sure it happened. Cabe
knew that.

He hoped the fact that the other two beacons were on
the boat meant Amy was on there too, and not dead. The
idea caused a wave of panic like he'd never experienced.
If they had, on the other hand, thrown her overboard
alive, there was still time to save her. The water wasn't
cold enough to kill her, though swimming alone in the
dark was as terrifying as it could be liberating. Plus shit,
even though it was rare, great white sharks had been
sighted off San Onofre State Beach, which they were
closing in on.

"Bearing adjusted," Buddha said through the comms
unit. "Target heading straight for international water."

Gaz, an expert at steering the inflatable, turned the boat
to a bearing of three-fifteen degrees. "We'll cut it off."

Now it was simple math. The yacht had to travel the
shorter distance at a slower speed. And they had to power
through the longer distance to intercept it, but at the faster
speed. And he didn't actually have the patience to do the
math. He just had to pray that the team had it covered,

which for a man who hated being out of control at the best of times was a new level of agony with Amy's life on the line.

"Three miles to international waters," Buddha said.

The boat hit the top of a wave, Gaz knowing to come off the throttle before hammering it again as they hit the water. Cabe tightened his abs, bending slightly forward, knowing from years of experience that the landings would hurt but ignoring the discomfort. His thoughts centered on Amy.

I'm coming for you, Ames.

He repeated the words over and over as they closed in on the vessel. Nobody would ever see them. The boat was black, and they were dressed in black. The yacht's engines would make enough noise to hide the sound of their approach. And when they got close enough, Gaz would bring the boat in behind the yacht. One thing about civilian sailors, they rarely looked behind. The captain would have his attention forward, as would the majority of the crew. The passengers might be looking port or starboard. But rarely did anyone look back into the wake of the yacht at night, a cool night at that.

"Two miles to international water," Buddha announced. "With an incoming boat just over one nautical out and closing, bearing ninety."

That must be the rendezvous boat. In their black inflatable, dressed in all black, they blended into the darkness, but he wanted to be on the back of Sokolov's boat moments before the two boats met. He, Six, and Jackson were going to take control of the boat Amy was on, and then Gaz would circle the boat around to get Mac, Harley, and Lite onto the rendezvous boat while using the inflatable to block any exit attempt.

Salt and wind burned the small part of his face that was exposed as he hung on, like the rest of them, for dear life. Approaching through the wake of the yacht made for an even bumpier arrival. As he squinted into the wind, Cabe noticed a subdued burst of light from one of the lower cabins. At first glance, it looked like a light bulb on the fritz. But none of the other lights were on. Nor was the flashing consistent. It was . . .

Holy shit!

"There's an SOS from the port side lower deck," he said, finding the place of calm he needed before he set foot on the boat. Torn between love and duty, Cabe wanted to blow off the plan and head straight for whichever cabin the light came from, even though he knew taking out their assailants first meant a better chance of success.

Gaz was able to bring the inflatable alongside the rear deck as the boat began to slow for the meet. Cabe was the first to climb between the two boats, landing with a thud against his ribs. He rolled out of the way, aiming his weapon at the stairs and then the upper deck. So far, nobody had noticed, but it wouldn't be long. Six followed, as did Jackson. Once situated, they proceeded to work their way along the boat.

A member of Sokolov's security team was looking toward the front of the boat, and with stealth that came with years of training, Jackson grabbed him and gagged him while Six continued to push forward. The mission statement was clear. Apprehend Sokolov and his business partners. Extract the hostages. Minimum force. And he'd adhere to that . . . for now. Because as soon as it became clear Amy was in mortal danger, all bets were off.

"One mile to international water," Buddha said through his earpiece.

Jesus Christ, they needed to stop the frigging boat before it hit the boundary. Jackson caught up with them, signaling that the man was now tied up on the lower deck. Cabe signaled in the direction of the bridge. On a yacht this size, there was likely a captain and a first mate, and probably a chief and a second engineer. Four people to secure, but their priority was the men in the main salon.

He glanced over the bow and saw Gaz line the boat up to the rear of the incoming vessel.

Cabe, Jackson, and Six rounded the salon, where two more men stood with weapons. With his fingers, he signed. *Three, two, one.* He burst forward from his crouched position and took down his target, feeling a sense of satisfaction at the crunch that occurred when the guy's nose collided with the deck floor. He let out a grunt.

Six's target yelled out a shout of warning, but Cabe couldn't worry about that now. Disarm, disable, move on. That was his focus. He tied the man's hands behind his back.

"Coast Guard has checked location of beacon. No sign of Amy. Nothing on thermal imaging," Buddha said.

Relief raged through him, a torrent of it. So much of his mental energy had been tied up with that single concern.

Another man rushed out of the double doors of the upper saloon and tried to fire his weapon down onto them, a bullet splintering the deck not an arm's length away. Cabe scrambled back, making the angle too difficult, but it was only a matter of time before he and his men were surrounded.

Cabe and Six kept their backs to the wall as they approached the main salon from the port side, Jackson from starboard. He'd take their three trained guns against any number of thugs any day of the week. Plus, it was Six. The guy had one of the longest confirmed kills in history, and had had his back since kindergarten. And Jackson could beat anybody down at the gun range.

Six crouched beneath the window line of the main salon. The fiberglass walls of the boat wouldn't stop a bullet, but they provided enough cover so Cabe could lean forward and pull the door open.

"Mac, position?"

"On board. Ready to press forward."

"On three. One, two, three."

They charged the room, Six yelling loudly for everyone to put their weapons on the ground. Shots were fired. One hit Cabe's bulletproof vest, winding him as he pushed forward, his eyes scanning for danger. And for Amy.

Sokolov was behind the bar. Cabe had seen him dive there—happy to hide behind the thick mahogany and the bodies of his men—when the second set of shots were fired. With his weapon raised, Cabe ran through the room, relying on Six and Jackson to cover his tracks. Take out the leader, and the lower levels of the organization would crumble. And there was no doubt in his mind that Sokolov was the top.

A bullet skimmed Cabe's hip as Sokolov attempted to take a shot, but Cabe returned fire, three quick taps on the trigger to ensure Sokolov was crouched low and off-balance by the time Cabe reached him. When they were within a foot of each other, Cabe threw his weapon over his shoulder and crashed down on top of Sokolov.

"I'll kill you," Sokolov yelled as he attempted to push Cabe off his chest.

Space was limited behind the bar as the two of them

grappled on the floor, but Cabe managed to get the upper hand just as an array of bullets hit the glass bottles on the bar above them, showering them both in shards.

"You think you can get away from me? You think you can do this to me and not get what is coming to you?" Sokolov raged.

With all his gear on, Cabe was well protected, and he knew there was no way Sokolov could tell who he was. The temptation was strong to rip off his headgear and let the fucker know exactly who had him flat on his back, but he resisted it.

Ignoring the injury the broken glass would cause to Sokolov's face, Cabe flipped him onto his front and tied his wrists. For good measure, Cabe also tied his ankles.

Keeping low, Cabe crawled to the edge of the bar. Six was providing cover for Jackson to move forward, tying up people as he went. Three men were down, notably Ivan Popov, who was lying painfully contorted by Six's feet.

Faulkner Woods was hiding beneath the poker table. Relying on Six and Jackson to lock everyone down in the main salon, Cabe ran to the other side of the room. He fell to the ground and put a knee into Faulkner's back.

"I'm innocent. I'm a victim too," he whimpered.

Cabe ignored his pleas and used the ties to bind Woods's arms behind his back. "Where are the women?"

"I don't know what you are talking about," Woods stammered.

"You don't want to mess with me right now," he grounded out through clenched teeth. "Where. The fuck. Are they?"

The man had gone gray, as if he was about to pass out, but right now, Cabe didn't give a shit. He needed to know

Amy was safe. He heard footsteps run along the deck but couldn't look up. His teammates had everybody covered. Cabe pressed the nozzle of his gun to Woods's temple. "One last chance, Woods," he said. "Where are they?"

"They're down in one of the staff bedrooms." The smell of urine filled the air. Cabe stood and raced for the staircase, weapon at the ready. "They're on the lower floor. Six?"

"Right behind you."

While Cabe wasn't sure exactly where those rooms were, he knew they were down. With the sounds of Six's footsteps following him down the stairs, he skipped the first deck he came to, assuming those rooms would be the more luxurious suites. Woods had said "staff rooms."

When he reached the next floor, he heard voices. The nervous ramblings of a scared man. "We need to get out of here."

"And do what? Go where?" a voice replied.

"The jet skis. Man, we could cut through the storage area and—"

"Fucking jet skis? And how far do you think we'll get on those. Sokolov will kill us himself if we let her—"

"Down on the ground," Cabe shouted as he turned the corner. What Sokolov would do to them was nothing compared to the icy fury that ran through his veins.

If they'd hurt Amy, there wasn't *anything* he wouldn't do to them.

Amy could hear the earth-shattering gunfire on the floors above. Her heart pounded with fear and with frustration over not being able to think through a way out of this.

They were unarmed and up against an unknown number of assailants. A part of her thought it might be best to barricade themselves in until help arrived, but she couldn't be certain that the shots fired above were from Cabe's team. She was certain their weapons would have silencers.

Though she was relatively sure it *was* Cabe and his team, she needed to remain cautious on the off chance that something had gone wrong in the meet-up and that the gunfire was, in fact, between Sokolov's men and whomever they were meeting.

"Start looking for anything we could use as weapons," Amy said to the others, a little louder now. With the commotion on the upper level, she was less concerned about being heard. She checked the door. It was still locked from the outside. "Anything you can use. What are your names?" she asked, yanking open the wardrobe in the small cabin bedroom. She knew who the women were, but she needed them active and alert. Thinking even. Names were innocuous, but having the women identify themselves would bring them into the here and now. There was nothing inside the closet except a couple of wooden coat hangers. She grabbed them. Anything was better than nothing.

"I'm Alison Berry," the slender blonde said, crawling on her knees to look under the bed.

"I'm Eve Canallis," the taller redhead replied, rubbing her wrists, which were red and raw. She'd obviously tried to pull the ties off. "Please tell me that's backup." Eve flinched as another round of gunfire went off above them.

"Hopefully it is. If it isn't, they are most definitely on their way. I'm going to need you to move. Check the drawers over there," Amy instructed.

"There are slats supporting the bed," Alison said. "A

couple of them are loose, if we could just lift the mattress."

Sonya stepped in to help as Amy checked the bathroom. There was a hairdryer on the sink. One of them could swing it, or they could use the cable to tie someone up. They were pathetic weapons choices, household appliances and pieces of wood, but they'd serve a purpose. Plus, looking for them was keeping the women busy and calming them down. *Two* of the women, she corrected herself as she stepped out of the bathroom. Eve still hadn't moved, her eyes trained on the ceiling as if the bullets might actually come through the floor.

"Eve, drawers," Amy said firmly. Panic and urgency were two different things, and all the women needed to show the latter. The gunfire was getting louder, sounding as if it had hit their hallway. "Stay away from the door," she instructed. The last thing the op needed was a stray bullet taking one of the women out.

"Ames," Cabe shouted from the hallway. It was faint, but she could hear him.

Thank God.

She raced to the door she'd just told the women to avoid and hammered on it. "Over here!"

"Ames?" His voice was getting louder, as were his footsteps on the wood floor of the corridor.

She pounded her palm against the door, ignoring the sting and pain that flashed along her forearm. "In here, but it's locked."

The handle turned as if being rattled on the outside. "Get everybody out of the way. Get back against the wall."

Amy pushed the three women into the bathroom. They stumbled and tripped over one another, but she had no time to be concerned. "Clear!" she yelled.

The frame of the door began to splinter, as did the area around the lock. The women behind her screamed, holding on to one another. Suddenly, the door burst open, obviously by Cabe having thrown himself at it. He tore into the room, weapon raised. She tried to imagine how the women must feel. What little she could see of Cabe's face was fierce, his all-black outfit intimidating, and his raised weapon terrifying.

He passed straight by her, and she noticed Six, a flash of blond hair from beneath his uniform giving him away, standing guard.

"Clear!" he shouted as he returned to stand in front of her. Swiftly, he bent and pulled a weapon from his thigh and thrust it into her hands. "Let's take the women up the stairs at the end of the hallway and—" He pressed his hand to his ear, the one with his earpiece. "Got it, Mac. We aren't clear over here. Leave Harley and Lite and make your way back over here." He paused again. "On it. . . . Sorry," he said, returning his attention to her. "We're going to take the stairs at the end of the hall, Jackson has the salon secure. Six'll give us cover, I've got your back." He pressed his fingertips to her cheek for a millisecond and then yelled for her to go.

"Quick," she shouted to Eve, Alison, and Sonya, who was now in tears. "We need to go." She ushered them out of the room and waved them in the direction of the stairs. She briefly wished she could take a moment to thank Cabe, to kiss him, to tell him what he meant to her. But they both had jobs to do, and he needed her to do her thing so he could do his, though her cheek still burned with his touch.

The women ahead of her scrambled up the stairs. Alison tripped at the top, but Eve helped her to her feet.

Woods was seated up against a wall, hands tied behind his back, as were all the men. His eyes were red and his pants were strained. She'd put money on him being the first to flip. Sokolov yelled at one of the other men in Russian, who yelled back.

She encouraged the women to move to the other side of the salon, behind the safety of a low dividing wall. All three of them sat down on a two-seater sofa, clinging to one another for what she imagined was a mix of safety and comfort. "We'll take your stories down once we get off the boat," she told them. "I'm not sure what the strategy is yet, whether you'll be airlifted off or whether the Coast Guard will come out and sail the ship back into the harbor."

Sonya reached for her hand, squeezing it hard. "Thank you." She jumped as they heard gunfire again, this time from beneath them.

Icy cold fear trickled down her spine. Six was still down there, and the idea that Cabe's men could still get hurt froze her to the bone. "You're welcome."

Once she was certain the women were at least comfortable if not calm, she headed over to Cabe, who had switched with Jackson to guard the targets. Sokolov looked in her direction and sneered, but she held his gaze.

Yeah, asshole, regardless of what comes next, you're going away.

He muttered something in Russian.

She leaned over to Cabe. "I wish we knew what they were saying," she muttered.

"You don't want to know, Ames," Cabe whispered, never taking his eyes, or his weapon, off the men. "But if he keeps it up, my finger might just slip on this trigger."

Despite the fear and worry for Cabe and Six below,

Amy raised an eyebrow. "Don't do anything stupid," she said, although the words held no heat. She knew he wouldn't do anything that wasn't aboveboard. "Words don't hurt, Cabe. You know that."

He looked her way for a millisecond, then returned his focus to the targets. "I know. Doesn't mean I can't imagine taking the bastard down though, right?"

Footsteps came from outside and she swung around, her weapon aimed at the doors out onto the deck. Mac pushed the doors open, and she let go of a deep breath she'd been holding. He ignored her and Cabe, running straight down the stairs as she assumed Cabe had told him to.

Goddamn, what where they up to? Why hadn't they locked it down yet?

"Steady, Agent Murray," Cabe murmured. "They've got this."

He looked so indifferent, so casual, yet she didn't doubt his focus for a second. He was made for this.

Was she?

She'd gone into this for her mother. To somehow give back, to feel useful, to move on. And she loved her work with the FBI. But was undercover work what she was meant to do with the rest of her life? She watched as Jackson, Six, and Mac brought the remaining men to the main floor. What would it mean for her relationship with Cabe? Huge periods out of contact. Could she do it? Or would it be better to go back to general fieldwork? At least with fieldwork she had contact with the victims, people she could identify with, had empathy with. Like the women on the sofa.

The thought remained with her as they waited for the Coast Guard, as she watched the suspects moved from the other boat to theirs. It didn't leave her as she saw the casual slap on the back and squeeze of the shoulder between the men on Cabe's team. They were meant to do this. She could tell that. They'd never panicked. And she'd place money on it that their hands had never shaken.

When Cabe climbed into the Coast Guard helicopter right after her, ditching his military equipment to pull her in his arms, she knew she'd need to talk to him about it at some point. But tonight was not the night.

"Shit, Ames. When the car went north instead of south, I—"

She pressed her lips to his, cutting him off, stopping the overwhelming display of emotion that had him on edge.

"I knew you'd come," she whispered fiercely. "It's what got me through. I knew you'd find me."

"A thousand times over," he replied, studying her eyes for just a moment. "I'd come for you wherever you were. The ends of the earth if I had to."

"I love you," she replied.

He had her back as much as she had his. "I love you too."

And he didn't let her go until they were home. In *his* apartment. In his bed.

Where she knew she belonged.

EPILOGUE

Cabe looked out through the double doors of the Windsor suite of the Hotel del Coronado and took a breath. The water soothed the deepest parts of him, as the desert soothed Amy. In the weeks since the raid on the boat, they'd gotten to Vegas, Amy to spend time with her dad and Uncle Clive, him to celebrate Six's last days of freedom. It had been more symbolic than a riotous bachelor party. There'd been no strippers or painful hangovers. Just some gambling and relaxing by the pool, where they'd sat shooting shit, just like the day they'd all met in kindergarten.

He wondered what Brock would have made of the three of them. Of where they'd ended up. There would be an empty seat at the long table behind him, just for Brock.

The palms swayed, the waves crashed, the sun shone. It couldn't have been any more perfect had a rainbow split the garden in half.

Every single person he loved was in the room behind him—except Six and Lou, who were taking their own sweet time driving the classic open-top convertible to the venue. Cabe's guess was they were driving all the way down Coronado and back.

Hands slipped around his waist, hands that were now familiar and as necessary as the call of the ocean. "You okay?" she asked.

Cabe turned and pulled her close. "Did I tell you how beautiful you look today?" He ran his finger along her shoulder, the strapless black dress that fitted her like a second skin leaving them bare.

"Maybe once or twice," she replied.

He kissed her lips. "Ow," he said as his mom slapped him on the arm.

"Behave," she whispered.

His mom always treated formal events with a reverence they really didn't require. It wasn't like they were in church. Six and Lou's wedding had been a small civil one, with just Six, Lou, and a handful of witnesses, where he'd proudly stood as Six's best man. But the reception was bigger. Delaney had her arm around Mac's bicep, leaning her head on his shoulder while Mac spoke to his parents. Six's parents were chatting with Louisa's mother, while Six's sister was instructing her boyfriend to help her move the favors table. Cabe's mom had just finished fussing over the wedding cake she'd made, while his dad and brother were shooting shit over sports stats. And the guys from Eagle who were in town and off duty sat looking uncomfortable in their suits, while a few of Lou's friends talked in the corner.

The cake was way too big for their party of twenty-six, and included three layers of cake done in all their favorite flavors.

Six walked up the steps toward them, leading his new

bride by the hand. His smile was nearly as bright as the glint of his wedding ring. As always, Louisa's head was down, and she gripped his hand as though her life depended on it. Cabe knew he'd brought her in through the parking lot and grounds so she didn't have to deal with all the people milling about the hotel. A new bride was a beautiful thing, and it was only natural for people to want to stop and wish the couple well, something that would make Lou desperately uncomfortable.

"Don't tell me, Lou," Cabe said. "He got lost, right?"

Lou laughed, her shoulders shaking. She glanced up at him briefly. "I told him to keep going," she answered honestly.

Six chuckled. "I told *her* I wasn't missing your mom's cake."

Everybody cheered as they stepped inside.

The photographer Cabe had picked snapped a photograph of the two of them. She'd been totally behind Amy's idea of no formal pictures, and Cabe had talked to her at great length about Lou's shyness. They'd come to an agreement that an almost invisible candid photography approach would be best. "You need to see this," she said.

She fiddled with her camera for a moment and then showed him a photograph that almost made him choke. At the moment the clerk had said Six could kiss his bride, Lou had put her arms around Six's neck and looked up at him, the long hair she usually hid behind had all fallen away from her face, leaving a beautifully unobstructed image of the two of them staring into each other's eyes with so much love and passion that he couldn't help but sigh.

"Beautiful, isn't it?" Amy said.

"It is."

He took Amy's hand and led them to their seats at the long table. White and Tiffany blue paper lanterns were clustered above them. Mac had found them after scouring the internet for days. Bizarrely, the tall vases of white flowers with Tiffany-blue ribbons had been his idea. Between the three of them, they'd cobbled together a half-decent party.

He smiled as he watched Lou change the place settings, moving her and Six from the middle of the table to the end nearest the view of the water. And as usual, Six watched and let her do whatever she needed to. It was only right.

Which was exactly why Amy would be taking on another difficult case starting Monday and he wasn't going to lose his shit over it.

Well, he was. Maybe a little bit when he saw her back in those ugly suits with a sidearm strapped to her shoulder.

But he wasn't going to tell her.

Because she was better than good.

And she needed to leave the house every day knowing he fully believed she'd come back to him. At least during this next assignment she wasn't undercover, something Amy had decided on her own.

Ivan Popov had taken a plea deal. In return for information on Lemtov and Sokolov, he faced lesser charges for the theft of the chemical weapon Louisa had developed and his role in her abduction. It had been an outstanding debt at Lucky Seven and his inability to pay it off that set all the wheels in motion.

Between pressure from the Assistant District Attorney and Woods's fear of life in prison, he'd confirmed nine missing women had been trafficked the exact same way they had planned to traffic Amy, Sonya, Alison, and Eve. The women had been picked for their looks and hospitality training because, as Woods had confessed, American women sold for a premium. While their actions had broken up the trafficking ring, their leads on the locations of the still-missing women were running dry. And Cabe knew just how hard it was for Amy to accept that they might never find them. Which was why Eagle Securities still had resources, at their own cost, looking for them. Harley and Lite were trying to find their trails, but there were days when it seemed unlikely they were ever going to find them. He shook his head, parking the grim thought for another day. Today was for celebrating and he was determined to focus on that.

"You want this, Ames?" he asked quietly. "Wedding, marriage, kids?"

He'd never asked, and suddenly it became imperative that he knew where she stood.

Amy smiled at him and placed her hand around the back of his neck, squeezing and massaging it just how he liked. "Yes. I do. I want to get married on a beach in the middle of nowhere with my toes in the hot sand. And I want to go back there for my ten-year wedding anniversary with two kids in tow and let them build sandcastles in the place I said my vows."

Her words soothed yet surprised him. "I would have thought you'd want to get married in Vegas."

She shook her head. "There's a reason Nevada's divorce rate exceeds the national average. Plus, it would be a circus. I don't have the challenges that Lou has, but I want it just to be about me and my husband and the start of our own adventure."

Just when he thought he couldn't love her any more, she'd encapsulated his own thoughts exactly. He didn't want to recreate the wedding he and Jess had planned to have, and if he was honest, it had always been more about what Jess had wanted. But now . . . he wanted the vision Amy had just laid out. The two of them on sand that was almost as white as Amy's hair, and the blue coming from the ocean, not paper lanterns or clothes.

He pressed his lips chastely to hers. "Let's do it," he murmured.

"Do what?"

"Go get married on a beach. Or at least let's take a trip and find the beach we want it to happen on. We can spend however long we need or want scouring the planet for the perfect place. I just want to go, with you . . . anywhere."

Amy sighed. "That sounds perfect, but without being the party pooper, we have jobs. I have a new case starting on Monday, and you're off to South America, right?"

Cabe pressed his forehead to hers. "Fuck. Being a grown-up sucks."

She cupped his cheek. "It does . . . but you know that conversation we've been putting off about where to spend Christmas?"

"The one I'm going to win?" he said with a wink.

"What if we didn't go to Vegas or stay here for Christmas? What if we went and found our first beach?"

He could see it. The two of them. Her in a red bikini sipping champagne on Christmas morning, away from the chaos of their jobs and busy lives. A time to get to know each other. That would be the best Christmas present of all. It was less than a month away, but they could pull it off. "You sure you want to do that, Ames? I don't want Uncle Clive buying a new shovel so he can dig a hole to bury me in."

Amy laughed. "Uncle Clive wouldn't dig a hole. He'd pay someone to do it."

Cabe kissed her softly. "Semantics, Ames."

"Can we do it?" she asked.

He looked up briefly and saw his mom smile at him. He knew his parents would be cool, that they'd understand his need to disappear, to travel. Then he looked back at Amy, those eyes of hers the very color of the oceans he was thinking about. "Let's look tonight at where we could go."

Amy shimmied in her chair, a little victory dance of excitement. "*Yes*. Costa Rica? Tahiti?"

He shook his head. He didn't give a shit where they went as long as it was together, but for kicks he responded. "Thailand? Seychelles?"

Her laughter was interrupted by the sound of Six clinking his spoon against his glass.

I love you, Cabe mouthed.

And his heart filled as she returned his words.